Immortal Outlaw

"Lisa Hendrix has a great talent and *Immortal Outlaw* is one book that will have readers riveted."
—*Fresh Fiction*

"The hero of *Immortal Outlaw* is very yummy and the heroine is one that any reader can easily come to love and really root for . . . Lisa Hendrix knows how to give you what you want . . . I just loved how this whole love story played out."
—*Night Owl Romance*

"Filled with action . . . The audience will relish Lisa Hendrix's enjoyable entry."
—*Midwest Book Review*

"Some terrific entertainment is packed between the covers of Hendrix's *Immortal Outlaw* . . . highly recommended to any fans of historical romances or paranormal romances."
—*The Good, the Bad and the Unread*

"Imaginative, fascinating, adventurous; a fantastic read. Hendrix knows how to blend myth and magic in a way that enchants readers . . . The second installment, based on the Robin Hood legend, has passion, adventure, history, and characters you'll treasure."
—*Romantic Times*

"A great installment in the Immortal Brotherhood series."
—*Book Binge*

Immortal Warrior

"Blending paranormal with historical and a touch of the comedy that she is known for, Lisa Hendrix gives us the first in a stunning new series bound to rocket straight to the bestseller list. Her heroine was smart and sassy, her hero was strong and patient, the subplot was awesome, and the twist at the end was completely unexpected."
—*Manic Readers*

continued . . .

"Gripping . . . I expect both this book and its sequels to find their way onto the must-buy lists of book lovers everywhere!"
—*Wild on Books*

"*Immortal Warrior* will sweep you off your feet . . . A fast-paced paranormal delight that will have you adding Lisa Hendrix to your must-buy list. Shifters, witches, Norse gods, and more make this series unforgettable." —*Night Owl Romance*

"A bold and beautiful fairy tale for grown-ups: an enchanted story of a stalwart warrior and a feisty lady . . . Not to be missed!"
—*Romantic Times*

"A sizzling and engrossing romance from the pen of Lisa Hendrix, *Immortal Warrior* should not be missed."
—*Romance Reviews Today*

"Five stars. Hendrix weaves this fascinating tale as seamlessly as the most skilled storytellers of old, with a lyrical quality to her writing that draws the reader in . . . *Immortal Warrior* is going straight to my keeper shelf. I highly recommend that you buy a copy for yours." —*Romance Novel TV*

"Absolutely stunning . . . Starts off a new paranormal series with a bang! *Immortal Warrior* is an excellent paranormal romance—but to the medieval lover, it is all the more exquisite . . . Bringing together Norse sagas, English history, and medieval fairy tales, Lisa Hendrix adds her own unique vision to this popular classic tale of magic." —*Medieval Book Reviews*

"Lisa Hendrix has struck immortal pay dirt with this novel and I, for one, will be anxiously awaiting the next installment of this saga . . . Five martinis for a story I could not bear to put down."
—*The Girls on Books*

"Lisa Hendrix has penned a winner . . . A fast-moving, thrilling tale that kept me up at night." —*Romance Reader at Heart*

IMMORTAL CHAMPION

LISA HENDRIX

BERKLEY SENSATION, NEW YORK

THE BERKLEY PUBLISHING GROUP
Published by the Penguin Group
Penguin Group (USA) Inc.
375 Hudson Street, New York, New York 10014, USA

Penguin Group (Canada), 90 Eglinton Avenue East, Suite 700, Toronto, Ontario M4P 2Y3, Canada
(a division of Pearson Penguin Canada Inc.)
Penguin Books Ltd., 80 Strand, London WC2R 0RL, England
Penguin Group Ireland, 25 St. Stephen's Green, Dublin 2, Ireland (a division of Penguin Books Ltd.)
Penguin Group (Australia), 250 Camberwell Road, Camberwell, Victoria 3124, Australia
(a division of Pearson Australia Group Pty. Ltd.)
Penguin Books India Pvt. Ltd., 11 Community Centre, Panchsheel Park, New Delhi—110 017, India
Penguin Group (NZ), 67 Apollo Drive, Rosedale, North Shore 0632, New Zealand
(a division of Pearson New Zealand Ltd.)
Penguin Books (South Africa) (Pty.) Ltd., 24 Sturdee Avenue, Rosebank, Johannesburg 2196,
South Africa

Penguin Books Ltd., Registered Offices: 80 Strand, London WC2R 0RL, England

This is a work of fiction. Names, characters, places, and incidents either are the product of the author's imagination or are used fictitiously, and any resemblance to actual persons, living or dead, business establishments, events, or locales is entirely coincidental. The publisher does not have any control over and does not assume any responsibility for author or third-party websites or their content.

IMMORTAL CHAMPION

A Berkley Sensation Book / published by arrangement with the author

PRINTING HISTORY
Berkley Sensation mass-market edition / January 2011

Copyright © 2011 by Lisa Hendrix.
Excerpt from *Immortal Defender* copyright © by Lisa Hendrix.
Cover art by Tony Mauro.
Cover design by Rita Frangie.
Interior text design by Kristin del Rosario.

ISBN: 978-0-425-23921-6

BERKLEY® SENSATION
Berkley Sensation Books are published by The Berkley Publishing Group,
a division of Penguin Group (USA) Inc.,
375 Hudson Street, New York, New York 10014.
BERKLEY® SENSATION and the "B" design are trademarks of Penguin Group (USA) Inc.

PRINTED IN THE UNITED STATES OF AMERICA

10 9 8 7 6 5 4 3 2 1

To Kristan Higgins,
Two-time RITA® Award winner and chocolate codependent,
who sorted through her Dove Miniatures
to find all the peanut butter ones
when I needed a fix to finish this book.

The Legend

WINTERS IN ENGLAND have ever been foul—fraught with bone-chilling cold, yet too warm for the snow to thicken on the roof and keep a dwelling snug and far too wet to let a man's clothing keep him truly warm. Through the ages, the men and women of this misbegotten land suffered through the cold months as best they could, huddling in their cottages as much as possible and often seeking work in castle or hall in order to enjoy the warmth of their lord's hearth.

There were those, however, who could find no such refuge, those who were not fully men, nor entirely beast. Cursed by dark magic wielded by the sorceress Cwen, whose son they had killed in a raid for treasure, these Norse warriors spent half of each day in the form of their fylgjur, their spirit companions, each man a different beast. Unable to settle amongst men for any length of time, they kept mostly to the wilds. And because Cwen had also made them immortal, they suffered in the raw damp for winter after soggy winter, century after bleak century.

Yet even in the depths of England's dismal winters, they

clung to some hope, for Cwen's magic had a flaw, a weakness. Her spell had been wrought upon the fylgja amulet each man had worn, and it could be broken on the same token through the power of true love. Knowing this, Cwen had sent her men to scatter the amulets across the land, thinking they would never be found. Yet two warriors had managed it, finding both their amulets and women who could love them even knowing what they were, and their victories left Cwen sore wounded and her powers weakened.

Furious at their triumph, Cwen set out to regather her magic, determined to keep the seven remaining warriors from breaking free of her curse, for it was her intention to make them suffer for eternity, to torture them, to strip away their hope for happiness in the same way they had stripped away hers, leaving her heart barren and empty. By late in the Christian year 1407, she had regained enough power to call a true winter down upon England, the kind of winter the Northmen had known at home.

But without the stout halls of Vass to comfort them, the warriors were not prepared for such a winter—and even less prepared were the folk of England. The cold settled over the land like death, week after bitter week. Snow blanketed the hills. Rivers and wells turned to ice. Birds died by the thousands, frozen where they perched.

And then came the wind, sweeping the roofs clean, blasting the branches off frozen trees, knocking over crofts and barns, and piling the snow into head-high drifts that blocked the roads and made it impossible to travel. In the villages, beleaguered peasants built their fires as high as they could afford and brought their most precious animals—the cows in calf, the best breeding sows and ewes, the hens, and the herding dogs—inside, where they could share the warmth. In the forests and on the moors, the wild things had no such protectors. Those creatures that could burrowed into their dens to sleep away the worst of the weather. Those that could not struggled and often died.

The beast warriors could neither sleep away the winter nor, because of Cwen's curse, find peace in death. They built rough shelters or took refuge in abandoned huts, but the cold went on and on, week after frozen week, and eventually even those dwellings proved too meager.

One who found himself freezing as the winter spun down harder and harder was Gunnar, son of Hrólfr, called Gunnar the Red, who spent his days as a great bull, suffering in the cold, and his nights as a man, trying to get warm . . .

—from the *Dyrrekkr Saga of Ari Sturlusson*
(E. L. Branson, trans.)

CHAPTER 1

"YOU SIT VERY close to the fire, *monsire*."

The soft voice lifted Gunnar's thoughts out of the flames. He glanced up to find a slip of a maid standing at his shield-side elbow, regarding him with wide, gray eyes that sparkled with curiosity. He'd noticed her before, here and there about the hall, but they'd never spoken.

He'd prefer it stayed that way. He picked up the flagon of ale that sat by his foot and took a healthy draught before answering curtly, "I like to be warm."

"Her Grace says sitting too close to the hearth leads to illness. It dries the lungs, she says." Hands folded at her waist, she stood there rocking up and down on her toes, waiting for him to comment on the duchess's notions of health.

Instead, Gunnar turned back to the fire and stretched his legs out, putting his feet even closer to the flames. Then to make it clearer that he had no intention of answering, he took another draught of ale and noisily swished it around in his mouth.

It wasn't that he wanted to be rude. He just wanted to be left alone.

He'd managed to pass five good, warm nights here at Richmond Castle without anyone noticing him, and he hoped to pass many more before he had to move on. But the ability to stay here before the fire each night depended on no one taking notice of him—or of Jafri during the daylight hours. It was difficult enough to disguise their odd comings and goings when no one paid them any attention. If someone grew too curious, they'd have to head back out into the woods.

And back into that devil's wind.

It was the wind that had forced them in toward Richmond to begin with. Roaring down out of the north like a snowslide down a mountain, it had blown in the roof of the old forester's hut they'd been sharing, burying Gunnar and the fire under a ton of frozen thatch and leaving him to spend the remainder of that already miserable night freezing his balls off in the dark as he dug out the gear and tried to get the fire restarted. The next morning, thank the gods, Jafri had looped a rope around the neck of the bull and led him toward the castle.

It was a risk, coming in so close. Someone might spot the wolf, the form Jafri took each night, lurking at the edge of the forest, and with so few wolves left in this part of England, the sight of one so close to the village would draw hunters, even in a winter like this one. But Jafri needed shelter as much as Gunnar, for the days were as frigid as the nights, and so he had apparently judged the risk to be worth taking. When Gunnar had shifted from bull back to man at sunset that night, he'd found himself within sight of Richmond and its welcoming hall. They'd been trading places each dawn and dusk ever since, waiting for the weather to ease. Until that happened, it was vital that their odd comings and goings remaining unnoticed.

"I would fear for the toes of my slippers, with my feet so close to the coals," she said. "Have you never burned your feet?"

It was one thing to ignore a statement, another to refuse to answer a direct question—people would notice that, of a certs, even if the question came from an annoying maid. Gunnar gave the ale one last swish and swallowed. "No." And then, because out of the corner of his eye he saw her frown at his abruptness, "My boots are sturdier than your slippers."

She stopped rocking long enough to lift the front edge of her emerald gown and held out one foot, showing off the toe of a plain slipper about half the size of his boot. "I suppose they are. Still, I should worry."

"And yet you stand here beside me, every bit as close as I," Gunnar pointed out.

"Not as close as your feet, *monsire*." She gestured toward his boots with her toe. "Not by a yard. You are quite tall, though I think the varlet who lights the candles is taller."

He turned toward the dais as though he'd heard something. "I think they call for the women to retire."

She cocked her head and listened. "No, not yet." She waited again until he gave in.

"So. Did you come only to talk about my height and whether I will burn my boots?"

"No, *monsire*. I was curious about you. I have seen you these past nights, but not before. Where do you hail from?"

"The north." He would leave it at that, but she arched an eyebrow expectantly and he added, "Near Alnwick."

"I have never yet been to Alnwick, but I have met Henry Percy. The younger one, I mean, not the old earl. *He* is a traitor."

"He is that," said Gunnar. "And he is no longer earl."

"True. You are not loyal to him, then?"

"If I were, I would be in Scotland."

"I suppose you would." The corners of her eyes crinkled in mischief. "Unless, of course, you are a rebel and a spy."

Three knights nearby looked up, frowning suspiciously, and Gunnar glared at her. "I am neither. You should be careful what you say, maid. That tongue could get a man killed."

She saw the knights staring and flushed. "Your pardon, *monsire*." She raised her voice so it would carry well. "I meant it only as a jest, but I grant 'twas a poor one. Please forgive me."

The men stared a moment longer, then relaxed back into their conversation, and Gunnar nodded a grudging acceptance of her apology, as little good as it would do him. *Curse it.* Now not only the girl had noted him, but those three had, and they would be keeping a close eye on him from now on. He either needed to find another place to sleep or give them some reason to stop worrying about him.

As he was considering how he might accomplish that, a clatter rose at the front of the hall, and the maid sighed. "Now that is the call to retire. Your pardon, *monsire*, I must go." She did him courtesy. "Do be careful of the fire. God keep you."

"And you." He didn't bother to watch her go, instead eyeing the suspicious knights. One of them had pulled out cup and dice and laid out a house of fortune on a bench, and the other two started scraping aside the floor rushes to make a space to roll. Gunnar grinned, seeing a possible solution to his problem in two small cubes of bone. He pulled a farthing out of his purse and tossed it on the seven-square to join the game, and by the time they all settled in for the night, he'd become just another traveler stranded by the weather, his place by the fire secure for as many nights as he could afford to continue to lose.

FIRE.

Even in his sleep, the word possessed Gunnar, drew at him. *Fire. Heat.* He stirred and, still mostly asleep, cracked one eye open just enough to see dim glow of the banked fire. By the gods, he loved the fine, big hearths the English built. His gaze shifted higher to take in the hour candle on the mantle.

Not yet half gone. Good. That meant more time to wallow in Richmond Castle's warmth. He stretched his feet toward the hearth, drew his cloak more tightly around his shoulders, closed his eyes, and drifted back down toward sleep.

Fire. The door slammed open, the sudden sound jerking Gunnar bolt upright. He was on his feet, knife in hand, before he came fully awake.

"Fire!" cried the watchman. "Fire in the bower! The duke! The women!"

The women. The sour taste of fear flooded Gunnar's mouth. As the hall erupted in chaos, he shoved his knife back into its sheath and leapt toward the door, plowing aside confused and sleepy men as he went. Outside, the air boiled with smoke and shouting and the screams of horses, and the red flicker of flames rose along the eastern wall of the two-story bower. He ran toward the building, pushing past frightened women who streamed out the door. As he entered, Edward of Norwich, Duke of York, appeared on the landing above wearing nothing but his braies. He started pulling women out through the door behind him, shoving them down the stairs one after another. As they stumbled down, Gunnar grabbed them at the bottom and pushed them toward the outer door. "Run!"

He lost track at a dozen, but still they came, women and girls and young boys, noble and servant alike, all fleeing for their lives. The smoke grew thicker, clotting in Gunnar's throat, and his eyes streamed with tears.

"Get out of there, man!" came a call from outside.

Gunnar squinted up to where the duke stood with smoke and sparks roiling around him. "Your Grace. Come."

Coughing, the duke peered back into the chamber. "I am not certain . . ."

Smoke already wisped up from the wooden treads, and Gunnar shook his head. "Now, Your Grace, while you can. There is no more you can do."

The duke took a final glance into the smoke-filled chamber, hesitated barely an instant, and then pounded down the stairs, swearing as his bare foot landed on an ember. Gunnar caught him as he stumbled, and together they ducked and ran as more embers rained down. They had just reached the door when Gunnar heard a scream behind him. A cold hand gripped his heart. *Kolla* . . .

He and the duke both turned at once. On the landing, nearly hidden by smoke, two girls wrestled. One was screaming, scrabbling back toward the bedchamber. The other clung to her, dragging her forward. "No. We cannot go back."

"Lady Eleanor." The duke started back.

Gunnar shook off the old dread and grabbed him. "Go, Your Grace. I will get them."

He shoved the duke outside, where a pair of his relieved men pulled him away, then Gunnar turned back. In that brief moment, the stair treads had started to burn in thin flames. There was no way the girls could come down. Ignoring the falling sparks, Gunnar hurried to a spot below the landing and held his arms out. "Jump. I will catch you."

His voice was enough to quiet the screaming girl, but she took one look down and backed away. "I cannot."

Coughing, the other girl shoved her toward the edge. "You can. Go on."

The screamer froze. "I cannot."

"Move!" Gunnar's bellowed order shook the air, and both girls yelped as larger embers showered down from the burning roof. When the screamer still didn't move, the other girl put her shoulder down and shoved. The girl seemed to float for a heartbeat before she tumbled into Gunnar's arms.

He started to set her down, but newly fallen embers spangled the floor and the girl screamed again as her bare feet hit the ground. She crawled up Gunnar as though he were a tree. With a growl, he dashed toward the door with the screaming wench, heaved her outside like a sack of grain, and turned back. By now, the smoke was so thick that he couldn't see the landing at all until he stood right below it.

He coughed and gagged, trying to muster a voice. "Jump, girl!"

No answer.

"Jump!"

No answer. A rock formed in the center of his chest. *He'd failed her.*

Again.

No. This wasn't Kolla. He could save this one. Choking on smoke and memory, he pulled the front of his shirt up over his nose and started forward. But as the flaming stairs towered before him, he hesitated. He'd seen the bodies of men who'd died by fire, fingers and toes and manhood burned away. What if he burned and the curse kept him alive, unmanned and crippled?

What if he failed again and was unmanned anyway, in spirit if not in body? He pounded up the stairs, bellowing in pain as the heat scorched his shins.

The girl lay on the landing, crumpled right where she'd been standing. The foul, heated air strained Gunnar's lungs, and he knew that if not for the perverse protection of the curse, he would likely fall beside her. As it was, he barely had the breath to bend over her. A tongue of flame flickered on her sleeve where an ember had landed and caught. He smothered the fire with his hand and scooped her up. As more embers showered down, he curled over the girl to protect her and turned to retreat back down the stairs. He'd barely taken a step when there was a loud crack and a section of roof crashed down just in front of him. The landing shook, then teetered wildly as the burning stairs came away from the wall.

Nearly smoke-blind, he peered down, trying to recall how far it was to the floor. Too far and he'd break his legs and they'd both lie there as the building burned around them. The window . . . but a glance over his shoulder showed him a chamber now fully aflame. There was no way past the blazing bedding and roiling vapors.

"Loki, you dog piss of a god, help her if not me."

He jumped, landing bent-kneed to take some of the force, then twisting to put himself beneath the girl as they fell. Pain sizzled through his back as the coals beneath him seared through his clothes. He forged to his feet with a roar and charged blindly toward the door and out into the blessedly cold night.

Men swarmed around him, yelling as they covered him with damp blankets. Hands dragged him farther from the burning building; more hands reached for the unconscious girl. Gunnar heard her gasp of breath as they pulled her from his arms, and he nearly sobbed with relief. His legs gave way and he collapsed to his knees, dragging at the clean air, then hacking and spitting as his lungs tried to clear themselves of soot.

"You are sore hurt," said the duke after a moment.

"No. I am fine." Gunnar blinked and scrubbed at his stinging eyes. "The girl?"

"She may live, thanks to you." He hauled Gunnar to his feet. "Go. Have your wounds tended."

"My wounds can wait, Your Grace. You need men on the fire."

The duke's jaw worked as he gave Gunnar a nod. "Then take up a bucket."

His Grace turned back to his duty, shouting instructions to the men to clear the horses from the stables. Gunnar took another moment to catch his breath and clear his sight, then ripped a soaked hide away from a lad too slight to wield it well, sent him to help in the bucket line, and stepped toward the fire.

The bower was lost from the first; they all knew that. The fight was to keep the flames from spreading to the rest of the compound, and in that they succeeded, though just barely. The keep proper and the main hall were in little danger because of distance and their stone walls and lead roofs, but the kitchen and stables were threatened more than once by flying embers, and flames licked parlous close to the armory before the duke's men beat them back. Fortunately, it was a quick blaze, the bower being well over a hundred years old—Gunnar had visited Richmond the year it was built—and so dry that it burned like a straw man. The building soon collapsed, and once they'd beaten back the cloud of sparks thrown up by that, it was largely a matter of keeping up the stream of buckets until all that was left was a mass of steaming coals.

Gunnar was still flailing at the edges of the fire with his hide when he felt a hand on his shoulder. He turned to find a grimy-faced man, black as a collier.

"Rest now, *monsire*. You have done more than enough tonight." Only the man's hoarse but recognizable voice told Gunnar it was the duke, now wearing a cote and boots, though they were every bit as black as Gunnar's own. "My own men can handle the rest of it. Go have those hands tended, lest they fester."

Gunnar glanced down toward his hands, the backs of which glistened with open burns. And his back stung like the very devil. He fingered a sore spot on his shoulder and found a hole where an ember had burned clear through. He flinched as he touched the open wound below.

"That will pain you tomorrow." The duke tugged the hide out of Gunnar's hands and handed it to a passing man, then tipped his head toward the keep. "Go and have it seen to. Go. I command it."

Gunnar glanced toward the east to judge how long he had until dawn. He was surprised to see it was snowing again; the weather had been the farthest thing from his mind while he'd been fighting the fire. Assured by the blackness that he had enough time, he nodded. "Yes, Your Grace."

He turned toward the stone keep, quietly cursing the fire. Now he was truly in the duke's notice. Snow or no, he and Jafri would have to head back out into the wilds and pray the gods would help them find some shelter.

Horses, still frantic with fear, milled around the upper bailey along with pigs and cattle that had been moved from the barn. Gunnar spotted his horses amongst the others and pointed them out to one of the boys who stood watch. "Catch those two and have someone find the gear I left with the stable master. I want them loaded and ready to leave within the hour."

The boy's eyes widened in the flickering torchlight. "In this weather, *monsire*?"

"Aye." Gunnar glanced back toward the fallen bower to make sure the freshening breeze wasn't making things flare up. "A man does what he must. Even in this weather."

Gunnar watched until the stableboy caught his pack-horse and started after the rouncey, then turned and climbed the slight mound toward the tower keep, where the women had set up a station to care for the injured on the first level. As he entered, someone recognized him and spread word of who he was and what he'd done. In moments, his smoky, singed clothes had been stripped away and his hands were soaking in cold buttermilk while a stout old woman sponged yet more soothing buttermilk over his back and several maids stood by fawning. He gave himself over to it, enjoying the fuss. It had been a long while since he'd been hailed as a hero—it had been a long while since he deserved it—and it felt good, even if it meant he was correct about the need to be away.

The old woman had just tied a cooling poultice in place over the burn on his shoulder when a page came up and bowed slightly. "Her Grace would see you upstairs, *monsire*."

"You cannot go to her undressed, *monsire*," said the old woman as he rose. She held out his shirt, grinning. "Much as she might enjoy it. Aye, you're a fair sight of a man, even with that back."

Gunnar grabbed for the shirt and quickly dragged it

over his head, suddenly uneasy even though neither the old woman nor the others had given any sign the scars disturbed them. He had never seen his back, but he knew from the comments of various wenches that it was bad. He bore all the scars of a warrior who'd lived far too long, plus the terrible, raking marks of lion and bear and wolf and dog.

Before they had resigned themselves to mostly solitary lives, all of the crew had suffered with attacks from the others as they swung back and forth between beast and man. Gunnar had been hunted as both human and bull in those first terrible years, and in the centuries since, he had more than once defended innocents from Jafri or Steinarr or Brand or one of the others. They were honorable scars, but to people who knew no better, they looked as though he'd been lashed as an outlaw. Or worse, as a slave.

"You will want to clean off some of that soot, too, *monsire*, if I can say it," continued the old woman, paying no heed to his discomfort.

More heat rising beneath the grime, Gunnar reached for the damp cloth the woman wrung out for him and quickly scrubbed his face, then pulled on his singed gown, buckled on his belt, and slipped his sword into its scabbard as the boy waited.

"Your name, *monsire*?"

"Sir Gunnar of Lesbury." He gave the name of the estate near Alnwick that passed from man to man amongst the crew, and then followed the lad out and around to the stair that led up the outside of the keep to the main hall. From there, they climbed up the inner stair to the solar, where the duke's lady sat in her tall-backed chair, surrounded as always by the score or so of young noblewomen who fostered with her. Now, however, she guarded a flock of dirty pigeons, the girls' linen kirtles gray with smoke and their smudged faces streaked by tears. As the page announced his name, Gunnar glanced around, unsure which one was the screaming Lady Eleanor.

Suddenly he realized the women had all come to their

feet. He frowned as the duchess stepped forward and dipped in courtesy.

"Ah, no, Your Grace," he protested. "I am only a poor knight."

"You saved us, Sir Gunnar," she said, her voice cracking with emotion. "We owe you all honor, as well as eternal gratitude. God must surely have brought you here tonight." She dropped still lower, then rose and stepped back as the younger women similarly knelt and murmured their thanks.

God had sent him? Perhaps. But surely a different god than the one who had let a fire start at night in a chamber full of sleeping women and children. Gunnar shook his head. "Any of your own men would have done the same. I was simply the first out the door."

"And the last out of the bower," said Her Grace. "You are too modest. Our castellan told me what you did for Lady Eleanor when his men bore her in."

"I could hardly leave her to die. Or the other one either. Her, um, serving woman?"

The duchess shook her head. "More maid-in-waiting than servant. A bastard cousin to Lady Eleanor from her father's brother, come to serve her during her fostering."

"A brave creature."

A furrow creased the duchess's high brow. "Lucy? Truly? I would not have thought it." She crossed the room, and a servant hurried to pull aside a tapestry and open the door behind it. "Come. Lady Eleanor wishes to thank you herself."

He had little interest in the lady's thanks, but he could hardly tell a duchess no. Mostly, though, he wanted to see how the brave maid fared. He followed the duchess up a curved stairway and down a short hall to a tiny chamber. A bed occupied one entire end of the room, and from behind the draperies issued great, wracking coughs, as though someone had the lung sickness.

As he and the duchess approached the bed, a maid

hurried out of the room while another, standing near the headboard, pushed the draperies aside and stepped back. As she murmured her thanks and dipped in courtesy, Gunnar recognized the girl from the hall.

Then he caught sight of the occupant of the bed and stopped dead. *Another one?* He glanced back and forth, confused. They were so similar, they looked like twins, with their midnight hair, ivory skin, and gray eyes. But the one in bed had her arm propped up on a cushion, a poultice covering a burn just where he'd put out the flames on a sleeve. So . . . the brave one was the noblewoman and the screamer was the bastard cousin. But which one had been pestering him earlier? And why had he not noticed there were two of them?

The lines of pain around Lady Eleanor's eyes faded as she looked up and saw him. "Here is my rescuer."

"Lady Eleanor de Neville, I give you Sir Gunnar of Lesbury. Do not linger too long, *monsire*. She needs to sleep, but would not, until she saw you were well."

Gunnar bowed to Lady Eleanor, and then to the duchess. "By your command, Your Grace."

The duchess backed away, and motioned for Screaming Lucy to join her by the door.

"I owe you my life, sir," said Lady Eleanor. "I am told you charged up the burning stair then leapt with me to safety. And here I worried that you sat too near the fire."

Aha. It had been her. He thought back to how he'd spoken to her earlier and flushed. "'Twas more of a fall than a leap, my lady."

"Perhaps that is why I ache so." Her voice was husky from the smoke but still managed to carry a ring of good humor. "Well, no matter. Leap or tumble, I will take it over burning. I wish to kiss your hand in thanks."

She held out her hand and looked at him expectantly. It was disconcerting, being under such close examination by eyes both so wise and so very young. Hardly more than a child—and yet her tone and manner were those of one used to having her requests honored by lessers. Aye, he should have heard that earlier, would have heard it, if he had not been so intent on chasing her off. She was noble for certs. And that she was called "Lady" meant she was married. Frowning at the thought of a girl so young being married off already, he glanced toward her hand. But her fingers were bare of rings, and the duchess did seem to be treating her like one of the fosterlings. Unmarried, and yet called "Lady"? And a *Neville*. How did he know that name?

Puzzling over it, he took too long and made her frown back at him. "Your hand, Sir Gunnar. I cannot reach it."

He abandoned trying to sort out who she was and offered his hand.

She started to take it, but hesitated at the sight of the blistered skin across his knuckles. She glanced at her arm, and gently turned his hand over to examine the matching burn on his palm. "I thought I remembered . . . No wonder you did not want me to kiss your hand, *monsire*. You should have spoken."

"'Tis nothing, my lady."

"Still, I would not hurt you further for the world. And yet I would kiss you." She squinted at him in the candlelight. "Your right cheek is unmarked, I think. Let me kiss you there."

"Your thanks are enough, my lady."

"You saved my life, Sir Gunnar. I owe you a kiss, at the least." She pushed herself upright with a slight wince and crooked her finger at him. "Bend close."

Shifting uncomfortably, he glanced toward the duchess, who nodded and smiled. "Let her kiss you, sir. I know her well. She has it in her mind, and she will not rest until she does, stubborn creature that she is."

"I suspect you are correct, Your Grace. I saw her amid the flames." He turned back toward the girl and scolded gently, "Brave to the point of foolishness."

"Not nearly so brave as you, *monsire*. You had a choice, where I did not, being already in the fire." Lady Eleanor's smile faded away at the thought. "And I am grateful for the choice you made. You might have left me, but you did not, and for that I am ever in your debt. Your cheek, if you please."

"Of course, my lady." He started to lean over, but realized he wouldn't be close enough, so he crawled half onto the bed and bent to her. She reeked of the acrid smoke, but as her lips touched his cheek, soft as a butterfly, he smiled at the sweetness in her kiss. A girl's kiss. Outside, a single bell tolled mournfully, calling the monks to prepare for Matins. 'Twas time to be gone.

"You are forever my champion," Lady Eleanor whispered as he straightened, and his chest squeezed a little at the idea of being champion to any maid, even one so very young. "I would have you sit beside me at dinner on the morrow."

"I would be honored, my lady, but I cannot. I must ride on."

"In this weather?" asked the duchess from across the room.

"Aye, Your Grace, and soon."

"But I would give you your proper due." Lady Eleanor frowned and then brightened as a thought struck her. "I know—the spring tourney at York. You will attend and carry my favor."

"I . . ." *I cannot*, he began, but she had that tone again, the one that expected obedience, plus the pain was starting to creep back into her eyes. He wanted her to rest, and so instead of the truth, he offered a lie. "I will try, my lady."

"You will come," she said firmly, easing herself back against the pillows. The motion, combined with the effort of speaking, brought on another fit of coughing. The screamer hurried over as her lady hacked, and Gunnar quietly backed away.

The duchess motioned for him to follow her out. As the door closed behind them, she shook her head. "She breathed far too much smoke. I fear it may have damaged her lungs."

Gunnar glanced back at the door, where the sound of coughing still echoed.

"She seems strong enough," he said, willing it to be so. She couldn't die, not after all that.

"She is, usually, but she already suffered a bout of fever this winter. And now this . . ." The duchess stopped midway down the stairs and faced Gunnar. "I would have a stronger promise that you will come to York, *monsire*. She needs something to cling to for strength. And *I* do not wish to lie to her."

Not that she would mind if *he* lied, her tone said. But there were lies, and there were lies. "I understand, Your Grace. Tell Lady Eleanor . . . tell her that she will see me again after she is well."

The duchess considered him through narrowed eyes, then a mischievous smile spread across her face. "Well done, *monsire*. I can use that without compunction."

She truly was fair when she smiled like that; the duke was a fortunate man. As they reentered the gallery, Gunnar repeated, "I truly must be away now, Your Grace."

"But I intended you to have new clothes to replace those. Let me call the steward."

"A kind thought, Your Grace, but I have no time." He tugged at the singed hem of his sleeve. "These will keep me warm enough. My cloak was not burned."

"But we . . ." She cast about as though looking for something. In the end, she twisted a large ruby ring off her thumb. "Here. Take this as thanks for your aid."

"But I—"

She pressed it into hand. "No. I would give you both new clothes and gold a-plenty, but my keys were in the bower and I can unlock neither treasury nor even my personal casket just now. Take the ring, though it be poor reward for one who did so much."

"I did my duty as a man, Your Grace. That is all."

"You helped us all, and you saved Lady Eleanor. A ring is little enough. Take it, I say, and sell it to buy yourself warm new clothes before the day is out. You cannot refuse me, not after I accepted that promise." That smile again.

Gunnar flushed as he slipped the ring on his little finger. "I would not dare refuse a lady so kind, Your Grace. And I am most grateful. By your leave."

She nodded, and he bowed and backed off a few steps before he turned and trotted down the stairs. Moments later, he'd retrieved his sword and was checking the girth straps on his horses, and by the time the clouds began to pale, he was in the glade where he and Jafri had been trading places each dawn and dusk. A dark, lean form slunk through the snowdrifts not far away, and Gunnar tied the still-nervous horses more tightly than usual, so they couldn't run from the wolf. He stripped off his clothes, and as he stowed them away for the day, a snowflake hit his cheek, conjuring a memory of Lady Eleanor's sweet kiss.

In the next instant, a gust of wind scoured it away and set his shoulder and hands afire anew with a blast of stinging ice crystals, and all he could do was stand there naked, freezing, until the pain of transformation overwhelmed the pain of his burns and beat him to the ground.

THE WATERS WERE stirring again—most strange when the whole of England was frozen.

Cwen stood in the doorway of her woodland cottage, staring out at a gray winter dawn so cold that the fog of her breath turned to ice and settled to the ground like snow. It had taken all her craft to call down such cold, and she savored every drift and shattered branch, knowing that the misery of it pursued the beast-warriors into their very lairs. Even if they'd found shelter amongst men, at this instant before sunrise, as at every dawn and dusk, they lay freezing and naked in the snow. Surely by now they must be begging for the death they could never have.

And yet so much was amiss.

Cwen turned back to the loom that sat in the corner and the nine colors of thread—one for each of the seven remaining men plus black spun from her own hair and a reddish brown dyed with her own blood—that hung upon it in tatters. When she had retired last night, the cloth had been all but done, a year's worth of labor woven into the interlocking figures and finely wrought chains. The elaborate spell had been a makeshift, meant to freshen the now ancient curse and hold the beast-warriors more securely while she searched for a way to recover the fullness of her powers.

But mice had come in the night as she'd dreamed, gnawing at both warp and weft like mad things, undoing it all. She'd not heard a sound, nor apparently had the magpie, her companion, who sat on his perch less than a yard away. Yet the magic so carefully woven with each pass of the shuttle was unbound, and the little beastlings, three of them, lay at the foot of the loom, struck dead by the very magic they had shredded.

It was a message, clearly, a warning from the Old Ones that yet another fragment of the old spell was on the verge of unraveling. And though disappointment and anger twisted inside her at the idea of it, she felt no surprise. She'd sensed it for years, a vague uneasiness as unseeable as the currents of air beneath the magpie's wings.

But this. This was clear.

It was time to act, to once again deal with the Northmen and their efforts to escape her vengeance. But how? She dropped to her knees before the loom and raised her hands in supplication to the gods, opening herself to their wisdom and aid.

Their answer came later that day when she had burned the ruined spell-cloth and purified herself in its smoke. As she trudged to the great oak that overshadowed her cottage and prepared to spread the remains of her magic-making on the snow beneath it, the wind lifted the ashes from the copper basin she held and swirled them high into the air, up through the tree's bare branches to where the magpie watched. Startled, the bird shrieked loudly and darted off, heading due west like a black and white arrow from blind Hodor's bow, the trail of ash swirling along behind in his wake.

Cwen smiled, then bowed low toward the tree. "I understand and obey, my lord."

She called the bird back to her with a sharp whistle and went inside, and the next morning she set about dispelling the fearsome cold and clearing the roads so that she could go find whatever awaited her in the west country.

CHAPTER 2

One month later

"AH, IT IS good to see you at your sewing again, Lady Eleanor. It tells me you are truly well."

"Your Grace." Eleanor started to lay aside her sewing to rise and do courtesy with the others, but the duchess held up a staying hand. In the days since Eleanor had been allowed out of bed, the duchess had gone out of her way to save her any extra effort. "I am well, indeed. Perhaps I might rejoin you in the gallery tonight after supper?"

"A few more days, I think. What is that you are making?"

"A cote-hardie." Eleanor held up the garment to show her. "I cut the cloth yesterday and began stitching after prayers this morning."

"And you have the shoulders seamed already? I hope you are taking proper care with your stitches."

"Of course, my lady. As you taught me."

The duchess came over and inspected the stitching, then fingered the thick brown wool. "Is this not the cloth Westmorland sent you to make a traveling cloak?"

Eleanor flushed at the mention of her father. "It is not to my taste. I felt it better suited to a man."

"To Sir Gunnar, perhaps?"

Suddenly self-conscious before the duchess's knowing smile, Eleanor smoothed the cloth across her knee and started sorting out the needle and thread, which had tangled as she'd shown the garment. "I heard he did not stay long enough to have new clothes to replace his burnt ones, and I thought to have something ready for him when he comes to tourney."

"*If* he comes—"

"You told me he promised, my lady."

Coloring a little, the duchess pressed her fingertips together before her chin. "*Promise* may have been too strong a word. You were ill, and I spoke to give you cause to heal."

Disappointment made Eleanor frown. She sought reassurance. "But he did say I would see him again when I was well?"

"Yes," admitted the duchess.

"Then he surely will come," said Eleanor. "He did not strike me as the sort who would lie."

"No. I suppose not," said the duchess, a bit uncomfortably for Eleanor's taste. "But there is no need for you to sew for him. I gave him a ring to buy himself new clothes, and if, eh, *when* he does come back, I will see that he receives more. After all, I owe him very nearly as much as you."

"But I wish to sew for him, my lady. By way of thanks."

"Of course," said Her Grace gently. "But you must not carry your thanks too far. Sir Gunnar is a simple knight, while you—"

"While you are so much more," said a masculine voice from the doorway.

This time Eleanor sprang up without hesitation, her sewing tumbling to the floor as she dropped into a deep courtesy along with the other women. "Your Grace."

The duke stepped into the room and his gaze raked over the others. "I would speak with Lady Eleanor alone."

The duchess clapped her hands, and the other women and maids, already on their feet, quickly departed, leaving their work where it lay. Her Grace started to follow them out, but her husband motioned for her to stay, then paced across the room and stood, fists on hips, looking down at Eleanor, who slowly straightened.

"You must look higher than Sir Gunnar, Lady Eleanor. And fortunately, I bring word of someone you may look to."

Higher than the man who had saved me? Doubtful that there could be such a man, Eleanor asked, "Who? I mean, if you please, Your Grace."

Smiling as though he had a pleasant secret to reveal, the duke took a folded parchment out of his sleeve. Eleanor's mouth went dry as she recognized her father's wax seal across the opening. Oblivious of Eleanor's pounding heart, the duke unfolded the message and looked it over, nodding silently to himself. "A husband. Your father and I have come to an agreement on your marriage."

"Marriage?" Eleanor blinked, stunned even though she'd been expecting it for some time. "To whom?"

"Richard le Despenser."

"Richard. Your nephew?" The image of a boy two years younger than she, skinny as a broom straw and pale as dough, sprang up in Eleanor's skull. "But I don't *want* to marry Richard."

The duke's smile vanished. "It is a good match. You should be grateful."

"But Richard is my cousin. The Church forbids—"

"He is only your second cousin," interrupted the duchess, coming around to stand behind Eleanor, who suddenly felt the precariousness of her position. "The Church has already given dispensation for the match. You should be pleased. You will be Lady Burghersh and eventually, Countess of Gloucester."

Eleanor glanced over her shoulder to the duchess, confused. "But his father was attainted, and the title deprived."

"The father is not the son, and Henry already realizes it," said His Grace firmly. "Richard is a good lad. He will be created earl once more."

"Earl or no, I do not like him, Your Grace. And he—"

"It is not about what you like," snapped the duke. "It is about what is good for Westmorland and York and the Crown."

"But Richard likes me no more than I like him," argued Eleanor. Her Grace laid a hand on her shoulder in warning, but Eleanor plowed on in her certitude. "He will not want to marry me."

The duke flicked a finger at her notion. "But he does want you, God help him, for he is clever enough to realize that you, my lady, are what will bring the earldom back to him."

"I? How?" And then, the truth hit her. "Oh. Because the king will not likely let me remain so low, despite my Beaufort uncles' sins. Is there to be no love in it at all, then?"

"Love? What does love have to do with marriage and matters of state?"

Eleanor lifted her chin and met the duke's gaze with defiance. "My lord grandfather married for love."

"Aye, eventually, but only after he'd done his duty to England. And still, see where his love got all of you." York flipped the parchment closed and shoved it back up his sleeve. "Enough. You will say your betrothal vows before we leave for Wales. Richard will serve his time as squire and earn his spurs and Henry's trust, and when you are both of an age, you will be married. And with luck and God's blessing, you will take after your lady mother and breed like a sow."

Eleanor felt the duchess tense at her husband's words. Her Grace had a son from an earlier marriage, but had produced no children, male or female, since wedding York.

Her inability to bear her husband an heir ate at her, and his words no doubt stung.

But the duke, in his anger, was either careless or blind to her distress. He glowered at Eleanor. "It is done, girl. Resign yourself and make ready."

He waited expectantly, his frown growing darker as Eleanor stood there, mouth agape. Finally, Her Grace squeezed her shoulder. "She understands her duty, husband. Do you not, Eleanor?"

Another squeeze, sharper, jerked Eleanor to attention. She closed her mouth and swallowed hard. "Yes, Your Grace." She dropped an obedient courtesy to the duke. "As you—and my lord father—command. I will make ready."

The duke stalked out and turned toward the hall. The duchess released her grip on Eleanor's shoulder and walked out without a word, turning the opposite way, toward her bedchamber.

Eleanor sagged back onto her stool and sat there, hands shaking as she considered her fate. Richard.

Richard!

She tried to wrap her mind around the notion of being married to Richard le Despenser. Scrawny, sickly, unpleasant Richard, who put toads in her sewing basket and picked his nose and started fights he couldn't even finish, much less win. And he fiddled all the time, his fingers constantly picking and twisting at things, never still. She despised him.

Perhaps if she thought of him as Earl of Gloucester . . .

But no. She could not see that Richard would ever bear the title. His father's murder of Thomas of Woodstock and role in the subsequent uprising had surely been too great a treason for Henry to forgive. Besides, Richard didn't even look like an earl. An earl, like a duke, should have a certain bearing. A certain dignity.

His Grace had it. Her father had it. So did John, her eldest half brother, who would be earl after her father.

So, for that matter, did Sir Gunnar.

The mere thought of the latter brought a smile to her lips. Simple knight or no, he possessed more nobility than Richard le Despenser ever would. She closed her eyes and conjured up Gunnar's image: broad chest, broader shoulders, that mane of copper-shot curls—in need of a proper cutting, but striking nonetheless. Strong, square jaw. That smile, barely there even when humor lit his green eyes, as though he begrudged his lips the right to reveal too much. He might be better than twice her age, but he was far, far more to her taste than Richard. If only her father would bind her to a substantial man like that. Or if only she were a peasant and could chose for herself.

Well, no, perhaps not a peasant. She wouldn't like that, but she wouldn't mind at all being the wife of some minor knight, if he were like Sir Gunnar. Her mind drifted for a moment over the possibility that her champion might return not just for the tourney but to claim her as wife, and the idea pleased her greatly. Far more than the idea of Richard. She would not, could not, resign herself to Richard.

The other women began filing back in, and with a sigh, Eleanor opened her eyes, retrieved the pile of cloth lying at her feet, and went back to work. Whenever Sir Gunnar did return—*Please let him return soon and carry me away from this contract the way he carried me away from the bower pyre*, she prayed between stitches—she intended to have his gift ready.

But the week came and went with no sign of her prayer being answered, and on Tuesday next she was summoned to the hall, where a handful of noble witnesses stood by while a cleric read out the contract and the duke and Richard le Despenser signed.

"Your mark," ordered His Grace, shoving a quill at her.

And since Sir Gunnar had not come and she had little choice in the matter in any case, she took the quill and carefully scribed her name beside Richard's and then went to the chapel to say the vows that promised she would one day become his wife. Her prayer was still unanswered a few days after that when Richard rode off to war, and it remained so when she next faced the priest and had to confess that in a moment of weakness—honesty, but weakness—she had also prayed for Richard to be killed while in Wales so that she would never have to marry him. By the time she finished the penance, her knees were raw.

Through it all, she continued to sew.

She soon finished Sir Gunnar's cote-hardie and moved on to a padded doublet for him to wear beneath it, then to a chemise for beneath that, choosing a thick, soft wool that would keep him warm in his travels, and then a linen for summer wear, and when those were done, she went on to make him some good, thick chausses and a lined mantle of sturdy stuff that would stand up to the vilest weather.

By then it was spring and they were back at York Castle, and the tourney came and went and Sir Gunnar still did not come. Even so, when all the other sewing was done, she dipped into her purse to buy cloth for a set of court clothes: a fine velvet houpelande in deepest blue with gold trimming; a jacket and a shirt of cambric so fine an angel would barely note its weight; hose—fine ones, this time— and a cap with gold trim to match the houpelande; and even court slippers and a braided belt. And all the while, still dreaming he might bear her away from Richard when he finally returned, she laid her work aside before each meal and stood peering down at the men in the hall, searching for those coppery curls.

In the end, the clothes she'd made, lying folded on a shelf in the cupboard, only collected dust. Before the moths could take an interest, Eleanor sprinkled everything with camphorwood and rue and tansy, wrapped them in silk and linen, tied them with cord, and then stored them and her dream of rescue away deep in the bottom of her chest, beneath a length of golden spiderwork the duchess had presented her for her wedding veil.

Then, as summer faded into autumn, she set out with

deliberate effort of thought to do as the duke and her father wished and resign herself to the idea of Richard le Despenser, who would, mayhap, one day make her Countess of Gloucester.

CHAPTER 3

Raby Castle, County Palatine of Durham, April 1412

A TOURNEY. AND a big one, if all those tents meant anything.

Gunnar looked over the broad meadow west of Raby Castle and grinned at his good fortune. He'd been hoping for a rich table, what with it being just after Easter and Raby being the seat of the Earl of Westmorland, but a tourney meant there would be true feasting. Even better, the crush of men would let him slip in, enjoy the best meal he'd had in many a month, barter for a few supplies, have a lie with one of the whores who would have gathered for the joust, and then slip back out unnoticed. Jafri could have a go tomorrow before they continued on to the coast, and they'd both spend the summer as happier men. The prospect of months alone in the woods always sat a little easier after a good meddle.

He checked to make certain the wolf hadn't followed him out of the woods, then turned his horse toward the castle. By the time he neared the walls, the fading light had brought the last of the day's combats to an end so that he could simply fall into the boisterous stream of men and women leaving the lists. He passed over the bridge and through the fortified gate, just one more in the crowd. No one even bothered to ask his name, and soon he stood in the castle bailey, staring up at a scaffolded tower, some ten yards high, that rose in the center of the yard. The pavilion at its top had wide windows on all four sides, but colorful draperies hid whatever or whoever was inside.

"Which favor will you vie for?" asked a voice at his shoulder.

Gunnar glanced at the speaker, a grizzled knight with a cropped beard. "Favor?"

"Aye. There." The man indicated a score of gloves and ribands and sleeves and veils arrayed on a length of paling wall whose still-green points showed the logs had been cut just for this tourney. "One for each of the ladies to be found in the Castle of Love."

"Castle of Love? Aren't those usually built out by the lists?"

"Aye, but Countess Joan wanted it close in. She's breeding." The man outlined a rounded belly with his hands. "She cannot go out to the gallery, so she called for the castle to be put here, where she can watch from her window. And she's declared her own rules, as well."

"What sort of rules?"

"She collected the favors from the ladies herself and had her varlet hang them, so no one knows which lady gave what, or even which ladies are in the tower for certs, for they climbed up while we were yet in the field. You're to retrieve a favor and make your way up—if you can, of course—to win a kiss from whichever lady owns it."

"Without knowing whose favor you have?" Gunnar raised an eyebrow. "What if you get up there and she's ugly?"

"Unless you're a fool, you'll close your eyes and kiss her like she's the fairest maid in the land," the fellow said, laughing. "For each lady has a silver branch for the man who claims her—but only if his kiss moves her to release it."

"Silver?" asked Gunnar, suddenly more interested. "Are these branches big?"

"Big enough that I wish I could climb." The fellow stretched his forefinger and thumb wide to show the size. "Sadly, I've no head for heights. I'd tumble down aswoon before I climbed halfway up. But you look the sort who could manage it."

Gunnar glanced from tower to favors and back, but shook his head. "I didn't come for the tourney. I don't even have my harness with me."

"You don't want armor anyway, not to climb," chided the man. "And as for not being part of the tourney, 'tis no matter. The countess has opened the contest to all gentlemen present, jousting or not. Even the squires and pages, provided they're noble-born. She wants a merry mêlée, she says, since she must miss the rest of the sport."

"But the fee . . ."

"Only a penny, and that to go to the poor. Our lady has left you no excuses, sir. You may as well have a try."

"I don't know," muttered Gunnar, but he was sorely tempted. He and Jafri could always use the silver, and a kiss from a noblewoman, even an ugly one, was surely worth a penny on its own. It wasn't often that a man like him had the chance to kiss a highborn lady.

And then there was the tower itself, soon to be swarming with men, every one of them vying to knock the others down. He hadn't fought in years . . .

"It might be good sport," he allowed.

"They're already up there, you know," mused the other man. "Likely watching us as we speak." He waved toward the unseen women in the tower, and a few giggles drifted down.

Gunnar's body tightened at the purely female sound. *Young. They sounded so young and sweet.* He squinted up, imagining he could see shadowed curves moving behind the draperies. "Where do I enter?"

Moments later, his name recorded by the herald and a

penny laid in the priest's palm, he handed over his sword and knife to the marshal of the tourney and in exchange received a leather truncheon, the only weapon permitted. Gunnar tested it a few times against his palm. It would hurt, for certs, but would do little lasting damage. Sliding the truncheon into his belt, he ambled over to the spot beneath the countess's window where a knot of men had begun to collect. He hung back a moment, watching the others until he saw one man lean over to whisper to another, then sidled in behind them.

"The blue sleeve, you say," one was saying. "How do you know 'tis hers?" asked one.

"I've seen her in them. I think."

"Hmm." The first tapped his cheek with a fingertip as he considered. "Well, the red one belongs to Lady Margaret. And of that, I am certain."

"Scrope will be after it, then, just as Tunstall will fight for the silver and black riband."

"Is that Lady Celeste's favor?"

"I think so. But more to the point, *he* thinks so. That's what matters."

"Your lord will be trying for it, too, then."

"Aye, and so will I. If I can best Tunstall, or help Lord William do so, I'll be knighted before the month is out."

Their talk shifted to boasting about what they'd not yet done, so Gunnar moved on, eavesdropping here and there, assessing his competition, eliminating some favors from consideration and moving others higher on his list.

By the time the shutter overhead was pushed open, night was fully fallen and torches by the score flickered around the walls and yard—and Gunnar had settled on a plain, dove gray glove that seemed to have escaped the interest of most of his competition. The knot of men was by now a small army, at least ten men for every favor on the wall. A roar rose from the watching crowd as a lady of massive girth appeared at the window.

"God's wounds, if she sneezes, the babe will land on our

heads," muttered Gunnar. Around him, men choked back laughter as the lady lifted her hand for silence.

"Welcome, all, to my Castle of Love." The countess's voice, thick with a French accent, pealed over the yard. "My thanks to my dear and dread lord husband for granting me the boon of this most especial entertainment. I have one further boon to ask, this one of you, our warriors: that you be as honorable as you are courageous in vying for both favors and kisses, for I wish to see all of you undamaged at the merry supper that awaits us afterward. To that end, I have a prize withal for the man who shows himself to be the most worthy, *le plus preux et gentil* of our victors: this golden apple to add to his silver bough." The little orb she held up, the size of a large walnut, gleamed in the torchlight and drew another cheer from the crowd. "Herald, read out the rules of combat."

The rules were much as the old man had said, with the addition of information on bounds and fouls. As the herald finished, Gunnar tore his eyes away from the golden apple to take a final look up at the Castle of Love. Lamps had been lit inside the pavilion, and he truly could see the shadows now, his imaginings come to life.

Suddenly, the concealing draperies were thrown back and there they were: women, all in a cluster, like fine, feathered birds in a nest. Waiting. He grinned and bowed to them, sweeping so low his fingertips scraped the ground. After all, one of them was waiting for him, even if she didn't know it yet.

And then the horn blew and he landed on his ass, knocked down in the trample of men that rushed toward the favors even before the echo died away. He rolled to his feet, ignoring the laughter of the watching crowd. He wasn't the only one caught unawares, but he was the only one who'd hit the ground and the only one who didn't immediately dash off after the others, instead taking a moment to brush the dust off his clothes and make another, deeper bow, this one to the lady in the window. As she clapped in delight, he turned and trotted over to the wall of favors.

Men were already piling up at the bottom, dislodged by the stronger or luckier, or by their own clumsiness. The skinny squire he'd overheard earlier was doing his lord proud, scampering up the wall like a squirrel to reach the silver and black riband well ahead of any others. As the lad untied the bit of silk, the next man below surged up to grab his ankle. The boy fought to hold on, but the lower man was heavier and dogged. Slowly, the boy peeled away.

"Lord William!"

The squire, barely clinging by one hand, swung wildly and dropped the riband off to one side. Tunstall—for that was surely who the attacker must be—released him and lunged, but the riband fluttered by just past his fingertips. A third man, lower still, reached out, snagged it midair, stuffed it in his shirt, and started down.

Overhead, the squire whooped with pleasure. "Go, my lord. Fly to your lady."

"Little whoreson." The foiled Tunstall snarled and lashed out with his truncheon, catching the squire across the shins so hard Gunnar could hear the crack. The boy yelped and lost his grip. As he fell, he struck his Lord William and carried him off the wall. They both landed with a whoomp on the growing pile at the bottom. Tunstall started down, clearly intending to retrieve the riband.

If there wasn't at least one broken bone out of this, 'twould be a miracle. With one eye on the men climbing and tumbling and beating at each other with their truncheons, Gunnar lined himself up with the glove and paced out seven long strides to the end of the wall. Then, stepping over a couple of fallen warriors, he walked around to the rear of the wall and paced seven strides back. It should be right up—he sighted carefully—*there*.

With no one to battle, it took him only moments to climb the back of the wall, reach over the top, and grope around until he hit something soft. He barely had hold of it, barely had the inkling it wasn't leather, when a hand closed around his wrist. He jerked back, bringing whatever it was with him, and laughed when someone swore. He glanced down at the glove.

God's toes. It wasn't the glove at all, but a wine-colored veil a good dozen men had had their eyes on.

No matter. He didn't know who the glove belong to anyway—and he little cared, just as he little cared about the curses and cries of protests that sailed over the wall after the veil.

There'd been nothing in the rules about the back of the wall being out of bounds, after all, and the herald's quick answer to the protests quickly confirmed it. Grinning, Gunnar shoved the scrap of cloth into his shirt, scrambled down far enough to drop to the ground, and set off to collect his kiss. Now the true sport would begin.

As he rounded the end of the wall, two men hit him hard, one high and one low. He went down, but managed to twist so he landed atop one, who grunted as Gunnar's bulk flattened him. A third man piled on, fists flying. A truncheon-tap to the head took the fight out of that one; Gunnar heaved him off, then jerked one arm back sharply to elbow the bottom man, connecting with his chin. He went slack, leaving only the man wrapped around Gunnar's knees.

Gunnar threaded his fingers into the fellow's hair and hauled up hard until he yowled and turned loose. He was hardly more than a boy—a squire, perhaps, or even a page. Gunnar hesitated, unwilling to beat a page, not for mere sport, and in that instant the lad clouted him in the nose, so hard it made his eyes water.

Sport be damned. Gunnar punched back—not too hard, but hard enough to make his point—and then put a foot in the boy's gut and sent him flying.

Gunnar scrambled up and started once more for the tower. A half-dozen other men with blood in their eyes spread out to block his way. With a roar of pleasure,

Gunnar lowered his head and hurtled into them. Two went flying, but two leapt onto his back. In a flash, the other two pinned his arms. He whirled, throwing one off, but another man stepped in, truncheon raised.

The world exploded and went dim and woolly. As Gunnar's knees buckled, he felt a swarm of hands plunge into his shirt, scrabbling for the veil and none too gently. Reeling, he wrenched one arm free and grabbed to save his prize.

He was too slow. The veil whipped past his face, and its captor sprinted off toward the tower. In an instant, the others bolted after the fellow, leaving Gunnar on his knees in the dirt, skull ringing, nose aching, and missing a fair portion of his chest hair, by the feel of it.

A fine fight, all in all, but now it was time to get serious. He'd spent a penny, after all, and he wanted his kiss, not to mention the silver that went with it.

He shook off the fuzziness, clambered to his feet, and squinted around in the torchlight. The battle was rapidly shifting toward the foot of the tower as the many who'd missed out on a favor fought to steal from those few who had succeeded. With the same thought in mind, Gunnar waded into the middle of the mêlée, cheerfully trading blows with whoever came to hand as he worked his way to the foot of the scaffolding.

Lord Tunstall had just started up the tower, but the determined squire was hard on his heels. The lad hurled himself upward to snag his belt. Tunstall strained for the next rung, but the boy, slim as he was, clung to him like a leech. Snarling, the bigger man twisted and reached down toward his boot. Gunnar frowned as Tunstall drew a fine dagger from a hidden sheath.

Knave. Without waiting to see how he intended to use the blade, Gunnar pitched his truncheon. It hit Tunstall square on the elbow. The noble bawled with pain, and the knife dropped from his nerveless fingers and buried itself to the hilt in the ground, narrowly missing a pair of pursuing knights. Cries of "Foul!" rose, far angrier than what Gunnar had earned for his little cheat.

"Forfeit. Lord Tunstall forfeits for carrying a banned weapon," bellowed the herald at the window. "Withdraw, my lord. Withdraw."

As boos and jeers echoed off the walls. Gunnar retrieved his truncheon and turned his attention back to finding someone with a favor to steal. Anyone . . . with any favor . . .

There. A man escaped a skirmish a few yards away, dashed to the foot of the tower, and started up. Two men charged out of the knot after him. Gunnar grabbed the nearest one by the back of the neck and tossed him into a cluster of men a couple of yards away. They all went down in a muddle.

The second one had managed to get one foot up before Gunnar disposed of him in similar fashion. That just left the man with the favor, whatever it was. *God's toes, he was quick.*

Gunnar threw himself up the wall.

He barely caught the fellow at the base of the pavilion itself, and only because the knight, his mind clearly fixed on the women, paused just long enough to run his fingers through his hair.

It was enough. In a flash, Gunnar yanked the cord from his hood and, as the fellow lifted his foot for the final step, looped the sturdy braiding around his ankle.

"Eh?"

Before the stunned knight could stop him, Gunnar lashed the man's foot to the nearest crossbar and pulled the knot tight. As the fellow struggled, Gunnar clambered up and plunged a hand into his rival's shirt in search of the favor.

"No!" The fellow twisted away and swung. His fist connected with Gunnar's cheek, but fettered so, he had no purchase, and the blow barely registered . Gunnar shoved to throw him off balance, and as the man flailed wildly in midair, Gunnar easily relieved him of . . .

The gray glove. Now that was good fortune.

"Dastard!" The knight lunged but came up short, like a puppy on a string.

Laughing, Gunnar clamped the little glove between his teeth, and reached for the window.

A wave of perfume, rich as a summer meadow, washed over the sill as he pulled himself up. A heartbeat later he was over and in, surrounded by excited squeals and giggles. And women. Tall and short, fair and dark, slim as reeds and plump as partridges . . . But young, every one of them.

A few men stood amongst them; he wasn't the first man up, by half, but it made no difference. He was here, and one of these toothsome creatures was his to kiss. He took the glove from his mouth and stood, scanning them all as though he could have his pick when, in truth, the choice had already been made. Which one . . . ?

A heavy hand clapped him on the back. Gunnar whirled, ready to fight off another challenger.

But it was only one of the other victors, a honey-haired beauty already on his other arm, and he was grinning. "Cleverly fought, sir. 'Tis clear you've taken a few towers in your life."

"One or two." Gunnar glanced at the scrap of wine-colored silk dangling from the man's belt. "Ah. You're the one that hit me. You have a good arm."

"You bear no ill will, I hope."

Gunnar gingerly touched the knot on his head. "'Twas part of the sport. And I wasn't after the veil to begin with."

"Indeed!" The lady of the veil pursed her lips as though she'd bitten into a worm. "Then I am glad you lost it, sir."

"I didn't mean . . ." Face hot, Gunnar stumbled to a stop, took a deep breath, and started again. "I would be pleased to have your kiss, my lady, had I earned it. But I fell on your favor by chance alone, so when it was taken, it seemed . . . just."

She sighed, a sound that was half vexation, half mollification, and her eyes flickered to the glove in his hand. "Well. So now you are left with *that*."

"So I am," Gunnar agreed. He held up his prize, fingering the doeskin. If he had any luck at all, its owner would be equally soft, not prickly like this wench. He backed away a pace, half turning. "Where is the lady who holds its mate? I would claim my kiss."

"*Là-bas.* Over there." The lady of the veil started to gesture, but there was a stir and the women separated, leaving Gunnar facing a black-haired maid with flashing eyes that matched the gray glove she held in her hand.

Ah, good, not ugly at all. A bit dark to his taste—he preferred the gold and cream of home over the look the French had brought to England—but pleasant enough. Quite pleasant, in fact. Pleased with his luck, Gunnar stepped forward. "My lady."

"Sir Gunnar." The slightest smile curved her mouth, as if she was privy to some jest. "Are you always so very late?"

CHAPTER 4

"YOUR PARDON, MY lady. Do I know you?"

Do I know you? Eleanor stared at the man she had watched for, waited for during all those long months of quashed hope. After four years, *this* is what he had to offer: *Do I know you?* Did he think she would be amused?

Her fingers tightened around the glove in her hand. She'd hurl it at him if there weren't so many people watching. Why, oh why, hadn't she kept her tongue when she'd spotted him amongst the combatants? Fool that she was, she'd crowed it out, certain that he'd come for her, thinking he would drop to his knee and beg her forgiveness for not returning sooner. Instead, this . . . tripe.

She broadened her smile, unwilling to let the others see her humiliation. "Ah, *monsire*, you do like your jests."

His eyes widened a bit and his forehead pinched with concern, as though he thought she might be mad. "Um, yes. I do, but . . ."

"'Tis mine, knave!" Two knights tumbled over the sill, pummeling each other as they fell. Women and pages scattered, but Eleanor, her attention fixed on willing Sir Gunnar to be silent, reacted too slowly. They rolled into her, and as she tried to jump back, her foot tangled in her hem. She teetered.

Strong arms swept her up before she fell; a broad body sheltered her from the tussle.

His arms. *His* body. She caught a whiff of sweat and straw that set her heart racing.

He set her firmly on her feet and stepped back. "Are you hurt, my lady?"

"Hurt?" Eleanor blinked at him. "No. No. I am fine. That makes twice now you have saved me, though of course, this time my plight was not nearly so dire."

The furrow reappeared. "Twice? I'm sorry, my lady, but . . ."

God's knees, could it be that he truly did not know her at all? Stung, Eleanor glanced past his shoulder, to where the others were, thankfully, occupied with separating the offending knights and welcoming two others, newly victorious. That wouldn't last, though. He *had* to remember. She had to *make* him remember.

"A clue, then. Bend close." She crooked an impatient finger, summoning him down, and as he neared, leaned forward to press a kiss to his right cheek. "We both smelled of smoke when last I did that."

The crease between his brows deepened as he straightened, and then he touched his cheek and his eyes met hers, recognition dawning at last. "The maid from the fire. Lady, um, Eleanor, is it?"

Her budding delight faded at his uncertainty. "Aye."

He looked down at the glove in his hand. "Yours. This is yours?" He sounded surprised.

She held up its mate. "It is."

"But it . . . I didn't know. I didn't even know—"

Eleanor saw her half sister, Anne, turn to watch. She put a hand on his arm as though teasing. "Silence, sir. You will turn my head with such flattery."

But it was too late. Anne had heard, and she swooped over like a hawk on a wounded quail, her champion and betrothed, Gilbert d'Umfraville, pulled along in her wake.

"Is it true, then? He didn't come for you after all? Oh, Eleanor." Anne's chuckle fairly dripped with venom, and Eleanor felt her cheeks blaze.

Sir Gunnar glanced to Anne then back to Eleanor. His eyes narrowed slightly, and he turned just enough to acknowledge Anne with a slight dip of the head.

"But of course I came for her, my lady." He turned his shoulder to Anne, directing his full attention on Eleanor. "It is only that I didn't realize I had found her. You see, the Lady Eleanor I carried in my mind was a child. This fair creature . . . is not."

Eleanor knew she wasn't meant to note that slight hesitation, nor the way his gaze flickered down to her bosom between words. But note it she did, and the warmth in his eyes and voice drew an answering warmth in her that melted away her irritation like summer snow.

"Some debate whether she has entirely left childhood behind." Anne sniffed dismissively and sailed away. Gilbert bowed, muttered, "Your pardon," and went after her.

Eleanor smiled up at Sir Gunnar, an honest smile now, as she murmured, "My thanks, *monsire*. I don't even mind that you lied to her."

His neck reddened up to his ears. "It should not have been a lie, my lady. I should have known you as surely as you knew me."

"Ah, but I have the advantage. You have changed not a wight, but for being unsinged." It was true. He looked exactly the same, other than his clothing. Even his face remained unlined by the intervening years, and his hair— still in need of a proper cutting, she noted—still gleamed of gold and copper, without the least glint of silver, even at the temples.

One last young man heaved himself over the sill and fell to the floor, limply waving a black and silver riband as he gasped, "I claim the lady whose favor this is in the name of William, Lord Ethridge, who lies injured below."

As the inmates of the Castle of Love clapped and urged the lady forward, the page assigned to keep count blew a horn.

Outside, the herald cried out, "All the ladies have now been won. The champions will retire to the great hall to claim their prizes."

The crowd flowed toward the gate in the rear wall, where a sturdy stair was being set into place with much clatter. Eleanor and Gunnar fell in with the others, and as they waited their turn to climb down, she stole another look at her champion, marveling at how unchanged he was. Truly, he looked no different at all. Why had she once thought him so very old?

"What is that smile?"

"Nothing," she said. "I merely find it difficult to believe that you are here, at a tournament and as my champion at long last. A part of me thinks you must be some phantom of my imaginings."

His expression grew grave. "I am many things, my lady, but I am no phantom."

"Phantom or not, I bless whatever Providence put my glove in your hand."

"Providence," he repeated softly, in a way that lifted the hairs on the back of her neck. The last of the others disappeared down the stairway, leaving only them, alone but for a single page. Eyes glittering like emeralds in the torchlight, Sir Gunnar put out his hand to help her down.

Eleanor hesitated, suddenly and inexplicably wary of touching him. No, that wasn't true. There was an explanation. Its name was Richard. She had resigned herself to marrying Richard.

Sir Gunnar waited, one corner of his mouth lifted in that odd half smile she'd held in one corner of her heart for all those years. "Shall we go down, my lady?"

"Yes. Yes, of course." She laid her hand in his, res-

ignation forgotten and four long years forgiven in a single
touch.

AH, BALLOCKS. RIGHT up there in front of everyone.

Gunnar watched the line of champions and their ladies
snake toward the dais at the front of the great hall. He
hadn't thought about that part of it, that if he succeeded,
he'd have to step forward to claim his due. Why couldn't
the prizes be given in the Castle of Love, instead of here,
before everyone?

It truly was everyone. Raby had the grandest hall he'd
ever seen, a huge chamber large enough to hold the army
of men who'd been on the wall as well as all those who'd
been watching.

And now they'd be watching him.

His shoulders tightened at the idea of putting himself
forward before so many. They would remember him for
years, every man of them. He'd have to avoid them all until
memories blurred.

Unless . . .

No, he couldn't think of that now. He must keep his
mind on what was before him lest he put both himself and
Jafri at risk.

Steeling himself with a deep breath, he led Lady Eleanor past the frowning Tunstall, and onto the dais with the
other couples. A page passed down the line, handing each
lady an identical silver branch.

"Well done to all our champions." The countess pushed
to her feet, more graceful than Gunnar would have thought
possible with that belly on her. "You entertained me greatly,
and now it is time to claim your kisses. I remind you to perform as admirably here as you did on the tower, so that you
impress your lady and earn your silver branch." She made
her way to the far end of the line, where she faced the first
couple. "It appears we begin with you, Sir Gilbert. Be ware
you don't perform *too* well. My lord husband watches."

As the crowd chuckled, the knight who'd claimed the jealous Lady Anne glanced toward the earl, hesitated, then overcame whatever misgivings the countess's odd warning had apparently raised, slipped an arm around the maid's waist, and claimed her with a deep kiss. The lady stiffened and her hands came up as though to push him away, but after a heartbeat, she softened in his arms, her fingers curling into his shirt, and Gunnar could hear her sigh even from where he stood at the far end of the dais. The delighted laughter of the crowd pulled the pair apart with a jerk, the lady blushing red as a beetroot.

But she gave Sir Gilbert her branch.

The next man took a different tack, offering the sort of kiss a man might give his sister. But for all its lack of fervor, it seemed to be the proper kiss for that lady. She turned as rosy as the first, and that man, too, won his bit of silver.

So it went down the line, some kisses as full of passion as any two lovers might share, others tender, a few clumsy but earnest. The young squire's Lord Etheridge managed to kiss his lady to a near swoon, balanced on one foot though he was.

The closer it came to Gunnar's turn, the more his stomach churned. This kiss he'd sought so blithely now seemed to bear some import beyond the moment's pleasure. He gnawed on his lip, trying to think how best to approach it. Beside him, Eleanor fidgeted, clearly as nervous as he.

And then, too soon, it was his turn. He turned to face Lady Eleanor, every eye on him, hers most of all. She stilled, waiting. Her lips parted slightly, moist, as though she expected a true kiss, a lover's kiss, and a part of him screamed to scoop her into his arms and oblige.

But no. Not until he was certain. For now, he needed both caution and something . . . special. Something just for her.

"My lady." He bowed slightly and dropped to one knee. Taking her hand, he turned it over and drew it slowly toward his mouth. He hesitated, letting the musk and spice perfume she wore at her wrist fill his senses, then bent and, as gently as he could, brushed a kiss into her palm.

A kiss like a butterfly. A snowflake.

Eleanor's fingers curled shut around the kiss, trapping it, and above him, her tiny, breathless *"ah"* told him more clearly than words that he'd chosen rightly.

"Très gentil, monsire." The countess nodded her approval as Gunnar pushed to his feet and collected his silver branch. "Even my lord husband can find no fault with a such a kiss. And now we will decide the champion of champions, at least in the ways of love. Ladies, come."

She led the maids off to one side, where they formed a tight knot and much whispering ensued.

Gunnar leaned over to the man next to him, the one who'd stolen the veil from him, and lowered his voice. "Why does the countess worry how her husband will react to the kissing?"

"You don't know? I thought you and Lady Eleanor . . ."

"I met her long ago, and only briefly. At Richmond. I know nothing about her."

"Ah." The fellow tipped his head toward the earl. "She's Westmorland's daughter. As are Lady Anne and Lady Margaret, though from his first wife, God rest her."

"Daughter?" A hazy memory floated up: the duchess's mention of the name *Neville*, and himself, thickheaded from smoke and exhaustion, unable to recall who that might be. Of course: the Earl of Westmorland was Ralph de Neville. By the gods, he had walked right into her father's hall without even knowing it.

Balls. He truly *had* forgotten her. He shouldn't have, but he had, letting his recollection of her slip into the morass of six centuries of memories.

As he stood there kicking himself for his foolishness, the countess made her way back to the front with the ladies. At her side, Eleanor slowly rocked up and down on her toes, her smiling eyes fixed on Gunnar, adding to the shame that bubbled uncomfortably in his gut. She was so pleased to see him, and he'd forgotten all about her.

Aye, he was both fool and ass.

"We have our decision. Oddly, the man deemed *le plus preux et gentil* is not amongst the champions here before us. Rather, he fought with great courage and fortitude, only to sacrifice his right to claim a prize to the knight he serves, all in the name of love." She held up the little golden apple. "By acclamation of the ladies, the prize goes to John Penson, squire to William, Lord Ethridge."

Some of the other champions looked aggrieved, and a veritable cloud of black formed around Tunstall, but most cheered as the beaming squire took a knee to receive his prize.

"If young John doesn't float up into the rafters, 'twill be a marvel," said Lady Eleanor, reappearing at Gunnar's side.

He watched the lad wince as he pushed to his feet, favoring the leg Tunstall had struck. "He's too sore to fly. He earned every grain of that gold, twice over."

"He had good aide, I think. My lady mother says you disarmed Tunstall, though I did not see it myself. She wishes me to present you before we sup." She leaned close, brushing his arm as she whispered, "She does not yet know who you are. Come, we must stand aside."

With the dais clear, a throng of servants rushed forward to produce the high table, drape it in yard upon yard of white linen, and set it with gleaming plate.

As the earl and his lady at last stepped forward to take their chairs, Eleanor turned to Gunnar. "Are you ready, *monsire*? My lord father can be . . . formidable."

"No more so than his daughter." Gunnar offered his hand. "I believe I have courage enough for both of you."

Smiling, she curled her fingers over his offered fist and firmly steered him toward the high table. As they approached, Westmorland turned. "Who is this champion who claimed such a chaste kiss, daughter?"

"Truly a champion, my lord, and a man I have long wanted you to meet. I give you Sir Gunnar of Lesbury. The knight who saved us from the fire."

"At Richmond?" Lord Ralph came up out of his chair to grasp Gunnar by the hand. "Welcome, Sir Gunnar, welcome at last."

"Eleanor! You should have told me," scolded the countess.

"I only discovered him during the mêlée, my lady. And it would not have been seemly during the award."

"Then *you* should have told us, *monsire*." The countess beamed up from her chair. "Why did you not announce yourself? You have been in my prayers every day since York sent word of how a brave stranger saved my daughter."

Gunnar shifted uneasily. "I did only what any man would do."

"No other man rescued her."

"Only because I reached the bower first, my lady. If I had not, another would have stepped forward."

"No, they would not," said Lady Eleanor. "I would have died in the flames if not for you, and Lucy with me. And you know it well. Now come, I can at last have you beside me at table."

She turned toward the long second table where the champions and their ladies were taking their places, but Lord Ralph stopped her. "Here at the high table, Eleanor. Your Sir Gunnar is a most honored guest in this household."

Servants scrambled to set a fresh place, and Gunnar soon found himself sharing a bench with Lady Eleanor. As she exchanged a few words of greeting with the lord and lady to her right, he took advantage of the moment to study her, comparing the maid beside him to the girl in his mind.

It wasn't simply the height and the full teats that were different: her face had changed as well, losing the blandness of childhood to become both strikingly female and uncommonly bold. She clearly took after her father: his high cheekbones and noble nose gave her face enough strength to balance a full mouth that fell just shy of being too wide. Beneath brows that flew off aslant like a blackbird's wings, her pale gray eyes—the only feature she seemed to have stolen from her mother—glowed from amid lashes so dark he suspected she might dust them with coal.

And that hair: still as bone-straight and glossy as he remembered on that girl by the hearth, but now caught back in an intricate net of braids that hung well past her buttocks, thick as his wrist.

Thank the gods her hair wasn't hidden away beneath a crespin or one of those bizarre horned arrangements that were the mark of married women these days. The braids meant she was still unwed. Hope surged through him once more at the thought; he pushed it down, still unwilling to give himself over to it.

And then the first courses were carried out, and he was saved, the lady all but forgotten as the aromas of onions, saffron, cloves, and freshly baked bread washed over him. His stomach rumbled like an oxcart on cobblestones, audible even over the music drifting down from the minstrels' gallery at the end of the hall.

Lady Eleanor averted her gaze, pretending not to hear, but Gunnar caught a snort of, what? Laughter? Disapproval? It used to be that a rumbling belly was the sign of a good appetite, just as a hearty belch after a meal was a sign that the food had satisfied, but now, and at a noble table . . . He supposed he needed to apologize.

He leaned close so he could keep his words private. "Your pardon, my lady. I have yet to learn how to still an empty belly."

"You have not eaten today?"

"I was traveling." That wasn't quite true; the bull had spent the day grazing, but that hardly counted.

"And then you fought, unfed? You must be starved." She motioned over the nearest serving man, who began spooning a savory soup of veal and onions over slices of toasted bread in a bowl. Gunnar picked up a spoon and dug in. He was nearly through the bowl when the meat was carried in.

Not just any meat. Roasted pig, crisp skin dripping with fat. Aye, just what he'd longed for, that and the custard, yellow with eggs and glistening with cream. As a boy passed by with a huge bowl of the stuff, he felt like leaping in. It was all he could do not to groan.

Lady Eleanor must have noted the food-lust in his eyes, for she saw to it that their trencher was piled with the richest dishes on the table, then held back as he ate his fill, pointing out choice morsels, buttering bread for him, and gently encouraging him to stuff himself. He obliged, and most happily.

As they shared a piece of the honey cake that finished the meal, the lord to their left, whose name Gunnar had already forgotten, leaned over.

"Your pardon, sir. Did I hear it said that you saved Lady Eleanor, here, from a fire?"

It was as though the lady had been waiting all these years for someone to ask. Before Gunnar could gather his words, she raced into her version of the events at Richmond. She was a lively if inaccurate storyteller, and soon everyone within hearing was caught up in her tale as she painted him a hero, her hands fluttering and swooping with her words.

Gunnar sat quietly, willing everyone to watch her and forget him. And it worked, too, until her tale ventured so far from the truth that it made him wince.

"What is it, Sir Gunnar?" asked Lord Ralph—probably the only man within hearing not enthralled by his daughter and her tale. "Does Eleanor have it wrong?"

"I would not dare call her wrong, my lord," said Gunnar carefully. "But she does . . . beribbon things."

"Beribbon." Chuckling with the others, Lord Ralph rose and came over to stand behind Eleanor, laying a hand on each shoulder. "A good name for her way. I have heard her 'beribbon' a story until it fell over from the weight of all the trimmings. Where did she go astray?"

"I did not soar off the balcony like an eagle, my lord. I fell off it like a sack of stones, all but killing us both."

"You told me you leapt," protested Lady Eleanor over the laughter. "That very night."

"You said leapt, my lady. I said fell, even then."

"How strange you so easily recall what you said when you struggled to recall me," she said tartly, shrugging off her father's hands. "I say we could not have fallen. I had barely a bruise."

"You told me that night that you ached, my lady," reminded Gunnar, laughing himself now. "And I know I did."

"Whatever aches you felt, they were surely less than the sting of your burns. Your very shirt was—"

"Aaah."

"Almost burned off y—" The groan carried Lady Eleanor to her feet mid-word. "*Madame?*"

"Joan?" Lord Ralph hurried back to kneel at his wife's side. They exchanged a few hushed words, and then he rose to scold her. "You should have told me, instead of trying to outlast both mêlée and meal. And *I* should have noticed. It isn't as though I haven't seen this before. Mary, Eleanor, the rest of you. Come, it is time. Someone fetch the midwife."

A page dashed toward the door, and Eleanor started toward her mother. She'd gone only a few steps when she stopped and turned back. "Forgive me, Sir Gunnar, but I am needed. You will still be here on the morrow, I hope."

Yes, he wanted to say, but it wasn't possible. He needed to see to Jafri's safety before he could deal with anything else. "I fear not, my lady. I have business to attend, but—"

"Not again! But I have a gift for you, and I cannot give it now." She glanced anxiously toward where her sisters and the other women surrounded her mother.

And that's when he saw it, the silver comb that caught her braid at the nape of her neck. He'd noticed it before, but now the light caught it just right, raising the image engraved into the wide spine: a maiden sitting on the back of a bull.

His heart stuttered in his chest, then started pounding like a fuller's stock, so loud he barely heard her say,

"You must come back."

Of course he must. He swallowed hard, trying to find his voice. "I will. As soon as I am able."

"I have heard that promise before." She balled her fists on her hips and faced him like a stubborn alewife. "What surety do I have that you tell the truth this time, so that I may attend my mother's labors without worrying that another five years will pass before I see you?"

"None but my word, but I give it freely. I will be back."

"When?"

He quickly calculated how much time it would take to do what needed to be done and get back to her, then held up a finger. "One week."

"And you swear it?"

"Of a certs, my lady. How can I not, when it is Providence?"

She gave him a smile so brilliant he felt its warmth in the pit of his stomach. "I believe you will," she said quietly, then whirled and hurried off after her mother.

Gunnar watched, bemused, until she vanished with the others down a passageway, then carried his cup of wine over to the hearth. The men already there made way for him, shuffling back to let him pass, to give him the best seat, to defer to him. Not good, whispered the part of him that demanded to stay hidden, but any chance of that had vanished. Consoling himself with the thought that most of those present were there for the tourney and would scatter before he returned, he took the offered seat, stretched his feet toward the fire, and settled in for an evening's company.

Only later, when the hall was dark and rattling with snores, did he have the peace he needed to try to wrap his mind around what had happened.

Of all the places he might have chosen to lay his head this night, he had been drawn here, to her. And of all the favors he could have chosen, he'd been drawn to *her* glove. It had beckoned him from the first, and even when he failed to find it, fortune conspired to put it into his hands. He'd been led to her in spite of himself.

He'd suspected it from the moment he'd realized who she was, but hadn't dared hope it was true. Now, he had no doubt, not after seeing the maid and bull.

Providence, she'd called it, using her Christian word. But he knew the truth: it was the *Nornir*, the Fate-spinners, who had woven their life-strands together. He might have been too dull-witted to see it when they'd set her in his path four years ago, but he could not mistake it now, not when she wore the confirming sign on her very body.

Glancing around to make certain the others truly slept, Gunnar rose and approached the fire to spill a measure of wine into the dying flames. As the coals hissed, he whispered a word of thanks to be carried aloft by the sweet, rising steam, the first of what he knew would be many such offerings.

For the gods had brought a gift to him, a boon for staying faithful to them through the long centuries. They'd given him a prize more valuable than any golden apple, indeed, more precious than all the gold in England: Lady Eleanor de Neville. The woman who could love him, even knowing what he was.

The woman who could save him and, in saving him, lead him to the life—and in time, the death—he so much desired.

He had much to be thankful for.

CHAPTER 5

"PUT THAT CHILD down. You hold him more than the wet nurse does."

"Forgive me, *madame*. I did not mean to wake you." Eleanor turned from the window, cuddling her new brother. "Edward was fretting and I thought to settle him. Look, he smiles at me." She tilted him slightly so her mother could see.

"Week-old babes do not smile. He has wind. Where is the wet nurse?"

"Below, suckling her own son."

"She is supposed to do that while Edward sleeps."

"He was sleeping. As were you. As you both still should be."

"It appears we have both slept enough for now." Lady Joan sat up and wrestled her pillows into shape before she eased back. "Did I dream it, or wasn't Mary here before?"

Mary Ferrers was another of Eleanor's half sisters, this one from her mother's first marriage—and very much more pleasant than those from her father's first marriage. "She was. But I wanted to sit with you, so I sent her off."

"You did? Truly?"

Eleanor nodded, paying no heed to the guilt that poked at her. She truly did want to be here, after all, though less for mother and child than for their windows: the lying-in chamber had clear glass windows that overlooked both inner and outer gates and the ward between. She could even see a bit of the road beyond the wall—the road down which Sir Gunnar was to ride today.

Except today was already over, the sun having set on a misty, cold afternoon with no sign of him. And despite full knowledge that the man had lied with his promises before, the more the light faded, the more this particular lie stung.

But her mother didn't know any of that, and she beamed up at Eleanor, happy. Eleanor could only smile back.

The baby started to fret again, tiny mewing sounds of distress, and her mother held out her arms. "Bring him here. There is nothing the nurse can do that I cannot. Except feed him, of course. I want you to watch. You will have babes of your own soon, God willing."

And God willing, they would not be Richard's. Eleanor carried the tightly swaddled infant over and laid him in his mother's arms. Lady Joan checked his clout to make sure he was still clean, then brought him up to her shoulder and patted his back until he produced a belch worthy of a smith.

"See? Wind." Her mother settled Edward into the crook of her arm, where he rooted at her bound teats a moment before sticking his own fist in his mouth and promptly going back to sleep. She patted the bed for Eleanor to come sit by her. "See, after twelve, I have learned a bit. You should have, too. You were meant to have experience of birthing and infants while with York."

"Her Grace cannot help that she is barren."

"She is *not* barren," said Lady Joan.

"But everyone said—"

"They always say it is the woman's fault, whether 'tis

true or not. Philippa produced a son for Fitzwalter with no trouble at all, while York has been swiving his way across England for years and has not a single bastard to show for it."

"How do you know?"

"If he did, he'd be bringing one forward as heir, wouldn't he? No, his seed is bad, mark my word. I doubt he could get even me with child, while all your father need do is walk past my chamber door to get me breeding. With luck, Richard will show similar vigor. Ah, there you are at last," she said as the door opened on a plump young peasant woman with teats worthy of her station as wet nurse. "Take him, and carefully, for he sleeps. And you, Eleanor, go down to supper. I think I heard the horn."

"Yes, *madame*." Barely containing a grimace at the idea of Richard in her bed, Eleanor made her courtesy and escaped—though to what and from what, she wasn't sure. Neither the man she wanted nor the one she didn't was here. In no particular hurry, she trudged down the long passageway past the family apartments.

By the time she reached the solar, it was empty but for Lucy, who stood by the grilled window that separated solar from hall. "I thought you would come sooner, my lady, to watch for Sir Gunnar."

"I have had enough of watching. It holds no more interest."

"No?" Lucy put her eye to the grill. "Then should I have someone carry his gift to him and say you are ill?"

The center of Eleanor went still. "What?"

"Should I send word you are ill? I could say your head aches. It might be best anyway."

"He is here?" Eleanor hurried the few steps to stand beside Lucy and peer through the wooden lacework.

There. Her eyes found him instantly, drawn to that thatch of red-tinged gold as though his curls were the tongues of a signal fire. "But I watched from the tower. How . . . ?"

"He only just came. You must have missed his approach in the gloom." Lucy paused a moment, then ventured a hesitant, "My lady?"

Below, Gunnar stripped off his cloak and sword and handed them to a varlet. Hardly able to breathe, Eleanor watched him join the line for the ewer. She should go down. She'd been waiting all day for him, and she should go down, but her feet were suddenly as heavy as millstones.

"My lady?" repeated Lucy more insistently.

"What?"

"As cousin and friend, I must remind you. You are betrothed."

Lucy's quiet words echoed the very thought that anchored Eleanor to the floor, the same thought that had dogged her all week: that Richard, confirmed as Lord Burghersh these three years past, would come to claim her someday soon.

But she was not yet wife, and her champion was here. *Here.*

All those months, watching for Sir Gunnar, dreaming of him, praying for him; all those years of struggling to resign herself to a marriage she never wanted; the past week of soaring hope; her mother's wishes for Richard's vigor abed; they all collided now in the face of the man below. He hadn't seemed real last week, come so suddenly and without intent.

But now he was here because he wanted to be. *For her.* She really should go down to him. Her feet stayed frozen to the floor.

"My lady." Lucy's tone was a warning.

"You watched with me, Lucy. Every night. You never worried about my betrothal then."

"We were girls. It was a game, like in one of the fabliaux. But I have watched you this last week, and I see your face now. I worry that it is no longer a game."

No. No, it isn't. Eleanor wiped her palms, damp with sweat, against her skirts. "Is the clothing I made ready?"

"You know it is, my lady. You have asked after it every day this sennight."

"Good. When it is time, bring it all here to the solar. He will have to try everything. I may need to make alteration." Oh, she did hope so. It would give her leave to be close to him, to touch him.

Lucy's frown accused Eleanor, as if she'd read her intent. "Be careful, my lady. 'Twould be sin to betray Lord Burghersh."

"I know that." *But it would be far worse sin to betray Providence.* The thought formed whole, as if dropped into her head from above, and in the same instant, the weights fell from her feet. "I know what I am doing."

She ran for the stair, sending a silent prayer to Heaven that she truly did.

THERE SHE CAME, sailing across the hall, the crowd parting before her like the sea before the prow of a fast ship.

Gunnar watched Lady Eleanor approach with a mix of anticipation and apprehension. Not one for the background, this one. If he was wrong about this, she would surely be the ruin of him.

As she glided to a stop, he commended his fate to the *Nornir* and bowed. "My lady."

"*Monsire.*" She stood there, wearing a pleased expression as she suddenly sprouted up an inch and settled back down. "Your business went well, I hope." Up and down.

"It did." He watched her rise and fall again. "Is something wrong, my lady?"

"No." Up and down she went. "Why do you ask?"

"You seem to be . . . bobbing." He waved his fingers up and down. "You do it often."

"What?" She looked down at her toes just as she sprouted yet again. "Oh. So I am." She settled firmly to the ground, embarrassment spotting her cheeks. "And so vanishes my pretense of calm and grace." She shot him a rueful grin.

" 'Tis rude of you to point it out, sir, when the cause lies at your feet."

"It does? How?"

"You are here."

"As I said I would be."

"Aye. But when the sun set and there was no sign of you, I thought you had failed me again. Thus my great pleasure at seeing you now." Another flash of smile. "And my bobbing. I fear it gives me away when I am happy. Your pardon while I wash for supper."

She slid into the front of the line, leaving Gunnar shaking his head in amusement.

They were soon seated once again at the high table. "Because we were interrupted last time," the lady explained. "Though for good reason."

"A very good one. Mother and child are well, I hope?"

"Very well, and thank you. My new brother is named Edward, and he already smiles at me, even if my lady mother believes otherwise."

She chattered on proudly about the babe. Gunnar tried to listen. Much as he wanted—needed—to keep his mind on the lady, the day's chill weather and travel had left him as hungry as ever, and the aroma of the food being carried in made him slaver like a mad dog. As a pair of men entered with a spitted goose, his stomach rumbled even more loudly than it had before.

Lady Eleanor glanced up at him, her eyes sparkling with humor. "I must be ware that my hand does not come between you and that gander, *monsire*, lest I lose it."

"You have your bobbing, I have my belly. They both betray us." He held up his hands in surrender while Lady Eleanor broke off a piece of bread, smeared it with butter, and handed it to him.

As he popped it in his mouth, she leaned near and lowered her voice. " 'Struth, my stomach often rumbles as loudly as yours. My lady mother despairs of it. She says a lady of royal blood should not make noises like a peasant."

Gunnar almost choked on his bread. He swallowed quickly and wiped away the crumbs with the back of his hand. "Royal? But . . ." He wracked his brain for what little he knew of Ralph de Neville. "The earl is not a Plantagenet. Or is he?"

"No. 'Tis my lady mother who carries the line." She raised an eyebrow. "Ah, you do not know her, and I did not make a good introduction last time. She is Lady Joan de Beaufort. Her father—my lord grandfather—was John of Gaunt, God rest him."

"Of course. I should have remembered," muttered Gunnar, stunned. *John of Gaunt!* It was a fruitless task, trying to keep track of the English and all their marriages and alliances from the forest deeps where he hid, but even he knew John of Gaunt, the third Edward's middle son, who had been Duke of Lancaster. It was Gaunt's son and heir, Bolingbroke, who'd deposed his uncle Richard to steal the throne and become the fourth king called Henry, but Gaunt had also sired a pack of bastards with his mistress in France. If the countess was one of those Beaufort byblows, that made Eleanor . . .

Ballocks. "King Henry is your uncle."

"So he is. Or half an uncle, at the least." Her lips thinned as she buttered a piece of bread for herself. "Or better said, an eighth part of an uncle, since he is only half uncle to half of us, and only acts like uncle to half of those. He has always greatly favored my sisters and me over my brothers."

Gunnar shrugged. The reason was obvious to him. "You and your sisters cannot claim the throne."

"Nor can my brothers. Parliament has said it."

"Nor could Henry, himself, by right," pointed out Gunnar. "Richard was the one born king. And yet there Henry sits."

Lady Eleanor's expression went flat. "Be careful of what you say, sir. Richard's supporters are not well suffered here. Nor Mortimer's."

"I supported neither of them. But truth is truth. If your brothers grow powerful enough, one of them might attempt what Bolingbroke himself succeeded at. Perhaps he keeps your brothers at a distance for fear he or Prince Harry will find themselves obliged to go to war against them one day. It is difficult to fight a man once you've coddled him as a child."

She looked down to where her brothers sat, and a crease formed between her brows. "My Beaufort uncles have certainly given the king cause to consider such a possibility. You surely have it right."

"I wish I did not, if it makes you frown so. I should have held my tongue and kept your smile."

"As you say, *monsire*, truth is truth. And your explanation does help me better understand the king. And my father," she added softly, almost to herself.

They both dropped silent as the varlets approached to fill their trencher. Despite the bread and butter, Gunnar's stomach rumbled even more loudly as the pile of food before him grew.

Lady Eleanor's face cleared, and she snatched up a sliver of roasted goose and held it up to him. "Here, Sir Gunnar, quickly, before you frighten the dogs."

Chuckling, he leaned forward to take the morsel and, with barely a thought, closed his lips over the tip of her finger and sucked.

It was something he'd done scores of times through the centuries, letting a bite of food shared with some wench lead to the "accidental" contact of lip to finger. 'Twas always an enjoyable moment, whether it led to more or not. But this time . . .

The surge of Gunnar's pulse was mirrored in the slight widening of Lady Eleanor's eyes. *Yes.* He released her finger before anyone could notice, but not before he ran his tongue around the tip. He grinned as he caught that sound again, that little catch in her breath he'd heard when he'd collected his victor's kiss. A warm, rosy glow flowed up from the neck of her gown, making her look less embarrassed than . . . aroused.

Beddable.

He'd thought of that all week, that wooing and winning her also meant bedding her. At first it had given him trouble; the image of her as a smoke-smudged child remained in his head. But she was eight-and-ten now, or very nearly so, a woman full-grown and more than ready for marriage. A fair, spirited woman who would surely be just as spirited abed.

A woman of royal blood.

Now there was a twist. He hadn't known that while he sat alone in the night forest, planning his campaign for her heart and body and spilling blood to thank the gods for this chance. He had no business considering a woman so high, not when he was what he was.

But even as the hairs on his neck lifted in warning, Gunnar found himself reaching to cut a slice of the goose, holding it out like a lure to a falcon soaring high over his head. "You should try a bit of the gander yourself, my lady. I am certain you will enjoy it."

Her color rose higher. She understood his meaning.

As Gunnar held his breath, she hesitated a moment, then slowly leaned in to take the bite. Her lips never touched him, but just before her teeth closed on the meat, her tongue brushed the tip of his thumb in a caress so subtle that he wasn't certain he'd truly felt it.

His blood was certain, though. Danger or not, it sang to life in his veins and rushed to his tarse, where he could easily imagine her tongue performing the same trick. By the gods. *Did she have any idea?*

Of course she did, her modestly lowered eyes notwithstanding—a conviction that was confirmed when she delicately licked a droplet off her own fingertip—the same fingertip he'd suckled—then looked up at him through those thick lashes of hers in a way that nearly made him groan aloud.

By the gods, if he didn't know better, he'd think she was out to seduce *him*. Perhaps winning her truly would be an easy thing.

But not if his lust got ahead of him. He needed her love, not merely her desire. He needed to take his time, to woo her, to make certain he had not just her body, but her heart. He needed to slow down.

A glance toward where her father sat beside his lady wife's empty chair provided some of the chill he needed: *Royal blood. Powerful father. King's niece.* If he fouled this, the whole of England would be after his balls.

Even so, it took him a while to shepherd his wayward thoughts back into line. Eventually, though, the weight at his crotch eased, and he managed to turn the conversation to safer subjects for long enough to get through supper. News of the waning campaign in Wales. The chill weather. Court gossip she might have heard.

He must have kept things too safe, however, because as they finished the wedge of gingerbread that ended the meal, she rose, apparently ready to retire.

"Forgive me, my lady," Gunnar rose, too. "I am too seldom amongst gentlefolk to recall how to be good company to a lady."

"What? Oh, no, you mistake me. You do not escape so easily." She lifted a hand and crooked a finger, and Screaming Lucy abandoned her place at the table with the fosterlings, collected a brace of serving women, and hurried off.

"My lord?" Lady Eleanor turned to her father. "I readied a gift for Sir Gunnar all those years ago and had no chance to give it. I would like to do so now."

"Of course. Have it brought."

"'Twould be better given in the solar. Do we have your pardon to leave?"

The earl frowned. "Will others attend you?"

"Of course, my lord. Lucy goes now with servants to fetch things and meet us there."

"Fine, then." Lord Ralph waved them off. "We will be along shortly."

Eleanor put out her hand. "Come, *monsire*."

As before, he found he had little choice but to obey. He rose in surrender, and let her lead him upstairs.

The solar of Raby Castle was larger than the hall of most manors and far more pleasant, what with ell upon ell of heavy tapestries lining the walls and what looked to be acres of thick rugs upon the floor. Enough candles lit the chamber to make it glow like a clear dawn, but as they entered, a servant, apparently stationed there for no other purpose, hurried to light more. As he worked, they stood silently, Eleanor rocking up and down on her toes in a way that belied the bland look on her face, until at last the man finished and vanished with his lighting rush, leaving them suddenly and unexpectedly alone.

Alone.

"Your woman is not here yet," said Gunnar.

"No." She lifted her chin to look directly into his eyes, challenging him with the slightest curve of a smile. "My lord father will not be pleased."

His pulse pounded in his skull, silencing everything but the voice that urged him toward her.

"Then we will not tell him," he murmured, and then somehow she was in his arms, her lips sweet and hot on his. With a groan, he lifted her against him, and her body melded perfectly to his, as he'd known it would.

"I dreamed of you," she whispered against his mouth. "So many nights, I wished you would come. Wished you would take me—" Muffled voices in the passageway made her stop short. "Ah, curse it. She is too quick."

She pushed out of his arms, whirling to face the hearth just as Lucy came in, followed by two maids whose arms were laden with clothes.

Gunnar stood there half stupefied, Eleanor's taste lingering on his lips, her words ringing in his skull. *Wished you would take me.* Oh, yes, he would happily do that. But the sane part of him, the part not in rut, said she hadn't finished the thought. Surely she hadn't been so boldly asking him to *take* her. Trying to regain control, he stalked over to the table and poured himself a cup of wine.

Eleanor turned to Lucy with an easy smile, the roses in her cheeks looking like they might well come from the heat of the fire. "You were quick."

"I knew you were anxious, my lady."

"Aye, I am. And so, Sir Gunnar, I may at last give you your gifts." Eleanor motioned one of the maids forward, her cool manner giving no sign of the heat they'd shared, a fair measure of which still clung to Gunnar like cobwebs. "First these. I began them when I heard that you had left without waiting for new clothes from the duchess. I knew yours were burned and that you would need something warm for your travels. However, I did not know it would take so long to give them to you."

Garment by garment, she showed him a heavy winter traveling cloak and a full set of clothes to go with it, draping each piece in turn over the high-backed chair that Lucy pulled near. Then the other maid stepped forward, and Eleanor showed a second set of clothing, finer this time, cut from velvet and figured silk rich enough for a great lord. Together, they made up more clothing than Gunnar had owned at one time since he'd left home. They must represent months of work. Perhaps years. His lust faded away as he absorbed it all.

"You sewed all this?" he asked, stunned, when she had finished. "For me?"

"For no one else."

"Every stitch by her own hand, *monsire*," added Lucy. "She would not accept even my help, beyond the measuring and cutting."

"My lady," said Gunnar, and then could say no more. *She'd sewn for him.* No one had sewn for him except for

pay since before he'd sailed. He swallowed hard, trying to
clear the lump that clogged his throat, but it only thickened.

She rescued him by taking the wine cup from his hand.
"Come. I had to guess at the size from what I remembered
and what Lucy could add. Let us see if I came close, or if I
must make changes."

"But I—"

"Try them, *monsire*," urged Lucy, and Gunnar found
himself shedding his worn gown. Lady Eleanor stepped
forward holding his new chemise. Ever aware of his scars,
he kept his back to the wall while he stripped off his old
one and pulled on the new in a single motion.

He smoothed and tested it and nodded in approval. "If you
guessed as well with the other things, they will fit very well."

"I used ties rather than hooks or buttons, as they are
more forgiving if I guessed poorly," explained Eleanor as
he reached for the long-sleeved doublet that Lucy held out.
"And everything fastens in front, to make it easier for you
in your travels."

"It will be that," he assured her. With each tie he tied,
the doublet formed itself to his body, until it fitted more
closely than any garment he'd ever worn. It was time, he
supposed. He'd been avoiding the new style of clothes in
the fear they would bind, but the old, loose gowns were
more and more the mark of cottars and not knights. When
he flexed his arms and shoulders, testing, he found more
than enough ease. "It is comfortable."

"You sound surprised. Have you no faith in my skills?
Let me see." She stepped around behind him and ran her
hands over his shoulders to check the fit of what she'd
made, a common gesture made uncommon by the way her
hands lingered. Gunnar closed his eyes and let his imagination play for a moment.

"It will do, I think. Lucy, the cote-hardie, if you please.
I tried to leave enough room for a second doublet beneath
for winter, but it was difficult to be sure without having

you there. I had to mark your height and the width of your shoulders against the frame of the door where you stood beside the duchess. I had Lucy do the same, and we had nearly the same marks, so I chose the larger of each." As she chattered, she helped him into the cote-hardie, then came around to tie the ties, deftly working her way down his chest. "Do I hear my father coming?

Lucy went to peer through the grillwork that over-looked the hall. "Not yet, my lady. He has called for the chessboard."

"Keep watch and tell me when he starts up. You two fold everything." Eleanor smiled up at Gunnar. "See if the cote pulls across the shoulders, *monsire*."

Ah. Grinning, he obliged, thrusting his arms forward. "A excellent fit, my lady. You guessed very well."

"Test it fully, sir." She glanced to his arms on either side of her and stepped closer to take hold of the hem of the cote-hardie and tug it down.

The gesture put her hands parlous close to his crotch, and a fresh wave of desire washed over Gunnar. *Wishing you would take me*, she'd said. Perhaps the thought had been complete after all. A glance over his shoulder told him that the maids were busy and that Lucy was still at the grill, watching. None of the three paid them any heed.

A slight shift put his back fully to Lucy, blocking her view of her mistress. Thus shielded, he crossed his arms midair behind Eleanor, enfolding her, embracing her with-out actually touching her. She tilted her head back to meet his eyes, and a slow smile curved her lips. She laid one hand on his chest, exactly over his heart. Her lips parted, ready for another kiss. *Take me . . .*

"Aye," he murmured. "A very comfortable fit indeed."

They stood there, his arms encircling her, her smiling up at him, hovering on the edge of that kiss, until Lucy cleared her throat. "The earl comes, my lady."

Eleanor's smile fell away with Gunnar's arms. "I think it will do."

She stepped away to retrieve the belt that hung on the chair, presenting it to Gunnar as her father and the other women came trooping through the door, then, as though nothing at all had passed between them, she drifted off, leaving only a whiff of her perfume in her wake.

Westmorland walked over and looked Gunnar up and down. "You made all these clothes yourself, Eleanor?"

"Aye, my lord. His were burned in saving me." Eleanor lowered her eyes, strangely tense. "Her Grace thought it a good gift."

"Mmm." As the women and girls began settling on the various stools and cushions, Lord Ralph stepped past Gunnar to finger the velvet houpelande and brocade jacket that lay over the chair. He picked up the other chemise and squinted at the stitching. "You have your mother's skill with a needle."

Eleanor's relief was plain, though the tautness remained around her eyes. "I am pleased you think so, my lord."

"And you, Sir Gunnar. Are you pleased as well?"

Fully aware of the obstacle Westmorland could present to his plans, Gunnar carefully kept his eyes off Eleanor as he buckled the belt. "Very much, my lord."

"Good." Lord Ralph took his seat and, as the maids cleared the trove of clothing and set it to one side, motioned Gunnar toward the other chair. "Go on. My wife has no need of it tonight, nor for some time to come."

"Your lady is well, I hope," said Gunnar, easing down. Lady Eleanor took a seat beside Lucy on the far side of the room. *Good. It was safer that way.*

"Aye, she brings children forth with little trouble, thanks be to God." Lord Ralph sighed with an odd heaviness. "And so I have another son who will need lands."

"There is always the Church," offered Gunnar.

"If he chooses it for himself. Otherwise, I must marry him to a title, which means finding yet another heiress. With so many children, it is nearly as difficult to find good wives for sons as it is to find good husbands for daughters."

"How many children do you have, my lord? I have been trying to count, but I think some are not here."

Lord Ralph chewed the end of his mustache as he considered. "Let me think. With Margaret there were Maud, Alice, Philippa, John, Elizabeth, Ralph, Margaret, Anne, and, um, Anastasia." He ticked them off on his fingers as he named them. "And then with Joan, there are Catherine, Eleanor, Joan, Richard, Thomas, Cuthbert, Robert, William, and now Edward. That makes eight and ten so far, and one other who died young. Plus we have her two from Ferrers with us now that their fostering is done. An old woman once told me that I would sire two dozens. I thought her mad, but look at me."

"Many men would envy you."

"They don't have to feed them all and marry them off. But come, we are here for another purpose. Bertrand?"

"Here, my lord." An aging retainer stepped forward with a small personal casket, which he placed on the table next to the sweets. Lord Ralph set aside his cup and took a ring of keys from his belt.

"I determined long ago that you would have this for reward. And now I am glad I set it aside, for it will suit that new houpelande." He unlocked the casket and pulled out a heavy chain of silver and gold links. He let the chain pool onto the table with a clatter, then reached in again to produce an unmounted sapphire twice the size of the ruby in the ring the Duchess of York had given Gunnar the night of the fire. "And this is from my lady wife. Both come with our thanks for Eleanor's life."

Gunnar held out his hands to stop him. "It is too much, my lord."

"To the contrary. It is far too little and, as my wife has reminded me, far, far too late. I should have had one of my men track you down years ago, but I thought our paths would cross. However, you are here now, and so you will have it." He dropped the chain back into the chest, placed the sapphire on top, and locked the casket. Taking the key off his ring, he pushed it across to Gunnar. "Take it. It is yours, as is Eleanor's little gift. Bertrand will see it is kept safe until you are ready to ride on."

"Thank you, my lord." Gunnar dropped the key into his purse and, as it clinked against the coins he'd gotten for the silver branch, became richer than he'd been in years. And that wasn't even counting the treasure that was Eleanor herself, smiling as she pretended not to watch from across the room.

Westmorland pushed to his feet. "I left three of my sons trying to best my marshal at chess, and I wish to see the outcome. Come. We will leave the women to their music and gossip."

Eleanor's smile faded with Gunnar's spirits. The earl strode off, and Gunnar had little choice but to follow him out, with no time for more than a general "God's rest" to the ladies. Eleanor nodded back. "God's rest to you as well, *monsire*."

So much for this evening of wooing.

Good thing he would be back.

CHAPTER 6

WITH MOST OF the tourney guests having moved on, things were different at Raby the next night. Supper was already half over when Gunnar arrived—likely the way it would be most evenings, since noble households tended to eat their second meal earlier than those who worked the fields—so after he washed, he slid into the first empty place he found amongst the earl's knights. The meat was less plentiful than at the high table, and the bread made of coarser meal, but it was still far better fare than he enjoyed most nights, and he ate it with just as much pleasure.

The only drawback was that he wasn't beside Eleanor, so instead of having another chance to woo her, he was left to perform the trick she had managed so well the night before in the solar: to watch without seeming to watch.

Fortunately, he had a perfect view, right over the marshal's shoulder. Anytime the man spoke—which was often and at length—Gunnar could feign attention and watch the lady instead.

In some ways, his position was better. He saw more than

he would have at her side: how easily she smiled, how she made those around her laugh with some jest he couldn't hear, how she picked over her food even though she didn't have him to share with.

How she glanced at him, then looked elsewhere as she delicately sucked the grease off a fingertip.

He was still contemplating that one when Screaming Lucy approached him after the meal.

"His lordship asks if you will join him in the solar, and . . ." She hesitated, picking at a loose bit of braid on her sleeve.

"What?"

"And my lady said to tell you she desires you say yes." She made a slight dip and flitted away.

My lady desires you say yes. He liked those words, *desires you*, and wondered if Eleanor had chosen them on purpose, as a reminder of those brief moments alone in the solar. It still took his breath away, thinking about the way she'd surged into his arms. There was a part of him that wished for the old days, the raiding days, when he could have thrown her over his saddle and carried her off without asking anyone.

But those days were long over. This was going to be about courtship, about subtlety and stolen moments, about the kind of coolness Eleanor had shown last night in the aftermath of their kiss.

Aye, she'd shown him the path, if he could just manage to follow her. It worried him. There were many reasons his *fylgja* took the form of a bull; shrewdness and cunning weren't amongst them.

Girding himself for the challenge ahead, he finished the last bites of his meal, picked up his cup, and headed toward the solar. Even though he was the last to leave the hall, Eleanor somehow—by accident or design?—ended up falling in beside him. Mindful of the many eyes watching, Gunnar offered her the sort of polite nod he would give her sisters.

"How went your business, *monsire*?" she asked as they started up. In the narrow confines of the stairway, her hand brushed against his. He bunched his fist and stretched it wide, trying to purge his senses of her touch before it made him want to reach for her.

"Neither well nor badly." *Nor any way at all.* He had no business, of course, excepting the need to hide what he was by day. "I fear it may take some weeks to finish it."

"Ah. You will be in the area some while, then. You will want to stay here at Raby."

They reached the top step, and he stood aside to let her enter the solar first. "It would make a convenient base, if the earl is willing to have me."

"Have you what?" asked Westmorland as they entered the hall.

"Rest here while he goes about his business, my lord," said Eleanor. "I would not speak for you, but—"

"Of course you can stay here," Westmorland said to Gunnar. "The marshal can provide a bed for you in the garrison."

"A kind offer, my lord, but I sleep fitfully and will be riding out well before sunrise most days. 'Twill be far easier on your men if I take my rest in the hall."

"Will it? Well, then, the hall it shall be. Bertrand!"

As her father turned to snap a few orders at his steward, a smile flickered across Eleanor's lips, quick as a midge, betraying her pleasure in a way her voice and manner had not.

Everyone from the earl's guests and grown children to the full complement of fosterlings and higher-ranked knights packed the solar this night. Pages bustled around pouring wine and filling ale pots, and servants produced gaming tables as well as boards for use by those who took their ease on the thick rugs and floor cushions. As a minstrel and his harper took up a tune in the far corner, Gunnar was called over to the earl's hearthside table to be introduced to some newly arrived guests. He found himself facing a lad of about twice ten years who looked vaguely familiar.

"You two know each other, of course," said Westmorland.

The lad inspected Gunnar closely, then shook his head. "No, my lord. I do not know him. Should I?"

Westmorland frowned at Gunnar, who was equally confounded. "How is this possible? Does Lesbury not lie within Alnwick?"

Of course. The lad seemed familiar because he was a Percy. He had the look of the old earl, who, if Gunnar was right, was this lad's grandsire. This boy would have been Earl of Northumberland, and thus lord of Alnwick, if his father and grandfather hadn't been such rebellious fools. Now they were dead, their lands and title forfeited to the Crown, and their heir, this boy, left with nothing but a tainted name.

"I was born while my parents were on pilgrimage, my lord," Gunnar hurried to explain. That was the story he and the others had always used to pass their bit of land from man to man over the centuries; he could only hope it would still suffice awhile longer. It became harder to maintain the lie as the English kept more and better records. "And I was left to foster in Guelders. I had not yet returned to take possession of my land when young Lord Percy, here, was still at Alnwick."

"Well, then 'tis time you met, even though he's not your lord any longer. Nor lord of anything. Henry Percy, I give you Sir Gunnar of Lesbury. He'll owe you fealty one day, if you ever manage to get your title back."

Percy nodded politely to Gunnar, but his eyes bore nothing but sharp steel for Westmorland. Another of the guests, a Lord Lumley from Surrey, took one look at Percy's frown and turned to the earl. "Shall I set up the chessmen, my lord?"

"Aye. I learned last evening that Sir Gunnar is a fair hand at chess. We shall have a small tourney, and I will challenge the victor."

Eleanor, who had wandered off for a moment, reappeared at her father's shoulder. "Chess again, my lord? I hoped we might play at cards. It has been a long while."

"Cards?" Lord Lumley perked up. "I do enjoy cards."

"Mmm. Perhaps." Westmorland turned to Gunnar. "Do you play, sir?"

"I, um, do not think so, my lord. 'Struth, I do not know what cards is. Are."

"Truly?" The earl drummed his fingers on the table, considering this. "They are new, but not so very new. Where have you been that you have never encountered them?"

In a wild dene, with a wolf. "Traveling, my lord, and to the wrong places, it seems."

"We can fix that."

"I'll fetch them, my lord." Eleanor quickly retrieved a small box from the cupboard, plunked it down in the center of the table, and flipped it open to remove what appeared to be a tiny, unbound book. Pulling one page free, she held it out to Gunnar. "These small leaves of pressed linen are the cards."

Gunnar took the leaf to examine it. It was a longish square painted on one side with a design of red and yellow flowers and on the other with six gilded chalices.

"This is a simple set," said Westmorland. "The king has far finer ones, of course. In fact, I gave him a far finer one last year."

As the earl boasted, Gunnar took another card and compared it to the first. This one had four silvered swords on the one side, but on the other . . .

"The flowers are the same," he said. "To the very line."

"They press the back of each with a carved block of wood covered in ink and then add the colors and gilding by hand," said Eleanor. "Or so my lord father tells us."

"Do you accuse me of lying?" her father challenged.

Eleanor became immediately contrite. "Of course not, my lord, I just have never seen it myself."

Westmorland snatched the cards away from her. "Well, I have. I watched a man do it in France when I bought these. He makes images for pilgrims in the same way, hundreds just alike. Even with the time spent carving, it is faster than any man can trace them." The earl plucked the other two cards from Gunnar's fingers, returned them to the book, and fanned them all out like a peacock's tail. "So. Will you play?"

"Gladly, my lord, if someone will teach me."

"Eleanor may show you." Lord Ralph casually split the book of cards in two and ruffled the halves neatly back together, a clever trick that made Gunnar want to try his hand at it. "She is a fair player for her sex, though she rarely bests me. Percy, you will be our fourth."

Eleanor dragged a stool over next to Gunnar, who quickly found himself learning about suits and what made a winning hand and how that ruffling trick worked—'twas more difficult than it looked. He also found himself learning more of Eleanor herself—and suffering for what he learned.

It was odd. Other than instructions on the rules of the game, she said little and behaved herself as any modest maid helping a guest, except . . .

Except that every time she reached to point to a card, she managed to brush against his arm. Like the contact in the stairwell, her touch seemed accidental, and she gave no sign it was otherwise.

But each touch sent sparks racing up Gunnar's arm, where they then dispersed to other parts of his body to set them aflame. Before long, it was all he could do to keep his mind on the most basic rules, much less absorb any hint of strategy. She might as well have been working to help her father win: her sweet tortures so distracted Gunnar that even playing the cards she indicated, he lost every hand to the earl. However, in the end, he threw down one particular card and Eleanor softly cleared her throat and signaled with her eyes.

He stared at the cards a moment before he saw it. "Aah. I think that that is triumph?"

"Triumph, indeed." Henry Percy threw down his cards in frustration. "First the earl and now you. The cards do not favor me tonight."

"You have picked up on the game quickly, Sir Gunnar," said Westmorland. "You're ready to play on your own, I think."

Gunnar shook his head. "Hardly, my lord. I owe this one small success to the lady's skill, not my own."

"Hold fast to Eleanor, Sir Gunnar," warned one of the earl's older sons, laughing from where he leaned against the wall watching. "My lord father tries to puff you up, so you will think yourself done with lessons and ready to wager on your own."

"He has done it to all of us," said Sir Gilbert from his spot by Lady Anne. "His lordship much enjoys winning."

"At everything," added Eleanor, and Gunnar thought he caught a hint of accusation beneath her light tone.

But if there was, Westmorland missed it. Laughing, he scooped the cards together to begin again. "Of course I enjoy winning. What fool wouldn't? Help him with another game or two, then, Eleanor, but don't jump so quickly to tell him what to play. Let him try it on his own first."

"Yes, my lord."

So the torture continued, made worse for its inconsistency. Not knowing when she would lean in to help, Gunnar found himself waiting, anticipating. It was far more difficult, he discovered, to steel himself to touches that fell like random drops of rain.

His head whirling, he pulled out the wrong card.

"Ah, no, *monsire*." She leaned especially close to point out his error, and he swore—*swore*—he could feel a pebble of hardness at the peak of the breast that pressed so firmly against his arm. Or was it merely a seam of her fitted bodice? If he could look, he might be able to tell, but with her father right there, not a yard away, and all her brothers and half brothers watching, too, he didn't dare.

And yet he so wanted to know.

Sanity battled desire. His crotch throbbed in time with the minstrel's music. Perhaps just a glance . . .

She shifted away again. "Do you dance, Sir Gunnar?"

The question, coming from nowhere as it did, shocked him back from the edge of madness. He shook his head and cleared his throat. "It has been far too many years since I had a chance to practice."

"A pity. Margaret, Mary, and I had discussed having dancing tomorrow after supper. If my lord approves."

"I'm sure he can manage a dance or two," said the earl, still unaware of what was really going on, thank the gods. "We will discuss it on the morrow. Just now, it is time for the women to retire."

"But it is early yet," Eleanor began. Her father glowered at her, and she quickly clamped her lips together. "Yes, my lord."

Gunnar stood and offered his hand to help her rise, relishing the excuse to touch her at last, to get a good look at her, to discover whether those eyes of hers held innocence or . . . no, mischief. Definitely mischief. *Had her color been that high all evening?* He held back a grin and gave her a bow. "My thanks for your aid tonight, my lady. God's rest."

"You were a most excellent student, *monsire*." Eleanor did her courtesy to Gunnar, to the other guests, and finally, to her father. "God's rest to you all, my lords."

Westmorland waved her off impatiently. He sat back until she and the other women left, then leaned forward, his expression avid. "Go on, Lumley, it is your play, and I wager you tuppence you cannot complete that suit."

THE WIND WAS rising.

Eleanor lay in bed beside Lucy, listening to the rattle of the shutters against the window frame alternate with her cousin's snores. Noisy as they were, wind and snores had little to do with the wakefulness that had dogged her all night; that she blamed on the remembered pressure of Gunnar's muscled arm against her breasts.

It wasn't his fault, by any measure. To his credit, he'd said or done nothing her father could take badly, remained so stolid, so impassive, in fact, that for a time she hadn't been certain he even noticed what she was doing. But then she'd watched him wiping his palms on his thighs to dry them, caught a sideways glance that he couldn't quite control, and known she was winning.

He wanted her.

And why not? She was young and fair—some even said comely—and she knew what she was doing, thanks to too many years spent watching ladies and knights play the games of love while she waited for Richard. She'd set out to make Gunnar desire her, and she had succeeded.

"Gunnar." She pronounced his name soundlessly into the night, testing its strangeness on her tongue for the thousandth time.

Sir Gunnar wanted her.

And she wanted him. She hadn't allowed for that, that in seducing him, she would seduce herself. Brushing against him had had far more effect on her than she would have guessed, the pleasure spreading like fire from breast to belly, growing hotter until she could think of little else.

She wanted Gunnar.

She wanted him with an urgency that kept her whole body trembling, making it impossible to sleep. If she could get up and do something—sew, read, anything—she might be able to distract herself, but what could she do in the middle of the night? Perhaps if she could just see him, she could . . .

No, that was foolish. But the notion wouldn't leave her be. It sat in her belly like common hunger, demanding satisfaction. A taste. A moment. She lay there wrestling the craving as long as she could bear it, then carefully crawled out of bed. Lucy mumbled and rolled over, and Eleanor froze, one foot on the floor, and waited until her cousin's soft snores started up again before she continued. Moving as silently as an owl, she found her slippers and a robe to pull around her shoulders, then took a stub of candle from the basket, lit it from the night lamp, and eased out the barely opened door.

Her tiny flame lit only the circle around her, leaving the far end of passageway in blackness. She hesitated, certain that what she was doing was not right, but hoping that if she saw him just for a moment, she'd be able to sleep. Careful that she made no noise to echo in the stone hall, she set out and found her way to the darkened solar and over to the grillwork where she could see into the hall below.

He was the only one awake, a solitary figure that sat staring into the fire. He'd said he slept fitfully, but as she watched his fingers work a length of rope, tying and untying knots like the sailors that worked her father's ships, she couldn't help but wonder if his wakefulness tonight was related to her own.

After a time, he laid aside the rope and stretched his long legs toward the hearth, much as he had done that night at Richmond. Eleanor smiled at the sight. She couldn't remember now what had drawn her to approach him that first evening, whether it was mere childish whim or some deeper augury, but now, standing here in the dark and looking back from a distance of years, it seemed she could have done nothing else.

The wind howled louder, raising drafts that sent shivers down Eleanor's back and set the candle flame dancing. Below, the shadow of the screen rippled and wavered against the far wall. Gunnar's head jerked up to stare.

With a start, Eleanor pinched out the flame, but it was too late. He'd seen it. He shot to his feet and spun, looking straight at her through the darkened screen. He knew it was she, she was certain of it, and that certainty was confirmed as he started across the hall. A moment later, his boots sounded on the stairs.

And then he was there, a phantom in the darkness, and even in the thin light that seeped through the grill from below, she could see the desire that glittered in his eyes.

Aye, he wanted her.

She shouldn't be here. She should go. But her belly tightened with anticipation, and she could do nothing but meet his eyes, his desire, with her own. She ran into his arms.

Gunnar caught her up and spun her back against the wall, his mouth covering her gasp of shock before it broke the silence. His tongue plunged into her open mouth and found hers. She'd never been kissed like that, devoured like that, but it seemed the most natural thing to devour him in turn, to challenge and parry and lick and suck like he did. His responding groan was a bare exhalation, almost without sound, but it set her blood pounding through her body so hot it drove away every sense of modesty along with the chill. Heated to the very core, she moved restlessly against him.

Somewhere far away, a door hinge squealed. Gunnar broke away, lifted his head, then put his lips by her ear. "Someone comes. You must go."

She cocked her head to listen, heard the door shut and the distant footfalls coming from the direction of the kitchen. *No, not now.*

"No time." She grabbed Gunnar's hand and led him across the solar into the retiring room, where they ducked behind the draperies that covered a hidden niche beside the window. Pressed together there in the dark, they listened to the footsteps enter and scuffle closer. Eleanor held her breath as a stripe of torchlight grazed their toes beneath the draperies. If they were caught, her father would have Gunnar's head on a pike. But the watchman, whoever he was, turned. He continued on his rounds and the light dwindled away.

As his footsteps faded into the distance, she started to part the draperies to leave, ready to forego this dangerous liaison, but Gunnar tugged on her hand, wordlessly pulling her back to him. In the blackness, he had to trace up her arms to find her face. He cupped her head and held her still, one thumb beneath her chin as he carefully lowered his mouth to hers.

This time his kiss was more careful, the exploration of his tongue slower. It was his hands that plundered her now, tracing over her boldly in the dark, down over her arms, breasts, belly, hips, and finally around to cup her bottom and pull her against him. She felt a leap of hardness against her where they touched and that was enough to plunge her back into the heat. It was she who pulled him back toward the wall.

There against its support, their hands and mouths were free to do their worst. The dark made their mutual assault both more difficult and more delicious, heightening every touch and taste. He taught her how to use it by example, trailing kisses everywhere, molding curves and planes with his palms, and silently encouraging her to do the same.

She'd touched him a little earlier, as she'd seen to his clothes, but not like this, not at leisure and with such awareness. His muscles were bulky but lean under her hands, his chest as hard as stone, and she knew that beneath his clothes, his skin must surely be as fevered as her own. Wanting to know, she slipped her hands up beneath his cote and found the gap between his doublet and hose. Flattening her hands over the narrow band of skin, she felt the heat that poured off him, sensed the quiver beneath her palms, and knew both the power she had and how badly she wanted that skin against her own.

He let her explore that small territory while he turned his attention to her breasts, slowly circling them with fingertips before he cupped them and dragged his thumbs over the peaks. She shuddered with the pleasure of it and pushed toward him. He pressed her back with one hand and held her while he kissed his way down her neck once more, then farther, past the neck of her chemise, to find the breast he still cupped. His lips closed over her nipple through the linen.

The flame that roared through her turned want into need. Her fingers clenched mindlessly, digging into his sides, and she lifted her hips toward him, searching for relief from that terrible, empty ache between her legs. With a barely audible growl, he drew her nipple into his mouth hard, his tongue working the tip through the thin cloth until she had to press her lips together to hold back a cry.

He shifted, forcing a knee between hers and lifting so she straddled him, his thigh hard against the place where she ached. The breath caught in her lungs, and she thought to say stop, but before she could, he shifted his hands to her hips and dragged her forward over his thigh. Every thought of stopping him vanished in the realization that this, this was what her body cried for.

His broad hands guided her, showing her the rhythm until she found it for herself. As she ground against him, searching for the perfect motion, the perfect pressure, the perfect end, his hands busied themselves with something else. And then they were on her, not through cloth, but skin to skin, her gown up around her waist, his palms on her belly.

She gasped, and he silenced her again, his tongue plunging into her mouth in the same perfect rhythm as her hips had discovered. One hand moved slowly lower, brushed through her woman's hair, then slid lower still, until his fingers slipped between his thigh and her quaint. Ah, yes. She recognized the touch, his intent, and moved to welcome him, the need worse than ever. Hanging on the edge of the unknown, she adjusted a little, putting his fingers to the exact spot, and thrust at him. Wanting. Close.

A footstep echoed somewhere beyond the draperies, the guard coming back through the solar, and the sound, the knowledge they could be caught, tripped her over the edge. Pleasure flashed through her like lightning and shattered her. The steps and light neared, sending her deeper into the spasms. A moan gathered at the back of her throat. She fought to hold it back, the struggle making her body quake harder. Gunnar quickly covered her mouth with his and curled his body around her protectively, holding her together as she shook.

By the time her senses came back to her, the guard was long gone. Gunnar still held her close, his hand curved possessively between her legs, his fingers moving in tiny, lazy circles that sent the last shocks of completion through her. He kissed her forehead, and she could feel the smile that curved his lips and raised a hand to trace it with her fingertips. A full smile, this time. She wanted to see it.

And she wanted to return the pleasure he'd given her. She stroked his cheek as she moved her other hand, still at the edge of his doublet, to tug at the end of one lace. It came free and she moved to the next. Something bumped her wrist in the dark. She jerked away, then realized it was his member, swelling and bobbing against the loosened cloth. She tentatively reached out, cupped him as he still cupped her, felt his deep sigh against her temple.

He entwined his fingers with hers and pulled her hand away.

She rose up on her toes to kiss him, using her tongue the way he'd taught her to show him how much she wanted to do this for him. The wind rattled at the shutters, now carrying with it, thin and high, the rooster's first crow, warning of a still-distant dawn. There was time. She reached for his laces.

This time, Gunnar's fingers bit into her wrist. "Stop," he whispered against her ear. "I must go."

"But—"

"I must. I'm sorry." He pushed the draperies open a crack and listened, and he was gone, like that, across the retiring room, out into the solar and down the stairs before she could even protest.

She stood there, mouth agape, stung that he could leave her like that, not understanding at all. She started after him, but he was already below, so she stood at the screen, angry and disappointed, and watched him gather his things. He looked up at her, just as he had earlier, and for a moment she thought he was coming back to her.

Then abruptly he whirled away and strode toward the door. As he pushed it open, another cock's crow blew in on the wind. Gunnar stood there a moment, tension radiating from his body as he battled something within himself.

She understood, then. He was protecting both of them by going off to do his odd business, whatever it was. If he didn't, the guard on the gate would note the change, talk might spread. Lucy might realize she'd left the bed.

If he turned back, they would both be lost.

So before he could lose his will, she snatched the candle stub from the table where she'd left it and ran, plunging into the dark hallway, only slowing when the faraway thud of the closing door told her he had gone.

Her heart pounded like a drum in her ears as she groped her way back to her room. Lucy still snored, thank the saints. Eleanor dropped the candle back into the basket with the other stubs, shed her robe, and slipped back into bed, grateful that no one would know she'd ever been gone, ever done anything so wonderful, so foolish, so utterly sinful. As the cock crowed again, she closed her eyes and pretended to sleep, knowing she'd made a terrible mistake and trying to ignore the soft, wicked voice that whispered that the mistake had been not in going, but in waiting so late to do it.

CHAPTER 7

"WHAT HAPPENED TO my riband?"

Lucy glanced up from the veil she was pinning into shape. "Is it caught in your gown?"

Holding the end of one braid, Eleanor twisted to look. "I don't see it, and this side is half undone already. Come and help me."

Lucy left the veil and went over to shake out Eleanor's skirts. "It must have fallen off earlier. I will retrace our steps."

"Later. See if you can fix this."

Lucy inspected the intricate arrangement of interlaced braids that cradled her cousin's head. "I'm not certain I can. Miriam did something different today, and I'm not certain where the plaits start and stop."

"Try, before they come out entirely."

"Yes, my lady." Lucy fetched a spare length of riband from the basket and, draping it over her shoulder, started trying to sort out one braid from the next as Eleanor jounced up and down, the way she was wont to do when she was happy. Unfortunately, Lucy suspected why she jounced, and it wasn't good. "I am going to undo a bit more. 'Twould be easier if you would stand still."

"I'm sorry. I shall try." Eleanor settled on her heels.

Lucy separated the various strands between her fingers and started rebraiding them. It seemed to go together correctly, but when she compared the results to the other side, the pattern didn't match. With Lady Eleanor beginning to jounce again, Lucy undid things and started again, tugging a strand to one side then the other without result. "This makes no sense."

"Then tie it off and fetch Miriam. The horn is about to blow for supper."

"And you are about to be married." Lucy clapped her mouth shut. She hadn't meant to say that aloud.

The braid flew out of Lucy's grasp as her cousin whirled on her. "Stop. We will not do this again."

Foolish, but now it was begun, she may as well finish. "I think we must, my lady, and that we must do it until you hear me. You and Sir Gunnar cannot . . ." Lucy stopped, hesitant to put a name to what she suspected. She wasn't sure if the fuzzy recollection of her cousin crawling over her into bed sometime near dawn was real or a dream. "Does he know you are promised elsewhere?"

Eleanor flushed. "The subject has not arisen."

"Then you must raise it."

"But he'll . . . He won't." Eleanor took a deep breath and started afresh. "He is an honorable man and he—"

"How do you know?" demanded Lucy.

"What?"

"How do you know he is honorable?"

"He saved us from the fire."

"And I am as grateful as you for that. But that proves only that he has courage, not honor. How do you know he is honorable?"

"Because I do." Eleanor touched the pit of her stomach. "Because when I look into his eyes, I feel it here."

Lucy raised an eyebrow. "An odd place to feel someone else's honor. And so to salute his honor, you lie to him?"

"I have not lied."

"A truth untold is as good as a lie."

"You sound like a priest." Eleanor made a sour face.

"I fear you *need* a priest," said Lucy. "And if I were wise, I would summon one. Why have you not told Sir Gunnar you are betrothed?"

"Because if he knew, he would do the honorable thing and ride away." Eleanor stared past Lucy's shoulder, her eyes fixed on some private vision. "I don't want him to ride away. Not unless it is with me."

"Surely you don't still imagine . . ." Lucy's voice trailed off in disbelief as she sank down onto the bed. "That was a phantasm even four years ago. Now it is dangerous folly. If you ride off with him, your father will hunt you down and have Sir Gunnar drawn and quartered before your eyes."

"No." Eleanor pressed her hands to her temples and shook her head, denying the bloody image. "No he won't. Not if he gives us leave to marry first."

"God's toes. You are mad! The earl will never let you wed him."

"Why not?"

"Because he's poor."

"He has land in Lesbury. My father has picked men as low for his other daughters."

"Not those from your lady mother. He wants you married well. To Lord Burghersh."

"Well, Lesbury is here and Burghersh isn't. Richard could have come for me three years ago when he was made lord, yet here I sit, still unwed. He wants me as little as I want him, and my father grows impatient with both of us. When Sir Gunnar asks for my hand, he will say yes, just to be rid of me at last."

"*If* Sir Gunnar asks for you."

"He will."

"How do you know?" Lucy cut off the answer with a

wave of her hand. "Never mind. I know, you 'feel' it. Well, whatever Sir Gunnar wants, you *must* tell him about Lord Burghersh. Else I will."

"You cannot. Please, Lucy." Agitated, Eleanor paced back and forth across the room, chewing on her lip. "I will tell him in time, but I want him to grow fond of me first, so he is ready to ask for me."

"And what if he doesn't? What if you are mistaken and all he wants is to bed you?"

"He doesn't." Eleanor blushed deep red. "But if he did, then I would change his mind."

"Every maid who ever spread her legs to a passing knight has thought the same thing."

Eleanor went redder yet. Lucy's stomach twisted. Perhaps it hadn't been a dream. She was going to have to try to sleep more lightly.

"You cannot tell me this is wrong, Lucy. I knew even at Richmond that I preferred Sir Gunnar over Richard, and as soon as I saw him take that bow after he was knocked over in the mêlée, I knew I still do. He has such a good humor to him. Can you imagine Richard able to mock his own loss of dignity so easily? Or that in mocking dignity lost, he could ever regain it?"

Staring up at a cobweb that waved lazily from a beam, Lucy debated what answer to give. She hadn't intended the conversation to go this way at all.

"Well, can you?" Eleanor prodded.

Lucy sighed. "If I am going to insist you tell the truth, I suppose I am obliged to do the same."

"You are."

"The truth then. I cannot envisage Richard le Despenser with any dignity at all. And if by chance he found some, surely it would be in such short supply he would dare neither lose it nor mock it."

Eleanor sagged down next to her, nearly sobbing with relief. "Then you understand."

"I do. I should not admit it to you, but I do."

Eleanor laid her head on Lucy's shoulder. "I need your help, Lucy, please."

"God's toes. I am not some simpleton you can bend to your will with those doe's eyes." Lucy squinted crookedly down at her cousin. "I won't help him to bed you. Nor you to bed him. And I won't lie to the earl, nor to your lady mother."

"I would not ask you to. Besides, my lady mother will be lying in for another month, and the lord, my father barely takes note of me, except when he wants something of me or is angry with me."

"He will take note of *this*," predicted Lucy.

"We will be discreet."

"There is an entire castle full of people, some of whom will be quite pleased to carry tales to the earl."

"Anne, you mean."

Lucy nodded. "And anyone else who wants to curry favor."

"We will misdirect them."

Lucy sighed. "In other words, we will lie."

"Then you *will* help." Eleanor threw her arms around Lucy. "I vow, you are a better sister to me than any of those who own the title."

"A true sister would stop you, as I should." Lucy pried herself free and started toward the door, muttering to herself, "I am the worst kind of fool."

"Lucy?"

"What?"

"I will tell him of Richard, I promise. As soon as I am certain of his heart."

Lucy stopped with her hand on the door and slowly shook her head. "That thing you feel in your belly, my lady? That is not his honor but your own guilt. I know, because now I suffer of it, too. I will fetch Miriam to fix your hair."

She did her courtesy without looking at Eleanor and headed off to the retiring room, where she'd last seen Miriam. But the maid had vanished, and none of the other attendants knew where she was. Lucy dispatched a page to hunt her down and started back, and as she passed back through the solar, she thought she might as well check to see whether Sir Gunnar had come yet. Eleanor was going to ask anyway.

He hadn't. She leaned her aching head against the screen and closed her eyes.

When she opened them a few moments later, it was to find Henry Percy leaning against the same screen, barely a yard away, watching her with a bemused expression. "Who is it that you pine for, fair Lucy?"

"No one, *monsire*. I was resting, not pining. I did not hear you come in."

"Because I was already here." He tipped his head toward Lord Ralph's high-backed chair, sitting by the fire. "I thought I might try it for size, having lost my own for the time being. You won't tell Westmorland, will you?"

He sounded much like he had when he had visited York as a boy and tried to get away with filching a sweet. "No, *monsire*, I will not tell. You are hardly Geoffrey the Bastard, trying on King Henry's crown."

"You remember that story?"

She nodded.

"Well, I feel like him." He shifted to peer through the screen as she had been doing. "I saw you on guard here last evening, too. Surely you search for someone. Or does Lady Eleanor send you to watch on her behalf?"

So, it began. At least she could handle Sir Henry without a lie. "She doesn't even know I am here."

"'Struth?"

"'Struth. She sent me to fetch the woman to fix her hair, but I could not find her. I thought to steal a moment before I go back."

"Avoiding a scolding, eh? Has the lady developed a sharp tongue? I remember her as quick-tongued, but sweet-tempered."

"She is for the greatest part. I watch because it pleases

me to see the hall fill up—though 'tis less interesting now the tourney is over."

"So you watch *all* the men."

"All of them and none of them."

"But no one in particular?" There was an odd quality in his voice, and Lucy studied him a moment before answering.

"No. No one holds my special attention, *monsire*."

"How unfortunate for the men of Raby." Straightening, he reached out to tuck the edge of Lucy's head rail back where it had fallen forward. As he pulled back, his fingers grazed her cheek. "Unfortunate indeed. Perhaps that will change someday soon. By your leave."

He bowed and sauntered off, leaving Lucy to stare after him and wonder what had gotten into the water, and who it was going to make go mad next.

By the way her pulse was racing, it might be she.

ELEANOR MUST HAVE convinced her father, because the next night after supper, they danced.

Gunnar had forgotten how much pleasure there was in dancing. The music. The jollity. The women.

Especially the women.

He hadn't touched so many women in one evening in all his accursed life. Granted, the touching was just hands and the occasional brush of veil or skirt as they glided past, but that was more than he usually enjoyed, and best of all, the touches were given freely. Most times, he had to pay for a woman to touch him, to buy her with a measure of silver or at the very least a sweetly spoken lie. These women touched him for no reason at all beyond the dance, and every one of them seemed more desirable than the last.

But most desirable of all was Eleanor.

His senses were full of her, alive to every movement and laugh and flick of her braids, even when she was on the far side of the hall. Yet as he trod heavily through the few simple hayes and round dances he'd picked up over the years, she moved in and out of his grasp exactly like the others, giving so little sign of what had passed the night before that he began to doubt his recollection. A dream. He must've fallen asleep for a few moments and dreamed it.

But then she passed by in a promenade, and her eyes met his and flickered unwittingly toward the solar screen, and he knew. 'Twas no dream at all. She had come down in the night.

And he'd had to walk away.

She likely thought he'd spurned her, when in truth he'd only left because he had to, lest he change right there in front of her. Cursed sun. Why couldn't it go down and stay down?

He had to fix this.

The music carried her away on the next beat, but when it carried her back, he was ready. He took her hand and led her around the circle.

"I had a dream last night," he said they turned into the center. "Near dawn."

Her eyes widened slightly, then crinkled at the corners as she understood. "Did you?"

"Aye." They faced each other and stepped back and forward. "In it, I was visited by a sprite, a wisp of cloud taking the form of a maid."

"Most strange." She feigned disinterest, glancing around the hall as though searching for someone.

"Most wondrous," he countered softly, and watched her blush.

"This dream," she posed a moment later as they turned shoulder-to-shoulder with each other. "Have you had it before?"

"No, my lady," he said as they wheeled around each other, clapping. "But I hope it visits me again."

She spun away, circled Henry Percy, and came back to him.

"Earlier," he said. He fell out of rhythm and bowed half-a-beat behind the other men.

She looked up, startled, as he caught up and they touched shoulders again. "What?"

"I said, I hope my dream finds me earlier in the night, so that I may fully . . ." It was his turn now to fly off and circle her sister Margaret. He left his words hanging till he came back to Eleanor. ". . . enjoy it before I must rise and ride away."

"Oh."

Another bow, another courtesy, and she passed forward to Percy while Margaret came up from behind to join him. They didn't come back together again before the final chord ended the song.

The master of the dance announced a turn Gunnar didn't know, and he quickly made his excuses and headed for the cup of wine he'd left sitting on a table. Dancing was difficult enough; playing this odd game with Eleanor while wrestling the music had all but drained him. He emptied the cup in one draught, had a boy refill it, and carried it over to where Lord Lumley and one of the earl's aging retainers studied a nard board.

Lumley looked up, grinning. "Made your escape at last, eh, Sir Gunnar?"

"Yes, my lord." He tipped his head toward the couples leaping and gamboling to the music. "I make a poor March hare."

"You're too big for it, is why," said Lumley. "That is a dance best suited to young, skinny lads like Percy there. There's no dignity to it or them."

Gunnar turned to watch. Henry Percy did indeed bound along with an energetic grace many of the others lacked, but it was his partner that caught Gunnar's eye: *Eleanor.* Cheeks glowing with good spirits, she danced and clapped the time, with eyes for no one but Percy. A sudden font of jealousy bubbled up, souring Gunnar's stomach.

He started to turn away and spotted Eleanor at her

father's side. "What?" He looked back and forth, sorting it out in his head. "Oh, that's Lucy with Percy."

"Thought it was Lady Eleanor, did you?" The retainer chuckled. "Most of us have been caught in the same error, sir. Especially when Lucy wears one of her lady's cast-off dresses."

Gunnar shook his head. "I can tell them apart up close, but from a distance . . ."

"Lady Anne once demanded that the earl require each of them to wear different colors, for that very reason." Lumley captured a piece and waved it beneath the retainer's nose. "There. I have you now, Fitzhugh."

Gunnar watched a little longer, then found a spot off to the side where he could watch and be left alone. That lasted only until Eleanor swooped by to urge him to rejoin the dancing, dragging along one of the fostering lads to blunt any appearance of impropriety. Gunnar obliged for those dances he knew, trying to take a position where they would meet in passing, where he might touch her.

The dancing went on into the small hours. As the last tune wound down and Eleanor came around to say her good nights, she was stifling a yawn behind her hand.

"You look tired, m'lady."

"Aye, and 'twill be a short night. My lord father does not hold with letting us sleep beyond the usual hour no matter how late we stay awake."

"That comes from dealing with men-at-arms. Left to their own, they would drink and wench all night, then sleep until Nones."

"I would be happy if he would give us till Terce." She yawned again. "Dawn is not far away. There will be little time for that dream of yours to find you."

"There will be other nights."

Eleanor glanced away, her forehead wrinkling in thought. "Perhaps. Dreams are odd and inconstant things. They do not always return when you command them. Sometimes, they do not return at all."

So she was rethinking her boldness. His chest tightened. There was much between them that needed the kind of privacy that could be found only in the dark of midnight and he very much wanted to urge her to come to him. But Lucy was right there, eyes sharp despite the late hour. Did they share a bed? Had she noticed her lady gone last night? It struck him that he should have been courting Lucy's goodwill, as well, in order to have access to Eleanor. Ah, shite. He wasn't very good at this.

"If this dream never came again," he said carefully, "I would still be thankful I had the one glimpse of it, but I hope it will return when the time is right."

Eleanor kept her eyes averted, so he couldn't see what was in them. "God's rest to you, Sir Gunnar."

"And God's rest, my lady." He bowed to her, then to her watchful cousin. "And to you, Maid Lucy. I hope you sleep well."

And soundly.

CHAPTER 8

The Welsh Marches

"I'LL GIVE YOU a mark for it, sir."

"The gold alone is worth twice that." Ari plucked the heavy gold chalice out of the smith's hand and held it up to tap his fingernail on the big amethyst in the bottom. "And that doesn't account for the drunkstone."

"That could be a piece of church glass for all I know of stones, good knight. And the gold itself is old gold. It may not be pure."

He was right about the age—Brand had found the chalice and a pair of equally ancient cloak pins while searching for their amulets—but that didn't make the smith right about the value.

"Assay it," said Ari. "Your fire is hot."

"I would, sir, but I don't have the proper waters. I ran out and haven't yet been to town to buy more. But I can give you one and three."

Ari snatched up the cloth and started wrapping the cup to go back into his scrip. Curse the vision that had led him to stop here, in the hinterlands of the Welsh border, at the house of a country silversmith. It was a wasted effort. "I'll go on to Shrewsbury, as I planned. A proper goldsmith will be able to tell the worth of the thing."

The smith, seeing his chance at a tidy profit about to ride off, chewed on his lip and hemmed a little. "I do have a touchstone. Let me see it again, if you would, sir."

He had him. Ari fought a grin as he unwrapped the chalice again. The smith pulled out a bit of slate and some tiny pins of gold of differing purities. He scratched the pins over the stone, then made a mark with the foot of the chalice. He and Ari both bent over the stone to see which pin mark best matched that left by the cup.

"You see?" said Ari, vindicated. "Pure. And for doubting me, the price goes up. Two marks and six shillings."

"Ach!" The man's mouth opened and closed a few times, then he put the chalice back on the scale. As he checked the weights, a dark-haired lad of about six years came in and peered into the pan.

"That looks very old." The boy scratched his head.

"I was just telling this good knight that very thing," said the smith. He bent over a wax tablet and scribed a few marks. "I can do one and six."

"You begin to provoke me, man. Two and two."

"One and eight."

Ari shook his head. "You know very well I can do better in town."

"Perhaps, sir, but it would cost you most of a day to ride there and back."

"I have all the time in the world."

The smith made a face and bent over his figuring again, counting on the fingers of one hand as he wrote. The boy took a step closer to Ari. "Have you killed anyone?"

"Mind your manners, boy. He's a noble knight and your better," said the smith without looking up.

"Sorry, *m'sir.*" The boy bobbed his head in a half bow. "Have you killed anyone, sir?"

"I have," said Ari. "But only when I had to. What is your name, boy?"

"Morvran, sir."

"Well, then, Morvran, are you Master Dafydd's son or his apprentice?"

"His son, sir. But I go to apprentice after harvest." He dug at his head again. Lice, no doubt. "I have something old, too."

"Don't bother the gentleman," mumbled the smith.

"He is no bother," said Ari. "What do you have that's old?"

The boy dug his finger under his collar and fished out a leather cord, at the end of which appeared a small bit of tarnished metal. A wink of red caught Ari's eye, and he looked closer.

His heart began to thud in his ears. *By the gods.* Could it be right here, on a child's neck? "Let me see that more closely, Morvran."

The child assessed him a moment, then pulled the cord over his head and lowered his treasure into Ari's open palm. *Ah.*

"'Tis a dragon, sir. See the red eye?"

"I do see it." Ari rubbed a thumb over the little garnet and then over the empty socket next to it. Blind in one eye, Gunnar had always said. He'd lost the stone someplace in the oat fields while plowing, long before they'd sailed. *Thank you, Odin.* Tears pricked Ari's eyes, and his throat tightened so that he could barely speak. "But this is no dragon. It is a bull."

"A bull," said the boy, clearly disappointed. "Are you certain, sir?"

"I am. I have a friend whose sign is a bull very much like it. How did you come by it?"

"I found it a while back." He glanced at his father, who looked up.

"He and Wat were chasing rabbits in the *waun* two summers ago," said the smith. "Found it in the dirt at the mouth of one of the holes, he did, like it had once been buried and kicked up by one of the beasties."

The boy, instead of confirming the tale, merely stared guiltily out the door and scratched some more.

"Hmm. You know, I think my friend might like the piece," said Ari, trying not to sound too interested. "I'll give you a penny for it."

"I don't want to sell it," said the boy. "I like it, even if it is only a bull and poor silver." He reached for it.

Ari closed his fist around the amulet, determined to take it. By force if need be. "Tuppence, then."

The smith stepped around the bench to stand behind his son. The boy thought a minute. "Four pence and 'tis yours, *monsire.*"

"Good lad," said Ari as the smith thumped his son on the back. "Four pence it is." He opened his purse and counted four silver pennies into the boy's palm.

The lad immediately turned around and handed them over to his father, who bit the coins to check them, then handed one back to the boy. "For all your own. We'll quarter it later. And the rest, I shall put aside for when you go off to Master Siarl."

"You have a wise father, Morvran," said Ari. "And if, in his wisdom, he will let you show me where you found the bull, I will let him have the cup for one and ten."

"Done," said the smith quickly. "Though I doubt you'll find aught of interest. I dug around a bit after, hoping there was more. All I found were coney turds."

"I only want to be able to tell my friend where the trinket came from." As the smith counted out coins, Ari broke the knot on the cord and handed the bit of leather back to the boy. He popped the little bull into his purse and stowed the purse inside his shirt, then put the smith's payment in the scrip to go on the saddle.

With the boy up behind, they headed out of the village. When they were well away from the smith's house,

Ari asked, "So, where did you really find it? Don't worry. I won't tell him."

"Eh?" The boy twisted to look back over his shoulder, as if he expected his father to come running after. "How did you know, sir?"

"It was in your eyes. It wasn't in the rabbit warren, was it?"

"No, sir. It were by the old fort on the hill. I told Father wrong because he'd told me and Wat not to go so far, and never to go up there at all. He says 'tis an evil place, where witches play at night. But it were near the mouth of a burrow. A badger's, I think."

"You're lucky, then. Badgers have nasty tempers. You might have been bitten and caught the mad fever. Will you show me? It is not night, so witches won't be about."

"Well . . . it were part of the bargain, so yes, sir. I'll show you. But could you ride toward the warren first, so my father doesn't know?"

Ari rode him 'round the warren and up the backside of the hill until the boy pointed. "There, *m'sir.*"

It was indeed a badger hole, and the fresh tracks at the entrance said it was still occupied. The beast had burrowed deep under the few remaining stones of a fortress so ancient it had probably been a ruin when the amulet was first hidden. It was only chance that the badger had kicked it up where it could be found, and more chance that the boy had stumbled upon it. But then the gods had stepped in to send that vision. For once they'd helped instead of hindered.

Ari had the boy show him just where he'd picked up the bull, then stood for a minute, marking the site well in his memory. There was little chance there would be another amulet in the area, but he'd come back anyway and dig, just to be sure.

But first, he had other, more important business.

He carried the boy back to his father, then rode deep into the woods to a clear pool. There he took his knife and laid his palm open to spill his blood into the water in thanksgiving to Odin and Vör for bringing him to this place, to this boy.

And the next morning, when he was man once more, he set out for the mountain cave where the bear was hiding, so that Brand could be the one to carry the amulet to Gunnar, as was his right as captain.

CHAPTER 9

Raby Castle

ELEANOR DIDN'T COME down in the night after the dance, nor in the next night, nor for a week after that. Perhaps Lucy didn't sleep soundly after all. Or perhaps Eleanor herself had taken heed of that momentary bout of good sense she'd expressed during the dancing—much as Gunnar wished for more time alone with her, upon thought, even he had to admit that love play behind the draperies was probably a poor idea.

So he was left sitting alone night after night, surrounded by snoring men and farting dogs as he reminded himself that it was her heart he needed and not her body. Over and over, he reminded himself, but it did little to relieve the ache in his balls.

Because whatever reasons kept Eleanor from presenting herself to him in private, they had no effect on the way she tortured him in public. Each evening when they retired to the solar—thank the gods Westmorland seemed happy to keep including him in that privilege—she found some new way to taunt him while looking utterly innocent to the others. One night, she selected a table for merels that was so small, their legs had to intertwine beneath while they played. On another, she leapt to accept Henry Percy's offer to escort her and Lucy for a stroll in the courtyard—a stroll that left Gunnar to squire her sister Margaret along behind, where the sight of Eleanor's hips swaying just out of reach drove him mad.

That very evening, after taunting him with her mere presence across the card table, she'd carelessly let a kerchief slip from her sleeve as she passed on her way out. Gunnar had scooped it up and handed it back to her with nary a word and barely a glance—her father was right there, after all. But the cloth had been so soaked in scent that even now, hours later, his hands reeked of her.

He buried his nose between his palms and inhaled deeply, letting the perfume's scent conjure visions of her amongstst the tousled furs of a great bed, her legs spread wide, waiting for him to bury his—

He stopped himself short, a wry grin twisting his lips. God's knees. Now she had him torturing himself.

He could find relief with one of the castle wenches, he supposed—the names of the most available were passed freely amongst Raby's men-at-arms, and he knew where at least one willing woman could be found even at this hour— but he'd never seen much point in tupping one woman when he wanted another. It just didn't have the same sweetness.

So he chose a time-honored path and wandered outside to find a dark corner and take care of the worst of the ache on his own, the scent of her perfume on his hands making his release that much more satisfying. As he retied his laces afterward, he reminded himself again of his true purpose. So long as he had one good hand, he could make shift without her body, but there was no substitute for her heart.

Unfortunately, her love was only half of what he needed, and his amulet wasn't going to turn up in the castle well, the way Ivo's had at Alnwick. Raby was far too new, and even the manor it had replaced had been built centuries too late.

Nor was it going to be part of some bastard's quest for land. No king was going to step in and—

He stopped dead.

What a fool he was.

Eleanor had given him the key herself: her veins carried the same Plantagenet blood as the kings of England, the same blood as those who had set things in motion in the past. Her royal lineage was part of the gift, not an encumbrance. Even as he had stumbled along in blindness, the gods had been moving the pieces into place. All he had to do was win the lady's heart, and they would surely bring the amulet to him.

Full of fresh hope and with considerably less ache in his balls, Gunnar went in, found his cup, and once again spilled a measure of wine into the fire in thanks.

Then he sat down and waited with much more patience than he'd had for at least a week, to see if by chance the lady would come down tonight before he had to leave.

She didn't.

Summer is a-coming in,
Loudly sing, cuckoo!
Seeds do grow and meadows blow,
And trees do spring anew . . .

Eleanor glanced up from her sewing. "You are in fine voice today, cuz."

"It is the weather, my lady. The day is glorious." Lucy stepped back from the open window and started the song over, swaying and spinning gracefully in time to the music. "Summer is a-coming in . . ."

Eleanor laid down the cap she was turning and went to the window to look down into the busy courtyard. *As she suspected.*

She caught Henry Percy's eye and surreptitiously motioned him closer. As she turned back to Lucy, she let her hand rest on the sill and started working one of her rings loose with her thumb. "The lord, my father told me he would like some stitching on the band of his cap. I was thinking a wreath of laurels."

"That would be too much," said her mother from across the room. "Just as that spinning is too much. Stop if you will, Lucy. You make me dizzy."

Lucy settled immediately. "Pardon, my lady."

"What should I do, then?" asked Eleanor.

"What about a single sprig? Right here." Lucy touched just over her right temple.

"He would like that," said Lady Joan.

"Or I could do rosemary for remembrance, so that he would—Oh! My ring." Eleanor leaned out the window to look down into the courtyard. "Halloo, I have lost my ring out the window. Sir Henry, can you find it?"

"I think so, my lady. I saw something fall." Percy winked at her before he squatted to pat around in the dirt. A moment later, he held up the ring between thumb and finger. "I have it."

"Ah, good. I will send Lucy down for it. Would you mind another favor, Harry?"

He pushed to his feet, fighting down a grin. "Of course not, my lady."

"I want some laurel to copy for my stitching. Will you escort Lucy around to the kitchen garden so she may cut a twig for me? With so many strangers about, I don't want her going back there alone, where no one can see."

Henry's eyes sparkled with the proper degree of mischief. "I am glad to be of service, my lady."

"My thanks. Lucy, would you also . . ." She meant to ask Lucy to bring a sprig of rosemary, too, but all she saw as she turned was her cousin's back as she flew out the door.

"I didn't know your ring was so loose," said her mother mildly.

"Only of late. I must see to it next time I am near a goldsmith. Pardon, my lady." Eleanor leaned back out. "Recall that you are a gentleman, Harry."

"I am wounded you doubt my good intent, my lady," said Henry, though his smile faded a bit. "Never fear. Fair Lucy will come back to you safe anon."

Not too safe, nor too soon, Eleanor hoped, though she refrained from saying that aloud. She waited until she saw Lucy at the door below, then went back to her sewing, confident that, whatever her mother thought of it, her life was likely to become a good deal easier if Lucy understood at least a little of the pleasure to be had with a man. "Does anyone know where my scissors are?"

SOMETHING WAS ASTIR. At this hour, the hall should be full of men finishing their meals or drinking. Instead, it stood nearly empty, with only a few of the higher-ranked knights and the family and fosterlings bunched together here and there.

Gunnar headed over to the washing station. A boy hurried over to pour for him, and as he scrubbed his hands, he felt someone step in behind him. Scent wrapped itself around him, and it was all he could do not to simply turn around and grab her. "Lady Eleanor."

"You are late, Sir Gunnar. *Again*."

"I often am. It is a wretched fault, my lady." Gunnar tossed the towel over the rack beside the washbowl and turned to discover a twinkle in her eyes that gave mockery to her stern tone. He bowed to her. "Much like rumbling bellies and bobbing. I take it that I have missed supper entirely today."

"The bishop of Durham came. He sent word ahead, and he likes to sup early, so my lord father accommodates him. I would have sent you word, if I'd known where to send to."

He ignored her unsubtle prying and looked around to see if one of the serving men was near. "I will need to speak to someone about food."

"There is no need. The steward recalled you were yet abroad and ordered a portion held for you." Motioning for him to follow, she led him to a table off to one side, where a wooden trencher holding a half capon and a loaf waited next to a bowl of honey-and-wine-soaked fruits, thick with nuts. "Will this do?"

"Very well and thank you, my lady." He sat, tore off the capon's leg, and began eating while she motioned for a boy to bring wine. "I'm glad I arrived before the earl called for you all to retire, lest I missed you entirely."

"I would not let that happen," she said firmly. "But the truth is, we have nowhere to retire to. His Grace has taken the solar and the whole of the rear tower for his party, and he and my lord have their heads together. They have left us all below for the evening and sent most of the men to the lesser hall."

"There's another hall?" asked Gunnar in surprise.

"On the far side of the watchtower, near the kitchen. Have you not ventured around the castle?"

He shook his head. "Remember that I am gone during the days. And of an evening, I have no interest in venturing anywhere." He glanced around to make certain no one was near. "At least, not anywhere that you are not."

"You flatter, sir."

"It is no flattery. You say we have some time without your father watching?"

"Yes. Though we must still be ware of the others. I want no one carrying tales to him. And to that end . . ." She rose and did courtesy, and spoke just loudly enough for her voice to carry to the nearest servants. "Your pardon, *monsire*. I must attend my lady mother for a little. Enjoy your meal."

She left him to eat his fill and contemplate this unexpected opportunity. As usual, the lady was a step ahead, able to see the next move in the game before he was even aware he was playing it.

By the time she returned, he'd worked his way through most of the capon, but still had no idea how he might take advantage of the moment. So he resorted to what he knew.

"And how is your lady mother?" he asked as she slid onto the bench opposite.

"She chafes at her confinement. She counted it out today and reckoned she has spent well over a full year of her life locked away because of childbearing."

"With so many babes, she needs the rest." He tore off a piece of bread and sopped up some of the juice on the trencher. "Come to think of it, the earl likely needs the rest, too."

She clapped her hand over her mouth to catch an un-ladylike snort. "You are a devil!"

"I?" He chewed thoughtfully. "I would like to be more of a devil, but how can I be, when I am always under such close watch?"

" 'Tis true. My lord father's admiration for you gives us little time to speak freely."

"Far too little, although"—he sniffed his fingers—"ah, no, the scent has faded. But I smelled of your kerchief the whole night through. As you intended, I think."

Her cheeks colored. "I am caught."

"You are. But so am I, for now I've told you that I noted it. The traces of your perfume gave me much comfort last night." *If she knew what kind of comfort, she'd slap him.*

The boy came with the wine again, and they both fell silent, avoiding each other's eyes while he poured. When the boy moved on out of earshot, though, Gunnar propped his elbows on the table and leaned forward. "So while we can speak, I may as well tell you, I have twice thought to kill Henry Percy."

Her eyes widened. "Twice?"

"Once when you walked with him. The other during the dancing."

Her brow wrinkled in puzzlement. "I did not dance with—ah, but Lucy did. You mistook her for me."

He nodded. "I did. It is not often cousins look so much the same."

"It comes from her father. He looks as much like mine

as Lucy looks like me. All but here, of course." She tapped the bridge of her nose. "You can always tell Lucy by her bump."

"And your bobbing. I wager Maid Lucy does not bob when she is glad."

"You would win. She hums—although she also hums when she is nervous."

"She hums a lot, then," muttered Gunnar.

Eleanor bit back a smile. "When she is truly happy, she sings and dances. I was reminded of that today."

"Something to do with Percy?"

"Ah, so you have noted it, too."

"It is difficult to miss." He uncurled a finger just enough to point across the hall, where Lucy and Henry Percy stood apart, talking. Percy looked like he was about to devour the blushing Lucy whole.

"I arranged for them to have a moment alone today. She came back all aglow and with a bruised look to her lips."

"Good. She needed to be kissed. How did you arrange this time?"

"I sent her to fetch some herbs from the kitchen garden, and asked Percy to go with her."

"The kitchen garden?"

"It is by the rear wall. Very few go back there, and it offers much privacy. Anne always goes back there with Gilbert when he is here."

He leaned back, contemplating her, until she shifted uncomfortably.

"Why do you look at me so?"

"I am wondering about a lady who would arrange for her maid to have a moment of privacy, but not arrange such a moment for herself. Why do you never go . . . herb picking?"

Her cheeks colored lightly, but she raised her chin. "Because you, sir, are never here by day, when the herbs want picking."

"Sadly true. It is not by choice that I leave, my lady." He leaned forward a bit more, so that his breath stirred a loose wisp of hair that lay by her jaw. "But they say some herbs are more potent when plucked in the dark of night."

Her lips parted on that faint gasp he liked so much, and the color in her cheeks spread and deepened. Pleased at finally being able to discomfit her in the same way she did him nearly every day, Gunnar pushed to his feet, stepping between her and the nearest watchers to block their view before someone noticed her blush. "If we do not want stories carried to your lord father, we should find something to occupy us that does not turn you so pink."

She pressed her hands to her cheeks. "You are not helping."

"I thought I was." He lowered his voice to a bare murmur. "It is better than telling you I want to kiss you into a swoon, is it not?"

"Hardly." She looked up. "Do you?"

"Need you ask?" He chuckled as a slow smile spread across her face. "That's better. Shall I call for a chessboard? A musician? I know. I'll challenge Percy to wrestle me. That should keep you entertained for a moment or two."

That made her laugh, Percy being half his size, and her embarrassment quickly faded. She pushed her bench back.

"The bishop travels with a most excellent storyteller in his party, and he has given him to us for tonight. Let us see what tales he has for us."

As she rose, she filched a scrap of the capon's crisp skin off his trencher and popped it into her mouth. She wiped her fingers on the napkin cloth this time, thank the gods, but a faint sheen of grease remained right in the center of her lower lip, as though she'd painted it there of a purpose so it could beg him to kiss it away.

By the gods. If he let her, she could turn his brain to custard on a whim. It would be a happy fate, if not so dangerous in her father's hall. "As you wish, my lady."

He followed her and her smudge of grease across the hall, where they joined a group that had gathered around a bearded old fellow who reminded Gunnar of one of the elder skalds back home, right down to the milky white stare of his blind eyes. Eleanor took a seat near the back, while Gunnar stepped around to a place where he could watch her without seeming to. The old fellow was just finishing a tale from their Bible, one about a drowning man swallowed by a whale and thrown up safely later. Clearly that one had been written by a man who'd never seen the inside of a whale. Gunnar had; he'd rather drown.

"Thus the story of Jonah teaches us that even at the darkest hour, so long as there is great faith, there is also great hope," said the old man. "I heard two more join us. Tell me who, please? The lady first. I heard light steps."

"It is Eleanor de Neville, Carolus. Do you remember me from York?"

"Only a little, my lady. My old mind grows too old and too crowded." He scratched his chin, thinking. "There was a man, as well. A big one. Over here." He waved his hand in the general direction.

"Gunnar of Lesbury, a guest of the earl. Do you only tell Bible stories, old man, or do you have other tales in that bald skull of yours?"

"Many others, *monsire*. Many, many others. Is there one you would like? Something from the olden times, perhaps." The old man swung his head, so those blank, blind eyes seemed to look straight at Gunnar. "Like when the Danes pillaged all of England?"

A cold chill ran down Gunnar's back and lifted the hairs on his arms. *How?* He shifted, setting his feet firmly, ready for a fight. "No. Not those."

"You know far older tales than that, Carolus," said Eleanor, all unaware. "You spent hours at York telling us of the ancients of Greece and Rome."

"I do not recall what I told, my lady, but I have learned some new stories just this year past. Would you like to hear them?"

Yeses rippled around the circle, but the old man kept his blind eyes on Gunnar. "And what say you, Sir Gunnar?"

"I don't know. Are they any good?"

Chuckling, the old fellow turned back to the others. "We shall see. Now, the first tale I'll tell is of how the Greeks believed their gods came to be. They were false gods, of course, but the ancients can be forgiven because our Lord had not yet sent Paul to give the Greeks knowledge of the One True God . . ."

He went on to tell of what he called the Titans and their battles for control of all creation, and of gods both great and small birthed from their foreheads and ripped from their thighs. It all sounded very much to Gunnar's ears like Ymir and Búri and how Vili, Ve, and Odin came to be, and slowly, as the familiar-but-not-familiar tale spun out, his wariness faded away. The old man was merely a skald, with the fey ways such men always had. Not so different from Ari, and for a while, Gunnar's mind wandered to his old shipmate and wondered what part of England he was plowing these days. Once he had Eleanor for his own, he would send Jafri to hunt down Ari and Brand and enlist the skald's visions to help him find his amulet.

And then he would put the amulet in Eleanor's hands and get her to say she loved him, and he would be free. Free. The idea of a life that was a true life, and the death that would properly finish it, was as sweet as honey wine.

When he came back to the present, the storyteller had moved on, telling of the ways the gods of Olympus dealt with their mortal subjects, again not so different from the way the gods of Asgard behaved, though the Greeks seemed to enjoy more tupping—especially Zeus and the one called Eros, who exercised their right to take any woman who pleased them more even than Odin did. For a monk, old Carolus seemed especially fond of those stories, going from one to the next to the next.

"One day, Zeus spied the fairest maid of them all bathing in the sea," the old man continued. "She was Europa, the youngest daughter of the King of Tyre, and the sight of her smooth skin and yellow hair inflamed Zeus till he could not contain himself. He wanted this maid beyond all others, but she was surrounded by her handmaidens. So Zeus drew on his powers and turned himself into a great bull . . ."

The chill went clear to Gunnar's bones, slowing his heart, turning his arms and legs to lead. *Run,* screamed a voice in his head, but he couldn't move. All around him, the others listened with rapt attention while Gunnar, frozen by the old man's words, struggled for breath and silently prayed, *Odin, help me. He gives me away.*

"And as the bull, Zeus wandered close to the fair Europa. Her handmaidens ran away in fear to hide in the woods, but Europa was taken by the beauty of the great beast and stayed behind, and the bull did her no harm, but instead let her stroke his head and breast. Enchanted by the animal's gentleness and nobility, Europa wove a garland of flowers and laurel and approached the bull to twine it about his horns. From the woods, her handmaidens called for her to come away before she was crushed or gored, but the beast only knelt down to her and let her climb, smiling, onto its back."

"It is the story from my comb!" Excited, Eleanor turned to the man next to her. "I have a silver comb with a lady on a bull. I never knew the story that went with it."

Her voice, so different from the old man's, shook Gunnar out of his stupor. He gulped down a huge breath, and the lead began to melt out of his limbs.

"Then it is good you hear it at last, my lady," said Carolus. "It is an important tale, and you shall see why. When the beast had Europa on his back, he plunged into the waves and carried her away across the seas to a beautiful island called Crete, and there he revealed himself, seduced the maid, and had his way with her. When he was done with her and she was with child, he left to return to his throne on Mount Olympus, but as her reward for being the fairest and sweetest of all his lovers, Zeus gave her as wife to the king of Crete, and she became queen and the mother of all the West, which is why today we call the whole of the Holy Roman Empire by her name, Europe."

"So, she was rewarded for her lack of chastity?" asked Lady Anne, tart as ever. She glared at Eleanor.

"A strange thing, I know," said Carolus, "But the ancients were of a different mind about such things. I cannot help but wonder what any of you ladies would do if a bull turned to a man before you."

"He wasn't a man, though," said Eleanor. "Not to Europa. To her, he was a god. She may have thought it an honor."

She sounded so reasonable about it. Could it be that she might actually accept such a thing? Gunnar's heart began to race. *Please, Odin, please.*

"Or she may have realized that she had little choice in it," offered Mary Ferrers. "Much as a lowborn woman has little choice today if her lord chooses her for his bed. Though a true gentleman would never force himself on a woman, no matter her rank." She looked straight at Henry Percy.

"A woman of true virtue would refuse, even unto death, as Saint Margaret of Antioch did," said Carolus. "The ancient tales also tell of such refusals. The fair daughters of the god Atlas refused Orion the Hunter for seven years as he pursued them." He shifted into this new story.

No, no, no. He was pushing her the wrong way now. Anger cleared the last of the cobwebs from Gunnar's brain. He didn't want Eleanor to refuse him. *Shut up, old man.*

But of course Carolus didn't shut up until he reached the end. "And in the end, Zeus turned them into stars, the constellation we commonly call the Hen and Chicks, but which is properly known as the Pleiades for the seven sisters. It shines in glory above us even today, as honor to their virtue." He turned to Gunnar suddenly. "Now what do you say of my stories, *monsire*?"

Gunnar's tongue was still thick in his mouth. He swallowed hard, and looked to Eleanor, still smiling, oblivious to any significance beyond a good story. Had the old man done him a favor or destroyed all hope?

"I think, old man, that you have talked a great deal." He reached into his purse and pressed the first coin that came to hand into the old man's palm without looking to see what it was. "And that someone should bring you some ale to wet that throat."

The listeners laughed and clapped, and a page scrambled for an ale pot. Gunnar pushed his still-unwieldy legs to carry him to the table on the far side of the hall, where he poured a cup of wine, drained it, and poured another.

"You did not like the stories," said Eleanor, coming up behind him.

He drained the second cup and set it down before he turned to face her with a lie. "I've heard them before."

"No, it was more than that." She held out a cup for him to pour for her. "You paled when he spoke of Zeus becoming a bull."

His hand jerked, sloshing wine over the edge of her cup. "Pardon." He took the cup from her and poured off to one side as she dried her hand on a cloth. He flailed around for a reasonable excuse for his behavior.

"It was his words, his, his, his, manner of sp-speaking." *Stop stuttering, fool.* He handed the cup back to her and formed his words more carefully. "I was suddenly reminded of someone I knew, long ago. It was as though I heard a ghost, and it caught me unawares. But it has passed."

One eyebrow went up slightly at that, but she didn't challenge him. "I am glad. I thought for a little you were going to retch on Carolus's head."

A snort of unwilling laughter escaped him. She was too close to the truth; he could still taste the bile in his mouth. "Perhaps it would have made his hair grow back. What of you—did you like the story of the lady and the bull?"

She sipped at her wine. "Very much, though it would be most strange to have a bull turn into a man before you."

"You told the old man it would be an honor."

"If it were a god. And if I were a pagan, to believe in such things. But I am not and I do not," she said firmly. "It was only an old tale."

"What if it wasn't?" he pushed, wanting to know—needing to know—her true heart in this. "What if such a thing could happen, and the bull were only a man, and you were only Eleanor?"

"I would run way in fear, for how else would a man become a bull, except that he was a demon?"

Gunnar turned away so she couldn't see his face. "He might have been enchanted through no fault of his own."

"I suppose that is possible. My nurse used to tell me of such enchantments," she mused. "Of good men changed to wolves or rabbits or foxes by those who deal in evil. If I were certain that was true, then I might not run. But how could I ever be certain?"

How indeed? But her question gave him hope. "I do not know, my lady. I will put some thought to it. Come, we should rejoin the others."

"Wait. Before we do, I . . . It is May Day in three days. Will you join me at the revels? The lord, my father never goes, and it is a very free day. It will be a chance to—"

"I cannot, my lady."

A shadow of hurt darkened her face. "Your mysterious business again. I have been most patient with you and your business, but truly, have you no time free of it?"

He lifted his hands helplessly.

"What sort of business could it be that takes you away every day, even May Day?"

"The sort that I have no choice in," he said, not answering her question because he could not. Not yet. "For if I did, I would spend every hour of sunlight striving to make you smile."

"Then do so. Delay your duty, just this once. You will find your task easy, for your mere presence at the revel will suffice to make me smile the whole day through."

He sighed heavily. "'Twould be a glorious sight, but much as I would like to see it, I cannot."

"I do not understand."

"Sometimes, even I do not understand," he said gently. "But it is what it is. Just know, my lady, it makes me no happier than it does you. Now come. The others grow too curious of us."

She didn't come down that night either, and for once, Gunnar was glad. It gave him time to think about what she'd said. To plan. To beg the gods to help him find some way to convince her he wasn't a demon.

For in three days, it was May Day.

And she'd said she might not run.

CHAPTER 10

"OH, NO. HERE she comes again," said Mary. "Up, everyone, to honor the Queen of May."

Eleanor laid aside the dried fig she'd been about to enjoy, conjured up a smile, and rose with the others to do courtesy and wonder for the thousandth time what had possessed their father to declare Anne, of all his daughters, queen. This must be the fourth, no, fifth time Anne had paraded through the revel, demanding honor from all her subjects.

"Be at ease," said Anne. "Why are you all out here? You should be in the pavilion, paying me court."

"It is too crowded, Your Grace. Your loyal subjects would not be able to approach," said Henry Percy. "You would not want to disappoint the good folk of your realm."

Anne glanced over her shoulder at the villagers of Staindrop, who had been bringing her a steady stream of flowers and good wishes in exchange for her blessings on their crops. "I suppose not, though I wish May Day and the tourney fell together. Then it would be dozens of knights laying garlands at my feet instead of dozens of peasants."

"They are good men and women," said Eleanor. "They deserve their holiday."

Anne's eyes narrowed shrewdly. "And at least they are here. It is so sad you find yourself without a companion, Eleanor, today of all days."

"But I have companions, Your Grace." Eleanor indicated Mary, Harry, Lucy, and the others gathered around. "Fine ones, including our brothers."

Anne barely gave Ralph the Younger, whom they called Raffin, a glance, much less the little boys. "Yes, of course, but not the one you want, I think, on this day when all the world sings of love. Where did you say Sir Gunnar is? I would call him *your* Sir Gunnar, but of course he is not and cannot be."

"Of course," said Eleanor as evenly as she could. She would've done better to keep her mouth shut. "His days are spent on business."

"It must be very dire business, that it keeps him from you even on a holiday. Or perhaps it is only that he knows what is *important*."

"Enough, Anne!" Red-faced, Gilbert inserted himself between the two of them. "It is time to go back. Your subjects await." He gripped Anne by the elbow and firmly steered her toward the pavilion.

They all stood there, staring in silent shock. Finally, Henry Percy whistled appreciatively. "Umfraville's found his balls at last."

That released the tension, and they all laughed. Lucy picked up Eleanor's fig and handed it to her, and Mary motioned for her waiting woman to start collecting her things. "Either we move someplace free of her royal presence or I am retiring to the hall."

"I'm for moving," said Raffin. "My sister annoys even me today. Pack the baskets, Cedric, and round up some men to move us."

"Yes, my lord."

The servants worked quickly, and soon the party was ready to move off.

"Where shall we go? Somewhere she won't trouble us."

"There's that big oak at the edge of the far meadow," suggested Eleanor. "I doubt she'll will venture so far, although I suppose she might ride over there just to torment me."

"I will see that she doesn't," said Henry Percy.

"She will take note of our leaving," said Mary.

"I will see to that as well," said Henry. "Lady Eleanor, may I borrow Lucy?"

"Harry . . ." Both Mary and Eleanor glared at him.

"She will cause a distraction in the pavilion and thus both hide what I do and cause Anne to think you are still within range of her royal whims."

"'Tis hardly fair to Lucy," said Eleanor.

"Oh, I won't leave her to Anne. That would a fate too terrible. No, I will rescue her in a little and bring her to you. I am, after all, a gentleman, and Lucy is your cousin." He gave Eleanor a wink, then put out his hand. "Come, maid, your lady has need of your succor."

Lucy took his hand, and they were off. Henry turned to call back, "Listen for my whistle, then make for the edge of the woods. We will see you at the oak."

Moments later, an outcry arose from the direction of the pavilion, followed quickly by a loud whistle. Laughing, they all dashed into the woods, where they paused to regroup. Raffin sent the servants ahead with the bundles and baskets, then turned to Eleanor.

"Shall we wait for Percy and Lucy?"

"If you were he, would you want us to wait?" asked Mary. "Sometimes, Raffin, I hold no hope for you at all."

The woods were pleasant, after the unfamiliar heat of the sun. As they skirted the brambles, the younger members of the party picked the few ripe berries. Cuthbert, one of Eleanor's own brothers, caught up with her and tugged on her sleeve. "I thought you were going to strike Anne. Were you?"

"No, of course not," lied Eleanor.

"Well, you should," said Mary over her shoulder. "She has been insufferable to you since Catherine left."

"She is jealous," said Raffin. "She has some cause. She thinks our father makes better marriages for his second family than his first."

It was a complaint Eleanor had heard herself, that Anne and her sisters had gotten short shrift, married off to the unremarkable sons of unremarkable families while Lady Joan's daughters got earls and dukes. It made little difference to Anne that most of their contracts had been made when their father was an unremarkable man himself, married to their even less remarkable mother. He was Earl Marshall now, and his second wife had brought a royal bloodline and powerful new connections. Anne, however, craved the same honors due his new family, even though she had no right to them.

"But all your sisters have lords," said Mary to Raffin. "And Gilbert is Earl of Kyme."

Raffin batted at a branch. "Kyme is a hollow honor. There are no lands with the title, and Parliament has never even confirmed it for him."

"Gilbert has served both the king and Prince Henry well. He will surely improve his position when the crown changes hands. But even if he doesn't, Anne will still be lady of both Harbottle and Redesdale."

"And Catherine is Countess of Norfolk and Nottinghamshire, while Eleanor will be Countess of Gloucester."

No, I won't, said Eleanor firmly, in her own head if not aloud. *No. I. Won't.*

Cuthbert, who was a clever boy though he was not yet seven, looked up at her and quietly squeezed her hand.

IT WAS WITH great relief that Lucy saw Henry Percy approaching from the direction of the horses. Dodging the morris dancers, he circled around to the far side of the open-sided pavilion, where he entered as though coming from the gaming field.

"There you are, Lucy. We have been looking for you." He bowed to Lady Anne. "By your leave, Your Grace. She lost a wager and owes Mary Ferrers a song."

Anne, occupied with yet another presentation of days-eyes, barely took note, waving her away. Lucy did her courtesy, and she and Henry strolled off toward where they'd left the others. The farther they got from the pavilion, the faster they walked, until, as they reached the edge of the revelers, they broke into a run and fled, laughing, into the wood.

"I heard you singing," he said as they slowed. He hummed the tune.

" 'Tis her favorite song. I told her it was my gift to her as Queen of May, and that Lady Eleanor didn't know I had come to sing for her."

"That pleased her, no doubt."

"She actually thought I slipped away from my lady for love of her." They walked a little farther before Lucy mustered the courage to ask, "What did you do to her mare, *monsire*? You didn't hurt her, I hope."

"I would never needlessly harm a good animal," Henry protested. His offended look shifted to one of mischief. "And you can confirm that, once they get her back."

Lucy half groaned, half laughed. "The poor groom. She'll have him thrashed."

"I made it seem the beast chewed through her tether. But if Anne insists on blaming the boy, I will confess my sins. They are already so many, this one will make little difference." His gaze traveled down to her breasts and back up. "And my sins will likely be more if I spend more time in these woods with you."

Lucy grew suddenly aware of how very alone they were, for having so many people nearby—far more alone than they had been in the garden, where the men on the walls could have heard her if she cried out. Lady Eleanor and the others were well gone, and the leaves muffled the sound of the revels, leaving them fainter than the buzz of the midges in the bushes. True privacy was such a rare thing in her life. Excitement thrilled through her, heated her blood.

"We should go, my lord." She took a step toward the path. "This way."

"This way, you say?" He started forward, then grabbed both her hands and tugged her around. "Or was it this?" As she started to laugh, he spun her the other direction. "Or this?" All the way 'round again. "Oh, no. This is it."

She was laughing so hard by now, she could hardly stand. She grabbed at his cote. "Stop, my lord. Stop."

He stopped quickly, his hands at her waist to steady her. With eyes locked on hers, he pulled her close.

She ducked around him and darted off.

"Ah, *that* way," he shouted, hard on her heels.

She might have outrun him if the path had been wider, but her gown caught on branches and brambles, and within a few paces, he had her. He spun her around and carried her back against the wide trunk of a tree, his body hard against hers, holding her there.

He skimmed kisses over her face, his breath warming her skin, his lips grazing cheeks, temple, brow in turn before lingering a hair's breadth from her mouth. "I have captured you twice now. I demand ransom."

She turned her head, so his kiss landed on her cheek. "I will not pay, sir."

He pulled away to squint at her. "Why not?"

"Paying the ransom would mean you must release me."

His squint narrowed, crinkled into a wolfish smile, and he gently cupped her chin to turn her face to his. "We shall negotiate that."

She didn't turn away this time, instead meeting his kiss head on, following his lead as he showed her how she might convince him. Her heart pounded in her ears, so loud she was sure he must hear, and indeed, he kissed his way down to where the pulse throbbed in her throat.

"Don't be afraid, fair Lucy."

"I am not."

It was a lie. She was terrified. It was a dangerous game, this, with no possible loser but she. She'd been thinking about nothing else since those moments in the garden. And yet she was elated, too, and when he shifted back her mouth, she threaded her arms around him, opened to his teasing tongue, and relished his groan.

They hung there against the tree, their kisses going from gentle to feverish and back again. Henry's hands began to wander, smoothing the length of her arms, measuring the span of her waist. Once again, he kissed his way down her neck, nuzzling aside the edge of her gown to nip at her shoulder before he moved lower.

The heat built in Lucy's blood as her imagination raced ahead. Breasts. He would find her breasts next, unlace her gown, and push it aside for his lips. Her nipples tightened, ready, and she knew, *knew* how wonderful it would be.

And she knew she couldn't let it happen. "Stop, my lord. Please."

"Ah, Lucy, I cannot." He held her pinned with one hand while the other came up to cup one breast and round it. He traced its upper curve with his tongue. "I want you so very much. Come deeper into the woods and lie with me."

She threaded her fingers into his hair. Temptation whispered in her ear, urging her to pull his head down, to lift to his searching mouth, to say yes.

"No." She tugged his head up. "No."

He shifted his kisses to her mouth. "I hear your words." Kiss. "But they make no sense." Kiss. "When your lips say yes."

"I do much enjoy your kisses," she admitted. "But—"

He stopped her mouth with another kiss, then found his way to her ear where he did some wondrous thing with his tongue that made her breasts ache for the same attention. She sighed.

"You will enjoy the rest as well," he whispered with

the voice of a fallen angel. "We will find much pleasure together, I promise. Say yes, Lucy."

"No. No, and forever, no." She tightened her grip on his hair and yanked.

"Ow!" In a flash, he grabbed her wrists and pinned them to the tree above her head. His eyes glittered with a mix of amusement and anger. "You dare hurt me, wench?"

"As you would hurt me, my lord."

He kissed her again, long and slow, releasing her hands and guiding them around his neck. "I would never harm you, Lucy-fair."

No, he wouldn't, not that way. For all his efforts to lift her skirts, Henry Percy was a good man. She felt it. She could see it his eyes. *Ah, la, Lady Eleanor was right.* "But you would."

"How?" He put a hand on either side and pushed away to look down at her. "How could I?"

"By taking the only thing of value I have in this world and giving me nothing in return."

"I would give you my heart." He flushed and fidgeted, as uncomfortable as a boy kneeling for confession. "I think you may already own it."

Lucy blinked furiously at the tears that welled up, unwilling to let him see that it was those words she both wanted and feared most of all. She strove to keep her voice light. "Little good it will do me. I am a bastard daughter of a second son and you . . . you are Percy of Northumberland."

"That means nothing just now."

"It will again, and when it does, I will find myself in possession of a heart far too high to take notice of someone of my station."

"Never. We are meant for each other." He cupped her jaw, his thumb stroking her cheek. "Can you not feel it?"

Oh, yes. "What I feel is of no matter."

"Then you *do* feel it."

She tugged his hand away. "When I marry, if I marry, it

will be to some small knight or merchant who doesn't mind a bastard wife with no land and only a small dowry. When you marry, it will be to someone high. Someone like my lady."

"Your lady would be a bastard once removed, but for Parliament and the Pope," he reminded her. "And I *am* a small knight, with nothing but my horse."

"But you will have Alnwick and the whole of Northumberland back one day, and with it a well-born bride from whom you will expect chastity." She watched his eyes as her truth struck home. "I owe the same chastity to my husband, whoever he may be, and I owe him my heart as well, if I can give it. If I present either to you, they will be gone forever." She swallowed hard against the lump that swelled in her throat and stepped away from the tree. "I am not for you."

When she looked back at him, his face was impassive. "We should rejoin the others."

He motioned her to go first, and she stepped past him and somehow put one foot in front of the other to lead the way through the strip of woodland that separated the two meadows. As they stepped out into the sunlight, she saw the group at the far side of the lea and sighed. Safe at last.

The thought had no sooner formed in her head than Henry's fingers closed over her shoulders. He pulled her back against him and put his mouth by her ear. "You *are* for me, Lucy-fair. Hear me and know it. And know as well that I will do whatever I must to have you."

He released her, and she fled.

SOMETHING HAD PASSED between Henry Percy and Lucy, that was certain. Eleanor took comfort in the knowledge that they hadn't been alone long enough for anything too rash—unless Henry had been an utter knave and forced himself on her, in which case Eleanor would personally see him lashed.

But Lucy bore no signs of struggle on her, nor any marks at all that Eleanor could see, except a mossy twig stuck in her hair, and she could've gotten that simply by walking through the woods. It was her wide-eyed distraction and the way she avoided Henry that hinted of more than a walk.

Eleanor desperately wanted to know whether the more had been good or bad, but with the others around, it was impossible to pry. After an unsuccessful attempt to lure Lucy off to one side—Mary interrupted with a request for Lucy's aid with a string game, a move which Eleanor suspected was deliberate—she decided to set aside her curiosity for later when she had Lucy alone in chamber. For now, she would lie back, pretend she didn't care that Sir Gunnar was missing, and enjoy the rest of the afternoon.

And a glorious afternoon it was, without Queen Anne to cloud it, full of sun and games and copious amounts of Portuguese wine that Raffin's man Cedric had liberated from Her Grace's stock. Late in the day, the bigger boys wanted to joust with reeds, so Henry and Raffin took them off to the other side of the lea, along with the younger ones to play at squire and varlets to serve as mounts.

As Eleanor wove together a few flowers, Mary coaxed Lucy into singing. Sadly, she was too distracted by avoiding Henry's looks to keep to the song. When she forgot the words for the fifth time, Mary signaled for her to stop.

Red-faced, Lucy twisted her hands in her lap. "Your pardon, my lady. Perhaps a different song."

"I don't think that will solve the problem," said Eleanor.

"It is not entirely Lucy's fault," said Mary. "The men are quite noisy. I do wish they'd gone off farther."

"No you don't," said Eleanor. "If anything, you'd rather they were closer, the better to watch Raffin pose for you."

Mary turned nearly as red as Lucy. "He does not pose, for me or anyone."

"He does, and you enjoy it," countered Eleanor, laughing now. The budding affection between Mary and Raffin pleased everyone around them, even if neither of them wanted to admit to it. Their marriage had been contracted long ago as a way to consolidate the Ferrers fortune, to which Mary was heir, with the Neville. The king himself had promoted the match as yet another boon of the Neville-Beaufort alliance. Since they had entirely different parents, the Church had no complaints—but then it seldom did when fortunes were involved, a fact to which Eleanor's own betrothal was witness. At least Mary would like her husband. "Go on. You can be the gallery and cheer for them."

"I suppose we may as well, as little peace as we have." The eagerness with which Mary rose betrayed the interest she pretended not to have. "Come along, everyone."

Lucy and the others got up, too, but Eleanor stayed seated. "You go ahead. I want to finish this." She held up the golden circlet of dent-de-lions she was weaving. "Tell them the champion shall have a golden crown."

They all set off except Lucy, who came back over and began collecting stray blossoms into a nosegay.

"What are you doing?"

"Staying here with you."

Eleanor was torn. She could take advantage of the time apart to quiz Lucy, or she could send her over near Henry—where it seemed she wanted to go, if those sidelong glances were any sign. Ah, well, there was always tonight. "There's no need for you to stay. Go. Enjoy yourself."

"And leave you alone?"

"I can hardly be alone in a meadow full of people. You will not even be out of my sight."

"But—"

Eleanor flapped her hand at her. "Go, I say."

"Yes, my lady." Lucy heaved a sigh that made it sound like she didn't want to go after all, then hurried to catch up with the others.

Apparently Lucy was as confused about what had happened with Henry as Eleanor was. Fortunately, Henry himself seemed not at all confused, flashing a broad grin as Lucy came across the field behind Mary.

Satisfied that she'd done the right thing, Eleanor quickly

wove in the last of the yellow dent-de-lions, set the completed crown aside, and lay back to enjoy her free moment.

Lulled by the sun-warmed cloth, the gentle buzz of the bees in the flowers, and the wine, she soon hung on the edge of sleep, her thoughts wandering unformed until they drifted into dream. An odd noise tugged at her, but not enough to rouse her, and in her dream, Carolus crawled out of a bee skep and began to tell of the bull that loved a maid.

The noise came again, louder now, a low, snuffling sound that drew her away from the story. Lazily, she rolled her head to the right and cracked one eye.

A bull, the one in the story she was sure, stood in the shadows at the edge of the wood, not a dozen yards away, looking at her. In her dream, Eleanor smiled at how clear it all was and sat up to have a better look.

He was an imposing beast, all blocky head and broad, muscled chest, with streaks of red in his curly yellow pelt. He would be terrifying if it weren't a dream, but it was a dream, because Lucy would surely be screaming if it weren't and because she could still hear Carolus's soothing voice. Cradled in that certainty, she picked up the crown of flowers meant for a champion and climbed to her feet.

Noble. Gentle. A god in disguise. Carolus's words followed her into the shadows and right up to the bull, where she carefully hung the crown over one dagger-sharp horn. The beast lowered his head, bowing to her, and the motion exposed his withers and the terrible scars that marked him. Eleanor gasped.

"Who did this to you?" she whispered, but of course he didn't answer, for bulls don't speak, even in dreams. The scars striped him all the way down his back, like some monstrous whip had torn him over and over. That any beast, even one disguising a god and in a dream, could take such cruel punishment and still have such a sweet spirit was a remarkable thing. Touched by his dignity, she knelt in a deep courtesy.

The bull lowed, a mellow, plaintive sound, and stepped

closer still, so close she could smell the grass on his breath and see the dark centers of his eyes. Unnerved, Eleanor put out a hand to fend him off, and as she touched him, an odd wave of contentment swept over her, so strong it washed everything else away, even Carolus's honeyed voice, leaving her afloat in some strange world that included only her and the bull and a deep sense of calm.

So when the great beast slowly lowered himself to his knees, it seemed natural. Proper.

"Zeus," she whispered, and still caught up in the thrall of the dream, climbed onto his broad, scarred back and let him carry her away.

CHAPTER 11

ELEANOR CAME BACK to herself with a start.

God's toes, what was she doing? Heart racing, she slid off the bull's back and scrambled away. He swung his head to look back at her and plodded on, unconcerned.

It seemed so dark. How long had she been riding that fool beast? More of the dream-thrall melted away and she realized with a shock how deep in the woods she must be, how very far off the path. Could he have carried her as far as the demesne forest?

She spun in circles, trying to get her bearings, but the trees grew so rank their branches blocked all but small patches of the sky, and after such a wet winter, every trunk hung thick with moss, confounding her efforts to tell north from south.

A branch snapped, and she jumped, but it was only the bull, still moving off into the murk. Beyond him, though, a faint glow painted the spaces between the trees. Hoping the bull knew where he was going, and that she wasn't being even a bigger fool than she already had been, she fought back the panic and followed him toward the light.

It was with a deep sense of relief that she hurried out into a narrow glade. Overhead, the scattered clouds glowed with the red and gold of sunset. Oh, good, west was that—

She froze.

Facing her, looking not at all gentle or noble, was the bull, who now appeared bloodred beneath the sunset sky, even to his glittering eyes. He pawed the ground and snorted, and she backed up quickly in the direction she'd come.

A scream behind her drove her forward again before she realized it was only a magpie on a low branch behind her. The bull lunged forward, a short feint. With a shriek, Eleanor scrambled behind the nearest tree, startling the magpie, which swooped down off his branch and fluttered around her head screeching like a mad thing. The bull lowered his head and charged.

Halfway across the glade, he crumpled, his legs going out from under him as though bow-shot. He hit the ground with a crash that shook the earth and lay there in a heap, shuddering and moaning.

The bull began to transform before her, his hulk spasming and shrinking as though the clay of his body were being wrenched away by some unseen hand. Hooves and horns receded, muzzle shortened, body deformed and flattened. His moans rose to an unnatural keening, a sound of such despair and agony that it sent terror streaming through Eleanor. Horrified, she tried to tear her eyes away, but she couldn't, any more than she could move, or scream, or even breathe. All she could do was watch, aghast, as the bull vanished, gradually replaced by what lay within.

Not a god at all, but a man. Then he arched back and she saw his face clearly, contorted in pain, and the truth slammed through her.

Gunnar.

An anguished howl tore from his throat and he writhed

as though being held to the flames of perdition. Eleanor dug her nails into her palms, silently pleading for the agony to stop, for whatever terrible power gripped him to release him. Finally, an eternity later, he collapsed, limp and unmoving, with only the sound of his groans to say he lived.

Tears streamed down her cheeks as she struggled with what she'd just seen. A bull become a man? Her mind rejected the very idea. It must be her dream turned nightmare, all part of the same madness that had carried her here to this forsaken place.

But no, she was awake now. That was one of the few things she was certain of. She didn't even have to pinch herself to know; the sting of her torn palms told her this was no dream.

But if she wasn't dreaming, then what was he? Demon?

Enchanted through no fault of his own. Gunnar's words echoed in her mind, and she recalled the hollowness in his voice as he'd said them. He hadn't been able to face her when he said them. Had they been lies? A demon would lie.

She tried her feet. They moved now. She could run.

She should run. She knew which way to go now, and she could be well away before he recovered his strength.

But then what? Even if men were searching for her, they would never imagine she had come so far, and she'd never find her way back to Raby before dark. She'd spend the night wandering the woods alone. Dread shuddered down her spine.

And what of Gunnar? The man she called champion, the man who had walked through fire to save her. He still lay there groaning in agony.

A demon could walk through fire, whispered that voice in the back of her mind. And if he was a demon, staying here could cost her. She should flee for her life, for her very soul.

No. She couldn't be that wrong. She couldn't. She'd told

Lucy that he was good, that she could feel it when she looked into his eyes. She'd felt the same deep-rooted good when she looked the bull in the eye, known it in her heart when she touched him, even through the dream. She couldn't abandon him now, when he might need help.

And so even though the dream no longer held her, even though she couldn't fully rid herself of the terrifying idea that he might be a demon, she made a choice, no doubt foolish, not to run.

Not yet anyway.

He groaned and moved a little, and she very nearly changed her mind, but in the end, she gave herself over to whatever was going to happen, said a quick but fervent prayer, and stepped out into the open.

"ARMUBDEM?"

The veil of pain that still enshrouded Gunnar so muffled things that he couldn't tell whether it was a man or woman who spoke, much less what they said. He worked his tongue, trying to make his mouth form a human sound. "Wha—?"

"I said, are you a demon?"

That voice. He prized his eyes open a slit and caught a glimpse of hem, and beneath it, the toe of a woman's slipper, Eleanor's slipper. Hope surged through him, clearing some of the cobwebs. "No. Not demon."

He forced himself onto his hands and knees with a grunt, gathered his feet, and pushed upright to face her as a man.

"Not demon," he repeated.

Eleanor stared at him a long moment, her eyes wide over tearstained cheeks, then abruptly turned away.

"Freya, please," he pleaded in Norse, then in English, "Don't go."

"If I were going, I would already be gone." Eleanor spoke

with sureness, despite the quaver in her voice, and that gave him even more hope.

He started toward her. "My lady, I—"

"You are naked, sir. Dress yourself."

Gunnar looked down at his body in surprise. His mind was still clogged with the bull's spirit, but he dredged up the memory and pointed to a nearby fallen tree. "I have clothes. There."

"Then fetch them. I will not run."

He found the bundle hidden in a hollow beneath the tree, and dragged on his chemise and braies. He had a harder time with his chausses; his hands were simply too clumsy to deal with them yet. As he struggled, Eleanor glanced over her shoulder.

Apparently satisfied that he was sufficiently clothed, she faced him with a determined expression. "If you are not a demon, what are you? And do not tell me you are Zeus."

"No, not a god either. I told you that night we heard the story. I am naught but a man, enchanted through no—"

"Through no fault of his own," she said with him. She shook her head. "That is not enough."

He understood what she was asking, and it was what he needed her to know. But for all the hours he'd spent thinking about how to explain it to her, he still wasn't sure he could. He finally got one stocking on, then drew on the second to buy himself a little time to get his thoughts in order. In the end, though, there was no escape. He began.

"I am Gunnar, son of Hrólfr, called Gunnar the Red for both my hair and the enemy blood I have spilled." Even spoken in English, the ancient form of naming made him sit up a little straighter. He was a warrior. *Gunnar inn rauði.* He could do this.

Her brows pinched together. "A Dane?"

"A Northman, as you would say it. I sailed to these shores as a raider long ago." He hesitated before he added, "In the years before your King Alfred."

"This is not the time for jests, *monsire*. Alfred lived before the time of the Conqueror."

"Long before," he confirmed. "It is no jest. I have lived in England these six hundreds of years."

She shook her head in denial. "That is not possible."

"You saw what I am, my lady. You know it is true."

"I saw the bull and you, but . . ."

"Six hundreds of years," Gunnar said harshly, and his jaw clenched with the memory of each wretched one. "Every day of it changing back and forth between man and beast, made immortal so the torment goes on and on."

Paling, Eleanor stumbled over and sagged down on the log not far from Gunnar. "But how did this happen?"

"A witch's curse," said Gunnar. Something prickled at the edges of his memory, something the bull had seen. He reached for it, but it flittered away.

"No. Surely even a w-witch cannot do such evil." Her fear of even the word was evident in the way she stumbled over it. She wrapped her arms around herself.

"She was a priestess of the dark gods," said Gunnar. "A sorceress of the old ways who held great power in her day. Called Cwen."

"She is dead, then." Eleanor sounded relieved.

"No." He got his doublet on and tried fastening the ties, but he was still having trouble with his fingers. He left it. "She lives. She has lost much of her power, but she clings to the same unending life she forces on us, so that she may enjoy our suffering and continue to hound us."

She wrapped her arms around herself and huddled there on the log, staring at the ground. "Why would she harbor such hate?"

"We raided in search of the treasure she guarded, and she sent her son to lead the fight against us."

"And you killed him," she murmured, her voice full of accusation.

"He died, as men do in battle."

"But by your hand."

Gunnar's jaw tightened. "It makes no difference whose hand struck the blow. I would have slain him if our swords had crossed. We each of us would. It was battle."

"You say 'we' and 'us.' Are there others?"

He nodded. "Nine. All that survived the fight. Two have found release. Seven remain."

"All like you?"

"Not bulls. They take other forms. Dog. Stallion. Hart. Raven." He stopped there, unwilling to name Brand's bear or Jafri's wolf. They were too frightening, too rare in England, too easy to find if someone knew to look for them. If he was wrong about her and she denounced them, the full wrath of Church and Crown would fall on them like Thor's hammer, and Brand and Jafri would take the brunt of it. *Please, Freya, do not let me be wrong about this woman.*

"We each wore an amulet to honor our *fylgjur*, our guardian spirits," he went on. "Cwen used them in her spell, to turn us to their image, each man to his own. Some of us are beast by day, others by night, but we all shift at the rising and setting of the sun."

Understanding dawned across her face. "The rooster crow. No wonder you left so quickly the night we . . . the night you had your dream."

"I did not want to go."

"I know. I knew then that you didn't, though I thought you left so quickly because we were about to . . . because you wished to protect my honor. Why do you tell me all this now? Is it because of old Carolus's tale about Europa?"

"Yes. The bull . . . I . . ." He struggled with the words. "I retain some measure of myself deep within the beast. Most times it is barely enough to bring it back to my clothes and horse each night. But if the need is great, I have learned to force myself forward, to know a little of what the bull knows and gain some power over it. When you said you might not run, I saw good reason to try."

"I didn't." She lifted her chin, a glint of pride in her eyes. Or was that a tear? "Run, I mean."

"No, you did not run, and for that, I am most grateful, my lady."

"I don't know why. I wanted to. A part of me still does."

Gunnar had nothing to offer her. A part of him wanted to run, too. In all the years of warring and raiding, he had never flinched from battle, but if given the chance, he would flee sunrise and sunset like the most craven dog.

"It frightens me," she continued softly almost as though to herself. "All this talk of curses and witches and men who become beasts. It is heresy, all of it. To believe such things puts me beyond the pale of the Church, and yet how can I not believe? I have seen you change with my own eyes. I know there are powers at work here, both good and evil, even if I do not understand them." She looked him fully in the eye. "Did you enchant me? Is that why I let the bull bring me here?"

He thought back to the prayers and to the little fallow doe he'd sacrificed to Freya just before dawn. "Not how you mean. I would never inflict on you what has been laid on me, my lady. But I need for you to know, and to know, you had to see, else you would never believe. It is May Day, a day full of the old magic. I asked for help and it was given." *Praise be to Freya.*

"May Day," repeated Eleanor softly as though she just recalled it. She looked up at the sky, now faded to gray except for where last light gilded the westernmost clouds. "It will be dark soon. They will come searching for me."

"The bull carried you into a deep part of the forest. They are not likely to find you here. I'll fetch my horse and take you back." Gunnar rose and tried the ties on his doublet again. He did better this time, but it was still a slow process, requiring all his attention. He finished the first tie and glanced up to find Eleanor watching him intently.

"Have you hurt your hands?" she asked. "You had trouble with your chausses, too."

"No, I'm only a little ham-fisted." He held his hands up and wiggled his fingers. "I regain my strength quickly most days, but when I struggle against the bull's spirit, it takes longer to find my way back."

" 'I asked for help and it was given.' " She repeated his words back to him, then stood up and brushed his hands aside. "This is a far simpler thing and requires no magic at all."

Her touch was shaky at first, then steadied as she finished the second tie and moved down to the next. "Do you suffer such pain every day?"

"Dawn and dusk." He stood there as she worked at his ties, desperate to hold her, to kiss her, to ask her if she could love him now, knowing what he was. But that was for later, after she'd had a chance to take in all she'd seen. There was one thing he must have from her, though, and he needed it now, before he took her back.

He covered her hands with his, pressing them against his chest to hold her there, where she had no choice but to look up at him. "You cannot tell anyone about me or the others."

Her brows arched up in surprise. "Who would I tell? They would think me mad."

"And then they would hunt us down anyway, out of fear you might not be. We cannot be killed, my lady, but we can be hurt, and we feel the pain of every wound as much as any man. Some would enjoy learning how much pain we can bear—and that, too, would go on forever."

"Torture? Dear God, no." Her hand went to her mouth. "No. Of course, I would never tell anyone. Not even Lucy."

"Especially not Lucy," he warned. "You will be tempted, lying there in bed with your cousin, talking in the night, but you cannot risk it. She is too frightened of the world to keep such a secret for long, and this one must be kept forever. Nor can you confess it. I must have your vow, my lady, that you will hold all this to yourself, whatever comes."

"It is my secret, as well," she said. "No one must know I was here, with you. We both must promise, and so I will begin. I vow I will never tell anyone what I witnessed here this even, Sir Gunnar of Lesbury. So far as the world will know, I was lost in the forest. Alone."

"And I vow I will never tell anyone you were here to witness it, Lady Eleanor de Neville. So far as the world will know, I never found you. I was miles from here."

"And to seal the vow . . ." Hands still pressed to his breast, she rose up on her toes and kissed him.

It was a chaste kiss, meant only as a pledge, nearly as innocent as that first kiss of thanks all those years before, but the touch of her lips to his was like putting key to lock. A door opened, and desire flooded through Gunnar.

He couldn't help himself. He kissed her back, lowering his head to follow her as she settled back onto her heels, pouring his hope and longing into her so that she might understand what her staying, her promise, meant to him. She sighed, and as their tongues tangled, he hardened, as ready for her as he had been that night in the solar. Readier. Sliding his hands around to cup the fine roundness of her bottom, he pulled her close, trapping his tarse between them. Her answering gasp went to his head like strong wine.

From somewhere came the wherewithal to warn her. He wrenched his mouth off hers. "If I don't fetch my horse now, you will not leave this place a virgin."

She arched back, giving herself distance enough to have a good look at him. Her expression was unreadable, and for a long moment he thought she was going to push him away. Instead, she threaded her arms around his neck.

"Then I will not leave a virgin." She pulled his head down and kissed him again, no sweetness in her at all, just a fierceness that took his breath away.

She must love him. She must. The need to test that, to possess her, became his reason to exist.

He explored every inch of her body he could reach without breaking the kiss, ending with the rich weight of her breasts in his palms. He dragged his thumbs over their peaks and then did it again because of how she shuddered against him. He'd make her do that while he was in her, he promised himself.

In her. Ah, how he wanted to be in her.

Flattening one hand over her belly, he slid it down between them to find his way between her legs, where he could stroke her through the cloth. A fevered moan rose from her throat, and he almost laughed at such an immodest sound coming from a maid.

Not maid for long. Even through the cloth, he could feel her warming and he knew how slick she'd be. Sensation mixed with memory, making him swell more, so hard now that it pained him. But what sweet pain. Eleanor pressed toward him, and through the thickening fog of arousal he knew she sought the same thing he wanted: release.

But not like this. No, this time, it was going to be the right way, and when he was done, she would be his.

"I'll be in you this time when your pleasure comes," he told her, savoring the rough intake of her breath and her incoherent whine of protest as he set her away for a moment. "Patience, sweeting."

He found the blanket his clothes had been wrapped in and made a rough nest in the grass. Eleanor watched, swaying and trembling like an aspen tree as she waited for him.

For *him*. Even knowing what she knew, she waited for him. The wonder of it made Gunnar dizzy with need.

It was nearly dark. He wanted to see her naked before he lost the light, and though the dress she wore was a simple one, little more than a kirtle with a half gown buttoned over it, there wasn't time for him and his still-thick fingers.

"Undress," he growled, "else I will tear that gown off you and then have to send you home like Godiva afterward, bare as a babe."

Her fingers flew over the buttons. He helped where he could, but mostly watched as she removed the overgown, slippers, and gartered hose, laying them all on the log. But when she began to gather her kirtle at her waist and exposed her legs, he lost the last bit of patience he had. With a growl, he stripped the yards of cloth over her head, tossed the kirtle atop her other things, and scooped her up to lower her onto her back.

He stood over her a moment, just looking at all that creamy flesh, radiant as the moon in the last glimmer of light, fair as a goddess. The harsh sound of her breath was like a slow drumbeat, urging him toward her. He peeled off the hose he'd just worked so hard to put on and slipped one toe between her knees, nudging them apart. "Spread your legs to me, Eleanor."

She hesitated, then obeyed, showing herself to him.

He nodded. "Wider."

He dropped to his knees between her thighs, put his hands to either side of her, and bowed to worship her with his mouth, kissing his way up over belly and breast to her lips, and then back down and lower, bypassing her quaint to nibble his way up the insides of her thighs.

By now it was too dark to make out much more than the faintest outlines, the light of the stars being far too thin and the moon not yet risen above the trees, but he could smell her musk and hear her moans, deeper and more urgent the nearer he got.

Finally he was there. He tasted her, gently, then plunged in to devour her.

With a cry, she arched up off the blanket, surging against his tongue, seeking. Not wanting her to finish too soon, Gunnar stopped and let her cool before he dove down again. She didn't thrust at him this time, but as he lapped at her, he could tell how close she was, and once more he stopped before she could go there.

She whimpered and grabbed for his head, twining her fingers into his hair to pull him back to her.

He loved how willing she was, how quickly she learned. The heat in her fed his own, driving him to take her, take her now. Instead, he shook her loose and shifted around to lie beside her. Working by little more than feel, he kissed his way from mouth to breasts, enjoyed both, then settled in on the peak of one to circle it with his tongue, over and over. As she began to pant, he slid his hand down to cup her.

She moved restlessly against his hand. "I want . . . Like before."

"Not this time. I told you how it will be. Say it."

"*Nnh*. You in me."

"Aye." He found the tight ring of her maidenhead and paused there, the tip of his finger barely in her. "In you here." He went back to her breast, working the peak with his tongue until she relaxed and let him in.

He fit a second finger beside the first, but his fingers were large and she was small and oh so tight. There was a stretch and a sudden give. She sucked at the air and clamped her legs together, trying to stop him.

"Stay open to me, Eleanor. You'll find more pleasure later if I do it this way."

Again, she obeyed. He took his time, and a little later felt her moisture flood over his hand.

"There you go, sweeting. Now, sit up and help me with my laces." He shifted back to kneel between her legs, continuing to move his fingers gently within her as he helped her upright. "I want my skin against yours when I take you."

She found his ties in the dark, and as she pulled at them, he worked a third finger in beside the other two, felt her maidenhead give again. She shuddered but didn't stop, and soon his doublet was loose. He had to abandon her for a moment to pull it off and rid himself of his shirt, but he went right back. She moaned aloud this time and wriggled more firmly onto his fingers, helping him now. Ready.

"Braies," he said, but she was ready for that, too, her hands already at his waist. She gave a tug, loosed the waist, and peeled them down.

His cock sprang free, and for one brief moment he thought of urging her to take him into her mouth, to enjoy that tongue she'd teased him with so often in the last weeks. She would surely do it, just as she'd done everything else he'd asked of her, and it would be sweet, so sweet. But not this time. This time, it was about possession, about binding her to him. Whatever pleasure he took from her tonight was only a boon—but a boon he intended to savor.

Releasing her, he kicked away his braies, pressed her back, and slid his chest up the length of her body in one long, slow motion, relishing the feel of every inch of her, from woman's hair and hard mound to silken belly to pebbled breasts. She beckoned him up, drawing him into her arms.

When he lay full on her, breast to breast, he kissed her deeply and began to move, not in her yet but against her. As before, she moved against him in search of what she wanted. Her hands slipped over his back and shoulders, her heels hooked behind his knees to pull at him.

He shifted and reached down to bring himself to the right angle, and she moaned and bucked up to meet him and he was in, the whole of him at once, her heat enveloping him as completely as the night enveloped their bodies. Her gasp was half pain, half pleasure, all his.

"You are given to me," he breathed into her open mouth, making his claim a part of her being. He repeated it in Norse so the gods would hear and knew he understood his debt to them. Then, remembering his promise to himself, he raked his thumbs over her breasts to set her quivering around him, and he thought, just for a moment, that he wouldn't mind living forever if he could pass the years buried in her like this.

They moved together, just the two of them, surrounded by forest and stars, beginning slowly and gradually coming to each other faster, harder. She was liquid fire, all slick, wet heat in his arms. He slid toward the edge, too fast. *Too fast.*

Summoning the last of his will, he made himself go elsewhere, think of things not-Eleanor, so she would have time to find what she needed from him. She built, thrashing, her nails raking his back, that wondrous, unmaidenly moan rising around him until finally it broke and she thrashed beneath him, her body clenching and pulsing in release.

A little longer she was killing him a little longer.

He held back as long as he could, until her spasms began to ease, then turned his mind to her, nothing but her, drove into her hard and let go, tumbling after her, out of control.

Finally, spent, he slipped into mindless nothingness. It was Eleanor's hand that drew him back, gliding across his cheek to find his mouth. He kissed her fingertips as she traced out his lips. "What are you doing?"

"Seeing if you are smiling. You never truly do, but I thought you did the last time we . . ." She was blushing, he was sure of it. He'd never known it was possible to hear a blush in a woman's voice, but he could now, and he knew just the shade of pink that colored her cheeks and breasts. She brushed a kiss across each corner of his mouth. "I think you do now, as well. I wish I could see it."

"The moon will be up soon. You can see it then."

"I fear it may vanish."

"Then you must help to keep it here."

She did her best, kissing and touching, soothing over the scars on his back. They lay joined a long time, the sweat drying between their bellies as they traded kisses back and forth. Eventually, though, he softened and slipped out of her and the night air grew chill, and even with him atop her to keep her warm, Eleanor began to shiver.

Still covering her, Gunnar groped around till he found cloth. "Here's, um . . . my doublet, I think. Put it on while I start a fire."

He helped her with the doublet and tucked the blanket around her legs, then pulled on his shirt and stumbled off in search of his gear. "Shite! Ow."

"What? Are you all right?"

"Fine. I forgot about a branch, that's all." Gunnar

rubbed his belly where he'd nearly impaled himself, then traced the branch to the fallen tree it was part of and followed the trunk to where he'd hidden his saddle and gear. He knew just which pouch his flint and steel were in, and he found them quickly.

The fire he started wasn't much, since all he had was what tinder and twigs he could find by feel, but it was enough to begin. He lit one of the candle stubs he kept in the pouch and handed it to Eleanor so she could start gathering her clothes. The first thing she did was hold the flame up to see his face.

"Your smile is gone."

"No it isn't. I'm smiling right now."

She closed her eyes and felt his mouth with her free hand, then shook her head. "That is only your common smile, the half smile. The real one must only come out in the dark."

"Or between your legs," he suggested, to which idea she made a sour face. Chuckling, he dressed quickly, lit a second candle off hers, and went off to gather more wood.

"You laugh, but the priests warn us women every year of the dangers of going into the woods with wicked men like you," she called after him. "Just this morning, Father Stephen charged us to avoid the sins of the forest."

"That's what he called it? The sins of the forest?"

"He did. I thought that of all those going a-maying, I was the least likely to stray, since you were not to be there. Instead, I am the most grievous sinner of all, and more so that I enjoyed the sinning so very much."

He stopped in his tracks. "Did you?"

"Surely you could tell."

"I suspected so," he admitted. "I hoped so." He carried a handful of sticks back to the fire and added a couple to the flame.

"I can barely tell if the proper side is out," complained Eleanor as she felt her way along a sleeve. "'Tis one thing if my clothes are disheveled when I return, another entirely if it is clear I've had them off. Can you not build the fire higher?"

"No. I don't want to lead someone here. The moon will be nearly full tonight. It will give us enough light soon, and I will help you sort them out," he promised. "Though if you were to leave them off entirely while we ride, you would see me smile for certs."

"You, *monsire*, are a ribald." She threaded her arm down a sleeve to turn it. "Is bedding always so pleasant?"

"If it is done right, between two people who are well matched in their desire."

"We must be *very* well matched, then."

The corners of his mouth twitched, as did his tarse, despite being so freshly and so thoroughly spent. "You may be right. Stay here by the fire. I'll get my horse."

Carrying his piece of candle, he went a stone's throw down a deer path to the tumbled-down gamekeeper's cottage where he'd tethered Ghost for the day. He led him back to the glade and, working by candle and firelight, saddled him, then left him to graze a little while he carried a small bag of shelled hazelnuts and another of dried apples over to Eleanor.

"'Tis a poor supper, but all I have with me," he said as he sat down beside her. She'd managed to get her clothes on.

"I like hazelnuts." She took a few nutmeats and a slice of apple and nibbled at them while he disposed of several handfuls of each. Silence stretched between them, but it was a companionable one, as though they'd known each other so long and so well that they found little need to speak. The moon rose after a time, and in its clear light, Gunnar inspected Eleanor's clothes.

"All looks well to me." He pinched out the candles, dropped them into the pouch with his flint and steel, and hooked the pouch onto his belt. "It is time we go, my lady, lest your father's men happen on us here."

"Aye. I like it far better when you call me Eleanor."

"As do I. But for now, you must remain Lady Eleanor

to me, as I must stay Sir Gunnar to you. It would be dire if either of us slipped before others." He rolled the blanket around the last of his gear, shoved it back into the hollow, stamped out the fire, and prepared to mount.

"Do you want me behind or before?" asked Eleanor as she reached up to him.

"Before," he said, and helped her up into the saddle proper. He swung up behind the saddle and pulled her back hard against him, and she settled into his arms.

He turned west, to circle around through a more open part of the forest where the moon could light the way. Even so, the going was slow. They rode a long way in silence, letting the surefooted Ghost pick his way through the forest at his own pace. Gunnar was in no hurry, content simply to hold Eleanor for as long as possible.

"I would think it difficult for you to live always in Lesbury," she said thoughtfully. "People would see that you do not age. I saw that you haven't changed since Richmond."

"The steward minds the lands, and I visit only when I must."

"Where do you live in between?"

"There is wild dene along the coast, east of Durham and a little south, that a friend and I call home. But we wander a lot, too. That is how I came to be at Richmond. And at Raby."

"Ah." She settled to silence again, and in time, they reached the main track and turned north and east, toward Raby.

"You never told me why," she murmured.

"I thought you slept." He pressed a kiss into her hair. "Why what?"

"I have been thinking about all that you said, and all that you did not. I come back over and over to the same question. Why did you want me to see what you are?"

There it was, the final piece. He hadn't expected she would ask for it tonight, thinking she would need more time. But then he hadn't expected most of what she'd done or said. The depth of her courage left him in awe.

But he still wasn't certain whether he should tell her or not, whether telling her that he needed her heart before she offered it herself would somehow change the love itself, weaken it so much the magic wouldn't work.

He found a path between. "I want you for wife. I am going to ask your father for your hand."

She nestled back against him with a sigh. "I hoped you would take me away one day. I have dreamt of it for years, since Richmond."

Take me. Ah, so she hadn't been talking about tupping at all. Not that it mattered now. "And now, knowing what I am, do you still dream of it? Are you willing to be mine?"

"I am already yours. Given to you, you said."

A place in the center of him glowed with satisfaction, but he pressed on. She had to understand and want him anyway.

"It will be difficult. I am not a rich man. You will have few servants, few of the fine things you have now. What you will have is a husband who leaves you before dawn every morning to spend his day in the field. I'm a bull, Eleanor. Think of that, and tell me you will be happy with a bull."

She pulled his arms more tightly around herself as though trying to stay warm. "I cannot pretend I am not frightened of that part of you and of the evil that created it. But I will be happy with the man who returns to me each night, and pleased to welcome him into my bed and my body. That is more than I—" She stopped and took a deep breath. "It is more than most women have from marriage. Speak to my father. I will affirm that I want you." A distant horn sounded over her last words, and she stiffened. "The search party."

"Aye." Gunnar reined Ghost to a halt and sat listening. "They are perhaps half a mile off. We will dismount here."

"You're not taking me back yourself? You will be named hero once more."

"I will be named defiler of virgins," he said as he swung down. He helped her off, but kept her in the circle of his arms. "I did not plan what passed between us tonight. I thought you would need time to come to peace with what I am, and I told the steward I was going to Durham. If we return together now, after a night in the forest, it will not matter what tale we tell. All will know. But if you are found alone and lost, and I return to Raby in two days' time as I said I would, no one will suspect."

"Two days! But—"

He stopped her protest with a finger across her lip. "It is better this way, my lady. Both you and your honor will be secure, and I will use the time to set things in motion, the quicker to carry you to Lesbury."

"I don't have to be truly lost, do I? I fear I have used up all my courage for this day."

She? Who had more courage than most men? Gunnar pulled her back against him and pressed a kiss to her neck. "No. I will see you safe until we near them, then I'll send you ahead to be found while I hang back."

He tied Ghost to a tree well off the track and they set out, moving carefully so they wouldn't stumble into a search party unawares. There was little chance of that; the various parties crashed through the brush in the distance, driving startled animals before them like beaters at a poorly organized hunt. When they closed on one party, Gunnar stopped in the deep shadows beneath a tree and pulled Eleanor into his arms so he could put his mouth by her ear—and so he could hold her one last time.

"Oh, God. I hear my father's voice amongst the others." She didn't sound happy.

But all Gunnar could think was that her father would see her safely home. "They will come out just there, I think." He pointed to the moonlit crown of small rise ahead. "Cry out and run toward them as though you just heard them. They will carry you home."

"Where will you be?"

"Here. Watching over you." He pressed a kiss to her cheek, gave her one final squeeze, and hoisted himself up onto a branch where he could see but not be seen. "There are the torches. Go, my lady. Be found."

"Two days," she whispered up to him. And then she was off, calling for aid, flying across the field into her father's arms.

CHAPTER 12

"OH, MY LADY!" Lucy rushed across the courtyard as Raffin helped Eleanor down from her father's horse. "I thought you were lost."

"I was, but—" began Eleanor.

"Later," snapped Westmorland as he leapt to the ground behind her. He grabbed Eleanor by the arm and stalked toward the door, barely giving her a chance to get her feet under her. "Your mother is half mad with worry. You will relieve her mind and then to bed. Wait in chamber, Lucy."

Lucy, who'd been scurrying along on their heels, fell behind with a weak, "Yes, m'lord."

He swept Eleanor through the hall, up to the solar, down the passageway, and up the tower stairs without another word. He'd barely said anything at all thus far. After making certain she was unharmed and asking how she'd become lost, he'd gone silent. From the way his fingers bit into her arm now, however, she knew he was angry, and she could understand, what with having to turn out the entire castle to search for her. At least he wasn't shouting. Yet.

He finally released her when they reached the lying-in chamber. "I will remain here to escort you to your chamber."

"There is no need, my lord. I have caused you much trouble already, and—"

"I will remain." He pushed the door open and shoved her inside. "Here she is, Joan."

"Eleanor! Thank the heavens." Lady Joan jumped up from her chair and hurried over to gather Eleanor into her arms. "What happened? No, never mind. I will hear it tomorrow. Tonight, nothing matters but that you are found."

"It was so foolish." Eleanor burrowed her face against her mother's shoulder, the better to hide her lie. "All I did was go into the woods a little way, and the next thing I knew . . ."

"The woods! Why?"

"To make water." Now that she was saying it for the second time, it sounded far too weak a reason to wander off, so she added in a mumble, "And the other. I wanted to be well away from where we were eating, but I went too far. I turned wrong somewhere."

"You certainly did. Poor dearling, you are shaking," said her mother, which only added to Eleanor's guilt. "Lucy should have gone with you."

"She bears no fault in this," said Eleanor quickly. "I sent her off to play with the boys before I realized I needed to . . ."

"Ah, well, what matters is that you are safe and hale." Lady Joan cupped Eleanor's face in both hands. "This is the second time we have almost lost you. Heaven must surely have plans for you, to bring you back safely each time."

"Whatever Heaven's plans are, they can wait," said Westmorland. "She should be abed, Joan, and so should you." He turned sideways in the door and waited, stiff as one of the family effigies in the church. Eleanor felt herself pale.

"Look at you. You are exhausted." Lady Joan kissed

Eleanor's forehead and felt it for fever. "At least you're not ill. I will send Amy to help with—"

"Lucy will see to her," said Westmorland. "Eleanor."

"God's rest, *madame*." Eleanor gave her mother a quick kiss and ducked out past her father, who bade her mother a curt God's rest before he tugged the door shut and grabbed Eleanor's arm again.

If his grip as he hauled her down the stairs was any sign, he was even angrier now than he had been on the way up. Eleanor quickly ran through what she'd said to her mother, but found nothing he could fault. Perhaps if she groveled a bit. He always liked it when people groveled. It had saved her more than once.

At her chamber, he pushed the door open so hard it slammed against the wall behind.

"Lucy, tell Bertrand I want two men on this door for the night. And when I am done, ready your lady for travel."

Lucy's eyes got wide. "My lord?"

"She leaves for Burwash at first light."

Burwash. Richard. "No!" Eleanor jerked forward, grabbing at his sleeve. "Oh, no, my lord, please. He has not even sent for me. He wants me no more than I want him."

He shook her off and snapped at Lucy, "Did you not understand me?"

"Yes, of course, my lord." Lucy bolted out the door. Before she'd gotten a yard down the hall, Westmorland grabbed Eleanor, yanked her into the chamber, slammed the door shut, and dropped the bar. Lucy had lit the room well, and the glow of the lamp and candles brought his icy, narrowed eyes and the white ring around his mouth into high relief.

His silence wasn't vexation, it was fury. Pure, raw, barely controlled fury. Wherever it came from, Eleanor realized, her only chance was to appease.

"I am sorry my foolishness caused so much trouble, my lord, and very grateful you found me. If you had not—"

"Silence."

"But I only meant to say—"

He hit her, a backhand so quick she didn't see it coming. It left her head spinning. Clutching her cheek, she looked up at him through tearing eyes. "What did I—"

"Was it Sir Gunnar?"

Oh, sweet Mother. Fear chilled her blood and thickened her tongue. Part of her, the panicked part, wanted to shout that Gunnar would be there to marry her in two days. The other, the part that knew her father's anger too well, recognized that such a claim would only make matters worse. "I don't know what—"

He hit her again, harder. Reeling, she stumbled against the wall and slid down partway. Grabbing her hair, he hauled her to her feet, ignoring her squall of pain. He pushed his nose into her neck and inhaled deeply. "I could smell him on you the moment I took you onto my horse. You stink of his seed, even now."

She reached through the fog of pain and grasped at the story Gunnar had told her. "Sir Gunnar left for Durham before dawn. I swear, my lord, I have not—"

He hit her a third time, a vicious blow that made something in her nose snap like a dry twig, and then he let her drop as her legs gave out. "Do not dare to lie to me. All it will take is a midwife to prove you were bedded tonight."

He loomed over her, his face a snarl. "You will leave at dawn for Clementhorpe to rest there with the holy sisters until the wedding is arranged. If Sir Gunnar follows, if you try to run, if he disturbs the wedding or you refuse Richard at the altar or later in bed, I will feed your knight his balls before you. And then I will see him hanged slowly, with a fire beneath his feet."

. . . and that, too, would go on forever . . .

The world spun and heaved, and she emptied her stomach onto the floor at her father's feet. She spat and wiped her mouth on her sleeve, her split lip and broken nose leaving a smear of blood on the white linen. "And if I do as you ask?"

"He goes on his way, his manhood intact, fit to spread some other maid's legs." He leaned down, intent on punishing her in every way. "No doubt he will find someone willing by the time Richard is spreading yours."

Her stomach twisted again, but she locked her teeth against the bile and ground out, "Your word. I would have your word that you will not harm him."

He stilled, and for a moment she thought he was going to hit her again. Then he straightened and tugged his cote smooth. "You have it, so long as I, and then Richard, have your obedience."

Someone pushed at the door, found it barred, and knocked.

"Stand up." He put his hand out. She hesitated and his lip curled. "Do you defy me already?"

"No, my lord. I only collect myself." She took his hand, and he pulled her to her feet and up against him in one motion. One hand cupped behind her head as he put his mouth to her ear.

"I know women have ways to deceive men of their virtue." His voice was harsh and barely audible. "Pray that one of the black sisters knows them and that they are convincing, for if Richard realizes he has taken a whore for a wife and annuls the marriage . . ."

"You gave your word," she whispered.

"Then see that I have no reason to withdraw it." He kissed her forehead, a mark of control rather than affection, then turned and walked to the door. When he pulled it open, Lucy was standing there wide-eyed, someone behind her. He shouldered past them with a grunt. "Attend to your lady. And clean the floor. She has been ill."

And as he vanished down the hall, Eleanor saw Anne, grinning in delight, turn to follow him.

NOW THAT WAS odd. Gunnar reined Ghost to a halt at the end of the moat bridge and sat looking at the lowered portcullis. The iron gate had never been down this early before. He checked the walls for extra men, then twisted around to scan the meadow and woods for any sign of attack, but saw nothing. Ah, well, perhaps they were greasing the channel. The gate had been screeching mightily of late.

"Entry," he called.

"Denied, Sir Gunnar," came a voice back. "The earl said you should wait there."

"Is that you, Owain de Breck?"

The grizzled knight from the tourney stepped up to show his face between the bars of the gate. "Aye."

"What is this about? Are the Scots on the prowl again?"

"The earl says to wait there," repeated Owain. He glanced over his shoulder. "He comes anon."

A few moments later, the heavy bolt was thrown on the adjacent man-gate and Westmorland strode out.

"My lord." Gunnar dismounted and met him mid-bridge. "Is there some trouble?"

"Not war, if that is what you ask, but I do wish a word with you." He glanced over his shoulder toward the guard tower and motioned Gunnar a little farther from the wall. "I have news, sir, regarding my daughter."

"Lady Eleanor?"

"Which of my other daughters would concern you?" Westmorland's voice carried an undercurrent of anger that raised the hairs on Gunnar's neck. "Eleanor is betrothed, sir, and has been these five years past, to Richard le Despenser, who is Lord Burghersh and soon to be remade Earl of Gloucester."

"Betrothed?" A leaden coldness weighted Gunnar's limbs, as though his blood was being drained away onto the verge. "But she never—"

"Never told you? I thought as much."

"But I . . . that is, she . . . I . . ." Gunnar struggled to put together a thought. "I have come to ask for her hand myself," he blurted out finally. "She said she would affirm to you that she wished it."

"When?"

"Your pardon?"

"*When* did she say that she would affirm it? When did she make this . . . assurance?"

The sharpness in Westmorland's question renewed Gunnar's wariness. Had he guessed what had happened in the wood? Keeping to the lie he'd agreed to with Eleanor, he answered, "Before I rode to Durham, my lord. Three, no, four days ago. I told her I would speak to you when I returned."

"Indeed." His narrowed eyes glittering with the fading light, Westmorland stared off into the west for a moment before he turned to Gunnar. "Hear me, sir, and hear me well. Eleanor is not for you. She never has been. She is meant to be a countess, like her lady mother, and she has long known it."

. . . dreamed you would take me away . . .

"She doesn't want to marry Lord Burghersh," Gunnar whispered, half to himself, wondering if she'd lain with him merely to get his help in breaking the betrothal.

Westmorland dismissed the idea with a wave of his hand. "She said the vows willingly and signed the contract with her own hand, all before witnesses. I have reminded her of her duty and she is contrite, as she should be. She will be married before the month is out." He leveled his gaze with Gunnar's and added firmly, "*Also* willingly. It is done."

Gunnar swallowed back the bitter taste that flooded his mouth. "Aye, my lord, it is. If I had known she was promised elsewhere, it would never have begun."

"Good. I would have had Eleanor make apology herself, but she knows she used you poorly and has no courage to face you. She is still young, *monsire*, and I fear she got caught up in the trifling leading to May Day. Forgive her, sir. And forget her."

"Yes, my lord," he said, though it was unlikely he would do either.

Westmorland clasped his hands behind his back and

pursed his lips. "I regret that Eleanor has caused us this trouble. I have greatly enjoyed your company. Perhaps in future, when she is well settled with Richard and surrounded by babes, you and I can be companions once more."

Never. "Perhaps, my lord. Tell the lady I wish her joy in her mar—" The words choked him, and he had to clear his throat and try again. "In her marriage to Lord Burghersh. I will not trouble her or you again."

Westmorland gave a curt nod and spun on his heel, leaving Gunnar to stare at his back as he strode across the bridge.

The man-gate shut behind him with a clang that echoed in Gunnar's belly. He remembered this feeling. It was the same gutted hollowness he'd felt when he'd learned that Kolla had begged her lover to carry her away.

Now he was the lover, and he'd almost let Eleanor persuade him to do the same thing to another man.

What he'd said to Westmorland was truth: if he'd known, he never would have stayed after the tourney, never would have pursued Eleanor. But how much pursuing did he actually do? Every little seduction she'd wielded against him came flooding back: the subtle touches, the perfume, the way she'd come down to him in the night without him even asking. Even the words she'd spoken as she gave herself to him in the forest.

There is a reason I'm here . . .

Aye, a reason, all right. She wanted out of a poor marriage contract. Treachery. Fire and treachery. She was no different from Kolla at all.

He swung up on Ghost and turned him toward the forest north of the castle, intending to put as much distance as he could between himself and Eleanor. He knew from experience that this strange, empty calm wouldn't last, and he needed to be well away before it broke, before all the frustration and anger and loneliness came boiling up from wherever it hid below the void, and he raged against the

Nornir for leaving him naked and alone, facing the agony of yet another dawn.

"COULD YOU HIT him from here?" Westmorland asked the captain of the archers, who stood beside him on the wall as he watched Sir Gunnar gallop away.

The fellow wet his finger and stuck it in the air to check the wind, then pulled an arrow from his quiver, fitted it to his longbow, and half drew the string. "Do you want him dead, my lord, or merely wounded?"

Westmorland hesitated.

"My lord? It is getting dark and he is nearly out of range."

"It is a difficult decision, good archer. He truly was a pleasant companion."

Pleasant but treacherous. It was so tempting to punish that treachery. But in the end, he kept his word to Eleanor and let her lover ride out of range and into the wood. "If you see him within a mile of Lady Eleanor before she bears an heir to Lord Burghersh, take him alive and bring him to me in chains."

"Yes, my lord." The bowman eased the tension off the string and stood down. "I will pass the word."

CHAPTER 13

"MOVE ON, NEWT." Gunnar flicked the little beast away and dragged the stool over by the fire to try to dry out.

It was a futile effort. He was damp to the skin, all the fine, warm weather of early May having vanished in a bank of fog that had rolled off the northern sea the self-same day he'd reached the dene, as though the weather was determined to mirror his mood. It had lain here ever since, over a fortnight now, squatting over everything like a great white toad, sucking the warmth out of everything and leaving the cave he and Jafri used as shelter even danker than usual. Moisture ran down the cave walls and dripped from the yews outside like rain. Moss bloomed in furry green mounds that covered every rock and log.

And then there were the newts. They'd always been plentiful, but with no need to hide beneath the forest litter to stay damp, they scuttled over everything like so many ants—even over Gunnar, if he sat still too long. Too bad the little devils weren't fit to eat. He could have his fill every day three times over for a year and there would still be plenty left to breed.

"But even you won't touch the foul things, will you?" he said to the wolf who had crept in behind him, so wet and miserable that he was willing to tolerate the close company of man to lie by the fire. Gunnar took one of the squirrels he'd snared and tossed it the wolf's direction. "There you go."

Watching warily through yellow eyes, the beast stretched his neck to sniff at the squirrel. Satisfied the offering wasn't a trick, he tugged it close and started tearing at the tender belly. Gunnar skinned the other two squirrels, skewered them on sticks, and propped them over the fire. He'd just begun scraping the skins clean for tanning when the wolf lifted his head, a low growl humming in his throat.

Knife in hand, Gunnar came to his feet and stepped to the entrance. The one good thing about the fog was the way it hid their fire. Day or night, no one would guess anyone was in the dene at all, unless they knew where to look.

So either someone knew or some fool was lost, because even with the blanket of fog muffling sounds, Gunnar could hear two horses picking their way up the stream bank from the direction of the sea, snapping twigs and kicking stones as they came. From the pen, Ghost and the rouncey whinnied nervously, and the approaching horses answered. Whoever they were, they weren't trying to be quiet. That was a good sign.

And then the squawk of a raven cut through the fog, followed by a man's voice. "Quiet, bird. They must be here. I hear the wolf growling."

"He always did growl a lot," said a second man. Gunnar hadn't heard either voice in years, but he knew both instantly.

Brand and Torvald. And Ari, of course, in the raven form he took each night. Gunnar's tension drained away, only to be replaced by irritation. Years without seeing them, and they show up now, when he most wanted to be alone. Ah, well, Jafri would find Ari's company pleasant, he supposed. With a sigh, Gunnar pulled a partly burning log off the fire and went out to guide his crewmates in. "Keep bearing this way. You're almost here."

The wolf gave one last growl, picked up his half-eaten squirrel, and trotted off into the fog, headed up the dene to finish his meal in peace. A moment later, the pair came riding out of the dark, Brand on a huge dappled horse, carrying the raven on his shoulder, and Torvald on a nondescript rouncey that would serve as a pack horse by day, when Ari would ride the white stallion that Torvald became. They exchanged greetings with much thumping of backs, then quickly unloaded the horses and led them into the pen to join his and Jafri's animals. As they collected the gear to carry inside, Torvald wordlessly tossed a bag to Gunnar.

He could smell it without even opening it. "Fresh bread?"

"Baked just this morning." Brand swung his saddle up over one shoulder and the packsaddle over the other. "We thought you could use it."

"Always. Was your journey good?" Gunnar asked as they stacked things in the back of the cave, away from the damp wall.

"It was till we hit this fog. 'Tis thick as cream up there. We rode right past the castle. I didn't even see the torches. I only realized where we were when we reached the sea."

"Fog or no, there are no more torches to be seen. The castle is empty now and already falling down, and the village burned. Yoden, too," he added, referring to the tiny hamlet that had lain to the north of the dene.

"War?" asked Brand.

"Plague. Two score of years ago. Maybe more."

"Has it been so long since we were here?"

"Aye." Gunnar upended a couple of unsplit logs near the fire and motioned for them to sit. "So many died, there weren't enough left to till the land. The last few burned the cottages and fled." He poked at the squirrels with the tip of his knife and decided they needed more time. "Men turn up now and then to knock down walls and cart off a few stones, but mostly things just sit. Another few years and you'll never know men ever lived there at all."

"That should suit you," said Brand. "Less chance of anyone seeing you if no one's around."

"No one ever came down here anyway. We had them convinced that monsters live in the caves and pool. Where have you two been?" asked Gunnar. The raven chattered angrily, and he amended, "I mean, you three."

"Shropshire and Wales," said Torvald, and left it for Brand to fill in the reason and flesh out the story.

As they talked, the squirrels finished roasting and they ate, stretching the meager meat to make a meal for three with thick slabs of bread, and washing everything down with ale from one of the skins Brand had brought. By the time they tossed the well-sucked bones into the fire, Gunnar knew about Brand's most recent effort to track down Cwen, the ancient treasure they had stumbled on instead of their amulets, where to find good hiding places along the Welsh march, and that Rorik and Kjell had finally abandoned their wenching in Hampshire.

"One of the king's huntsmen shot the hart in the flank," said Brand, touching his left side to show where Kjell had been hit. "He only escaped because it was near sunset. They decided things are too crowded and that they needed to move on. Last I knew, they were headed this way. I'm surprised you haven't seen them."

"Likely we missed them," said Gunnar. "We were in the west for nearly three years. We only just came back."

He told of their stay in Lancashire, but left out any mention of the tourney or his time at Raby. He'd spent the past fortnight trying to put Eleanor and her betrothal out of his mind, and he had no desire to explain any of it to Brand now. He took another draught of ale, swishing it around in his mouth before he swallowed. "So if Wales was such a pleasant place to hide, why are you here?"

"I needed to bring you something." Brand and Torvald exchanged a peculiar look, then Brand drew a small linen pouch out of his shirt. He stared at it a moment, weighing it in his hand before he tossed it to Gunnar. "Ari found it."

Gunnar knew what it was as soon as he felt the oblong lump in the corner. He'd spent so much time fingering it through the cloth of his shirt that even now, all these hundreds of years after Cwen had ripped it off his neck, the size and weight and shape remained burned into his memory. As he dumped the little bull's head into his hand, the single red eye caught the firelight and confirmed it was his, sending his stomach sliding sideways. *Eleanor . . .*

"Where?" he asked.

"A few leagues from Shrewsbury. Ari went to sell off some of the treasure we found and spied it around the neck of the smith's son."

"When?"

"What was it, four weeks ago?"

"Five," said Torvald.

Around the time she'd come down to him in the night.

Gunnar saw her in his mind's eye, in that shadowed moment before she'd run into his arms. A sprite, he'd called her. A wisp of cloud. His fingers tightened around the amulet, pressing the bull's horns into his palm.

"It is your turn," said Brand, grinning like a fool, so clearly pleased for Gunnar. "All you need is to find the woman."

"All I need," echoed Gunnar hollowly. Then the hollowness filled with rage, and he stood up and flung the stool. It hit the wall over Brand's head and shattered. "Piss on you. Five weeks to get here? Five? You could have been here in two. Less! Jafri would have sent you to . . . I could have been done with this."

He stormed out, plowing blindly into the fog, careening

from boulder to bush as the light of the fire receded to nothing, until finally he blundered over a root and fell.

Pain added to his fury. He exploded, driving his fist into the offending tree over and over, beating it as he wanted to beat Brand, Westmorland, the gods, Burghersh, Ari, Cwen, and himself, most of all himself, for still imagining she had actually cared. Only when his knuckles were a bloody pulp did he stop and sink to the ground at the foot of the tree, Eleanor's name a groan on his lips.

He wasn't sure how long he'd been there before he heard footsteps, just yards away.

"You can hit me instead, if you want." A torch came looming out of the dark with Brand attached. "You'll do less damage to your hand on my jaw than against that oak."

"Begone."

Brand squatted beside Gunnar. "Not until you tell me about her."

"About who?"

"Whatever woman has you murdering this poor tree. Who is she?"

"No one," he said, but Brand waited, torch in hand, just squatting there as if he had nothing else to do for the next hundred years or so, and eventually, Gunnar began to talk. He told of the fire at Richmond, the Castle of Love, the clothes, the flirtation, the cards, the dancing. Everything.

When he was done, Brand sat quietly for a little, stroking the bottom of his chin as though he still wore a full beard. "So . . . she saw you change. And she didn't run?"

"Only into my arms," said Gunnar.

"Your arms . . . You mean she lay with you?"

"Aye."

"Right there in the forest? That night?"

He never should have told that part of it. "Aye. That night."

"Balls, man, why didn't you carry her away then, and keep her till the amulet turned up?"

"Her father would have hunted us down. What would I

have done by day to keep her?" Gunnar leaned back against the tree and thumped his head against the trunk a couple of times, using the pain to steady himself. "I needed his leave to wed her. I feigned a journey to Durham and waited two days, so he wouldn't suspect I had been with her. But when I returned to ask for her hand, he met me at the gate and told me she was betrothed and that she had been all along."

"Betrothed." That brought Brand up short, but then he brushed it off. "So what? What difference does it make?"

"None, in the end. She doesn't love me." There. He'd said it aloud. "There were things she said . . . She didn't want to marry the man she was tied to. She only wanted someone to get her out of the contract. If I hadn't come along, she would have found someone else and seduced him."

"Bah." Brand pushed to his feet and stood squinting down at Gunnar by the light of the torch. "Have I forgotten, or were you always this thick?"

Rage still clinging to him, Gunnar popped up and squared off with Brand, nose to nose, his fists bunched and ready. "You really do want to be hit, don't you?"

"Hit away, if it will make you think. She gave herself to you." Brand stabbed one finger into the center of Gunnar's chest. "*After* she saw what you are."

"She only meant to fetter me, so she could persuade me to carry her away." Gunnar batted Brand's hand away. "She all but told me so."

"That is shite. I don't care how foul a marriage looks to a woman, she's not going to lie with a man she's just seen turn from bull to man merely to get out of it. She no doubt thought you were some sort of demon."

"Aye," conceded Gunnar. "Till I told her I wasn't."

"And she believed what you said, just like that."

"Not fully. She thought I might have enchanted her, and she feared the magic."

"Yet she let you tup her—unless you forced her." Brand's voice hardened. "You didn't force her, did you?"

"No. Of course not."

"Then she was willing. And no woman born would willingly lie with a man who she knows is a bull, who she suspects has enchanted her, who she fears is a demon, unless beneath it all, she truly loved him."

Loved him. Gunnar pushed back against the surge of hope. "Even if you're right, it doesn't matter. She's betrothed. She's on her way to him by now."

"Then stop her," said Brand.

"You mistake me for Drengi Fastarrsson," Gunnar growled. "I will not steal another man's wife!"

"Ah, there it is. We get to the bottom of it at last. That she was in a fire makes you toss her and Kolla into one pot, and now you think she also lied like Kolla. But that is just more shite. Lady Eleanor is not that whore you married. This is not a moment's lust on her part, nor do you seek revenge against her man for some imagined slight by taking her away. You *need* this woman. The gods put her in your path, in your very arms, in almost the same moment they led Ari to the amulet.

"She is the one, Gunnar," Brand insisted. "Claim her. Whatever it takes, claim her and be healed. We will worry about the rest later."

The world, askew since his confrontation with Westmorland outside Raby, straightened with a bump, leaving him lightheaded with hope. *Claim her. Whatever it takes.*

"You're right. I am thick." Gunnar headed toward the cave.

"We all are, sometimes." Brand fell in beside him. "Where are you going?"

"To pack my gear."

"Good. You may have a fight on your hands, you know."

"There is no 'may' about it," said Gunnar grimly. "Her father will try to take her back, as will her betrothed if he's any sort of man at all. I will need your help to keep her."

"You know you always have my arm, but in this, I will

slow you too much. Jafri and I will stay here. Take Torvald and Ari."

"Take us where?" asked Torvald as they entered the cave. He stood up and whistled the raven to his shoulder.

"Back to the old days." Gunnar found his saddlebag and started shoving gear into it. "We ride to Raby to steal a woman for me."

BUT SHE WASN'T at Raby. Ari found that out, slipping into the castle by day to see where things stood. With that easy way of his, he convinced some maid or other to tell him Eleanor had been packed off to a nunnery at Clementhorpe even before Gunnar had spoken with Westmorland. So they hurried to Clementhorpe, only to learn she'd left there, as well, some ten days before, headed for Burwash, in Sussex, to be wed. Even at the speed a bridal train traveled, they would have already reached London. Perhaps even Burwash.

And so they headed for Burwash, and as they raced south along the Great Road, Gunnar was glad Brand had stayed behind. As much as he would have liked to have his captain and friend at his side, the bear would have slowed them badly, forcing them to hide deep in the wilds every day because of his strangeness and the danger he posed to others. With Ari along, they were able to travel during daylight hours—more slowly, granted, because he had to lead the bull along, but still travel. And sunrise and sunset only required a place private enough that they weren't caught changing.

And of course at night, he and Torvald could ride hard, pushing the horses as fast as the moonlit roads would allow while the raven flew overhead. Even with having to skirt around London, they reached Burwash early on the fifth night after Clementhorpe.

They sat in the deep shadows of the village churchyard, staring at the manor across the way and listening to the music that drifted across the road on the evening air. The manor was a large, handsome hall, surrounded by a low stone wall that gave proof to the fact that this part of England had long been tamed, unlike the north, where even poor men needed high walls and towers to protect them from Scots and reavers and outlaws.

Lord Burghersh was no poor man, though. If the grounds of his manor didn't prove it, the amount of clear glass in his brightly lit windows did. A fresh wave of doubt washed over Gunnar, different this time, but just as bitter.

"How can I ask her to leave this?" he asked Torvald. "What kind of life I can offer, on the run and in hiding?"

"You'll be healed. You can carry her back home, start a new life with her by your side." Torvald turned his horse toward the gate. "Wait here."

So Gunnar waited, his mind turning over all the possibilities. He didn't have long before he found out which was true. Torvald came back with the grim news. "She is married. Three days ago."

Three days. The words cut Gunnar like a dagger. In three days, the marriage would surely have been consummated. His stomach roiled at the idea of Eleanor beneath another man, especially one she didn't want. And whether she loved him or not, she surely had *not* wanted Burghersh. If he'd forced her, if he'd hurt her in any way, he would die, Gunnar resolved coldly. Whatever else happened, Burghersh would die.

"Is Westmorland there?" Gunnar half hoped he was. He could kill him at the same time.

"The guard said he left for London yesterday. But I saw an archer in Westmorland livery. He must've left men behind. Would they know you on sight?"

"I was there for over a fortnight. I spoke with most of them at one point or another." Gunnar drummed his fingers on the pommel of his saddle. "I don't want her caught in the middle of a fight. We must find a way to get her out safely."

"Perhaps. Or perhaps we don't have to get her out at all."

"Of course we do. That's why we're here. I need her."

"You need her love, not her hand," said Torvald.

"What are you talking about?"

"Steinarr was freed not when he married his woman, but when she said she loved him. The same for Ivar. It is the love that defeats Cwen's magic, not the vows."

"You're mad."

"No. I have been thinking about it along the way. You need only for her to say she loves you, with the amulet in her hand, touching you."

"Why didn't you say anything about this before?"

"I wanted to see how things were. If she was still unwed . . ." Torvald's slight shrug was his way of saying he would've helped Gunnar take her, no matter what. "But she's not, and no matter how much she cares for you, she may not be willing to break her vows."

"Balls. I don't even know what I'm doing anymore."

"Find out what she wants," said Torvald, as though that would be an easy thing to do. "Then we will make plans."

Gunnar jerked his chin toward the archer pacing the front wall. "I'll need a way past Westmorland's men. I don't fancy an arrow in my arse."

"Done." Torvald reached behind his saddle, untied a bundle Gunnar had been wondering about, and shook it out.

"What are you doing with a monk's robe?"

"I long ago discovered that there's always room for a wandering monk. I told them I found you on the road and asked if we could stay. We have entry. Just keep your head down so Westmorland's men don't see your face."

A little later, a monk in robes a shade too small followed a wandering knight to the gate of Burghersh Hall

"Ah, good, you fetched him, sir," said the guard at the gate as he passed them through beneath the watchful eye of Westmorland's archer. "Welcome, Brother, welcome. You are out and about late for a monk."

"Aye, and I will feel every hour of it on the morrow during prayer." Gunnar pitched his voice a shade higher than normal and mumbled a bit, in case the archer was listening. "My ass fell down dead on the road and it is only through the offices of this good knight and his animal that I am safely here at all." Gunnar gave Torvald a little bob he hoped looked monk-like.

"Well, the hall is too crowded already from the wedding party, so you'll have to make your bed in the hayloft, the steward says. But you can go in and take supper. There is food and plenty for all."

Gunnar bobbed his head again and followed Torvald into the yard.

A stableman appeared almost immediately. "I'll see to your animals, sir."

"We will leave before dawn," said Torvald. "I want them close at hand."

"I'll put them in the first pen, then, *monsire*. Shall I show you where?"

"Aye."

"Perhaps you can show me where the garderobe is while you're at it," said Gunnar.

"Of course, Brother. Just follow us." The man took the horses and beckoned them forward. As they rounded the end of the hall, he pointed toward a torch flickering in the far corner of the yard. "There's plenty of clean straw just outside."

"My thanks," said Gunnar and headed that way. Once in the shadows, he veered off and, after checking that no one was minding him, went off to explore the warren of outbuildings, making note of all possible routes out.

He described the layout to Torvald when they met outside the hall. "One of Westmorland's archers stands guard on the rear tower, and another walks the wall."

"The groom says he left ten men. That's three watches, plus a captain. That means four in the hall, perhaps seven if the third watch is awake."

"They won't have their bows with them."

"No, but they'll have their eyes and their knives. Keep your head down and that hood well forward."

"Of course, sir knight. I am a very humble monk," said Gunnar, and headed for the door.

But when he got inside, he couldn't help but look for her. For an instant, he couldn't find her in the crowd on the dais. His heart fell, thinking that she must have retired already, that she would be bedded again before he could stop it.

Then a bulky merchant stepped aside and there she was, her eyes stark in her unsmiling face, the faint shadow of a bruise marking her cheek. And her nose. What was wrong with her nose? He squinted at the crooked bump that had never been there before. If Lucy wasn't standing over her shoulder fidgeting, he'd swear it was she with her hand in Burghersh's.

Had Burghersh beaten her? The fading yellow of the bruise said it was old, but Gunnar studied the slight, brown-haired fellow at Eleanor's side with suspicious eyes anyway. All this time, he'd been imagining an older, powerful man on the verge of being made earl. But this was a boy, so young that his jaw bore no shadow of a beard. He wasn't old enough to be a knight. He wasn't even as old as Eleanor, perhaps six and ten at the most.

"Look at him," he muttered under his breath. "I could snap that twig with one finger." He would, too, if he'd hit her. He'd kill the little weasel. Slowly.

"Head down," said Torvald.

Gunnar yanked the monk's hood forward and they went to wash hands, then took places as far from anyone wearing Westmorland livery as they could manage. It was all he could do to sit there and pretend to eat when she was just yards away, especially with that scrawny prick running his fingers back and forth along her wrist in some misbegotten effort to seduce her. But pretend he did . . . until he couldn't stand it any longer.

He leaned over to Torvald. "Either we do this now, or I'm just going to slit his throat and be done with it."

"Are you certain she won't betray us? Even by mistake?"

"She is quick and steady. She will be fine."

"All right, then." Torvald took a last swill of ale, clumsily spilling a measure down the front of his cote. He rubbed the ale in well and then stood.

"How will you get it to her?"

"Just be ready," said Torvald and, pulling a scrap of parchment from his sleeve, pushed into the crowd, heading for Eleanor.

CHAPTER 14

RICHARD NO LONGER picked his nose nor played with toads, but he still fiddled with everything constantly, and if he didn't stop trifling with her wrist like that, she was going to scream. Eleanor nodded at the next well-wishers to come forward, trying to ignore her husband's irritating touch, just as she'd been trying to ignore almost everything he'd done for the last three days and nights. Just now, it wasn't working.

Finally, she jerked her hand away, pretending an itch on the opposite arm that needed thorough scratching. Richard merely glanced over and turned his hand palm up, waiting for her to be done and come back to him. She scratched as long as she could, then found some reason to fuss with her veil, but eventually she had to give in. This time, though, she laced her fingers with his. At least he couldn't tickle her that way.

Richard smiled, pleased at what he apparently assumed was her affection or interest. "Patience, wife. Only a little longer, and we can retire."

She nodded. He had no idea how ill that thought made her, just as he had no idea that the archers her father lent him were there not for his convenience but to keep her prisoner, or that the smear of blood on his sheets two nights ago had come not from his earnest assault on her maidenhead but from a scrap of raw chicken liver she'd had Lucy filch from the kitchen. She could only hope she came up breeding quickly, so she didn't have to suffer his attentions any longer than necessary. Produce an heir, her father had assured her, and his men would depart, leaving her free to deal with Richard however she chose.

Oh, and would she deal with him.

That she could bend him to her will, she had no doubt. She already understood that her father had chosen Richard as much for his weak nature as his prospects, intending, she was certain, to gain power over him and his fortunes through her.

Well, let him try. She was here and her father wasn't. The last two nights beneath Richard had hardened her to the truth of her situation and sharpened her resolve to take something of value out of this devil's bargain. Give her time. Her father would discover who had the true power at Burghersh. And then in Gloucester.

She nodded and spoke whatever words came to mind, and the miller and his wife moved on. The next man stepped up, a lean knight with hair so pale it was nearly white. He appeared to be more than a little drunk.

"My lord and my lady." Ale fumes rose around them as he clumsily took a knee. "I come to offer my best wishes on your marriage and my thanks for your generous table."

"Who are you, sir? I do not know you," said Richard.

"A simple knight on his way to Portsmouth, who found his way to your door." He slurred through his speech, swaying like a birch in the wind. "And to your generous table. And to your ale."

"So I see." The corners of Richard's mouth twitched as

he fought back a laugh. "Well, go back to my ale, and with my blessings."

"Table and ale and blessings. You are a good and generous man, my lord. But now I must away." The knight started to rise, tilted off-balance, and sprawled full across Eleanor's lap. As he thrashed around in an effort to rise, he grabbed her hand. Eleanor felt something press into her palm, and he looked up at her and said plaintively, "To the garderobe."

Richard was on his feet in a flash, grabbing the knight and flinging him to the floor so quickly his men had no time to react. Red-faced and no longer amused, he stood over the fellow, scowling down.

"I should have you lashed for assaulting my wife." Richard squared his shoulders and got himself back in hand—something, Eleanor had to admit, he wouldn't have been able to do as a boy. "But it is my wedding celebration, and so I will show some forbearance."

He motioned two men-at-arms forward, and in the commotion of them hauling the man to his feet, Eleanor stole a peek at the scrap of parchment the man had pressed into her palm. Her heart squeezed at what she saw: a crude drawing of a tiny bull with a maid on his back.

He is here.

Her father's grisly threat rushed up from the place she'd kept it buried these last weeks, nearly bringing her stomach with it. She closed her eyes for a moment, struggling to settle herself, and when she opened them, Gunnar was the first thing she saw, a figure in a monk's robe that was so clearly him, even with that hood pulled low to hide his face, that she didn't know how she'd missed it. Ten steps, and she could be in his arms. Ten steps.

She pulled her eyes away quickly so as not to give him away. She tugged down her sleeves, tucking the scrap of parchment out of sight as she did so, then smoothed her skirts and plucked away an invisible thread to further distract any watchers.

"Throw him in the trough," Richard was saying. "Let the water and fresh air sober him."

His men grabbed the knight, one on each arm. As they dragged him out the door on his heels, he was still shouting, "To the garderobe, men. To the garderobe."

The hall roared in laughter. Richard's steward stepped forward, a worried frown creasing his face. "Forgive me, my lord. I should never have granted him entrance."

Richard waved off his apology. "I would not have you refuse my hospitality now of all times. But he'll no doubt piss in the trough. Have it emptied and filled with fresh water tomorrow."

"Yes, my lord. At first light." The steward backed away, clearly relieved.

"Are you all right, dearest?" asked Richard, turning to Eleanor. "Did he harm you?"

"No. No, I am fine," she said as the monk who wasn't a monk followed the others out the door. She saw him turn left. *Toward the garderobe.* "He was of merry spirit. He meant no harm."

"You always did have patience, even when I inflicted toads on you at Richmond," said Richard. "But you look pale now. His assault has wearied you. We should retire."

"No! That is, all these good people still wait." She motioned at the villagers bunched off to one side, waiting to greet her and do her honor as their new lady. "Give me a little to collect myself and get some fresh air and I will be fine. Perhaps our drunken friend had it right. A trip to the garderobe would do me well just now and save me the chamber pot later. Lucy?"

"Yes, my lady."

Richard started to raise his hand. "I'll send someone to—"

Eleanor grabbed his hand, stopping him with a smile she didn't know she had. "I am within your walls, surrounded on all sides by your men, Richard, no harm can come to me. I need only Lucy to attend." She took a steeling breath

and pressed a kiss to his knuckles in an effort to charm
him.

It worked. Richard relented with an easy smile. "Of
course."

To ensure no one suspected any connection between her
and the drunken knight, Eleanor stopped to exchange a few
words with several of the ladies who had come from neigh-
boring manors to attend the wedding, marking time until
the men-at-arms came back in. Once outside, she didn't
even glance toward the trough, and she took her time cross-
ing the yard, too, so the men on the wall would lose interest
in her progress.

No one can know, she told herself with every deliberate step. *No one can suspect.* As they entered the shadowy
lane between buildings, Eleanor threaded her arm around
Lucy's waist and leaned close, putting her head against her
cousin's. "Lucy, do you love me?"

"Of course, but—"

"*Shh.* I am going to tell you something, and you cannot
breathe a word. Not now. Not ever."

"Of course, my lady. Your secrets are mine, as always."

Eleanor lowered her voice even more. "Sir Gunnar is
here."

"Here?" Lucy squeaked.

Eleanor clamped her hand over Lucy's mouth and
shoved her into the darker shadows beneath the overhang
of the smith's shed. "Hush."

Lucy nodded and slowly peeled her hand away. "Is he
mad?" she whispered. "Are you? Lord Ralph's men will
kill him."

It would be far, far worse than that, thought Eleanor.
"He cannot be found out. You must stay here and remain
quiet."

"Oh, my lady, even I prayed he would come in time. I
know how unhappy you are." Lucy had seen tears no one
else had these past weeks, most especially the ones the
morning after the wedding. "But you are married now."

"I know that far better than you. But I have to . . ." The words caught in Eleanor's throat. "I beg you, keep silent, no matter what you see or hear. Swear it, on my life and his."

Lucy hesitated, but in the end she drew a cross over her heart. "I do swear, my lady."

She was clearly unhappy, but Eleanor had no choice but to trust her. With another warning to stay put, she left Lucy by the smithy and hurried down the alley, heading once more for the garderobe, knowing he waited there, someplace. As she passed the corner of the tack shed, a hand snaked out from the shadows and grabbed her wrist. She let him pull her into the darkness, into the narrow alley between the shed and the smaller barn.

And as she moved into his arms, the only arms in which she had ever belonged, she could think of only one thing to say.

"You are late, *monsire*."

Eleanor's bleak whisper tore at Gunnar's heart and told him every thing he needed to know. He gathered her close.

"It is a terrible fault, my lady." Surely she would not feel so right in his arms if the gods had not meant her for him. "But one I will correct. I will carry you away from here. From him."

She pressed a kiss to his chest and slowly pushed out of his arms. "You cannot."

"I know it looks impossible, but we will find a way."

"You and your drunken friend? He is . . . like you, isn't he?"

He nodded. "Torvald. And we brought another, Ari, who is man by day. He will keep you safe when I cannot. We need only—"

"I am married." She blurted out the words as though they couldn't be contained, then added more reluctantly, "And the marriage is consummated."

Thinking it had been bad enough. Hearing it from her own lips made it ten hundred times worse. Gunnar gripped Eleanor's shoulders and held her so he could make out her eyes in the wedge of moonlight that sliced between the buildings. "I saw the bruise on your cheek. Your nose. Did he strike you? Did he force himself on you?"

"No. The marks are from my father's hand. Richard was . . . He was patient. Even kind. But he is fully my husband, and I am fully his wife." Tears sparkled like stars on her lashes, refusing to spill over. "I should have told you I was betrothed, but I hoped . . . Forgive me. But I cannot go with you. I am bound."

How could he have ever thought she was like Kolla? And yet he found himself acting exactly like Drengi. "Come with me. Once we are away from here, it will not matter. You are mine, Eleanor."

"I cannot be," she whispered. "You must leave now, before you are caught. Please. I could not bear it if you were caught."

"We can—"

"Go!"

She wasn't Kolla. She had honor, and she would never run away with him, and that left him only one choice, one chance to grasp at the deliverance she could offer. "Why?"

"What?"

"Why couldn't you bear it if I were caught? Tell me, Eleanor."

"Just go," she said.

"Not until you tell me."

Her shoulders sagged. "Do not make me say it. The answer will only pain us both."

"I know, but I need to hear it. Why?"

She pressed her lips together and slowly shook her head, but in the end, she surrendered. "Because I love you."

She loved him. *Thank you, Freya, for this much, at least.* Gunnar drew Eleanor's hand up to press it over the amulet that hung beneath his shirt and braced for the pain. Brand had told him what it was like, the agony he would suffer as Cwen's evil flowed out of him, far worse than the daily changing. "Even knowing what I am?"

"Even knowing, I do love you. And that is why you must go."

Nothing happened.

Ah, she wasn't actually touching the amulet. That must be it. Gunnar ripped open his shirt and pulled her hand into the opening, trapping the bull's head firmly between her palm and his chest. "Tell me once more."

"Ssst." Torvald rounded the back end of the tack shed, still dripping trough water. He pointed toward the hall. "Someone comes."

Eleanor started to pull away, but Gunnar wouldn't let her go. Couldn't. Not yet. "Tell me again that you love me."

"I do love you," she whispered. "But it is no use. I cannot go with you."

Gunnar waited. Nothing.

A voice called out, "Eleanor!"

"Richard," breathed Eleanor. "Oh, please go. If he sees you, if anyone realizes you are here . . ."

Torvald edged closer. "Gunnar. Now. Let her go."

"Again." Desperate, Gunnar mashed her hand against his chest, forcing the bull into his skin. "Say it again."

"Go. Please go. I love you, but please go." She shoved at him, her words dissolving into ragged panic as she fought to escape. "Please go. Please. Please go." With a final effort, she wrenched free and backed away. Gunnar reached for her.

Torvald blocked him. "It is no use."

"My lady? Are you there?" A wide-eyed Lucy appeared at the end of the passageway, her whisper urgent. "Your lord husband comes."

"Go. Oh, God, make him go!" With a final plea to Torvald, Eleanor bolted toward Lucy.

"Lucy, is that you?" Burghersh was nearly on them. "Where is Lady Eleanor?"

Torvald grabbed Gunnar by the monk's cowl and propelled him back into the shadows, flattening him against a wall with an arm across his throat and a low growl into his ear. "Quiet for her sake, if not your own."

Burghersh appeared in the same instant that Eleanor burst out of the alley.

"Richard. Oh, thank goodness." She grabbed his arm and clung, burying her face against his shoulder, the way a wife might with a husband she cared for. Gunnar clamped his jaw against the howl of outrage that would have betrayed them all, and looked skyward, silently begging the gods for the strength to bear this.

"God's knees, Eleanor, why were you down there?" Burghersh squinted down the alley and both Torvald and Gunnar held their breath.

Her answer started out muffled, then cleared as she raised her head. ". . . separated from Lucy and took a wrong turn."

"I was looking for her, my lord," offered Lucy with a shaky voice.

"I have been groping around in the dark like a blind woman," lied Eleanor, far too easily for Gunnar's comfort. Kolla had been a good liar, too. "I fear I do not know the way as well as I thought."

"It is a maze back here," said Burghersh. "That's why I wanted to send others with you."

"I should have listened. Now I have left all those people waiting."

"Never mind them. They can come back another day. It is you I am concerned about."

He didn't sound like a prick. Gunnar wanted Burghersh to sound like a prick, wanted some ready excuse to slit his throat now and carry her off, no matter what she said she wanted. Instead, the bastard put his arm around Eleanor, trying to comfort her, acting like a decent man, a good husband. *Patient*, she'd said. *Kind*. May Hel take him for being kind—but he'd damned well better stay kind.

"You've had a difficult evening, what with that drunkard

and now this," soothed Burghersh. "Come, I will take you to bed."

There was the excuse. Gunnar reached for his knife. Torvald tightened his grip and braced to stop him.

"No," said Eleanor, saving her husband's life for the moment. "My foul sense of direction should not disappoint your people."

"They are your people, too, Eleanor."

"Which is why we must return to the hall. What would they think of their new lady if I abandon them now?"

"I care not."

"But I care. They must respect me. I have a duty to them, just as they have a duty to me." Her back grew straighter and her voice firmer with every word. She turned her head slightly, so her voice carried down the alley straight to Gunnar's ears. "We cannot always do what we wish. None of us."

"No. No, you're right. Come, then, we will see to our people. Together." Burghersh gently turned her toward the hall, Lucy falling in behind. "York was right, you are going to make me a very fine wife."

She would, Gunnar thought as their footsteps grew faint. She would turn that half-grown lad into a man and fine lord, make him fit to be earl. And in time, she would be his countess, as she was born to be. He would be kind to her.

And she would lie with him and bear him children and . . .

He shoved Torvald off and started after them. Torvald's quiet voice stopped him. "You cannot kill him. Not right now."

Gunnar stood there sucking at the air and rubbing at his breastbone, trying to rid himself of the rock that had formed in the center of his chest and which was growing larger by the minute. It wouldn't go away, though, and eventually he gave up and stalked off toward the pen where the boy had put their horses. Torvald followed.

Working in silence, they readied their animals and rode out, letting the guards at the gate believe that Torvald's supposed drunkenness had made them unwelcome—a notion bolstered when Torvald stripped off his cote and wrung out the last of the trough water over one man's head before he rode out.

The guard joined his fellows in good-natured laughter, but as Torvald swayed off down the road, the man's smile faded. "I don't care if he is a knight, he's a pig's arse and I'm glad he's going. Are you certain you want to go with him, Brother? You would still be welcome here."

"I doubt that," growled Gunnar and rode after him.

Torvald was waiting at the edge of the churchyard. He fell in alongside Gunnar. "I'm sorry, my friend. I must have been wrong. We'll figure out how to get her away. She can have the marriage annulled and—"

"No," said Gunnar. "It is done. She is wed, and 'tis clear she wishes to stay that way. She's not the one."

"But she is. She loves you."

"No. She is young. What she thinks is love is only gratitude. Or simple lust." That was his fault. He'd taught her of lust, just as he'd taught Kolla of it all those years ago. "Or perhaps I was right to begin with, and she was so set on getting away from Burghersh that she was willing to do anything to do it, even lie with a man who is a bull. But now that she knows her husband, she realizes he's not as bad as she thought." *Kind . . . And now that twig would enjoy the lessons she'd learned so willingly.*

"Gunnar . . ."

"It is done," he repeated. He stripped off the monk's robes and tossed them at Torvald, and rode on.

They were at the far edge of Etchingham when Gunnar spotted a torch-lit cottage from which poured a bawdy song and realized what he needed. He reined Ghost toward the tavern.

"I'll pay," said Torvald.

"Aye. You will. And I hope you're strong enough to

carry me, too, because by dawn I don't intend to be able to walk."

THERE WASN'T ENOUGH ale in all the taverns of England to wash out of his skull the image of Eleanor in her husband's arms, but that didn't stop Gunnar from spending a good portion of the trip back trying. He made his way tavern to tavern, and Torvald proved his strength more than once, throwing a well-soaked Gunnar over his horse so they could make a few miles before dawn. As a result, it took much longer to ride back than it had to go south.

Eventually, though, somewhere along about Saint Swithin's Day, they reached the dene. In the fullness of summer, the fog had long since cleared and the valley was in its glory, as fair as ever it had been, green and rich with life, the ground beneath the trees awash in a rainbow of wildflowers that made the salty air sweet with their perfume. To Gunnar's mind, it was the fairest wild place in England, the place he and Jafri had called home for most of the last hundred years.

And he couldn't stand it.

"It is too close to Raby," he told Brand and Torvald as they sat around the fire that first night, after they'd told Brand what had passed in Sussex. "I am tempted already to go hunting her father, but I can't do that to her, no matter how things stand between she and I. I need to go off somewhere till my anger cools."

"You could come with us," said Brand. "Help me hunt Cwen."

Gunnar shook his head. "I already carry enough scars from the bear."

"Most of yours came from the lion." Brand sliced another chunk off the flitch of ham Ari had bought along the way and handed it to Gunnar, then cut another piece for himself. "Besides, the bear's claws are no longer a problem. We have a wagon now." Brand's face pinched a little as he added, "One with bars."

Gunnar froze with the meat halfway to his mouth. "A cage? Shite, Brand."

"No pity," ordered Brand. "'Twas my idea, and I use it willingly if not happily. It lets us go where we could not go before. People think the bear is being taken somewhere for baiting, and we can stay closer without danger to anyone. It give us more hours to work and saves a good deal of running back and forth."

"I can see it would," said Gunnar. They'd learned early on to separate widely at dawn and dusk; those who took dangerous forms ran a mile or more on foot before each changing to keep from harming the others or their own mounts. Not having to do that would save hours in every day. "But still . . . a cage."

"Aye, a cage." Brand chewed a bite of ham, then grinned. "But every morning as I turn the key behind myself, I remember that Ari must pass the day as a carter instead of a knight."

"That might make it tolerable," agreed Gunnar, smiling for the first time in a long while. A half smile, she'd called it, and he had to lock his fingers in his fist to keep from feeling the corners of his mouth to see. "Where is this wagon? You didn't come with it."

"We left it in Easington. I saw no point in bringing it up the dene until we were certain you were here. I fetched it after you left. Because of it, Jafri remains safe and uneaten, as will the bull."

"How did you get it down here?"

"Brought it up from the beach. We couldn't get it all the way up, so it's down past the lower cave, but it's close enough. So, will you come with us?"

"I don't know . . ."

"It will be good. As we travel, the bull will make the baiting story look even more true."

"Where would we go?"

"Lancashire, east of Morecambe. On the way north Ari had a vision. Dark dealings, he said. I want to see if it's Cwen."

"Lancashire isn't safe for the wolf any longer," said Gunnar. "It is too well hunted. We must stay farther north."

"Then you go with Brand, and I'll stay here with Jafri," suggested Torvald.

Gunnar shot him a sideways glance. "He never liked you that much, you know."

Torvald laughed. "We'll never see each other anyway."

"True enough."

"Come with Ari and me," urged Brand. "You need the company and so do I. I tire of Torvald's monkish ways. A talker would be a good change. Not to mention a drinker."

"Gunnar *is* that," said Torvald.

The idea of more time spent with a friend tempted Gunnar. Monkish or not, it had been good to have Torvald's company these past few weeks, and Brand and he had always enjoyed an even easier friendship. In the end, though, Gunnar shook his head. "Jafri is my responsibility."

"I never understood you," said Brand. "Kolla treated you like a turd, and yet you insist on seeing to her brother."

"He became my brother, too, when I married her. That didn't change when she died. Anyway, I like him, or did the last time I talked with him. We'll go up into the hills along the marches this time, maybe even into Scotland proper. Wherever we can find a thick patch of forest without too many hunters."

"You won't like Scotland," predicted Torvald.

"I don't like any of this cursed island," muttered Gunnar, and reached for another piece of meat.

CHAPTER 15

Autumn 1414

SCOTLAND PROVED AS unpleasant as Torvald had warned, though Gunnar couldn't figure out why. The people carried a fair measure of Norse blood in them, after all, and the weather was more like home than that of England. Yet the Scots seemed unfamiliar, and the land constantly reminded them they were neither in England nor truly at home. Jafri and he moved deeper into Scotland's wild westlands trying to find a place they liked, but in the end they lasted but two winters and a miserable spring before they exchanged messages agreeing to return to the dene by summer's end.

By then, Gunnar's anger had faded enough that he could grant Westmorland his due. The man was Eleanor's father, after all, and it had been his right to contract her marriage as he saw fit and see that contract fulfilled. If Gunnar had a daughter who had been sporting in the woods with some errant knight, he likely would have done much as Westmorland had. If their paths ever crossed, Gunnar thought he might not be able to avoid a fight over the beating he'd given Eleanor, but he no longer had the urge to go hunting the man. That would have to do.

He and Torvald slipped back across the border mid-August and finished out the month in the Cheviot Hills before heading east toward the great road that would take them south, taking advantage of their nearness to Lesbury to stop and see that the steward was doing his duty. The forests around Alnwick still stood thick enough to hide the wolf, and Alnwick itself had herds and fields so vast that another bull went unnoticed.

They quickly fell into the roles they had set on their only other visit, Gunnar as the knight who hunted all day, every day, and Jafri as his wastrel friend who lazed about until midday because he was off every night tupping some woman in Alnwick town. After the bleakness of Scotland, the little vill of Lesbury and its manor seemed a fine place indeed, and with harvest and threshing in full swing, no one paid them much heed. They decided to stay until Michaelmas, when the year's accounts would be settled and Gunnar could collect what was owed him as lord.

A sennight passed peacefully, until one evening on the way back to the manor when Ghost picked up a stone. As Gunnar dismounted to remove it, he heard a distant rumble and saw the dust of a large group of riders coming his way from the direction of Lesbury. Not wanting to be seen by any more people than necessary, he quickly flicked the stone out and led Ghost deep into a stand of trees, then slipped back to the edge of the wood where he could watch from the shadows.

York. Gunnar recognized the red and blue livery of some of the outriders as soon as they came into view, and the royal arms carried by the herald confirmed it. He spied the duke himself, looking older and a little heavier, like a man just reaching his prime, riding alongside another nobleman that Gunnar didn't recognize. Gunnar remembered many of the flanking knights from those evenings before Richmond's fire and was glad he'd hidden.

Behind the duke's party, bright gowns and fluttering

veils announced a smaller party of women on horseback, surrounded by more knights and men-at-arms, and behind them came wagons bearing serving women and baggage. With a party so grand, the duke clearly intended to rest at Alnwick for some time.

As the cluster of women drew closer, the high-pitched twitter of girlish voices confirmed that the duchess still led her gaggle of fosterlings. And then one voice, husky and lower than the others, caught Gunnar's ear. Heart thumping, he scanned the group.

There. Eleanor.

Her fine black mare pranced along on the far side of the train, where he might not have seen her if he hadn't heard her voice—*thank you, Freya, for letting me hear her*—and she listened attentively to the swain who rode at her side. Jealousy bubbled through Gunnar, growing even more bitter when he realized that the man beside her was no swain, but Burghersh himself, grown a good hand's breadth and filled out a little.

Her husband. She was here with her prick of a husband.

The blood thundered through Gunnar's skull, deafening him so he could only watch as she smiled at something Burghersh said and twisted around to speak to the woman on the near side of her. The move let Gunnar see her face straight on, and her evident pleasure in the moment was a spear that went straight to his gut.

He should turn away, he told himself, not torture himself. But just as he hadn't been able to keep from kissing her that night in the glade, he couldn't keep his eyes off her now, absorbing every gesture and expression. He knew those lips, those hands, that sweetly curved body. And he knew the hair that hid beneath that silver caul and crimson veil, too, the raven mass her husband would let down each night when he bedded her.

Wrapping his fingers around the tree trunk as if it were Burghersh's neck, he silently dared the man to betray any hint of discord, any sign he was unkind to Eleanor.

But the husband looked even happier than the wife, clearly doting on her every word, and when Eleanor reached out to touch his knee as she spoke, Gunnar understood. She played her love games with Burghersh the same way she had with him, wielding that potent mix of innocence and seduction to snare him. No wonder the man grinned like a fool.

Did she feel his smile in the dark to see if it was real? Gunnar wondered. Did she shudder in pleasure at his touch? Did she claim to love him?

He tormented himself with questions until he could no longer make her out amongst the others in the dusk, not even her crimson headdress, and as the wagons at the back of the procession creaked past, he retrieved his horse and rode the few miles to Lesbury, where he wrote out a message for Jafri telling him exactly what he wanted him to do.

"DINNER, MY LADY."

Eleanor kept her eyes on the stitchery she was sorting out for one of the duchess's young fosterlings. She'd been picking at the girl's tangle since after chapel and she finally had the knot almost undone. She carefully worked the needle into the wool and gave a little tug, and the final knot loosened and came apart. "There. You are back to where you went awry."

The girl sighed with relief. "Will you show me the proper way, Lady Eleanor? I have had to pick it out three times already."

"That is why your yarn looks so worn. And why it was so difficult to untangle this time. You should end it here and start a fresh strand."

"My lady." Lucy grew more insistent. "They have already brought out the ewers. Lord Burghersh asks after you."

Eleanor pinned the needle into the edge of the cloth and laid the piece in the girl's sewing basket. "We will attend to it later. For now, run ahead, and if Her Grace scolds, you may tell her I kept you."

"Yes, my lady. Thank you, my lady." The child did her courtesy and hurried off. Eleanor just sat there.

Lucy came closer, concern pinching her face. "Do you feel well, my lady?"

"Yes. I am only weary." So very weary. Of the journey. Of the false smiles. Of pretending. Of all of it.

"Perhaps it is less weariness than riding right past his hall," ventured Lucy. "We should not have come to Alnwick."

Eleanor frowned. Lucy had said nothing the day before as they'd ridden through Lesbury, and Eleanor had thought—hoped—her cousin had forgotten that it was Sir Gunnar's home estate. Apparently, she had not. She motioned for Lucy to come sit by her in the window nook, where their words wouldn't carry.

"You know it was never my intent to come here. I agreed to accompany Richard only as far as Warkworth," she said quietly. It had been Her Grace who insisted the women come to Alnwick with the duke.

Lucy shook her head. "Even Warkworth was too close."

"I didn't know that," Eleanor protested. "I have never been so far north. It was merely a name to me. I thought only to keep York from gaining too much influence over Richard. He schemes to control him very nearly as much as my father does."

Lucy sighed heavily. "I know, but . . ."

"If it eases your mind, Sir Gunnar once told me he seldom visits his lands. He is unlikely to be here."

"I hope you are correct. I beg you, my lady, be wise about this."

"I have been wise for better than two years. Why would you think I would suddenly change?" She rose and shook out her skirts. "Now come. As you said, my lord husband waits."

As they went downstairs, she pinched her cheeks, so

that she entered the hall with a healthy glow and a smile on her lips. Richard responded as he always did, grinning like a happy pup. That pleased her enough to make her smile come more easily; as long as she kept him enraptured, she had some power.

"There you are," he said, motioning the ewerer back. "What kept you?"

"Forgive me. I was entangled in a string." She quickly explained to the table as she washed and dried her hands in the rosemary-scented water.

"You were good to help her. I remember how demanding Her Grace was of your stitching." Richard introduced her to the men at the table as the first course was carried out. She knew many of them by name if not face; they rode for one of her royal cousins, John, Duke of Bedford, who was holding Alnwick on behalf of his brother, the king. It was Bedford that York had come to visit, for reasons to which Eleanor was not privy.

Dinner itself was a leisurely meal, the many courses occupying a goodly portion of the midday hours. However, the moment York and Bedford had finished the last bite of sweet, they were ready to ride to the hunt. The men excused themselves, Richard included, and they all trooped out.

All but one dark, whip-thin knight who seemed to be attached to neither Bedford nor York, nor even Alnwick. There was something familiar about him, but though Eleanor stared at him, she couldn't quite put her finger on it. To her consternation, he seemed just as interested in her, studying her from across the hall.

A varlet came by collecting the spoons from the table. As he reached for hers, she motioned with her eyes. "Do you know yon knight? The one with the hungry look about him."

The old man barely glanced at where she pointed. "That would be Sir Geoffrey, my lady."

Eleanor waited, expecting more, but the man went back

to dropping spoons into his basket. She prodded. "And just who is Sir Geoffrey?"

"A friend of Sir Gunnar's, from over Lesbury way."

"He's here?" Her voice cracked, making the fellow look up from his work. She quickly lowered her voice. "I mean, is Sir Gunnar at Lesbury now?"

"Aye, my lady. I ween he came a week back or thereabouts. You know the gentleman, then?"

After the way she'd reacted, he'd know it was a lie if she denied it. "I met him once, long ago."

"You must have met Sir Geoffrey, too, then, for he always comes and goes with Sir Gunnar." He worried his cheek with his tongue. "Though I don't believe I've ever seen them at table together."

Ah, God. Not Geoffrey. *Jafri.* The friend Gunnar had mentioned.

He'd been at Richmond, she realized now, a lean, ravenous man who'd been as fond of the meat during the day as Gunnar had been the fire at night. She'd taken note of him as a strange face in the hall, just as she'd taken note of Gunnar, but for whatever reason, she'd never approached him. And she'd certainly never linked him and Gunnar in her mind.

She suddenly realized that the varlet was eyeing her curiously, waiting for some answer. "Pardon, what was that you said?"

"That I've never seen them together, m'lady. He and Sir Gunnar."

"They, um, keep very different hours, as I recall. Though as I said, it has been a good many years since I spoke to either of them."

"Did you not pass through Lesbury when you came here, my lady?"

"We did not stop." Oh, thank the saints they hadn't stopped. Out of the corner of her eye, she saw Lucy rise and head her way. She quickly dismissed the man with thanks. He dipped his head and went back to his spoons, jangling away with his basket to clear the next table. Eleanor dared a glance at Jafri and caught him still watching her. Assessing her.

He knew who she was, she realized. If he told Gunnar she was here . . .

"My lady?" Lucy came around the end of the table carrying a bunch of grapes. "Is something wrong? You are very pale."

"I . . . I . . ." She stared up at Lucy, unable to tell her. "It is too close in here."

"Perhaps we should go out for a breath of air."

Outside, where she just might be able to spy a noble red bull in the fields. Outside, where she could be in Lesbury before dark, even on foot.

It was only three miles—she'd counted them out as they rode—and from what York had said, less than thirty to Scotland riding cross-country or forty by the road. They could be across the border almost before Richard realized she was gone. She could be with him.

As though he knew her thoughts, Jafri stood up and started to work his way across the hall toward her.

Oh, sweet Mother of God, what was she thinking? Her father's archers still lurked about waiting for Gunnar to show his face. If he even so much as tried to catch a glimpse of her . . .

She couldn't go outside. She couldn't stay here at all. She jumped to her feet.

"My lady," the dark knight began. "I have—"

"Your pardon, *monsire*. I feel a sick headache coming on." She grabbed Lucy's arm and dragged her toward the door. "Come help me to bed. I will be going nowhere today."

SINCE THE DAY she'd been brought to serve Lady Eleanor at the age of seven, Lucy's afternoons had belonged to her noble cousin. There was always sewing and embroidery to do or the lady's wardrobe to attend to, or she might be called on to run errands in the village or simply to pass time with Eleanor herself, reading or singing. Her duties were never unpleasant or difficult, they were just always there to be done, and they always had been.

But now, banished by Lady Eleanor's demand for darkness and silence because of her sick headache, and with no service owing elsewhere because they were away from home, Lucy found herself free, her only obligation to herself.

She wandered the village the first day of her lady's illness, and the mill and tannery the next, but on the third day, when threshing began and tawny clouds of chaff and dust rose over everything, she kept to the castle grounds, where the air was a little cleaner. She didn't expect to find much of note; in the years of trailing around from place to place after Eleanor, she'd learned that a castle was a castle, and that much the same thing went on in every one. But at nearly five acres all told, Alnwick's baileys were larger than most. Perhaps there was something new to see.

She visited the stables and smithy, where she watched the men bend the iron for a window grate, then found her way to the herb garden, where she broke off a stem of mint to suck on and spent a pleasant while sitting on a stone bench watching the bees as they hurried to gather the last of the summer nectar. The sun was warm and the gentle buzzing lulled her, and after a time she found her head nodding. After a quick glance around to confirm she was alone, she leaned back against the wall, closed her eyes, and let herself drift, balanced on the edge of sleep, only vaguely aware of the odd noises that strayed over the garden wall.

"Tread carefully, Stephen." The male voice was almost on top of Lucy. Startled, she shot to her feet—and right into a pair of strong arms that caught her up. "You never know what fearsome creatures you may find amongstst the Mary-golds. You can see how they spring upon a man without warning."

Lucy found herself looking into Henry Percy's grinning face. "Sir Henry! I didn't know you were at Alnwick."

"I only just arrived." Keeping his hold on Lucy, Henry gave a nod to the page at his heel. "Stephen, go and tell His Grace that I have been attacked and will see him when I have escaped."

"I have my balance now," said Lucy as the boy hurried off. "You can let me go."

"Why would I want to do that, when I can hold the sweetest maid in the castle?" He pressed a kiss to her temple. Flustered, she closed her eyes and he added a trail of kisses over her eyelids. "And the warmest, I vow. It is like holding the sun in my arms, if the sun smelled of mint. Were you sleeping?"

"Nearly. I did not expect an invasion from Scotland."

"Invasions most often come when you least expect them." He demonstrated by kissing her, his tongue plunging in to take her mouth in a full-on assault that sent ten hundred sparks skittering through her body like so many warriors, intent on breaching her defenses.

And they very nearly did. Would have, if Henry hadn't broken off the kiss on his own. Lucy opened her eyes to find him looking at her with an odd expression that made the breath catch in her throat.

A moment passed, then another when anything might have happened, and then he cocked his head toward the clash of practice weapons that echoed across the bailey. "I believe I hear the men of Alnwick drilling against just such an invasion. Have you watched them?"

"A little."

"Are they any good? No, never mind, I shall see for myself. Come. Walk with me." He grabbed her hand and tugged her along before she had a chance to say yea or nay, leading her across the bailey to the foot of a stone stairway.

"We're going up on the wall?" Her voice came out with a squeak.

"Yes, my little mousekin. It is the only way to truly see

so many men at once," said Henry as he motioned for her to start up before him. "You sound like you have never been up on a wall before."

"Only once. Lord Ralph doesn't like women on the wall. And at York, we were kept too busy to go up."

"Um. Busy," mumbled Henry. Lucy glanced over her shoulder, and found that he lagged a few steps behind her, just far enough to put his eyes on the same level as her bottom. A sudden awkwardness made her stumble, and Henry quickly reached out to steady her. His hand landed on her bum, cupping it as though he'd intended this all along—a notion reinforced by the way he winked up at her. "How is Lady Eleanor? I heard she is ill."

Lucy reached behind and removed his hand. "You can only have been here less than an hour. How can you possibly know . . . ?"

"Spies. *Is* she ill?"

Lucy nodded. "She has been abed with a sick headache for three days now. She wants no noise and no light."

"Ah, that is why you are free to nap in the garden."

"You knew I was there before you found me, didn't you?"

"Aye. I told you, I have spies." They reached the top, and he took her hand and led her off to the east, toward the round tower, a structure that perched on the edge of the ravine that provided a portion of Alnwick's defenses. As they passed the guards who walked the wall, many greeted him by name, enough calling him Lord Henry to remind Lucy of the chasm between them.

"You were right, my lord, there is an excellent view of the men from up here." She tugged her hand away. "But I have neglected my lady too long. By your leave."

"Leave not given." He caught her around the wrist with just enough force that she would've looked foolish trying to wrest herself free. "You just said your lady wants quiet."

"She may need something."

"If she does, there are a dozen servants within reach

of her voice." He turned her hand over and studied it as though he'd never seen a hand before, then traced a line down her palm and first finger with one fingertip. "No, this is not about Eleanor." Without looking up, he started a second line, shifting so it trailed the length of her middle finger. "This is about me. You are trying to escape me."

"You're right. I am," she admitted. She tugged again, but might as well have been shackled, for all the good it did.

Her whole hand tingled as he started another line. He stopped on her third finger right where a ring would go. "Why? Did you not enjoy my kiss?"

"It is not that," she said with a sigh.

"Then what?"

"You know."

"You must tell me."

He started off toward the tower again with her in tow, just as the man on watch on top spied them. The fellow leaned over the edge. "Welcome home, Lord Henry!"

"That," said Lucy under her breath.

"James. I take it your eyes are still good. Best watchman in Northumberland," he explained to Lucy.

"No longer mere watchman, my lord. I am now sarjeant of the day watch."

"Well done." Henry tipped his head toward the door of the tower. "Anyone in there?"

"There shouldn't be, my lord. The men always stay off Hotspur's seat in case you should come. 'Tis ready for you." He glanced at Lucy and nodded. "That is, for you and your lady."

Laughing, Henry led her inside. The tower room was surprisingly bright, its interior lit by both arrow shafts and a wide, unglazed window on the interior wall. Suddenly solemn, Henry dropped Lucy's hand and went to the window niche, not looking down at the men in the bailey below, but staring instead at a stone seat cut into the wall beside the window. He bent and ran his hand over it, tracing the outline of an area that was worn slightly smoother than the rest.

"This was my father's favorite place," he said as Lucy came up behind him. "Every day, he would sit here and watch the men drill and call down orders."

She stepped around him to look down into the wide bailey below, where both knights and men-at-arms fought with blunted weapons. "Look. There is Lord Burghersh."

Henry wrapped his arms around her waist and rested his head on her shoulder. He studied the fighters for a moment. "Does Lady Eleanor have a great many headaches?"

"No, never. Why?"

"I was just thinking that, were I a woman and married to Richard le Despenser, I would find cause to have a headache every night."

And so the lady would, if only she could, thought Lucy—but that was not something to discuss with Percy. "You are too familiar, sir."

"Come now, Lucy-fair, you cannot tell me that your lady is happy with that wisp of straw. I remember him as a nose-picker."

"He is her husband," she said firmly and changed the subject. "Did you often come up here with your father?"

"Hmm. Yes. I used to sit right there." He took her hand and swung it to point just to the right of his father's place, then drew it up to press kisses to her fingertips.

"You should try your father's seat."

He looked at the seat and slowly shook his head. "Not till it is mine by right. But when I do have Alnwick back, it is the first place I will sit."

When, not if. He had a cockiness to him, that was certain, but he was a Percy, after all. They were born to cockiness and to the trouble it bred. If there was one of them in the whole history of the family that hadn't rebelled against his king at some point, she'd certainly never heard of it.

"Lucy?"

As she twisted to look up at him, he spun her within his

arms and pulled her away from the window, into the shadows where they couldn't be seen from below. Pressing her back against the curved stone wall, his hands shifted to her waist to better hold her.

"My lord . . ."

He stopped her protest with a long slow kiss, his invasion unhurried this time, the lazy explorations of his tongue keeping time with the leisurely wandering of his hands. She clutched at his shirt, knowing she should push him away but wanting so much to pull him closer, and he lifted his head and looked down at her, as though he knew the conflict in her soul.

"Kiss me, Lucy-fair," he whispered. "Hold me." And she did, not simply because he commanded it, but because she wanted to, because he made her want to, simply by being there.

Hesitantly, she ran her hands over his shoulders and back. Beneath his doublet, his body was all angles and lean muscles, the body of a well-trained warrior. Dangerous.

And especially dangerous to her, because of the thoughts those muscles inspired.

"We cannot do this," she said, then traced down the length of his strong arms anyway.

"And yet we both of us must." His hands slid up her ribs, his thumbs traced the lower curve of her breasts. The peaks swelled and hardened, preparing for his touch, but he moved no farther, only stroking, back and forth, back and forth. It was all she could do not to scream at him to touch her, for God's sake, touch her.

"We should stop."

Another kiss, as his thumbs arced back and forth, taunting. "You don't really want me to."

No. But she found her good sense anyway and locked her fingers around his wrists. "I have told you, *monsire*—"

"*Shh.* Let me complete my argument." He let her push his hands away from her breasts, but started a line of kisses down the side of her throat, nudging her veil and braid aside so he could find the curve where neck met shoulder. He raked his teeth across her skin and sucked, setting off another round of those distracting sparks.

She closed her eyes, trying to concentrate, trying not to sigh and melt against him. "That is hardly a fair argument."

"I am no more unfair to you than you have been to me these last three years. You have left me thinking of no woman but you."

"That is"—*wonderful*—"not my fault."

"So you have thought of others?"

"Yes," she lied.

He blew across the spot he'd made tender, sending shivers down her back. "And yet I can make you tremble in my arms, even so."

"You give me a chill, *monsire*. That is all."

His chuckle teased the hairs along her neck. "Have you dreamed of me, the way I've dreamed of you?"

Every night. "No."

He found an even more sensitive place just beneath her ear and traced a circle over it with his tongue. "Have you pleasured yourself in the night, imagining it was me?"

Lucy blushed to the roots of her hair. "My lord! We have not seen each other for over two years. Why would you even think to speak to me so?"

"Because I have. I have imagined your hands on me. Everywhere," he whispered, and she understood what he meant and felt heat rush to the place between her legs where he would soon complete his invasion if she let him.

"You have enchanted me, Lucy. Bewitched me with those misty gray eyes of yours." He drew his hands up the length of her body from hip to breast in one smooth, possessive attack that ended with him finally, finally capturing her breasts.

"Tell me you do not feel the same desire," he challenged. He flicked his thumbs over the peaks, tearing a moan from her lips that was half surrender, half unwilling helplessness. "Convince me you don't want me, and I shall leave you alone. But if you cannot, I intend to make you mine."

He shifted toward her mouth again. If she didn't stop this, he'd have her on her back right here in the tower.

She twisted away. "You are still Percy of Northumberland. I am still a bastard. Nothing has changed."

"Not yet. But our new king loves me far better than the old. He summoned me back here, to meet with York and Bedford. I think I am to have some of what is mine back again. Perhaps Alnwick itself."

She gaped at him, appalled. "You have kept two dukes waiting while you seduce me?"

"*Am* I seducing you?" he asked, ignoring the rest of her words.

"Go, before they change their minds." She shoved at him. He barely budged. "Oh, you're mad!"

"Mad with love. I knew the moment I saw you sleeping there in the garden. Marry me, Lucy-fair."

She flapped her hands in his face, trying to get him to move. "Don't be a fool. Go! Get your title back."

"I will. But come with me to the chapel now, before I become beholden to the fickle will of dukes and kings once more. Marry me, and when I bed you tonight, you will be lady of Alnwick."

"And the king will know you for a fool."

"Then give me a scepter and a belled cap for your wedding gift, for I will make a grand one."

"Don't be an ass, Percy."

They both froze.

The Duke of York stood in the doorway, his hand still on the door, his face grim in the shadows. "You should listen to the maid. She has far more sense than you do."

He stared at them until they broke apart and each did courtesy, then stepped into the chamber. "Leave us, Lucy."

"Yes, Your Grace."

"No." Henry grabbed her by the sleeve and pulled her out of her courtesy. "I want her for my wife."

"She's the bastard daughter of a second son." York barely glanced at Lucy as he paced over to stand in front of Henry. "If she were Westmorland's own bastard, it might be different, but she is not. Bed her if you must and if she'll have you, but do not think to marry her. We have grander plans for you than that."

"But Your Grace . . ."

"Or shall I tell the king you prefer Scotland after all?" York's color darkened, and Lucy was suddenly afraid for Henry, even if he was too foolish to be afraid for himself.

"I am the king's loyal friend and subject and have always been so," said Henry. "But Lucy—"

"*Lucy* knows her place, even if you do not." Lucy jerked out of Henry's grasp and backed away. "It is not at your side, my lord. It never has been, and I have always known it even if you forget. My thanks to you, Your Grace. By your leave."

She did another courtesy and ran, pelting along the wall to the nearest stairs as though Henry were after her. But of course he wasn't. He couldn't be.

It was only when she reached the privacy of the garde-robe that she let herself cry, and only when the tears were done a good while later that she slipped back into Lady Eleanor's chamber. She sat in the dark, hiding, and by the time Eleanor chased her out again the next morning, Henry Percy was gone, sent off to do homage to the king as Baron of Alnwick, someday soon to be remade Earl of Northumberland.

And she was still a bastard maid, her virtue intact, even if her heart was not.

BY THE FOURTH day, Eleanor's headache had become real, a combination of apprehension, sadness, and the gloom that came rolling in as the days shortened. Good husband that he was, Richard visited her every evening, standing just inside the doorway in order to disturb her as little as possible. He grew more worried day by day, until finally he came to sit on the edge of the bed.

"I should like to help you, if you will let me," he said. "Just tell me how."

Finally. "Take me home, Richard. I want to go home."

"To Raby?"

"No. That is no longer home. I want to go back to Burwash. I cannot bear it here. The autumn is too raw, the hall too smoky. I cannot spend a winter here. Your duty to the Crown is met for this year. Ask York to release you and take me home to Sussex before the weather changes. Please."

He sat for a moment, chewing on his lip as he absorbed her request. "Eleanor, are you breeding?"

"What makes you ask that?"

"The castellan suggested that might be what bedevils you. His wife grows restless and ill each time she is with child." He took her hands in his. "Are you?"

The denial was on her lips when she realized he'd handed her the key. She grabbed at it. "I don't know. Perhaps."

His face lit with pleasure. As she looked up at him, tears welled up out of nowhere, shame at what she was doing to him combined with her ever-increasing fear for Gunnar. "Just take me home. I want to go home."

"Of course, dearest." He wrapped his arms around her and held her as she sobbed. For all the tears she'd shed in the years she'd been his wife, these were the first Richard had seen.

He did admirably well with them, stroking her hair, as gentle as a wife could ever hope a husband would be, and it only made her cry harder.

"Forgive me," she hiccupped between sobs. "I cannot seem to stop."

"*Shh. Shh.* Whether you're with child or not, 'tis clear you need to be home. I will speak to York in the morning."

York was reluctant, but his lady intervened on Eleanor's behalf, and they started home as soon as the baggage could be packed and an escort arranged. As much as she wanted to see her mother, Eleanor convinced Richard to hold strictly to the great road and bypass Raby entirely. She held her breath until they reached York, well away from both Lesbury and the dene Gunnar had told her about, and then promptly told Richard her courses had started after all.

As might be expected, he was disappointed—but no more so than she had been every month for the past two years, when her bleeding only served as notice that she must suffer another month of lying with a man she didn't want. He would surely survive more easily than she had.

With her guilt eased and Gunnar safe, her headache faded away and she began to enjoy the journey a little. The sky was overcast but dry, the hostels overflowed with travelers hurrying to get wherever they were going before the roads turned to mud for the autumn, and Richard seemed somehow less irritating than usual. If not for the presence of her father's archers, she could almost, almost, imagine she was a good wife to a good man on her way back to a beloved home.

But the weather didn't hold. The autumn rains finally caught them between Royston and Ware in a downpour that carried the chill of the coming winter in every drop. By the time they found shelter, the entire party, from Richard and Eleanor on down to the lowest porter, was soaked to the skin and shivering. The hostel had good fires, however, and by the time the next morning dawned clear and fair, they were all dry once more.

But as they prepared to mount, Eleanor heard Richard cough. Having struggled with her own lungs after the fire, she immediately put her hand to his forehead. "We should remain here. You can rest a few days."

"Do I have a fever?" he asked.

"No, but—"

"Then there is no reason to rest." Richard pulled her hand away from his forehead and pressed a kiss into her palm. "I have a kittle in my throat, is all, and 'tis less than a day to London and but another to Burwash."

"If this is some misbegotten desire to see me home because I asked you, then please pay it no heed. Whatever was wrong with me has eased since we started back."

"And I am glad for that." He tucked her hand into the crook of his arm and turned to lead her toward her palfrey. "But we can be home in two days if we hurry, and I will rest far better in my own bed."

"Are you certain?"

"As certain as I am that the Earth lies at the center of the Heavens."

So they pushed to London, where they passed a night with the gray friars. The women were lodged separately from the men, of course, but in the still of the night, Eleanor could hear Richard's worsening cough echo through the stone cloister. The next morning when they met at the gate, she was shocked by the dark circles under his eyes.

"You are ill. Let me send for a physician."

"No. I cough only because London's air is so foul. Give me the fresh air of Burwash and I will be hale soon enough."

"When did you grow so stubborn?"

"I have learnt it from my lady wife."

"Then you must know I am stubborn enough to hold you here." She turned to Richard's body servant. "Tell the Lord Abbot we need a physician and the use of a chamber for a little longer."

"Yes, my lady." The man rushed off without waiting for Richard's leave, a sure sign he was as concerned as she. The physician soon arrived and, despite Richard's protests, examined his eyes and throat and listened carefully to his chest.

"You should be bled, my lord," he said, straightening. His guarded expression made the hair rise on Eleanor's neck. "And you most definitely should *not* ride. The air is already chill and there will be frost tonight. It will not be good for your lungs."

"All the more reason to leave now, so we're home before the frost lays in."

"Be sensible, Richard," urged Eleanor. "We cannot reach Burwash by nightfall when we start so late. Stay here today and rest, and we can leave on the morrow. I will ask the abbot for broth and wine."

"Why waste his wine when I am so near my own?" He turned to the physician. "This from a woman who was so anxious to return home that we rode the length of England in a fortnight."

Guilt pricked at Eleanor for the way she'd lied to further her own ends, but there was no way to correct it now. She concentrated on doing right by Richard now, today, and folded her arms stubbornly across her chest. "Ah, but I am fickle as well as stubborn, and I tell you now, I will *not* ride to Burwash today."

"Shrew," said Richard with a grin, but his chuckle set off another round of coughing.

The physician frowned at the way he hacked. "My lord, I must agree with Lady Burghersh."

"A compromise, then." Richard wiped the corner of his mouth on his sleeve. "We will go only as far Merton today."

"Merton? In Surrey?"

"A cousin on my mother's side has a fine new hall there," said Richard. "He will provide us with warm beds, and tomorrow when I show you that I am well enough, we will be poised to reach Burwash. Agreed?"

Eleanor looked to the physician and, when he nodded his acceptance, said, "Agreed. And when you show me you are well enough, I will apologize for being a such a shrew in this."

"That alone will be worth getting well for," said Richard, a teasing smile curling the corners of his mouth, making her think of how he'd always looked right after he'd put a toad somewhere abominable. "Now, someone kindly ready my horse."

CHAPTER 16

ON THE FIRST Saturday of the following April, Eleanor stood in the choir of the abbey church at Tewkesbury, and watched them transfer Richard's body into his finished tomb.

They had never had made it to Burwash. The lung fever had worsened in the course of the short ride to Merton, and unable to continue his pretense of health, Richard had taken to bed immediately. The best physicians were summoned. When their leeches and medicines failed, Eleanor called in the village healers. Their herbs and possets and poultices eased Richard's breathing, and for a few days, she'd thought they'd won.

But one night he had declined abruptly, sinking into a stupor as his fever raged and boils broke out over his face and chest. Terrified that he suffered from plague, his cousins and the servants refused to come near. It was left to Eleanor and Lucy to sit with him, to feed him, and to clean him when he soiled himself.

They tried everything they or anyone else knew to do, but nothing worked and they were forced to watch him fade away, until near dawn on the seventh day of October, in the year of Our Lord 1414, his dying rattles went silent. He had been two months shy of turning eight-and-ten.

And so Eleanor found herself a widow at barely twenty, and may Heaven forgive her, after these months of mourning, all she could think of as she watched the workmen slide the massive stone lid onto Richard's tomb was that she was finally, truly, and most blessedly free.

Her childish prayers notwithstanding, she would not have wished Richard dead for all the gold in the Exchequer. But now that he was, law and custom gave her rights as widow that a maid did not have. She intended to exercise every one of them to its fullest, especially the right to marry as she chose.

She had chosen so long ago . . .

As the priest began the final prayer commending Richard to Heaven's care, Eleanor closed her eyes, forced her thoughts back to Richard where they properly belonged, and tried to muster some wifely grief.

She failed. It simply wasn't in her and had never been.

He had tried to win her heart, he truly had. He'd been generous and kind and had striven to please her, even abed. Yet although she had grown more tolerant of Richard and even found a measure of peace with their marriage, she had never warmed to him, had never had a heart free to give him. Whatever sadness she felt now was for the cousin who had bedeviled her as a boy, for his suffering in his last days, and for the years lost. Not a whit of it was out of the kind of love a wife was meant to have for her husband. Poor Richard. He had never had the best of her.

Now, in death, all he would have of her was this fine tomb and a Mass each day for the next year, both funded from her own purse in an effort to assuage her guilt. With no children of his body and no male relatives in the line, the barony of Burghersh passed to Richard's younger sister, Isabel, Lady Bergavenny, whose husband would add it to his list of honors. The lands went with the title, of course, less the dower portion that was Eleanor's to keep. It was a generous portion; her father had seen to that, the one good he had done her in all this.

"Flox crescit et mox evanescit," said the priest, ending his prayer with the words carved on Richard's tomb. *A flower grows and soon passes away.* "In nomine patri et filii et spiritus sancti. Amen."

"Amen." She crossed herself and said her thanks to the priest and father abbot. The tomb and masses were already paid for, the keys and accounts in Isabel's hands, and her own things long since removed to the dower hall at Upton on Severn. It was done.

She stepped outside, unsteady in the giddiness of her new station, and tilted her face up to the bright spring sun. Eyes closed, she drew in her first breath as a fully free woman, sweeter than any air she'd known for years. She wanted to throw her arms out and spin like a child until she was so dizzy she couldn't stand.

The feeling buoyed her the six and ten miles back to Upton on Severn, right up until the gate of Dunn Hall swung open to reveal the sea of red that filled her yard. Westmorland red.

No. No. No. No. No.

The metallic taste of panic filled Eleanor's mouth. Her fingers tightened around the reins, ready to wheel her mount away, to run. Only a glimpse of her father's big bay courser stayed her; the beast could run her mount to ground within a mile, and then what? No, she had to stay and find out what her father wanted, to play his game, whatever it was, until she could find her way clear. God's knees, but she was tired of games.

"What can he want with you now?" fretted Lucy.

"Perhaps he wants nothing," said Eleanor, trying to convince her hands to stop trembling before anyone could see. "Perhaps he only comes to visit."

"Perhaps," said Lucy doubtfully. "But what if it is more, my lady? What should we do?"

"We will make him welcome, of course. He is my lord father." She turned a warning eye on Lucy. "And you will say nothing to him of consequence."

"I will say nothing to him at all if I can help it, my lady. And I will smile while not saying it. But—"

"Then put on your smile," said Eleanor as they rode through the gate. *Now, if only I can do the same.*

Of course she could. A smile was a simple thing compared to some of what she'd had to do over the past years. So as the door of the hall opened—her hall, curse it, *her* hall—and her father strolled out like he owned the place, she conjured a broad, welcoming smile out of naught but thin air and sunbeams and turned it on him.

"My lord! Welcome." She let a groom help her down, then shook the dust out of her skirts before she approached to do courtesy. "Forgive me for not being here to welcome you properly."

"You had good reason." Westmorland stood aside so she could enter the hall past some of the selfsame archers she'd sent home last fall in one of her first acts as widow. "I take it Richard is properly laid to rest now."

Her smile fell away and she stripped off her gloves. "Aye. At his father's side."

"You should have had him put elsewhere. Thomas le Despenser was a traitor and a fool."

"And he was Richard's father. It is what my husband wished. I owed him that honor." She passed her gloves and traveling cloak to the serving woman who stood by silently. "When did you arrive, my lord?"

"Midday. I thought to ride out to meet you, but I was told you would be back by halfway Nones. You are late."

"My mare picked up a stone. I am starved, Lucy. Have them lay the tables immediately."

"I would prefer to sup alone with you," said Westmorland.

Alone. The last time she'd been alone with her father, he'd beaten her half senseless. Ignoring the phantom pain that throbbed in her cheek and nose, she turned to Lucy. "Have our meal carried up to the solar. And we shall have a measure of the Poitou wine, as well."

The corner of Lucy's eyes tightened, but she smiled and nodded. "Yes, my lady."

Upstairs, Eleanor settled into her chair with a sigh that belied the knot in her shoulders and motioned her father toward the other, a subtle gesture that reaffirmed her as lady and he as guest. "'Tis good to be home, even though I have been gone only the one night. My lady mother is well, I hope?"

"Very. She insists she will birth this one by the end of the month, the sooner to try the new mare I bought her."

"A new mare? Oh, tell me about her."

Family and horses—he'd also presented young William with his first mount—provided safe talk through the meal as servants carried dishes in and out. At last a plate of honey cakes arrived, and as the boy left and pulled the door shut behind him, Westmorland pointed at Eleanor's middle. "I was hoping to find you round with a posthumous child. Richard had better than two years to get you breeding. Did he not do his duty as husband?"

"Richard's dedication to the task was never in question, my lord. Nor was mine, if that was your next question. We swived like pigs every night the Church did not forbid it." She met her father's rude bluntness with her own just to watch his eyes widen in shock. "I never caught. It seems I am barren."

"I questioned that, but your mother says it is too soon to know. Pray you are not, lest you leave Alnwick without an heir, too."

"Alnwick?" A chill settled over Eleanor, colder than the rain that had killed Richard. There it was, the reason he had come in person. "You mean for me to marry Henry Percy."

"I do. 'Twas Bedford's idea, but I favor it, as does your mother. The two of you are well suited, and it will help us bring Percy back into the fold. We need his influence with Albany and . . ."

Her father's voice faded away, muffled by the drumming of Eleanor's heart. *Not again. And not Henry. Never Henry. Oh, poor Lucy. How could her mother be a part of this, knowing it would break Lucy's heart? How could Henry? Unless he intended to marry her in order to have Lucy within easy reach. Was he truly so scurvy?*

As her thoughts raced, Westmorland watched her as though she were a mouse and he an owl, his sharp eyes all but daring her to speak one word of protest, to show one glimmer of refusal.

But she had learned much about hiding her true feelings in the past three years, so even as her dismay turned to fury, she let a slow smile spread over her face. "Will Henry come here, or shall I go to him?"

"You are in agreement, then?" He sounded vaguely surprised he'd won her over so easily.

"Why would I not be, my lord? He is Percy of Northumberland, and he is my friend, Henry. As little as he and I have been around each other, we have always found ourselves like-minded." She grasped at bits of honesty where she could find them, the better to hide the larger lie. "An alliance between our two houses can do nothing but good for both. A woman would have to be a fool not to welcome such a match."

"Exactly what your mother said."

"I assume you—and she—have plans for bringing the earldom back." A knowing smile curved her lips. "Perhaps a request from my lady to convince her nephew, the king, to return the county to Henry?"

"Already written and awaiting her seal. I will send it by fast horse as soon as you are wed. I doubt it will be a struggle. The king and Percy were fast friends as boys. The king is much disposed to forgiving what his father was so anxious to punish."

"I'm sure Henry will be appropriately grateful. And if he is not, I will remind him. When is this all to happen?"

"I will carry you to Raby straightaway to help your mother with the birthing, and then on to Durham to meet with Henry and sign the contract. You can marry in the cathedral there."

"That would be agreeable, but . . ." She tilted her head as if a new thought had struck her. "Would it not be better if we marry in Alnwick? The village has a lovely church, and if I am to be Countess of Northumberland, I should marry on county soil, before Henry's people. It will better serve his cause with them. And thus our own." And give her that much more time to find a way out of this snare.

"Quite right. Quite right," said Westmorland, rubbing his hands together. His clear avarice almost made Eleanor laugh aloud. His plans to bend Richard to his will had been one thing, but did he truly think he could trifle with a Percy? "You have become quite cunning in your widowhood, Eleanor."

"I have had good instruction, my lord," she said blandly. "Now, your pardon, but I must retire. I am tired from my journey and must rise early to begin preparation for the next."

"Of course." He rose with her and held his arms wide. "Come to me, Eleanor. It has been too long since I had a kiss from you."

Of course he would want a kiss, if for no other reason than to prove she was well and truly in his palm. Once more the lessons she'd learned with Richard came into use, as she went easily into his arms and made him believe the kisses she traded with him were sincere. For an instant as he looked down at her, his smile seemed to hold honest affection, almost as though he loved her as a daughter and not as a pawn on his chessboard. Alas, she didn't believe it for a moment.

"I'm glad the bargain meets your approval." He pressed a final kiss to her forehead and released her. "I expect you to present me with a grandson within the year."

"I pray I can oblige you." *Not that she meant for it to be Henry Percy's get.* "Good night, my lord."

"God's rest to you."

As soon as the door closed behind her, she let her smile fall away. Knave. Just because he'd sired her, he thought he could still whore her out to increase his power.

Lucy met her in the passageway. Her brows drew together when she saw Eleanor's scowl. "Was it terrible, my lady?"

It was certainly going to seem so to her. Eleanor assessed her cousin quickly. Lucy had learned a great deal about hiding things and lying in the last three years, too, but this would test her sorely. If she failed . . .

No, she had to trust her. There was no one else. She curved one arm around Lucy's waist and gave her a reassuring hug. "Come, I will tell you where we have some privacy. We have much to do."

Cunning, indeed.

He had no idea.

LADY JOAN GAVE birth to a healthy girl—her sixteenth child and her husband's twenty-third—on the third day of May, producing the infant with so little labor that the midwife nearly didn't arrive in time.

Anxious as she was to slip away and go find Gunnar, Eleanor stayed for the confinement afterward and bided her time, continuing to play the willing bride in order to lull her father into relaxing his guard. Lucy mostly avoided him.

One evening a fortnight later, Eleanor was holding little Cecily when she caught her mother watching her with an oddly wistful expression. "What is that look?"

"Nothing. Nothing. I was merely thinking how well you look with a child in your arms. But then everyone looks well holding Cecily." A proud smile lit Lady Joan's face. "She is by far the fairest of all my babes."

Eleanor shot her a teasing frown over Cecily's head. "Why, thank you, *madame*."

"Oh, you were all fair enough. Excepting poor Robert. He was a most awkward infant—all ears and nose."

Eleanor thought of her young brother and grinned. "He still *is* all ears and nose, and I fear he always will be."

"Alas, you are likely correct. But look at Cecily. Skin like a peach, a rosebud of a mouth. And those eyes. Blue as cornflowers."

"Do not all babes have blue eyes?"

"Cecily's will stay blue," said Lady Joan firmly. "She shows her Plantagenet blood, through and through. There is a grace to her, even to her hands."

"Stop, *madame*, lest you make her too proud." Laughing, Eleanor chucked the baby beneath her too perfectly dimpled chin. Her mother was correct about the babe's beauty, down to the tiny, flawless fingernails. "Do not listen to our mother, Cecily. Whatever she says, remember that you are bald beneath that chape. And you have no teeth."

"She will have, and they will be as perfect as the rest of her. And her hair will be pure gold."

"And her clouts will stink only of rose water and cloves," added Eleanor, biting her cheek to keep a straight face.

"Oh, I do love rose water and cloves," said Lucy as she came in the door at the end of the sentence, sending Eleanor, her mother, and the attending maids into fits of laughter. Flushing in confusion, Lucy bent a knee to the countess. "The earl waits in the hall, my lady. I reminded him you are lying in, but he said—"

"He comes to speak with me, Lucy, not to bed me. Let him in and then leave us, all of you."

Eleanor handed little Cecily over to her nurse and

gathered her sewing to leave with the others, but as her father came, he motioned for her to stay. He did not look happy, and he wasted no words explaining why.

"I have just had word that the king will sail for France this summer. He will likely order Percy to go with him to prove himself. I want you married and a child on the way before he leaves. I just sent word to Percy to meet you in Durham. You are to start north as soon as you can make ready."

Did he intend to go with her? Eleanor couldn't tell. She edged toward the door. "By your leave, then. I have much to do before we start."

"Not we," said her father. "You."

"Pardon, my lord?"

"I will not be going with you."

"But you said—" her mother began.

"Things have changed." Westmorland pulled a folded parchment out of his sleeve and waved it irritably. "Henry also says that he wants me at court within the week. If I delay, I both risk his ire and increase the likelihood I will have to sail to France to attend him. Eleanor is happy with the arrangements. She can give herself."

To Eleanor's ear, he put a slight stress on those last two words, a subtle reminder, perhaps, that he had not entirely forgotten what had happened with Gunnar.

But if he meant to shame her, his effort went awry. Just the thought of that giving, the one and only time she had truly given herself, made Eleanor's body sing to life. Hoping the heat in her blood didn't show in her cheeks, she looked up at her father with pleading eyes and murdered the last of his suspicions.

"Can you not ride at least to Durham with me, my lord? I can be ready in only a day or two, and—"

"In two days, I shall be past York. No, you must go without me. But I shall send Sir John Penson to accompany you. You need an extra man or two anyway, and he can go all the way to Alnwick to witness the wedding and then carry a true copy of the contract back here for safekeeping."

God's toes. Even supposedly trusting her, he sent along a surety. Eleanor had to bite her tongue to keep from cursing aloud, but her smile never wavered. "Ah, good. Sir John has a fine singing voice and will keep me well entertained along the way. Thank you, my lord."

"So, then, it is done." He seemed mildly confused by her easy agreement. Good. "I leave at first light. Come, Joan, let us say our farewells now, then you needn't rise so early."

Eleanor watched her mother bid her father good-bye with a tender kiss, then offered her own farewell. "I pray you have a safe journey, my lord."

"So solemn. Come, give me a kiss."

Once more she traded kisses that meant nothing with a man she didn't love. The last time, she hoped.

The next morning, she climbed to the scribes' room at the top of the west tower and watched from the window as her father rode south across the lea and disappeared into the morning mist. Three days later she rode out herself, turning the opposite way out the gate, an apparently willing widow-bride headed north with her baggage and servants to a new husband.

As she turned to wave back at her mother, an unexpected sob balled up in her throat. The farewells they'd exchanged had been full of promises for future visits, but if this adventure succeeded, there was a good chance she would never see her mother again. The sadness of that was almost enough to make her change her mind.

Almost. But there would be such a great a price to pay for the privilege of a few visits, and she'd paid it for far too long already. She pushed away the sorrow and rode on.

They reached the great road by late morning and turned toward Durham. Eleanor waited until she was certain no one else was following them—it was not beyond her father to order a detail of guards to trail after without saying anything—before she pulled up short in the middle of the road.

"I have ridden this path once too often and find myself already tired of it. I wish to go by the sea road."

Sir John wheeled his horse around and rode back as the carts squeaked to a stop behind her. "The sea road is in a poor state, my lady. The carts will bog down."

"Then the carts can stay on this road, but there is no reason Rosabelle and I must crawl along with them." Smiling as the mare's ears swiveled around to the sound of her name, Eleanor lifted a hand and summoned her marshal forward. "Edwin, choose some men to ride with me." She started to turn her mare toward the east.

"Hold, marshal." Sir John reined his horse across Eleanor's path. "I cannot let you do this, my lady."

She raised her chin and looked down her nose at him. "You cannot? My father is an earl, my cousin the king, and I, myself, *une baronesse douagiere* bound today to marry Lord Percy. When, pray tell, did I become subject to the commands of a knight of no rank at all?"

Sir John flushed at the insult. "You are . . . that is, I . . ."

"I believe Sir John meant to say he cannot let you go without good escort, my lady." Edwin, her marshal, edged his horse up to face off with the young knight. "Perhaps he thinks I cannot do the job."

"No, no, it is not that, Marshal. But Lord Westmorland bade me stay at the lady's side all the way to Alnwick."

"Then ride with me, by all means. But recall who is in whose service and do not think to tell me what to do. Edwin, put a good man in charge of the train and tell him to await us in . . ." She grappled for the name of a village. "In Bowburn, if we do not find him sooner. I want to ride into Durham in proper state, in the event Lord Percy is already arrived."

As Edwin selected five men and snapped a few quick orders to those who would stay with the baggage train, she pointed to one of her maidservants. "You, Amy, is it? I need a woman with me. Get yourself up behind Will."

Lucy's jaw fell open. "But I should be the one, my lady."

"I want you with the train, to see to my things."

Miriam, whom her mother had lent her to arrange her

hair for the wedding, stood up in the wagon. "Begging your pardon, my lady, but Amy is far too young for such duty. I will go with you."

"She will do well enough, and far better than you on the back of a horse." Eleanor wanted the girl precisely because she was so young. She would be malleable when the time came.

But Miriam was stubborn. She tucked a stray strand of hair into her caul, kilted her skirts up into her girdle, and bumped Amy aside to slide on behind Will. "I have ridden behind longer than you have been alive, my lady. Your lady mother would have my head if I let you go with naught but a child with you."

Her father's man, and now her mother's woman. This was getting more complicated by the moment. She would have to move quickly once she found Gunnar. If she found him.

"Fine, then. Lucy, get my heavy cloak and give it to Miriam."

Sir John watched as Lucy dug her squirrel-lined traveling cloak out of a chest. "Where are we bound, my lady, that you need a winter cloak in June?"

"It is often cold so near the sea, even in summer. I would rather be too warm than too cold." Plus she'd sewn a few gold florins and jewels into the corners and hems. "Can we make Middleborough before nightfall?"

"Aye, my lady, and easily, without the carts."

"Good. We will rest there tonight, then start north along the sea tomorrow," she said firmly, and turned her mare toward the east and freedom. Toward Gunnar.

Please let him be there, she prayed silently, hoping there was some saint or angel sympathetic to a hopeful sinner like her. Her chest squeezed so tightly, she could scarcely breathe, scarcely think beyond the moment. *Please let me find him.*

Edwin fell in on her right and Sir John on her left, and by the scowls and sighs and sideways glances that trailed her down the road, neither was very happy with her or each other. Though she felt much the same about them, Eleanor flashed her most charming smile, hoping to ease the mood. "Never fear. We will reach our goal soon enough."

And please, please, show me some way to be rid of these good men before we do. And Miriam. Amen.

CHAPTER 17

"THERE MUST BE strangers coming," said Jafri as he and Ari rode back from hunting one afternoon.

"Mmm?"

He pointed at Ari's shield hand, the one he kept gloved most of the time. "You've been scratching at that hand all day."

Ari glanced down and wiggled his fingers. "Have I?"

"Old Forkbeard used to say that an itchy sword hand meant money coming, but an itchy shield hand meant strangers. Either that or you got into some nettles."

But Ari was lost again, squinting out across the rolling, open ground to the south.

Jafri made a sour face at him. "You know, when Brand came back last week, I thought he might have brought along someone I could talk to, a man who was fond of words and knew how to use them well, like a skald or something. Too bad we never had anyone like that on the crew."

"Mmm." Ari looked down at his hand again and back up at Jafri, his eyes finally connecting to his wits. "Sorry.

There may be strangers coming. I saw something move. Over there."

Jafri studied the distant line of trees Ari indicated, then shook his head. "Was it elf fire?"

"No. It was . . . I don't know. But I saw something."

"Well, then, let's stay out of sight until we know who they are."

They moved into the woodlands and worked their way along the edge, where they could keep an eye out with little chance of being seen themselves. Jafri was the first to spot riders cresting a rise, already much closer than Ari had said.

"There. They must've been riding down in the burn. It looks like they're headed for the old castle." He stopped his horse under the nearest tree and swung up into the branches to get a better look. "There's a woman with them."

"Knights escorting their lady?"

As Jafri watched, one of the men reached out toward the woman. She jerked away. Her mount spooked and surged forward but came up short against a rope, and she made an awkward, two-handed grab at the animal's mane to catch herself. "It looks like her hands are bound. And they are headed for the ruins."

"That doesn't sound good," muttered Ari. "Let's go get her."

Jafri glanced to the western horizon, where the sun hung barely a finger's width above the horizon. "We don't have time."

"Brand and the others can to see to it, then." Ari dug into his saddlebag for a stub of charcoal and one of the scraps of parchment he kept at hand for his incessant messages. He scratched a few lines of runes across the skin and blew the loose dust off. "I'll put this where Brand will find it as soon as he changes. Come on back down."

In the scuffle, the woman's head covering had fallen off, and as she twisted away from her captor again, Jafri caught a glimpse of black hair gleaming nearly blue. He couldn't make out her face yet, but there was something about her . . . "Shite."

"What is it?"

Jafri scrambled higher to get the clearest view he could. What he saw made him fling himself out of the tree, breaking branches on the way down. "Get off the horse."

"What? Why?"

"Get off!" Jafri dragged Ari off the stallion and leapt into the saddle. He jabbed a finger toward the message in his friend's hand. "Make sure Gunnar and Brand see that right away. I'm going to get Torvald as close as I can before we change."

"What the devil is going on?"

"Get them," repeated Jafri. He reached back to make sure Ari's bow and quiver were tied to the saddle. Torvald would need them. "I may be mad, but I think their prisoner is Lady Eleanor. Gunnar's woman."

OHGODOHGODOHGOD. PLEASE, VIRGIN Mother, help me. All I wanted was to chose for myself. Please don't punish me for that.

As the sun sank in the west, Eleanor huddled beside the stingy fire her captors had built and tried to pull herself together. Things had gone sour so quickly. One moment she'd been riding the coast road listening to John Penson sing, and the next she'd been surrounded by swords and blood and death.

Now she was prisoner, and the outlaws who'd taken her stood a little way off, arguing about what to do with her. She couldn't make out the words, but she didn't like the tone. Didn't like it at all.

She looked around the bailey of the abandoned castle, trying to spy some way out, some weapon, but the best she could come up with was a fist-sized cobble, half overgrown with grass, that lay just out of reach. As her captors' argument became more heated, she worked the stone loose with her heel, drew it close, and hid it with a quick flip of her skirts.

A stone. She was reduced to arming herself with a stone. But it was something, at least, and with luck, she could crack at least one skull before they stopped her.

And then . . . She didn't want to think about then. She pushed the thought, her terror, all of it, aside and set her mind to coming out of this alive.

The argument ended abruptly, and the skull she'd most like to crack started toward her. It belonged to Simon Tunstall, no longer lord of anything except this band of outlaws, having been caught in further cravenness after his poor show at the Castle of Love. She'd heard that he'd hied off to Scotland in disgrace; by the accents of his men, the rumors were true.

He stopped in front of her and made a slight bow. "Are you comfortable, Lady Eleanor?"

Show no fear. She glanced up at him briefly, as though he little mattered. "I am sitting on a rock in the middle of nowhere, Tunstall. How comfortable do you think I am? Return me to Raby. Immediately."

"I think not." He shook his head, his expression growing almost rueful. "I did not start the day planning to kill anyone, you know."

"And yet they are all dead." Eleanor's stomach twisted at the memory of the bodies Tunstall's men had dragged off into the gorse for scavengers to dispose of. "Even my poor serving woman. Such brave men you are."

Tunstall's neck went red. "Blame that fool Penson. He shouldn't have drawn on me."

"His sword didn't even clear his scabbard," she accused. "He only thought to protect me. They all did."

"They did a poor job of it, then. My intent was only to relieve a party of travelers of their silver. Instead, I find myself with a different sort of prize."

"Ransom me quickly, then. Westmorland will pay."

Drawing off his gloves, Tunstall squatted down beside

her. "Sadly, there is a small issue of a noose. However, I have been thinking on it as we rode. Even murder might be forgiven if I were married to the king's cousin, don't you think?"

She gaped at him. God's knees. Yet another man who hoped to find fortune and forgiveness between her thighs. Did England breed no other kind? "How unfortunate there is no such cousin willing to marry you."

"But there is, my lady, one my men and I rescued from John Penson."

"Rescued!"

"The treacherous cur had killed your marshal in an attempt to take you hostage. By chance, I was traveling the same road, and I caught him before he could do you injury." He leaned in so close his breath stirred the loose strands of hair that lay against her neck, sending shivers down her back. "In your gratitude, you offered me your hand and we were married—will be married tomorrow—in the next village."

"No. I am already married. You stole the ring off my finger yourself."

"A ring does not make a wife. Richard le Despenser is dead half a year past." One corner of his mouth twisted wryly. "We are not totally without news in Scotland."

"But I am now bound to Henry Percy." She shifted her tale quickly, ready to use Henry to get to Gunnar, just as Henry intended to use her to get to Lucy. "The contract is made. I am on the way t—"

"You changed your mind because of my bravery. With the village priest as witness, Westmorland will have no choice but to accept our marriage. He will settle land on me as your husband, and our good king, your cousin, will welcome me back into England's loving bosom."

"No. Absolutely not."

"You may not want to refuse so quickly. My Scots friends over there argue that I should share you—especially those two big hairy fellows. Donal's never had a noblewoman and very much wants to try one. And Malcolm, there, thinks you owe him certain . . . comfort since that lad your marshal killed in the brawl was his nephew." Tunstall reached out to trace her lower lip, and the combination of his threats and the stench of soured glove leather that clung to his hand made Eleanor gag. "No, I am your sanctuary, my lady, just as you are mine. They are willing to forego your favors in exchange for my consideration later as lord of whatever your father gives me, but if you refuse me . . ."

"Percy is to have Northumberland back upon our marriage. He will pay you a fortune for my safe return. Take me to him. I will affirm that it was Sir John who tried to capture me. You will be acclaimed heroes and well rewarded. All of you."

"And then we will ride away with our gold, and you'll tell him the truth."

"No, I won't. I swear it."

"Forgive me, my lady, but I do not believe you. You will tell and the hunt will be on, and between Percy and your father, there is no place in all of Christendom that would be safe. No, I must keep you and the truth of what happened under close guard."

"In a locked chamber, you mean."

His shrug was confirmation that she would be more prisoner than wife. "So, there is your choice: me and a few words before a priest . . . or *them*. And me, too, of course."

She spat at his feet. "You vile pile of dung."

"I have been called worse," he said mildly. He pushed to his feet and stood over her, his eyes boring down until it was all she could do not to waste her stone by throwing it at him. "As simple as your decision should be, I can see that you need time to come to it. You have until after we—"

A horse screamed somewhere beyond the western wall.

"Eat. What the devil?"

Another cry, more human, rose from the east. Muttering

words like *murder* and *demon*, Tunstall's men drew their swords and edged toward the gate.

The sounds rose and blended one into the other, the human cry sliding into a beastly howl, the horse's scream melding into a man's fading groan. The hair on the back of Eleanor's neck lifted in a mix of horror and excitement. She'd heard that kind of agony before, that shifting from animal to man. It wasn't Gunnar and the bull, but . . . *Please, oh, please, Holy Mother, let it be some of his friends.*

"OW." GUNNAR SWATTED at whatever it was that was pulling at his hair. The pain stopped for a moment, then came back with another sharp yank. "Stop it."

He rolled onto his belly and lifted his head to find himself looking into a pair of beady black eyes from barely a footlength away.

Odd. The raven seldom came to him, and never so soon after the changing. But it was there now, hopping up and down, screeching, and flapping its wings against his head. Gunnar took another swipe and the bird fluttered out of reach, but continued to caw. Something had Ari going—a stranger who'd come too close, perhaps, or maybe just rats in the food stores. Wouldn't be the first time for either.

"All right. All right." Gunnar heaved himself to his feet, scratched his arse, and twisted to stretch out some of the cricks. The raven circled his head, then landed on the hilt of a knife stuck in a tree trunk right in front of him and squawked. Still fuzzy headed, Gunnar stared at the bit of parchment pinned to the bark with the knife.

The bird leaned over to peck at the scrap, then looked at Gunnar and shrieked like he was trying to raise the dead.

It worked. Gunnar's heart kicked in his chest, the rush of blood clearing his head. He ripped the parchment free and, with a growing sense of foreboding, picked through the runes as quickly as he could. Balls.

Balls.

"Brand! Brand, now!"

He ran for his clothes and weapons.

By the time they reached the castle, it was nearly dark and Gunnar had molded his fury into an icy, practical calm and a basic plan: Get in. Get her out. Send her back to her husband unscathed. This wasn't about him. It was about saving Eleanor, if it even was her.

Now that he had time to think, he doubted that it was. Jafri had only the one look at Eleanor last fall, and there was little chance he'd recognize her from afar, nor any reason for her to be near the dene to begin with. It was just some other black-haired woman who had the misfortune to fall into outlaw hands. They'd still do the honorable thing and save her, of course, but it wasn't Eleanor. It couldn't be.

They left the horses hidden in a stand of trees and approached the castle on foot. Torvald spotted them and waved them toward a fallen-down section where they could scramble up easily.

"Well?" Brand's voice barely carried the arm's length between them.

Torvald held up ten fingers. "Two on the front gate. The others are by the fire, eating."

"The woman?" asked Brand.

"Also by the fire. Unharmed, as yet, but . . ."

But Gunnar was already on his knees, peering over the inner parapet, and what he saw threatened to crack the ice. He closed his eyes a moment, willing it to hold. "It is her."

The stark whiteness of Eleanor's face told him how frightened she was, but the fact that she was picking at a biscuit, even so slowly, said she was safe for the moment.

He took a look at the outlaws themselves, and one face jumped out. The ice flashed to steam in the furious heat that rose within him. "That whoreson."

"You know one of them?" Brand peeked over the edge.

"Aye. It's that bastard from the tourney. The one with the knife. Simon Tunstall."

"The one who tried to kill the squire?" asked Torvald, but Gunnar grabbed Ari's bow and quiver and was gone, crouching low to stay out of sight as he ran toward the front wall. Shaking his head, Torvald looked to Brand. "He's still Gunnar."

"Aye," said Brand with a grim smile. "We'd better go."

They ran for the horses.

ELEANOR FORCED HERSELF to break off another crumb of biscuit and put it in her mouth, even though each stale bite was harder to swallow than the last. Her appetite was a fiction meant to drag out supper as long as possible, to give whoever was out there—please let there be someone out there—time to mount a rescue before she was forced into the choice both she and Tunstall already knew she'd make.

But delay carried its own risks. The men had already finished eating, and some of them were staring at her, their eyes keen with ale-fueled lust. Tunstall barely had them in control. If they drank much more . . .

One of them jabbed a finger toward her. "She's eatin' slow of a purpose."

"Of course she is. You can hardly fault her, when she has such a solemn decision to make." Tunstall popped a morsel of cheese into his mouth and grinned at the complaining man. "Grant her this small victory. She'll fill up soon enough."

The man sitting next on the other side of Tunstall nudged him with an elbow. "*I'd* like to fill her up."

"Watch your mouth," snapped Tunstall. "She is a noble lady and soon to be my wife."

"'Struth, I'm hopin' she refuses you." Another man directly across the fire from Eleanor made a show of sniffing the air, then grabbed his crotch to adjust himself. "Even from here, she smells so very fine and womanish, I'm all but squirtin' meself."

"That's no great news," said Donal. "You do that every time you smell a sheep."

The first man raised his middle finger, and insults flew back and forth, each rawer than the last. Malcolm and Angus drifted over from the gate to join in the sport, and the mood quickly grew darker, the words more tinged with violence.

Shaking in earnest now, Eleanor struggled to swallow the last bite of biscuit, but it had gone dry as sawdust and refused to go down. She choked, unable to speak the words that might put a stop to this before it was too late. Promising herself she'd kill him the first chance she got, she spat the bite out on the ground and prepared to tell Simon Tunstall she would marry him on the morrow.

"Who's that?" Malcolm's sudden question cut off the insults and carried all of them to their feet, even Eleanor. He pointed toward a half-tumbled section of wall. "There."

In the cleft stood a man, a phantom lit from behind by the rising moon, his hair a fire-tinged halo. His face was little more than a shadow, but she knew him at once.

Gunnar.

She clapped her hand over her mouth to catch her cry of recognition and relief. He was here. He'd come for her.

Tunstall glanced around at his men, then screwed up his courage and took a couple of steps forward. "Who are you? What do you want?"

"I am here for the woman."

"So are we," said Angus, and some of the others laughed that nasty laugh that made her skin crawl.

"Give her over unharmed and you may live."

Anger rumbled through the band, and Donal raised his sword high and shook it in challenge. "Come down here to take her and you may get to watch us fuck her as you die."

As the others hooted and thumped their chests and each other's backs in agreement, Gunnar raised a bow and drew, lightning fast. There was a faint whisk and thump, and

Donal's eyes widened in shock. Eleanor followed his gaze down and gasped.

An arrow sprouted from Donal's groin like some odd, feathered member. He stared at it, uncomprehending, then with a wail, grabbed at the shaft and wrenched.

"Donal, don't!"

Malcolm's warning came too late. The arrow tore free, and blood fountained over Donal's thighs, pulsing with every beat of his heart. He folded to his knees, shrieking, clutching at himself, trying to catch his life in cupped hands as it darkened the earth before him. They all stood staring, aghast, and for the space of a breath or two, there was nothing but the horror of Donal's screams.

Then he toppled over, the screaming fading with his life. In the frozen silence that followed, a low rumble rose beyond the walls. Tunstall's head came up.

"The gate," he shouted as the rumble turned into approaching hoofbeats. He ran toward the opening, waving frantically for his men to follow. "Fools. You left the gate unmanned!"

His shout jolted the men out of their trance and they raced after him, hurrying to form a rough line before the opening. In the moment of chaos, Eleanor, realizing she was unwatched, snatched up her rock and started backing away.

Before she got more than a few steps, two riders tore through the gate, their swords flashing as they swept into the ragged line, their battle cries echoing off the stones.

The larger of the two took out the nearest outlaw with a single, clean blow that sent the man's head bouncing off into the dark like an unwanted ball. The other rider disposed of a second man in like fashion, and they each charged after another.

From the wall, Gunnar took out another man with an arrow, then dropped his bow and hurtled off the wall with a bloodcurdling cry. The remaining outlaws broke and ran,

scattering like dust before a broom. Gunnar ran one to
ground, sword high.

Still frozen in awe, Eleanor saw Tunstall break away
from the group and pelt across the yard—not just running,
she suddenly realized, but coming straight for her.

"Gunnar!" She turned to run, but Tunstall was already
on her. He snagged her braid and brought her up short with
a jerk. She rounded on him, swung, and clipped his forehead with her stone, just enough to make him wince. She
swung again, and felt the satisfying clunk of stone on bone.
He grunted, and blood welled, then streamed down his
temple. He stumbled, but held on.

"Bitch." He yanked again, harder, this time ripping her
hair. She pitched into his chest with a yelp of pain, and
before she could recover, the tip of his sword bit into the
side of her neck. She froze.

"Drop it." He pulled the blade, just a little, and she cried
out. As blood streamed down her neck, she let her only
weapon fall.

"That's better." Twisting his hand into her braid, he
dragged her around the corner of the keep. "Now, we are
going to fetch my horse and ride out of here."

IT WAS A short, brutal fight, over before the blood could
fully slake the white heat of Gunnar's fury. When it was
done and the moans of the dying had been silenced, he,
Brand, and Torvald stood in the bailey, breathing hard and
looking over the gore-covered things that had once been
men.

"They weren't very good fighters," said Brand, echoing
Gunnar's thought. Brand cut a scrap of fairly clean linen off
the body at his feet and used it to wipe his blade before he
sheathed it, then passed the cloth to Gunnar. "We'll deal with
the bodies and meet you back at camp. Go find your lady."

"She is not my lady." The words tasted as bitter as they

sounded. Gunnar cleaned his own sword and wiped the blood off his hands. "One of you should see to her."

"Gunnar . . ."

"No. I will be poor company. I still want to kill something." He put his sword away and tossed the cloth to Torvald. "I almost wish there had been more of them."

"There were."

"What?"

Holding the scrap of linen, Torvald turned a slow circle, frowning as he scoured the bailey. "Did one of you kill a man someplace else?"

Brand and Gunnar looked at each other and shook their heads.

"There were one and ten counting Lady Eleanor. She's . . . wherever she is. I see only nine dead."

Gunnar counted quickly and came up short, too.

"Shite. Eleanor. Eleanor!" He ran toward the last place he'd seen her, by the fire.

As he neared the spot, a flash of movement toward the rear of the bailey caught his eye. Gunnar ducked behind the keep and peered around the corner. He spotted Eleanor untying one of the horses; an outlaw held a sword at her back.

Not just any outlaw. Tunstall.

Gunnar signaled Torvald and Brand to send them circling around the far side of the keep to come up from behind, then flattened against the wall, where the shadows would hide him while he crept closer.

"Over by the block," Tunstall ordered, prodding Eleanor with his sword.

There was no way Gunnar was going to let this asp ride away with Eleanor in his hands. The bastard had been ready to kill a squire for a kiss and a bit of silver. The gods only knew what he'd do to save his own life. But with that blade at Eleanor's back . . . Gunnar said a brief prayer to Baldr to make her as quick-witted as she had been at Raby.

He stepped out into the moonlight. "Hold or die, Tunstall."

The man turned with a start. He squinted toward Gunnar, and recognition dawned across his face. "You!"

He wrenched Eleanor away from the horse, holding her before him as a shield. Moonlight flashed off his blade as he waggled it at Gunnar, threatening. "Back away. You already cost me one prize. You won't take this one. I'll kill her first."

Eleanor met Gunnar's eyes, then moaned faintly and collapsed, seemingly having swooned away. Tunstall caught at her limp body, but it was like holding water. She oozed through his arms and pooled at his feet. With a cry of frustration, he grabbed for her.

Gunnar threw himself at Tunstall, carrying him away from Eleanor before he could touch her again. They landed amongst the horses, hooves flashing around their heads as the animals shied away. Gunnar threw the outlaw off and rolled clear, but the other man, lighter and quicker, was up and running before Gunnar could get to his feet.

Torvald and Brand ran out of the shadows behind the keep, blocking Tunstall's escape. Snarling like a cornered fox, Tunstall whirled back toward Gunnar and rushed at him, sword held high in two hands. Gunnar parried the blow to the side, reached beneath his blade before Tunstall could recover, and thrust deep between his ribs, a quick in, twist, and out.

Tunstall froze in mid-stride and looked at Gunnar with that surprised stare men have in the instant they realize they're dead. His sword sagged as the blood drained from his arms, and he swayed like a willow in an autumn storm. He looked down at the gaping hole in his chest where air and blood foamed together. "You have killed me."

"I have."

"Good." Eleanor appeared at Gunnar's side, her face hard. "I am not your prize," she spat at Tunstall. "I am no man's prize. I hope you burn in Hell."

Fury roared up out of Tunstall's throat, giving him a last burst of strength. He lifted his sword to strike. Gunnar shoved Eleanor aside and blocked the blow, then struck. Tunstall's guts spilled and he collapsed, dead.

Brand threaded his way between the horses and took a look at Tunstall, then at Eleanor, standing white-faced behind Gunnar. "Get her away from here, Gunnar. It is not the place for a woman."

"I told you, I cannot." He spoke in Norse. "You take her, Torvald."

"Gunnar . . ."

"Take her," snapped Gunnar. He couldn't. She wasn't his, and if he held her before him on a horse the way he had on May Day, so long ago, he would never be able to send her back to her husband. "I will follow after we are done."

Shaking his head, Torvald stepped forward. "My lady. Come with me."

Eleanor ignored the hand he offered and stepped around Gunnar to look down at the body. Her eyes were hooded, her face as blank as a death mask. She stood there for a moment, then turned away and walked off, stiff backed. She got about a dozen steps before she stopped. Her shoulders sagged and she covered her face with her hands and began to cry.

In three steps, Gunnar was at her side, scooping her up, holding her, sheltering her. She curled against him and clutched at his bloodied shirt, trying to say something, but the words came out so muddled with tears he couldn't understand.

". . . dead . . ." he thought he heard. ". . . couldn't . . . Henry . . ."

"*Shh*. You are safe. I have you." He kissed the top of her head, and she sobbed harder.

Torvald gave him a nod. "I'll get your horse."

"Just bring him when you come back," said Gunnar, and carried her home.

By the time he waded through the creek at the bottom of

the dene, Eleanor had stopped crying and started shaking. He'd expected she would. He'd seen enough men get the shakes after the heat of battle faded—had even suffered them himself a few times—to know they were coming and that they were no sign of weakness. Eleanor might not have borne weapons, but she had fought a battle, the gods only knew for how long, and now that it was over and she was safe, the strain was catching her unawares.

"You need something warm in you and then a sound sleep," he said as he settled her on a stool beside the dead fire and draped a blanket over her shoulders. "I'll be as quick as I can."

She nodded, and he went to work, gathering his flint and steel and laying a fire in the thin light that filtered through the mouth of the cave. Despite working mostly by feel, he soon had a good ember, and he tipped it into the tinder and breathed over it until the flame flared to life.

"It is y-you."

Her whispered exclamation made him look up. She was staring at him, eyes round and bright as silver pennies in her ghost-white face.

"Aye, it is," he said gently. He so much wanted to hold her, comfort her, kiss away the fresh tears that trickled down her cheeks. Instead, he fed a few twigs and sticks into the fire. "Did you doubt it?"

"I j-j-j-ust . . ." She surrendered to the chattering of her teeth and simply shook her head and pulled the blanket tighter around her shoulders.

Gunnar kept adding small wood until the fire burned hot and true, then added three fat logs to keep it going and make enough coals for proper cooking later. He sloshed a good measure of the wine Brand had brought into a kettle and nestled the pot into the space between the logs to warm. "I don't have spices to mull this properly, but it will do you good anyway."

He got no answer, and when he turned to look, Eleanor was lost in the fire, barely blinking at whatever she saw in the flames. He sat back on his heels and took a good look at her now that he had enough light. Other than a shallow cut on her neck that had already stopped bleeding, she appeared unharmed.

Thanks belonged to Jafri for that. If he hadn't seen her, if Ari hadn't brought the message, if Torvald hadn't been there, if Brand and he hadn't . . .

His own hands began to shake as he considered the many ways this night could have gone sour.

What the devil was she doing out here? How had she fallen into Tunstall's hands? Where were the men who should have been protecting her?

He had a hundred questions—and no right to ask them, any more than he had the right to reach across the narrow space between them and brush that tear-dampened wisp of hair off her cheek.

Those rights belonged to her husband, the careless fool who had let her wander into danger. Had he made her Countess of Gloucester yet? he wondered, that prick of a husband she would return to.

Anger propelled Gunnar to his feet. He grabbed the leathern pail, muttered something about needing water, and escaped out into the night.

He filled the pail, then stripped off his blood-spattered gown and anchored it in the edge of the stream with a heavy stone so the current might wash away the stains, then plunged his head into the water as well, in the hopes it might carry away some of the darkly possessive desire that seethed inside him.

It helped. When he hauled the water back inside, his head was indeed clearer and the wine had begun to steam. Eleanor, however, still sat staring. He placed the pail near the fire to take the chill off the water, then poured some wine.

"My lady?" Nothing. "Eleanor."

She flinched and came partway back from wherever she was to meet his eyes.

He held out the wine. "Drink. It will help."

She nodded and cupped the bowl between two hands. She still shook badly, but she managed a sip, and then another, and then she heaved a great sigh, drained the bowl in one long draught, and held it out. "More."

"I told you it would help." He poured more, and watched her drink that, too, though considerably more slowly, and when she'd finished, he took the bowl, dampened a clean cloth, and offered it to her, indicating the side of her neck. "You are hurt."

Eleanor touched the wound, wincing, but didn't seem to register what she should do with the cloth.

Gunnar hesitated, unwilling to step right back into temptation when he'd only just escaped it, but in the end, he took away her wine and set to work, gently tipping her head to the side so he could daub away the blood without reopening the wound.

By the time he'd wiped the tear streaks off her cheeks, the wine was making her sag and yawn and his senses were so full of her he could hardly bear it. He tossed the cloth aside and tugged her to her feet. "Come, my lady."

"Where?"

"To bed." He caught her as she swayed. "Before you fall over."

He led her a few steps to the recess where he slept, when he bothered to sleep. He'd built a rough bed years ago, a simple frame of pegged logs and netted rope that served to keep a straw pallet off the damp floor, but which could be broken down and hidden away when he and Jafri moved elsewhere. It was not the sort of fine bed she was used to, but it had blankets and furs and a mattress of sweet grass hay. She would be warm in it, and she would be safe, and that was what mattered for now.

Gunnar flipped back the furs and motioned for her to sit, then knelt before her to unbuckle her boots.

Tugging them off unbalanced her. She reached out to steady herself, and her hand flattened against his bare chest. For all that she shivered, her fingers burned like hot irons, marking his flesh as hers. Gunnar closed his eyes, struggling to remember his place, to remember she wasn't his and couldn't be, to muster the will to turn away. But as he won, as he started to pull away, he heard a quiet plea.

"Don't go."

"I go nowhere but the fire." He pried her fingers off his skin and pressed her back onto the bed. It was all he could do not to follow her down. "Close your eyes, my lady. Rest."

She stared at him a moment, then her eyes drifted shut. An instant later, they popped open. "I c-cannot. He is there, inside my h-head."

"He is dead."

"They are all dead. His men. My men. My waiting woman. All of them. And it is my fault." Her voice slurred with exhaustion and wine and the threat of fresh tears. "If you hold me, maybe I won't see their faces. Or him."

Hold her? He couldn't. He mustn't. "My lady, I—"

"Please."

That single, bereft word went straight to Gunnar's soul, breaking him, shredding his resolve. With a groan of surrender, he lay down beside her and wrapped his arms around her. Three long years turned to smoke.

She burrowed against his chest, weeping in earnest. He could do nothing but hold her and let her cry until her tears went dry and she fell silent, then longer, until her breathing said she slept.

He told himself that asleep, she no longer needed him, that he should get up, concede the folly of this night, and move away from her. He had no right to hold her, to take such pleasure from her weight in his arms and the warmth of her cheek against his breast.

He should get up . . . but he might wake her. Or she might catch a chill, or a nightmare might find her.

He gave himself one excuse after another to keep holding her, until finally he simply admitted to himself he didn't want to let her go and pulled her closer. She murmured something and burrowed against him, and as the night sky spun outside the cave, he whispered his gratitude to Freya for letting him have her in his arms once more.

Even for just this brief while.

Even knowing she wasn't his to keep.

CHAPTER 18

BETWEEN THE EXHAUSTION, the wine, and the blessed sanctuary of Gunnar's arms, Eleanor slept long and hard. By the time she found her boots and crept out of the cave, eyes gritty and mouth tasting like the inside of a witch's stewpot, the day was well along.

"Stirring at last, are we?"

The unexpected voice made her jump, then wince as her brain rattled inside her skull. Shading her eyes with one hand, she squinted around trying to find the speaker. "Hello? Where are you?"

"Over here, my lady, beneath the tree. Good day to you."

She got her bearing and spotted him at last, a lean, dark man on the far side of the stream. The hand he raised held a shuttle-like net needle, and across his knees lay a fishnet he was mending. He looked like he desperately needed to get it fixed so he could have himself a good meal.

"I know you. You are J- . . . J- . . ." She shrugged helplessly, unable to get to his name through the haze. "You are his friend from Alnwick."

"Jafri," he said. "I suspected you knew who I was that day when you fled so quickly. But how?"

"I recalled you had been at Richmond. One of the Alnwick men confirmed you were his friend."

"Mmm." His grunt said nothing, but the tiny shake of his head reeked of disapproval. "Are you hungry, my lady?"

"I have more thirst than hunger." She started to kneel by the stream.

"Don't drink there. If you will let me finish this knot, I will pour you some ale. Or if you truly want water, I'll fetch a pail from the burn down the way. It runs pure and sweet."

"What's wrong with this water?"

"Usually nothing, but Ari's up at the pool. He is, er, *bathing*."

The way he said it made it sound like far more than bathing. Eleanor wrinkled her nose in distaste. "I shall wait for ale, then. Or better yet, tell me where to find it, and then I can pour for myself and you can keep at that net."

"Inside, to your sword hand. There's a skin in the nook."

She found the ale and a bowl that looked clean enough and carried them out into the light. As she wrestled the unwieldy skin up to pour, she asked, "Why do you sit there, Sir Jafri?"

"To watch over you, m'lady."

"I mean, why *there*, so far off?"

"Ari said it would be better if you did not wake to find a strange man skulking over you."

"It was a kind thought." She sealed the skin and laid it aside, then took a tentative sip from the bowl. The ale was thin, but not bad. She'd certainly had worse, even at her father's table. She took a deeper drink, then carried her bowl over to sit on a weather-bleached log from which she could see Sir Jafri easily. "Who else is here, besides you and this Ari?"

"Today, just us. Tonight there will be two besides Gunnar."

"The horsemen." Images from the previous night

crystallized along the border between nightmare and dream. "The thin, pale knight who came to Burwash."

"Torvald."

"And a big man I have not seen before. Even bigger than Gunnar."

"That would be Brand."

"They saved me. They and Gunnar."

"Aye, they did that, and they did it three against ten." A begrudging grin twisted his mouth. "I wish I could have seen it."

"I wish I had not," she murmured as an unattached head tumbled past her mind's eye.

"Pardon?"

"Nothing. I am only thinking to myself. Are all of you . . ." She hesitated, not knowing how to ask. "Gunnar told me there were others who change like he does."

His smile faded, and his eyes narrowed in suspicion. "Aye. We change."

"Ah." His chariness warned her against the next, most obvious question, about what sort of beast he was. She filled the awkward silence by taking another draught of ale, then looked to the slim strip of cloudy sky visible overhead. Was that the glow of the sun upstream? But if the stream flowed east to the sea . . . A sudden sense of disorientation swamped her. "What hour is it?"

"Well past halfway-Nones."

"What? I thought it was yet morning." She shook her head in denial. "No. I cannot have slept the whole day through."

"You did. If you were up top, you might hear the Vesper bells at Monk Hesledon anon."

"A whole day . . . I have never slept through a day when I was not ill. You should have woken me."

"Why? After yesterday, you needed the rest, and you'll want to be awake for Gunnar anyway. And he'll most assuredly want *you* awake," he added, bringing heat to her cheeks.

She finished her ale in silence, then searched out a

willow for a twig to rid her teeth of the fur and the stewpot. By the time she'd finished, Sir Jafri had tied the final knot in his net. He trimmed the line and stood up to stretch the net wide to inspect his work.

"There. Even Ari can't complain about that. He's the best fisherman amongst us," he explained as he collected his things and came hopping stone to stone across the stream. "But he's particular about his casting net."

"You would be, too, if you had to fish for Brand." A golden-haired man came strolling around a bend upstream, looking like a misplaced young god from one of old Carolus's tales except that he was dressed all in red. He gave Eleanor a wink and a pretty bow. "He gulps herrings down like a great whale, dozens at a time. Good day, Lady Eleanor. Are you well?"

"Well enough. You must be Sir Ari."

"I have often thought that I would prefer to be elsewise, but if such a fair lady says I *must* be Sir Ari, then how can I not?"

"Oh, shut up." Jafri tossed the casting net over Ari's head and gave the draw cord a pull, trapping his friend like a crayfish.

"Hey!"

Jafri said something Eleanor didn't understand. Ari answered with a laugh, but as he fought his way free, she noticed him favoring his left hand. She looked closer and spied a bloodstained strip of linen peeping out from the edge of that glove. He started gathering the net into proper folds, and the tone of their conversation grew more serious.

"She just now awoke," said Jafri, shifting back to English. "You see to it. I'm heading out."

Ari raised a brow. "So early?"

"I must go farther tonight." He nodded to Eleanor. "Good night, my lady."

"Good night, sir. Will I see you on the morrow?"

"If you are awake, you will. But whether you are or not, I will be here to watch over you." He looked at Ari and spoke in their language again, some kind of warning, by the sound of it. Ari rolled his eyes and waved him off. With a final look of caution, Jafri recrossed the burn, trotted a few yards upstream, then cut between the rocks, following a barely visible trail up the steep side.

"I thought I heard horses neighing downstream earlier," said Eleanor.

"You did."

"Then why doesn't he—"

"Because he goes on foot. Are you hungry?"

So, he wasn't going to tell her anything either. Fine, then, she would deal with something less interesting but far more pressing. "No. But I do have need of your garderobe."

Ari snorted back a laugh. "*Garderobe* is far too fine a word, my lady. We have a pit. Come, I'll show you."

She fell in beside Ari as he started downstream. "When we come back, perhaps I could tend to that hand for you?"

He glanced down, frowned, and poked the bloody bit of linen up into his glove so it didn't show. "My hand is fine. However, if you wish to make yourself useful—"

"I do. I need distraction," she admitted.

"Then I will find you some small chore to do."

"Good. Do you think you could you find me a comb as well?"

"I'm sure I can. This patch of moss is slick. Watch your step."

"I always do, *monsire*."

IT WAS THE most beautiful thing he'd ever seen.

Gunnar crouched behind a rock on the slope of the dene, staring at Eleanor across the way. She sat on his three-legged stool at the lip of the cave, her black hair spread around her like a mantle, the rose of sunset mixing with the fire behind her to set the wisps at her temple a-glint with ruddy bronze. She held an ivory comb he had never seen before—probably Ari's, popinjay that he was—and she worked it through her hair one long strand at a time, seven strokes each before moving on to the next.

Seven. Seven. He counted with her, his pulse slowing to match the rhythm of her comb, as even and steady as a monk's chant. Seven.

She surely hadn't meant for anyone to see her like this, head uncovered, hair unbound. She'd waited until dusk, after all, when she could expect to be alone for a time. But the bull hadn't wandered far afield today, and Gunnar had thrown on his clothes and all but run back, anxious to see that she was safe and well.

It was when he'd paused to retrieve the gown he'd left lying on a rock to dry that he'd seen her there combing. He'd ducked down before she'd spotted him, wanting to watch.

He was glad he had. She'd seemed so fragile last night, so broken, but tonight . . . Perhaps it was the power of this simple ritual, but she did not seem broken after all. Sad, yes, of course, but whole, both body and spirit intact despite that bastard Tunstall and his men. Fury bubbled within him at the thought of them laying hands on her, then faded as she continued to comb. Seven. Seven.

She finished at last and laid aside the comb to braid her hair, her fingers catching the hanks and weaving them into the sort of simple, fat plait women often wore when they had no maids to attend them. She tied off the end and dropped it over her shoulder, then folded her hands in her lap and sat, waiting.

For him.

How many times had he imagined coming down the path to find her waiting there like that? Even after Alnwick, even having seen for himself how content she was with her husband, a part of him had clung to the dream that she would someday come back to him, that she would lie with him, not in lust but in love, and heal him after all. Perhaps that was why she was here, a hopeful voice whispered in the back of his skull, and the idea of losing himself in her had him hardening in an instant.

Shite. He couldn't go down there like this, so full of desire. It had been difficult enough to hold her without demand last night, and still worse to leave her this morning, but now . . . Now it would be impossible even to be near her. Torturous. He would just have to stay here and wait for Brand and Torvald to return. They could watch over her in his stead tonight, and Jafri and Ari could carry her to safety tomorrow. He should have told them to take her back today before he'd had to face her again. He didn't need this torment.

Wings ruffled the air above, and the raven swooped down and landed on the rock in front of him. Gunnar reached up to snap the bird's beak shut. Too slow.

The raven's kaugh echoed through the gorge.

Below, Eleanor jumped to her feet. "Gunnar?"

Shite. Now he had no choice.

And a part of him—the foolish, hopeful part—was far happier about that than he should be. *Shite, shite, and shite*.

"I'm going to pluck you and roast you for dinner," he muttered as he flapped his hand to send the raven soaring off into the evening sky. Shoving his dream of deliverance and lovemaking down deep where it belonged, next to childhood fantasies of killing a fireworm, he straightened.

"Aye, my lady. It is only I. Be at ease." He slid the last few paces down to the bottom, yanking his gown over his head, making sure it covered his swollen tarse before he stepped out where she could see him clearly.

The wariness left her in a sigh and she took a tentative step forward. For a heartbeat he thought she was going to run into his arms the way she had that night in the solar, and he willed her not to, knowing that once he touched her, what little control he had left would turn to mist.

To his relief and his agony, she only stood there, staring at him. "It *is* you."

"I thought we settled that last night."

She nodded. "We did. But there is yet a part of me convinced I only imagined you. That I am even now mad."

He knew the feeling. He hadn't suffered the ordeal she had, but he craved a chance to touch her, just to be sure she was real, to know for certain that it had been her in his arms last night and not some wraith. Could a real woman's skin possibly be as warm and soft as hers had been? He leaned toward her, needing to know.

He caught himself and jerked back. "Brand and Torvald should be here any moment."

"Aye. Sir Ari said you all would be hungry. Especially Sir Brand."

He turned to the pot and pulled the lid off. "This smells good."

"It is pease with ransoms and salted pork."

"Did you—" *Did you make it?* he started to ask, but of course she hadn't made it. Countesses didn't cook; they gave orders for other people to cook. "Did you have some?"

"No. Not yet."

"Didn't Jafri and Ari feed you?" He reached for a dipper and bowl. "They were supposed to take care of you."

"Do not fault them. They both offered, but I—"

"Of course. You are too distraught from what happened to eat."

"No. I just . . . I wanted to wait for you."

"Well, I'm here." He filled the bowl and shoved it at her. Her fingertips grazed his as she took the bowl, and he jerked back, burning, and quickly circled the fire, putting it between himself and temptation. "Now eat before you make yourself ill."

She gaped at him like he'd grown horns. But of course he did grow horns, every single, damnable morning—and he had the tender spots on his head to prove it.

And yet she'd once said she loved him, even knowing. And she was here, and he wanted her so much.

Shite. Shiteshiteshiteshiteshite.

Brand's voice came echoing up the dene. Thank the gods. Saved.

Eleanor heard him, too, and set her bowl aside, and as Brand and Torvald and the damned traitorous raven came into sight, she stepped forward to meet them with a deep courtesy. *"Messires."*

"Lady Eleanor." Brand looked from her to Gunnar and back, as though expecting something. When whatever it was didn't happen, he gave her a brief nod. "I am called—"

"Sir Brand," she said with him. "And Sir Torvald. There can never be thanks enough for what the three of you did last night. I don't know how you knew I was there, but if you had not found me . . ."

"Ari first spotted the riders," said Brand. "And Jafri realized it was you."

"But I spoke to them both. Neither of them said a word of it."

"That is Jafri's way, though it surprises me Ari said nothing. He seldom keeps his mouth shut about anything."

"I begin to think the disease has spread," said Gunnar, dropping the lid back on the pot so hard it rang like a bell. "Stop standing around and let the woman eat."

Brand and Torvald glanced at each other, but went off to fetch their bowls and a quarter wheel of cheese, which Torvald sliced while Brand poured ale. They filled their bowls and settled in around the fire, the three of them and Eleanor, and for a while there was little but the sounds of eating and drinking.

Then Eleanor cleared her throat. Gunnar looked up to find she had done little more than nibble at a sliver of cheese. He frowned. "Is something wrong with the potage?"

"No, but I—"

"Then why aren't you eating? You need more than that little bit of cheese. You cannot get your strength back that way."

"My strength is fine," she said as Torvald got up and disappeared into the cave. "It just that—"

"You must eat," insisted Gunnar.

Torvald returned and silently handed Eleanor a horn spoon.

"My thanks." She gave Gunnar a sideways glance as she dug in.

"Why didn't you say something?" he demanded.

"She tried. You didn't give her a chance," said Brand in Norse. "You're acting like a fool. Again. You need to just bed her and be done with it."

"Fuck you." Gunnar got up and stalked off.

He'd barely gone a dozen paces when Brand's hand clamped down on his shoulder and whipped him around. "Stop it. She's here. You have your amulet. It is time. Claim her."

"What good would it do?" Gunnar ground the question out between jaws clenched so tight his teeth creaked.

"Bah. The *Nornir* have woven your lives together so firmly that you cannot escape her even hiding in this hole. The gods have put her in your path three times now."

"Four."

"What?"

"Four times. I saw her last autumn, when we stopped at Lesbury. Just from a distance, but . . ."

"Balls, Gunnar. What else must they do to convince you? The gods will not stay patient forever. If I were you—"

"You're not." He hadn't seen her with Burghersh, smiling at him. Touching him.

"If I were, I'd claim her tonight, lest the gods decide I was too thickheaded to bother with anymore."

"How can I, when she's already married?"

"Bed her, wed her, make a blood pledge with her beneath the moon. I don't care. Just find some way to show the gods you intend to hold on to her this time. They have brought her to you time and again. They must have cause."

"Aye. They like watching me suffer," Gunnar muttered.

"Who can fault them when you make it so easy for them?" Brand turned around and stomped off toward the cave. "Grab your gear, Torvald. We're moving down to the lower cave before I end up beating him bloody in front of his woman."

"Good idea." Torvald slurped down the last of his pottage and rose to follow Brand into the cave. There was a moment's rustling about, and then they both came out toting bedrolls and weapons and food.

"We'll come back for the rest tomorrow. And for supper." Brand stopped at the fire to light one of the tallow-dipped rushes Gunnar kept on hand for when he needed a quick torch. He gave Eleanor a nod. "My lady. Rest well."

"Where are you going?" Eleanor jumped up and hurried toward Gunnar. "Where are they going? Did you tell them to leave? Why?"

"I didn't. Come, Brand, there's no need for this."

"Yes there is. There are some things in the small cave that I think are hers. The bundle with the saddlebags right in front. You'll see." Brand snagged the ale skin, and he and Torvald started off downstream. As they headed off into the black, he called back in Norse, "Your *fylgja* is a bull, Gunnar, not a jackass. Try to remember that."

And then they vanished, and it was just him and Eleanor, staring at each other.

"I don't understand," she said.

"Brand is being Brand, that's all. It is nothing. Just . . . Just eat your supper."

"If my supper is of such concern to you, *monsire*, eat it yourself," she snapped, and stalked off into the cave.

ELEANOR SANK DOWN on the bed and hugged herself, trying to hold herself together. She felt as thin and fragile as an old silk gown, ready to shatter from being used too hard.

Seven brave men and a good woman were dead, plus Tunstall and his band, and all their bodies lay at her feet. She had lied to her mother, defied father, king, and Church, risked all that she was, all that she owned.

And for what?

This?

Gunnar might be right outside, but he seemed every bit as distant as when they'd been half a country apart. She could hear him right now, pacing back and forth, angrily kicking stones at the trees.

She didn't understand. She'd wanted him so much, been so certain he wanted her in return. That certainty had buoyed her through the years, carried her through all those nights beneath Richard. Had she been that wrong, that foolish? Was he angry that she'd come here?

Or was it something else? Perhaps Heaven had decided to punish her after all, for her arrogance in assuming she was destined for him and the destruction she'd wrought trying to get to him. Perhaps she wasn't meant to be here after all.

Outside, Gunnar stopped pacing, and for a heartbeat she hoped that he was coming in to her, that they would work their way past this awkward . . . whatever it was. But his boots scuffled in the gravel, moving away up the dene. A sob slipped past her defenses and echoed off the cave walls sounding more like laughter, as though the very stones were mocking her. She hugged herself harder, trying not to weep.

She was still sitting there when she heard him crunching his way back down the stream bank a while later.

Closer.

Closer. *Please, Holy Mother. Please let him be coming back to me.* She held her breath, waiting.

"My lady?"

Thank you. His voice came from the cave mouth, but if she looked up, if she so much as moved, she would surely fall apart. She took a deep breath. "What is it?"

"I, um, have this." His toes appeared just at the edge of her vision, and he dropped a cloth-wrapped bundle at her feet. "'Tis what they took off of Tunstall. Brand thinks some of it belongs to you."

"Ah." She reached for it, but her hands shook so badly, she couldn't pick the knot loose.

"I'll get it," he said brusquely. He knelt at her feet, tugged the bundle open, and started laying out the pitiful remains of Simon Tunstall's life.

"What did they do with him?"

"Tunstall?" Gunnar looked up, and he was right there, so close she could see the flecks of gold in his green eyes. "You don't need to hear that, my lady."

Eleanor, she wanted to shout. *Call me Eleanor.* "Yes, I do. Tell me."

"His body was put down the well with the others."

"All of them? What if someone finds them?"

"They won't. The well was old and beginning to collapse. Brand and Torvald just helped it along. Tunstall and his men are well buried and they will stay that way."

"Then they got better than they gave my men."

Gunnar's expression softened a little. "How many did you lose?"

"Eight." She didn't want to think of their faces right now, so she motioned toward the pile of gear. "I think Simon put what he took off me into his saddlebags."

"Let us see." Gunnar unbuckled the bags and tipped the contents out on the edge of the cloth closest to Eleanor. "There's your knife."

"Aye." Eleanor plucked it off the pile and returned it to her belt where it belonged, then picked out her silver chatelaine and keys, three rings with bruted stones that Tunstall had ripped off her fingers, and her purse. As she lifted the last, the coins within jingled, a sound far too merry for such grim business.

"Is that all of it?" asked Gunnar.

"Aye. They were too busy arguing over what to do with me to divide the other spoils." The coppery taste of fear flooded her mouth and set her heart racing. She pushed back at it in anger and starting shoving her rings onto her fingers. "There is one other thing. A cloak that Miriam carried for me."

"Miriam?"

"The woman my lady mother lent me for the trip north. She was to do my hair."

"Oh. It wasn't Lucy, then. Last night, when you said your woman had been killed, I thought . . ."

"No, thank the saints I sent Lucy with the wagons. She is safely on the main road."

"I'm glad, for your sake and hers." His sympathetic smile faded into a scowl. "But *you* should have been on the main road with her."

"If I had been, I would not have found you."

"You were the one found, m'lady, and if you had been where you belong, there would have been no need to find you."

"Where I *belong*? What does that mean? Why are you so angry with me?"

"I am not angry," he said, even as his clipped voice proclaimed him a liar. He reached down into Tunstall's leavings and pulled out something shiny. Grabbing her hand, he turned it over and pressed his find into her palm. "There. You missed something, *Lady Burghersh*."

Eleanor stared at the plain gold band that had shackled her to Richard for so long. It had served its purpose, keeping her father at bay, and she supposed she should keep it to honor that good use, if not her husband's memory. But she couldn't. She just couldn't. It would be like a prisoner keeping his chains to honor his gaoler.

She tossed it back amongst Tunstall's things, and as it left her hand, a small portion of the freedom she'd felt after Richard's entombment came rushing back to her as if by some conjuration. She smiled, perhaps the first true and honest smile that had touched her lips since her father had invaded her hall at Upton.

"I have no use for it. Sell it."

GUNNAR STARED AT Eleanor, unsure what this blithe dismissal of her wedding ring meant. "Do you care for your husband so little?"

"I cared as much as I was required to. I am done. And you can stop calling me Lady Burghersh, as well. The title belongs to Isabel."

A roar like an incoming storm filled Gunnar's head. "I don't understand."

"What is there to understand? He is dead, and the title passed to his sister, and by right of her, to Bergavenny."

"Dead," he repeated dully. "Richard is dead?"

"Yes. Yes, of course Richard is dead. I told you that."

"No, you didn't."

Eleanor gave him that horn-sprouting look again. "It was almost the first thing I said to you last night, that Richard is dead, and that I couldn't bear to marry Henry."

Something in the shape and rhythm of her words brought it back. The revelation buried in her sobs propelled him to his feet. "That's what you were trying to say? That *Richard* was dead?"

"Now it is I who does not understand. I did say it."

"You were crying so hard. I thought . . . Ah, shite. Brand is right. I am an ass." He paced around the fire, pounding his fists against his skull, trying to knock loose the idiocy that had possessed him. "I thought you were talking about your men. Or perhaps Tunstall. I don't know. I just didn't . . ."

"Oh. O-Oh. Of course." The confusion on Eleanor's face faded, replaced by something he could only describe as wonderment. "You thought I was still married."

"Aye."

"I am not." She stood up and cocked her head to study him a moment. "You thought I was merely a traveler waylaid nearby by chance."

"Aye."

"I was not. Well, I was waylaid, but . . ." She swept Tunstall's gear aside with her foot and started toward Gunnar, and his mouth went dry with hope. "You thought that where I *belonged* was with my husband."

He nodded.

"I did not." She stepped in front of him. "*Ever.* And you

were angry with me because . . . I am uncertain of this one. Why?"

"Because I didn't want to send you back to him," he growled, agonized even to say it. "And I knew I must."

She made a tiny sound of surprise and sympathy, and lifted one hand up to cup his jaw, comforting him. The faintest smile curved her lips. "I *told* Lucy you were an honorable man."

He turned into her hand, pressing a kiss into her palm, and as his beard ruffled over her fingers, it occurred to him, too late, that he had not shaved in far too long. "Did you also tell her I am the biggest fool this side of Gotham?"

"No bigger fool than I." She curved her fingers into his jaw, just a bit, drawing him down until his lips lingered barely an inch over hers. "Let us both stop being fools. I cannot bear it any longer."

"Gladly, my lady."

"Eleanor. I want to be Eleanor again. I want to be yours again." She rose that last inch and touched her lips to his, a sweet kiss that nonetheless poured through him like brandewine, melting away his last ridiculous qualms and leaving him drunk with need. "Make me yours. Let me feel alive again."

Dizzy, he reached for her. "Most gladly, my . . . Eleanor.

She came into his arms with a sigh that opened her mouth to him. He remembered that taste, the velvet softness of her mouth, and the way her tongue met his so willingly. He remembered her curves, too, and he traced them as they continued to kiss, finding the places where she was still slim as a girl and those where her body had grown riper and more womanly, more tempting.

So very tempting. He scooped her up and carried her to the bed. The long drop as he sat broke their kiss and drew a surprised yelp from Eleanor that made him chuckle. He nestled her more securely onto his lap. "I have you."

"I know." Her eyes glittered like stars in the flickering light, and for a moment he thought she might be crying again. The notion vanished as she slowly traced a line down his neck and across his shoulder. The heat her fingers left behind spread over his skin like a ship's wake, vanishing even as it left its path forever changed. He tensed, his body anticipating more heat, so much more, and as her trail dropped over the edge of his shoulder and she found the bunched muscles of his arm, she smiled. "You are too strong to let me fall."

CHAPTER 19

IN THE NEXT breath, they were on each other, hands everywhere, stripping away clothes as quickly as they could in the rush to join. Gowns and shirts flew across the cave, followed by boots and shoes and hose, until Eleanor sat on his lap in nothing but her chemise.

Even that was too much. Together, they wrestled at the yards of cloth, drawing the gown up to be rid of it. As her bare legs came into view, Gunnar groaned and dragged her around to face him.

When she shifted, the hem pulled free. Unfettered, she wriggled around and straddled him, the cloth bunched around her waist, his hardness rising against her, barely restrained by the thin linen of his braies. With a growl, Gunnar grabbed her bottom and moved her until he pressed up against the sweetest spot, then followed bare skin up, beneath cloth, over hips and waist, and higher.

And all the while they kissed, wildly, deeply, the hunger so thick and heavy that when they broke apart even for an instant, her belly ached with it. He found her breasts beneath the linen and gathered their weight in his hands and thumbed over the tips, over and over until she couldn't stand the pleasure of it anymore and had to push him away. Chuckling, he let her, then pulled his hands from under the cloth to find hers and guide them to his waist cord. A quick tug, some awkward pushing and pulling, and he was free, against her, flesh to willing flesh, ready to enter her. She closed her eyes, letting the want pour through her.

"Wrap your legs around me."

Richard always said that. A cold weight settled into the middle of all the heat, like a block of ice thrown on a fire, doing little at first until it melted and the water doused the flames.

Eleanor opened her eyes to reassure herself. Not Richard, Gunnar. This was Gunnar, the man she'd dreamed of for years, the man she'd held in her mind and heart, pretending it was he in her bed whenever Richard had come to her. Now he truly was here, in her arms, and she was thinking of Richard? A laugh bubbled up, half sob, bitter with mockery.

Gunnar stilled. "What is it?"

She couldn't tell him. She shook her head and reached for a smile, as she had so many times.

With Richard.

No. No! She refused to let him come fidgeting his way between them. He'd had his turn with her. It was Gunnar's time now. It was *her* time.

She let the smile fade away and fixed her attention on the man before her, running her hands over his bare skin, watching herself trace a path across his rippled chest, up those huge arms, across shoulder and up into curve of massive neck. He was so different. New and yet familiar, so very unlike . . . She pushed back at the name.

"Gunnar," she reminded herself, and threaded her fingers into his too-long curls to pull him close for more of those heated, wild kisses. Eyes wide open so she would remember who this was, she drank him in greedily.

Only Gunnar tasted like this, felt like this, touched like this. His hands wandered over her hips and belly and breasts, baring skin as he worked her chemise up and stripped it over her head to be tossed aside with the rest. Growling, he grabbed her hands and pulled them behind her back, catching her wrists in one hand, forcing her breasts forward to meet his seeking mouth. Unable to touch him, she watched him work back and forth between her nipples, saw his tongue curl around the tips, taking each into his mouth in turn to draw the pleasure from her body. He slipped his free hand down to touch her and fit himself to her. The heat poured through her, left her wet and open. Ready.

"Gunnar. Take me, Gunnar. Now."

"At your pleasure." Holding her gaze with his, he released her hands, grabbed her by the waist, and pushed into her in one driving thrust that tore a gasp from her lips. She grabbed his shoulders, her nails cutting into his skin.

"Big," she breathed when she could say anything at all. They began to move together, gently then harder. He bent to her breasts again, and she closed her eyes and threw her head back, giving herself over to the sensation. Big and hard and so deep in her. Nothing like—

Her eyes snapped open. "Gunnar."

"Aye, Gunnar. It is still I." There was mischief in his eyes as he suddenly lifted her free and twisted around, flipping her down onto the narrow cot. He took a moment, barely a heartbeat, to kick his braies off, and then he was kneeling between her legs, not in her but looking at her so intently she felt herself blushing. She fought the embarrassment and looked back, and what she saw stole her breath.

Gunnar. It was Gunnar. She watched as the mischief faded, replaced by pure, raw heat as his gaze fixed on her quaint. Watched as he dragged her hips up onto his thighs and spread her knees wide to expose her to him. Watched as he rubbed his member over her until it shone with her juices and she was quaking with need.

Watched as he spread her wide with his thumbs and took her again.

Oh, how she'd craved this. She hooked her heels behind his butt and drew him deeper. His hands played over her belly and breasts, stirring her senses, setting her trembling. She rose up on shaky elbows to see how they looked joining, over and over.

"Lie back," he urged. "Close your eyes. Give yourself over to it. To me."

She couldn't, not yet, so she reached to touch the place where his hardness stretched her, her explorations drawing a moan from him that hummed through her core. Her fingers came away slick, and on a whim, she traced a damp line up his flat belly and chest, clear up his neck to his face.

He caught her fingers and sucked them into his mouth, tasting her. A groan ripped from his throat. He fell on her, carrying her down, and as he moved over her, in her, she felt every sinew of her body begin to tighten. Tighter. Closer. So close. If she could shut her eyes . . . But not yet.

He arched back to look down at her, and the move put him just where she needed him to be. His next strokes sent her over the edge, and as her eyes fluttered shut, she arched back hard, pleasure pounding through her as she thrashed.

He stayed with her as the spasms carried her past pleasure to the edge of pain, letting go only when she slipped into pure bliss and her body went limp. His shout echoed off the stones, and as he collapsed atop her, their bodies spent and soaked with sweat, there was only one face in her mind, only one name on her lips. As it should be. As it should always have been.

"Gunnar."

THEY LAY STILL and silent for a long time afterward, holding each other while a nightjar churred in the distance and the fire burned down. The coals had begun to fall into embers when Gunnar finally gave in to one of the many questions that had started prodding at him as soon as his blood had cooled.

"How did Richard die?"

Eleanor stiffened against his side. "No. No, don't."

"Don't what? It is but a simple question."

"And I will answer it, I swear. I will tell you all you wish to know." She pushed up on one elbow, so tense he could have used her as a bowstring. "But not here, and most especially not while I lie in your arms. Please. *Please*."

"*Shh, shh*." He wrapped his arms around her and lifted her more onto his chest so he could better see her eyes in the dim glow from the coals. "You're right. I should not have brought him into bed with us."

"It must be our sanctuary," she said firmly. "Ours alone."

"Aye, our sanctuary," said Gunnar. He was about to pull her down for a kiss when he thought of something, one of the Church tales a monk once told him about a different sanctuary. "You know what they call this place, don't you?"

"No."

"It used to be *Jodene*, for its yew trees, and that is how I still think of it in my head. But as the old tongue faded away, the name shifted, first to Yoden, which was what they called the village, and then to the name they gave the castle, the name it bears now. Eden. This is Eden Dene."

"Eden." She breathed the name in wonder as she leaned down to him. And though the blanket fell forward and hid her face in deepest shadow, he knew she was pleased because could feel her smile as she kissed him.

And his was just as broad.

BRAND STOOD WITH his fists on his hips, staring up the dene toward where Lady Eleanor was poking a fresh log into the fire. "What do you think? It's only been the one night. Do we dare walk back into that mess?"

"She's smiling," said Torvald. Being more surefooted,

he'd clambered partway up the cliff face for a better view, and it was still light enough that he could make out Lady Eleanor's face with no trouble.

"Is she? Well, then, either he's made up with her or she's chased him off entirely and is pleased with herself."

Torvald edged back down from his perch. "She may have decided to go back."

Brand shook his head. "No."

"You can't be certain." Torvald hopped off the last ledge and brushed the rock grit off his hands.

"She's *not* going back," repeated Brand. "Even if I must tie her down. Or tie him down. Or tie them to each other, and the both of them to the rocks. Naked. Face to face."

Torvald chuckled. "I know where Jafri keeps their best rope."

"Good. We may need it," said Brand sourly. "Ah, there comes Gunnar. Let us see what passes."

They watched their friend pick his way down the trail, and they both grinned when Eleanor ran to meet him at the brook's edge.

"That's better," said Brand as Gunnar picked her up and spun her around, then bent over her for a long, possessive kiss. "Come on. Ari planned to go fishing today, and I'm hungry as a bear."

"Imagine that," said Torvald, and they started upstream.

ELEANOR WATCHED IN awe as Brand split, roasted, and ate enough shad to supply a small monastery with Friday dinner, well over twice what Torvald, Gunnar, and she ate put together.

As he stripped the needle bones out of yet another fish, she suddenly realized he was watching back, an amused grin on his face. Blushing, she snapped her mouth shut. "Your pardon, sir. I have forgotten my manners."

All three men laughed.

"You're not the first to stare," said Gunnar. "I used to

wager on how many herrings or eels he could eat at one sitting. I won every time."

"Untrue, my lady," said Brand. "He laid his coin against me the first time. I took half a mark from him."

"No doubt you did. Sir Ari said you liked fish. I just didn't think . . ."

"No one thinks it until they see it. That's what makes it a good wager." Gunnar turned to Torvald. "You could pick up a few extra shillings that way, if you were of a mind."

Torvald nodded. "I just might."

"Well, I'm done for tonight, so no wagers won or lost." Brand popped the last morsel into his mouth and sucked the oil off his fingers. "Lady Eleanor, Ari said you woke up in time to help Jafri sort out your men's horses from the others."

"I did, but . . ." She stopped, confused. "Sir Ari said? How? I thought you and he never saw each other."

"We leave each other messages, my lady. Well, mostly Ari leaves me messages. He can start taking the outlaw horses to market tomorrow, one or two at a time."

"Jafri said he would take them all to different markets so no one will notice where they came from."

"Aye."

"Except for Tunstall's gelding, there is little chance anyone might recognize them," said Eleanor. "The others are Scots horses—and scurfy things they are, too."

"They are that," agreed Brand with a chuckle. "But they'll still be worth a mark or two each. That little black mare is a fine animal. She is yours, correct?"

She nodded. "Her name is Rosabelle."

"She favors her right foreleg," said Gunnar.

"She got caught in the gorse when I tried to escape Tunstall. Jafri put a poultice on it, and it already begins to heal. Richard died of fever last autumn." The last came blurting out unexpectedly, her mind somehow going from poultices and healing to Richard on its own. The three faces around her looked as surprised as she felt. "I'm sorry. I didn't . . ."

"I have been wondering how you came to be here," said Brand.

"I do owe you explanation after all you did."

"But I thought . . ." Gunnar began, but he shook his head. "Never mind. You may as well tell us all together."

She began with that May Day night at Raby, her father's unholy fury, and the way she'd been dragged off to Clementhorpe the next morning before the sun had even cleared the horizon. Brand and Torvald listened patiently, if with frowns, but Gunnar got more agitated with every word, until finally, he shot up off his seat.

"Bikkjusonr!"

"He is her father, Gunnar. Speak with more respect," said Brand.

Torvald caught her eye and answered her unspoken question. "It means son of a . . . female dog."

Gunnar paced back and forth within the circle of firelight, pausing just long enough to kick a cobble that shot off in the dark and cracked against the far wall of the dene. He turned to Eleanor. "He told me you had decided to honor your betrothal of your own accord. He said you were too ashamed to face me, that you went *willingly* to Richard."

"You had just warned me to silence about your curse by telling me the Church would torture you, and that the torture would go on and on without end. My father used exactly that threat, almost as if he knew it would most terrify me." She met Gunnar's stark eyes across the fire circle. "I did what I must to keep him from hunting you down. I went to Richard obediently, but I never went willingly."

Pain rippled across his face, and she knew he understood—that they all understood—and she hurried on before the shame of them knowing could stop her.

"My father left men with Richard, with orders to take you alive if you came near before I produced an heir. They were still with us at Alnwick. When I realized you were at Lesbury, I feared you would try to approach, so I contrived an excuse to make Richard carry me home, and I fled." *An excuse—what a thing to call a babe, even one who never existed.* Still abashed by that lie more than any other she'd told, she wanted nothing more than to curl up and hide behind her hands like a child. Instead she sat up straighter and knotted her fingers together so her hands wouldn't shake, and told of Richard's illness. "It was my fault he died."

"No. The fault lies with that knave who sired you, and with the man he married you to."

"Lord Burghersh made his own decisions," said Brand. "You could not have pressed him to travel if he didn't wish to."

"No, sir, there you are mistaken. Richard made few of his own decisions. My father, York, Bedford, the king: they all tugged him this way and that at their whim. But none twisted his will so much as I. The only time he refused me was when he insisted upon riding on to Burwash, and he did that only because I had bedeviled him so about going home to begin with. No, his death is on my head."

Gunnar stopped his pacing. "Did you say he died in autumn?"

"October." She understood where his thoughts were taking him and hurried to explain. "I wanted nothing more than to fling myself onto Rosabelle and race to find you. But winter was coming, and Richard was my cousin, as well as my husband. I owed him some measure of mourning for that, if nothing else. And I was uncertain of where you were. I decided to have his tomb built while I waited till the weather softened so I could search the denes. But I waited too long." She told them about her father's unexpected arrival at Upton on Severn and what had unfolded since.

"But you're a widow!" blazed Gunnar. "You get to choose for yourself."

"Even I know that is the custom amongst you English," said Brand, his anger finally showing in the set of his jaw.

"Aye. But it is my lord father's custom to get what he

wants even if it means whoring out his children to get it. I am not the only daughter traded for power and riches with no regard for her happiness, just the only one who dared look elsewhere. Had I refused him, I have no doubt he would have beaten me again and then carried me to Percy bound and at sword point. So I feigned agreement to gain his trust, even as I searched for a way to slip his trap. When the king, God save him, summoned him to court, I felt the saints were at last on my side. But no sooner had Westmorland ridden out of my life than Tunstall rode in. And more men died because of me."

"You take far too much on yourself, my lady," said Torvald.

"Aye. You could just as well lay the blame on my shoulders," offered Gunnar. "I was the one who set all this in motion when I rode into Raby for tourney and cheated to win your token."

"The tourney." She met his eyes with a pained apology. "You remind me. One of those in my company was John Penson, from the Castle of Love."

"The squire I helped?"

"Aye. Grown into knighthood, and now lying unburied and unshriven a half-day's ride south of here." *Because of me.* It hung there unsaid at the end of her words.

Sadness and anger tinged the silence that settled over the four of them.

The weight was broken by Brand rising. He whistled, and the raven sailed over from his perch and landed on his shoulder. "You have courage, my lady, more than many men. But I think you two have more to talk through. We will go now."

Torvald lit a rush, grabbed the ale skin, and gave Eleanor a little bow. "My lady."

"God's rest, *messires*."

They returned her blessing and made their way off to their other camp, leaving Gunnar and Eleanor staring at each other, questions and expectations swirling up around them like the sparks from the fire.

"I should never have left you that night in the forest," he said at last. "I put you right into your father's hands."

"You thought to keep me safe."

"I made things worse for you. And then I believed his lies and made them worse yet. I could have ridden after you. I could have stolen you back before you wed. Even afterward, I could have saved you the years of Richard . . ." He closed his eyes against the image that must surely be there. "Why did you not let me carry you away from Burwash?"

"The archers . . ."

"Arrows do not frighten me. We could have done it, Torvald and Ari and I. We would have, somehow, if you hadn't told me to go. I should have taken you anyway. I was supposed to be your champion."

"You were. You are."

"No, I have failed you in so many ways. All these terrible things you say lay at your feet should properly be at mine. It should all come back to me."

"Instead, *I* have come back to you," she said softly. "Dragging along all my sorrows and all my sins. The question is, now that you know what I have done, do you still want me?"

CHAPTER 20

THE QUESTION DRAGGED Gunnar to his knees before Eleanor. He cupped her face in both hands and met those silvery, fire-lit eyes. They reflected back his own pain and shame, but also his hope.

Richard and his ghost be damned. She was his now.

"Foolish woman." He feathered kisses over her brow and cheeks, then covered her mouth. There was a moment of hesitancy and then she melted into him, her soft moan warming his mouth. A deep need welled up, and he rose and held out his hand. "Come lie with me, and I will show you how much I want you."

She let him lead her away from the dying fire to the bed, where they took their time undressing each other, each revealed bit of skin earning long, exploring kisses. Finally they stood clad only in shift and braies, but when Gunnar reached to remove her last garment, she stopped him with a hand to the center of his chest. "Do you have a candle? Or perhaps a lamp?"

He nodded.

"Would you light it? The fire already grows dim."

He raised an eyebrow, but nodded again and turned to find the lamp and the flask of oil. It took him a moment to fill it and trim the wick properly. "When did you become afraid of the dark?"

"I'm not. I just want to be able to see you."

He fished a brand from the fire and touched it to the wick. The flame flared and smoked, then settled into a good, steady light that flickered slightly in the evening air. "Your lamp, m'lady. Where—"

He stopped mid-turn, brought to silence by the sight of her pulling the riband from her hair. She dropped it on the pile of clothes and began unraveling her plait. Gunnar held the lamp high to let the light spill down over her and just watched, wondering if she knew what she was doing to him, letting down her hair before him.

Not that it made the least difference whether she taunted him innocently or a-purpose. He hardened, his tarse raising the front of his braies like a tent. His tongue went clumsy, and he had to work it over his teeth before he could re-form his question. "Where would you like this?"

"There, if you please." She indicated a rock ledge not far from the head of the bed. He stepped past her to wedge the lamp in place and turned back just as she pulled out the last of the plait and raked her fingers up through her hair from underneath, shaking the strands free to spill down past her waist. It was all Gunnar could do not to groan aloud.

Or maybe he did groan aloud, because she gave him a slanted look that made him think that maybe she did know what she was doing, then quietly turned her back to him, presenting that fall of dark silk like a gift. Gunnar stepped up behind her and filled his hands with it, scooping it up to bury his face in the lustrous mass. Faint traces of her musk and spice perfume still clung deep in the tresses, and he inhaled the sweetness as the heavy locks streamed through his fingers.

He regathered her hair, this time into one thick hank that he coiled around his fist and tugged to one side so he could kiss her from ear to edge of chemise and back again. The tender curve where her shoulder met her neck tempted him, and he bit down and sucked. She whimpered, but he didn't stop until he'd marked her.

"You are mine," he whispered, soothing the spot with a kiss.

Eleanor brought her fingers up to the darkening bruise. "I am yours." She turned to look up at him, and her eyes held a glow that made his heart stutter. "I have always been yours, Gunnar."

He almost asked her then if she loved him, but her hands went to the cord at his waist and lust clouded his mind and thickened his tongue. Loosened, his braies slipped over his hips and fell to the ground, and his cock sprang free, swaying as he kicked them aside. He reached for her.

She stepped back, just out of his grasp. "I want to see you first. I need to see you."

She saw him all right: rigid and throbbing so hard his tarse bounced with each beat of his heart. She stood there a long time, just watching it bob, her expression as serious as if she were gazing at some holy relic. It was unnerving, having a woman just stare at his cock like that, unnerving, that is, right up to the point where her tongue flickered out to moisten her lips.

Oh, yes.

She slowly lifted her eyes, raking them over belly, chest, neck, and finally up to meet his, and then, as she held his gaze, she stepped close and silently dropped to her knees.

He groaned as she took the tip, her mouth every bit as hot and silky as he'd known it would be. She lingered, and it quickly became clear he wasn't going to be able to stand this long. It took all his will not to grab her head and force himself deep into her throat. But he gritted his teeth and let her explore at her own pace, and she did, inch by glorious inch, until she took him all and his knees buckled and he swayed, moaning. Her name came out in a strangled plea for release. "Eleanor."

She abandoned him at the last instant, but, no, not really,

for her hand curved around him, the pressure different enough to bring him back from the edge. She came gracefully to her feet but he caught her up and lifted her high to let her slide down his chest. When her feet touched earth, she wrapped her arms around his waist, and laid her head against his chest with a sigh. "Your heart is as strong as your arms."

"Why did you stop?" he asked when he could speak.

"Because I want you in me." She said it so matter-of-factly that he almost laughed.

" 'I want a lamp.' 'I want to see you.' 'I want you in me.' " He cupped her bottom and ground against her, craving the pressure. "You seem very clear about what you want, my lady."

"I am." She thrust back at him, writhing a little as she did, and Gunnar nearly tipped her onto the bed then. "I have put much thought on it. Haven't you?"

"I have," he admitted. "But my wants are simpler than yours, I think."

"And what are they?"

"You naked and spread out before me."

She arched back and looked up at him. "How odd. That is part of my wants, as well."

Was she teasing? He considered her through narrowed eyes and decided she wasn't. "I am already naked, vixen. But I see one impediment to us *both* having our will."

She looked down and plucked at the laces of her chemise. "This? Then it should go the way of your braies."

"Are you certain? It is cooler tonight than it was last night. I think there will be fog."

"You will keep me warm."

"Aye. I will that."

He gathered the cloth and stripped her, and when he had her naked, he lay down on the bed and pulled her down atop him and dragged the blanket up to cover them.

Where last night had been fire and urgent possession, tonight was honeyed seduction. They went back to the beginning, trading slow kisses and slower touches, enjoying the feel and taste as they gradually built toward each other, until at long last the time was right and he pushed her upright and guided her into position.

He was suddenly very glad she'd made him put the lamp near the head of the bed, for it showed him how beautiful she was, poised above him like that, her skin flushed, her legs wide, her quaint slick and ready.

"Naked and spread before one another," he said, and grabbed her waist and slowly pulled her down.

"Gunnar." She gasped his name and threw her head back as he filled her, but even then she kept her eyes open. He didn't understand this need of hers to see everything, but the hunger building on her face left him half crazed with the need to make her yield. He reached for her breasts, teasing the peaks hard, then shifted one hand down to that spot he knew would make her shudder.

Her breath caught in her throat. She pushed at his circling thumb, hips swirling, searching until she found what she liked and settled on it. He smiled as she moved faster, driving toward release, pleasuring both herself and him in one beguiling dance. Her eyes lost their intensity and slowly drifted shut.

"Gunnar," she whispered, almost to herself, and then she arched back and she was there, tightening around him until he thought her strength, her need, would break him.

When it was over she collapsed, and he caught her and pulled her down. As she settled upon him, thigh to thigh, belly to belly, breast to breast, he knew that if there were a way keep her there forever, he would do it, even if it meant spending eternity aching with unslaked need like this. And for a while she granted him his wish, keeping him within her as she slowly came back to herself.

But after a time, she began to move again, unhurried at first, then more insistently, pushing him toward release the way he'd pushed her. He held back as long as he could, hoping she would find release again with him, but in the end she rose up a little, just enough to be able to touch him freely. Her hands, smooth and cool, traced over his chest, and when her nails flicked across his nipples, the near agony of the pleasure arched him off the bed and he came.

She stayed with him, riding him as he spilled into her, his mind emptying with his body, and by the time she'd finished with him, there was little left of him but a deep sense of peace.

But the peace faded quickly after he reached to pinch the lamp out. Memories crept out of the dark and wavered past his vision: Eleanor clinging to Richard in the alley behind Burghersh Hall. Eleanor reaching over to lay a hand on Richard's knee as they rode past at Alnwick.

And behind those, memories of Eleanor touching *him*, taunting *him*, dropping a perfume-laden kerchief that drove *him* half mad with desire.

He knew women did that, used their sex to turn men to their will; he understood that Eleanor had done it to wield what little power she had. But he didn't like thinking she might have used her wiles on him the same way she had on her prick of a husband, and a part of him wondered if she'd lain with him these last two nights to get something from him.

He rejected the idea in the next instant. The only reason the notion was in his head was because she had spoken of Richard, and the only reason she had spoken of Richard was because he'd been fool enough to raise the man's specter in this very bed.

Eleanor was in his arms because the gods wanted her here. She was his, meant to set him free.

And so he simply held her, pushing aside the whispers of doubt as they traded kisses and drifted in each other's arms. The lingering fog was already beginning to glow with light when Gunnar slipped out of bed and sorted out his clothes from the jumble on the ground.

"So soon?" She rolled over and sat up, the blanket pulled up around her breasts. "The nights are too short."

"They will start getting longer in a few days. But perhaps it won't matter."

"Why not?"

"Midsummer magic," he said, and though she cocked an eyebrow in question, he left it there and quickly pulled on his clothes and boots. "Now sleep, and I will see you this evening."

TEARS STREAMING DOWN her cheeks, Eleanor stood in the fog-filtered light of breaking dawn and watched Gunnar being wrenched into the bull's form. It was every bit as horrible as she remembered, the pain hammering him to the ground as his groans gradually shifted into the beast's agonized bellows.

She had ignored his instructions to sleep and instead followed him away from the cave to see exactly this, in the process gaining a new respect for the men who spied for her father's armies. No matter how lightly she trod, every step seemed to crack another twig or rustle another leaf. That Gunnar hadn't caught her amazed her. He must have been too distracted by the approach of this terrible torture.

And he faced it every dawn and dusk with no more complaint than other men offered over washing their hands and faces before dinner. Such strong metal Gunnar must be forged of—he and his friends. More tears streamed down her cheeks, thinking of their courage. Of what they went through. All of them

The bull, fully formed now, lay in a quivering heap where Gunnar had stood only moments before. Its nostrils flared wide as it sucked at the air, but gradually its breathing eased and its muscles grew less rigid. Not long after, it recovered enough to lurch to its feet. Eleanor froze, suddenly realizing she was alone with a beast that could easily kill her if Gunnar had no control. But to her relief, the bull, still far too disoriented to pay her any mind, staggered off in the other direction and vanished into the mist.

Eleanor wiped her cheeks dry, pulled herself together, and started toward the trail that would take her back to camp. But as careful as she'd been to note her way, the shifting fog and light made things look different now. She missed the trail.

When she realized her error, she cut back and forth a few times, searching for the path, but with no result. After a moment's consideration, she decided to follow the edge of the dene seaward until she found another way down. Surely the land fell off as it neared the water, so there should be some easier way down, and then she could always follow the stream back up. Working her way east, she eventually found what appeared to be a gentler slope, with a far gentler path, and started down.

"Would you like some help, Lady Eleanor?"

She jumped and squeaked like Lucy before she recognized the man looming out of the fog. "Sir Ari? Oh, thank the saints. Yes, please, I would like your aid."

"Come this way. There's an easier path." He led her back the way she'd come for a dozen yards, then cut through the brush to where a narrow but well-marked deer path angled down through a thick stand of yews.

"How did you know I was up here?"

"I saw you follow Gunnar," said Ari as he put out a hand to help her down a big step, and she realized he meant he'd seen her as a raven. "You watched him change, didn't you?"

Eleanor nodded. "I needed to see him go from man to bull for myself."

"Why?"

How to explain? "When I saw him change the other way, from bull to man, I was . . . It was as if some magic held me, that I was bewitched or dreaming, or at the very least drunk. It did not seem real. I knew here it was." She touched her heart. "But here . . ." She touched her head.

"You wanted to see it with your wits about you." He started off again. "A wise thing."

She followed him, but continued to explain, as much to herself as to him. "This curse is such a great part of Gunnar, of who he is and why he does what he does. I need to understand it. I need to know what it means when he leaves me each dawn, what he faces—what all of you face, since it seems you are all a part of my life now. It is a cruel thing."

"Aye."

"Is it as bad for you and the others?"

Ari shrugged. "Each suffers in his own way, some worse than others. As terrible as it is for Gunnar, it is far worse for Brand, not just the changing but all that goes with it."

"I don't know what sort of beast he becomes. Nor Jafri."

"No." He came to a fork in the trail and stopped to stare up the track that led toward the head of the dene, then looked the other way, toward the ocean. He ended by looking at her, but his indecision was clear, even in the dimness.

"I know you are the raven on Sir Brand's shoulder," she said, hoping to sway his mind in her favor. "And Torvald, I think, is your white stallion."

Ari shot her a look that was half dismay, half amusement. "Did Gunnar tell you, or are you that quick? Never mind. It matters little how you found out. If you're going to begin wandering away from camp, you probably need to know all of it."

"I have known what Gunnar is for nearly three years and even my cousin, who is both waiting woman and dearest friend, has never heard a word of it. And she never will, nor will anyone else. I swear it, *monsire*."

"I pray you are good to your word, my lady. Follow me." He set off along the seaward path.

They came out in a broader, shallower part of the dene, and Ari led her along the stony stream bank until they rounded a bend. The bright red and yellow of a players' wagon jumped out from amid the green of tree and bramble. No, not a player's wagon, but a bear-baiter's wagon, and inside it—

A beastly roar rattled the air and set the wagon rocking.

Eleanor jumped back, but Ari caught her by the sleeve. "He cannot escape, my lady. Come closer."

She edged a little closer and found herself staring into the almond-shaped eyes of the great bear that stood trapped behind the wagon's iron bars. "Is th-that Sir Brand?"

"No. Never confuse that, my lady. He and the bear are not nearly the same," said Ari as the beast roared again. "This is close enough."

Eleanor had seen bears before, doing tricks on the green or chained to a pole for baiting, but never one as big and with such frightening demeanor. She was quite certain he would eat her whole if given a chance, and as if to prove her right, the animal reached between the bars, raking the air with a paw the size of a trencher and claws as big as grappling hooks.

"Oh." She spread her hands, fingers curved, and matched by sight the distance between her nails and the bear's claws. "Gunnar's scars. Those claws are what marked him."

"They are what have marked all of us, much to Brand's torment. He is not like Gunnar and the rest of us. He cannot keep any piece of himself within the creature, no matter how hard he tries, and thus he knows nothing of what the bear does each day until he slips its hold that night. Fear of what it has done and might do again is what makes him shut himself in that cage each morning."

"How terrible for him."

"More terrible for everyone if he does not. You must stay well away from the beast, my lady."

"Be assured, I will." The bear clawed the air again, straining to reach her. She backed away. "You don't actually bait him, do you?"

"No, but it makes a good guise for travel. A bear-baiter is welcome anywhere. But of course, we are always passing through to somewhere else, by order of Lord Thus-and-such." A twinkle of devilry made Ari look more like a boy than a knight. "We have even used Westmorland's name to move through the west counties."

"Pray my lord father does not hear of it, sir. He would not be pleased." She watched the bear for a little longer, then they started up the dene, headed back toward camp.

"Brand is as big as a bear and roars like one when he angers," she mused aloud as they walked. "Gunnar is clearly a bull in both strength and temperament—calm until he suddenly is not. Torvald is noble and full of quiet fire, like that stallion—and his hair is as silken as the animal's mane. And you—"

"Take care, my lady," warned Ari, chuckling. "If you tell me I have a big beak, I may weep."

"Your beak, sir, is handsome, as you doubtless know. A chattering tongue would be your raven's trait. That and a good deal of mischief-making, I should think."

Ari's laugh echoed off the rocks. "Chattering? I think I shall take offense after all. But you have it right. The spirits follow us according to our natures."

"Then Sir Jafri must be a wolf, for he is lean, hungry-looking, and wary."

"God's knees, you *are* quick."

"Perhaps not so quick as you think," she confessed. "I heard howls outside the castle the night they rescued me. At the time, I thought dog, but . . ."

"There is a dog amongst us, but he is elsewhere now. You heard Jafri because he rode the stallion to the castle, so that when Torvald came back to himself, he would be near enough to keep watch over you until Gunnar and Brand arrived. Jafri is the one who spotted you, with those keen eyes of his."

A sudden flux of tears caught her off guard. *These men saved her, guarded her, knowing nothing of her except that she was Gunnar's.* She blinked furiously to be rid of the tears before they choked her. "I knew already that he saved me. But for all that, I think he does not much like me."

"It is not just you, my lady. He does not easily trust. He and Gunnar keep to the deep wilds for good reason."

"The wolf bounty."

"With the wolves nearly gone, it grows more difficult for him to hide with each passing year. Gunnar and Torvald can escape notice amongst the cattle and horses of any manor with little trouble, and I am always just one amongst many ravens. But if someone heard that there was a man who became a wolf, or one who became a bear, they could hunt them down with little doubt of what they had found."

"And then they would torture them as devils. I understand, sir. No one will learn of them from me."

"I think I do believe you, Lady Eleanor." They reached a waterfall that tumbled down through a gap too narrow to pass, and Ari pointed to the way they would go around.

"You asked if I hurt like the others." He stayed close at hand as she clambered over the rocks, ready to catch her. "For me, the torture lies not in the changing—though I would happily cut off my right arm and hand it to you if that would let me be done with it—but in the magic surrounding it. I am fey, my lady. Born to magic."

"A sorcerer?"

"A seer, when it suits the gods to send me visions. But Cwen's magic has somehow muddled my own. The visions come less often and less true with each passing year."

She reached a broad area from which she could see the section of the dene where Brand and Torvald were making their camp, and the sight of the pen full of horses reminded her that he was supposed to be taking animals to market, not playing squire to her. But this was the first time one of them was speaking to her about the curse so openly, and she wasn't willing to give up just yet.

"Is there nothing that can be done about your magic, *monsire*?"

"Only breaking the curse."

"Breaking it?" Excitement coursed through Eleanor. "I didn't know it could be broken."

"Of course it can. Did Gunnar not tell you?"

"He told me how the curse was laid, and that two had escaped it, but not that they had broken the curse. I thought he meant they had somehow died despite it." She could tell by the way Ari rolled his eyes that he was disgusted at Gunnar for some reason and tried to make an excuse. "Perhaps he didn't know they broke it?"

"He knows. We have all known for more than three hundreds of years, since the first of us found freedom."

"Then tell me, how is it broken? Can I help him somehow?" He considered her for so long, she thought she might have said something foolish. But it didn't matter. She pressed. "Truly, sir, I will do anything. Just tell me. Please. I love him. I want to help him."

A slow smile dawned across his face. "Ah, fair lady. You have brought joy to this tired heart today."

"How is that?"

"Simple. You have said the magic words."

CHAPTER 21

GUNNAR HAD HIS amulet and his woman who loved him. All was in place—and yet something wasn't right.

Ari sat with Jafri outside the cave where Lady Eleanor slept the day away, barely able to concentrate on the game of dice they were playing. His left hand burned as though he'd poured salt in the wounds. He raked at it through the glove, but the leather kept him from finding much relief. He made so many mistakes and poor bets that Jafri finally scooped up the dice and put the cup behind his back.

"Hey."

"You're going to owe me the price of a good destrier if you don't stop," said Jafri. He dropped his voice low. "What's wrong? Is there something about her?"

Ari glanced toward the cave and shook his head. "I don't know."

"You told me things are good. That she is ready."

"She is. It's just that . . . It is not right. None of it. I've known for months that something is coming, but I cannot . . . It should not be this difficult." Wincing, he ripped his glove off and stripped away the bandage so he could get to the itch.

"Balls, Ari. What have you done to yourself?" Jafri gaped at his bloodied palm with its lines of knife cuts, some so close together that the skin between them hung in tatters. "You are flayed. You will cost yourself a hand if you keep that up. Your visions cannot be worth such a price."

"But there lies the problem—I have no visions. None. I have been calling and calling, and they won't come. They haven't come in months. Nay, years. I think the last one was the one that got me Gunnar's amulet. Perhaps one after that."

"Then you're not meant to have them right now. Or you're trying too hard. Let them go, and when the time is right, the gods will give them back to you."

"I cannot wait for the gods. We are on the brink of something. I sense it and I don't know what it is, or even whether it is good or bad. I feel like a blind man groping his way around a dungeon. All is black on black. I must . . . Aw, shite." He pushed to his feet. "I'm going back to the pool again."

"Don't. Let it go."

"I cannot. We need to be ready, and it is my lot to discover what we must be ready for. Leave a message for Brand, will you. He needs to know. And he may need to come fetch the raven. His wing . . ." He held up his hand.

"What about Gunnar?" asked Jafri.

"I don't know," said Ari. "I told the lady all would be well. Hope for her sake and Gunnar's that it is."

So he set off to go slice his hand open yet again in the hope that his blood would buy him a single glimpse into the future.

Just one. Please, Vör, grant me just one.

ELEANOR WAS WAITING at the stream's edge when Gunnar came back that evening, and she wore a look that made the hairs rise on the back of his neck.

"What is it?"

"You are late. Again."

He grinned at her little jest. "It is a fault, my lady."

"You have many faults, good sir, one being that you are a bull." She reached into the neck of his shirt and found his amulet. He grabbed to stop her, but she pressed it into his chest. "But even so, I do love you."

His heart stuttered and began to race. "Eleanor."

"I love you, Gunnar," she said again.

Free. He was free. Yes, oh yes, oh yes.

Nothing happened.

Eleanor tugged the amulet out where she could see it. Her expression was pure confusion, but a cold, distant part of Gunnar understood.

She wasn't the one.

Whatever she thought she felt, whatever he wanted . . . It wasn't his turn after all.

"I don't understand," she murmured. "Ari said this is how it is done."

"Ari? He put you up to this?" Disappointment flashed to anger in an instant. "He should have kept his nose out of it."

"I asked him how to help you. He said that all I must do is say I love you with your amulet in hand and the curse will be broken."

Interfering ass. "Not just say it. *Mean* it."

"But I do mean it. I love you."

Anger at Ari. Anger at Eleanor. It didn't matter. He lashed out. "There is no use in lying."

"'Tis no lie," she snapped back. "I love you."

"If that were true, the curse would be broken. That is how the magic works. Either you lie, or you just think you love me. But you do not."

"Do not dare to tell me how I feel. I love you."

"Lust is not love. Need is not love. Wanting to escape your father and Burghersh and Percy is not love."

"I could escape my father by becoming a nun. It would

be far easier than dealing with you and a cave. But I *want* to be here. I risked all to be here. I know what love is, and I love you. I have loved you for years. I did everything I did because I love you."

"Let Richard bed you, you mean? Oh, yes, that is surely love, my lady, letting another man fuck you like that."

She slapped him.

In his madness, he barely felt the blow, but it was enough to stop his mouth. He turned and walked away.

His seething rage carried him up the dene until the pool and upper falls blocked his way. He stood a long while, watching the water gush through the narrow gap and into the pool below, letting its roar drown the roar in his head.

Why couldn't Ari have left things alone? At least there had been hope. Now even that was gone once more.

Gunnar ripped off his clothes and plunged into the pool.

The water wasn't as cold as he wanted or needed. Last night's fog notwithstanding, the weather had been gentle of late, and the water lacked the bite that might have cooled his wroth. He swam beneath the fall and stayed there, letting it beat at him in the hope that would help. But the water chattering against his skull sounded like mad laughter, as if the very spirit of the dene mocked him.

And well it should. He had a woman who, if she did not truly love him, at least did not fear what he was, who was willing to welcome him into her bed, into her arms, into that sweet, sweet body. He should be happy with her gift. Instead, he'd all but called her whore. His disgust with himself grew and exceeded the disgust he felt for Eleanor's lie. He roared his agony back at the torrent. "She was mine!"

"I *am* yours." The words echoed back to him, as faint and watery as a poppy dream. He ducked under the surface to wash them out of his ears, then pushed toward the edge of the pool.

Dream met reality in the moonlight of Eleanor's eyes and the stubborn set of her jaw. She stood at water's edge, waiting for him, and as soon as he saw her, he knew it didn't matter. Any of it. Not Richard, not the years of waiting, not even his amulet and the prospect of freedom. It all faded away in the way she looked at him.

With forgiveness. With passion. With certainty.

With love.

How could he have been such a fool? "Eleanor."

She stripped out of her gown and hose more quickly than he would have thought possible. She soon wore only her linen kirtle, and then that, too, flew aside, leaving her clad only in a robe of pale light, like Máni's bride.

She waded into the pool and headed straight for him. As the water closed over her hips and back, she gasped at the chill, but kept coming.

"I am yours," she whispered as she moved into his arms and kissed him. She was fire in water, heat in the dark winter of his soul, and he burned with a need that went beyond reason or thought. He pulled her close, locking her to him, and the warmth of her body hardened him despite the cool water. When she felt him rise against her, she curled one leg around his waist, lifted herself up, and pulled him in. As she began to move on him, she leaned back in his arms to meet his eyes. "Surely you must know that I am yours."

Gunnar's gaze fell to the line where the water lapped at her body in a delicate series of arcs that spoke of womanliness in a way that he'd never seen. Fascinated, he put one finger to where the waterline curled against the side of her breast, then followed it around the full mound, into the valley between, and over the other breast. She shuddered and pressed to him, and he reached down and touched her where they joined.

She shattered instantly, arcing back again his arm, and her pleasure took him over the edge with her, not in the violent release he usually knew, but something different. More tranquil. More satisfying. They clung to each other, both trembling, the water around them fracturing into a million shards of moonlight then coming back together.

Like his heart.

"I had a wife back in Vass, all those years ago," he began as their bodies finished with each other. It was the wrong thing to speak of at such a time, but something dragged it out of him anyway. "She betrayed me with a man who was first my friend and then my enemy, and when I went to take her back, he and I fought. In the midst of battle, a fire started. I could do nothing to help Kolla but listen to her die. I thought of her when the fire began at Richmond. I thought of her when you chose Richard over me. And every time you say you love me . . ." Shame strangled his voice.

"She told you she loved you and then betrayed you, so when I say the words, you think of her, too, and you think I lie like she did," Eleanor finished for him, understanding in that quick way of hers. "When the magic fails, you are certain of it.

"I am not she. Be certain of *me*, Gunnar, not this bauble, no matter what power it is supposed to have." She flattened her hand over the little bull that lay against his breast and rose up to kiss him, whispering against his mouth, "Magic or not, be certain that I love you. That I always have and always will."

There was a crackle, like distant lightning, and the water began to glow and surge around them. Pain slammed through Gunnar's body, and the bull rose up within him.

He shoved Eleanor away in an effort to protect her, but the bull receded, then rose again, receded then rose. Each time the pain wracked him, as though the bull's spirit couldn't get out. Each time he felt his body being ripped, as though the creature tore at him from within with dull horns.

"Odin, please!" The bull rose again, tearing at him in its need to escape. Gunnar's knees buckled with the agony of it and he sank into the pool, screaming. Water filled his mouth and nose. He began to drown.

"Gunnar! Oh, God, help!" screamed Eleanor. She grabbed for him, caught his hair, and dragged him up. He gasped for air then slipped under again as she shifted for a better hold under his arms. She hauled him back up again. "Help! Someone help us!"

She struggled toward the water's edge, but the closer she got, the less the water supported Gunnar's bulk. Thrashing, he slipped away from her once more, and by the time she could pull him back, he'd gone limp, and his eyes had rolled back in his skull. She gripped his water-slick skin and leaned back, hauling with all her strength, then shifted her grip and hauled again. Inch by inch she dragged him, until she had him in the shallows and his nose and mouth were clear. All the while the pool, glowing with that eerie light, boiled around them.

"Breathe. Oh, please, breathe." She shook Gunnar until he groaned and gasped for air. A quick thanks to Heaven crossed her lips, and then another shout. "Help! Help us!"

"What magic is this you wield?" The voice hissed out of the darkness, dripping with venom.

Eleanor twisted around to see a dark-robed figure stride out of the trees, face hidden deep within a hood. Fear, deeper than any she'd ever known, rippled through her, and though she'd only heard the name that once, so long ago, she didn't need to be told who this was. "Cwen."

"I say again, what magic is it you use?"

Eleanor scrambled up to put her naked body between the witch and Gunnar. "No magic. Only love."

"That is not enough."

"It is. He has his amulet and he has my love. That is all he needs. Begone, witch. Your power over him is done."

"No, my lady, not nearly done." Cwen pulled a slender chain out of her robes and dangled a silver charm from which blinked a single red stone eye. Eleanor's heart sank as the witch chuckled in delight. "Good. You know it. The Old Ones led me to it not long after the fire that brought you and he together. I had it remade. The one your bull wears is a twin, a false copy placed where the raven would find it."

A moonshadow passed over Cwen, drawing her gaze skyward.

"Yes, you, Raven, and my thanks to you and your visions. You make things so simple." The bird circled awkwardly, squawking, and Cwen threw her head back to laugh. Her hood fell way, revealing her face.

"Miriam?" Eleanor gaped at the woman who had dressed her mother's hair for so many years, who had dressed her own more times than she could count.

"Yes, Miriam," said Cwen, slipping the amulet back into her robes. "Most trusted Miriam, weaving spells with your own hair to summon the bull back to you. Whispering in your father's ear to warn him of the bull-knight who was spreading your legs in the woods, after the magpie and I watched you rutting with him. Telling him he must force you to marry before anyone could discover your sin, even if he must beat you into it. I hope your husband got as good use of you as your bull does."

"But you're dead," said Eleanor, still too stunned to care about the hatefulness spewed at her. "I saw you die."

"You saw me fall and watched them drag me off. You never saw me die. Nor did they." Cwen paced a few steps back and forth. "It is almost a shame the wolf and raven spotted those outlaws so quickly. It would have been most entertaining to watch your bull had Lord Tunstall's men raped you. He would never have forgiven himself."

"Just as you have never forgiven yourself for your son's death."

It was only a guess, but Cwen's lip curled into a snarl. "Do not speak of what you do not know."

"I know enough to tell you that their pain does not lessen yours. It never will."

"And yet I do enjoy it so." The grin that twisted Cwen's face was like some perversion of saintly ecstasy. "To take away their hope and their future the way they took away mine gives me such delicious pleasure. It is nectar to my soul, watching them ache from my vengeance. And this one has been especially juicy, eating his own heart out with little help from me and much from you. Best of all was when he realized how willingly you spread your legs for that husband of yours."

"Any willingness came from my love for Gunnar." The water stirred with her words, lapping at Eleanor's heels where she stood at its edge. She understood very little of magic, good or evil, but she realized she must indeed hold some power in her love. If so, it was her only weapon, and she must wield it like a sword. She straightened, feeling suddenly potent in spite of her nakedness. "It drives you mad, doesn't it, that a woman could love any of them the way I love Gunnar."

"Love him?" Cwen sneered down at Gunnar, who lay at Eleanor's feet still laboring to breathe. "He is a bull. You lie with a beast. Your Church would burn you if they knew it."

"And you alongside me, witch. In my arms, Gunnar is only a man. The man I love." The water pulsed with light, a little stronger each time she spoke the word. Gunnar moaned and stirred behind her.

But Cwen heard him, and her eyes went to the water. She clutched at the amulet beneath her gown as though to assure herself that it was still there. "This is not possible. The true charm is mine."

"The true charm is love," said Eleanor. The glow got brighter, and Gunnar groaned. "I love him with all of my heart."

"There must be more to it. How do you work this magic of yours? Tell me."

"I could tell you the whole night through, old woman, and you would not hear it through your bitterness. There is nothing more than love."

"Liar!" Cwen drew back her hand.

"No!" Gunnar surged up and dragged Eleanor down just as a bolt of lightning sizzled past. She screamed as she fell, and he caught her and rolled clear of the water just as the lighting struck the pool and danced over its surface.

Cwen pulled her hand back to strike again. Gunnar curled over Eleanor, shielding her with his body.

A fearsome roar echoed off the rocks and Brand came charging out of the dark, sword high, Torvald on his heels.

"You!" There was a boom and a flash as bright as the sun.

"I am blinded," shouted Torvald. "Where is she?"

Mad laughter echoed through the dene, coming from nowhere and everywhere at once. As Brand roared his fury to the skies, the wolf appeared out of nowhere and shot past them, snarling, into the forest.

"Guard them." Brand crashed off after the wolf, hacking at the bushes as he went. "Show yourself, witch." The sounds of their hunting faded into the forest.

Torvald backed toward Gunnar and Eleanor, turning and twisting to watch the whole area. "Can you move?"

"Yes," said Eleanor, sitting up. "But Gunnar . . ."

The effort to save her seemed to have used the last of his strength, leaving his body more pain-wracked than before, every muscle a knot.

"I love you," said Eleanor, trying the only thing she knew. The water boiled and heaved, seeming to reach toward Gunnar. He jerked away, clenching his teeth against the scream that rose from his gut.

"Forgive me. Oh, God, what can I do?" She looked to Torvald. "Please, there must be something I can do."

"If there is, I do not know it." Torvald sidled over to the pile of clothes she'd abandoned. Catching her kirtle on his toe, he kicked it up to his shield hand and tossed it to her. "Dress, my lady. We may have to run."

"I will not go without him," she said, but she started gathering her gown. As she was about to pull it over her head, the raven came fluttering down out of the night sky, something shiny in its beak. He dropped it at the edge of the pool and landed a few feet from Eleanor with an excited *kaugh*.

"Oh. Oh. God's toes, 'tis his bull." She dropped the gown and dove for the amulet. "Ugh. It is sticky. I think it is blood."

"The witch's, no doubt," said Torvald. "He surely tore it from her neck, else she would not have given it up. Do not put it to Gunnar that way, my lady. It will be tainted by the blood magic she works."

"Of course." She quickly rinsed it in the pool, using the edge of her sleeve to scrub it clean before she threw herself at Gunnar. Heaving him onto his back, she held the newly washed bull to his chest with both hands. "I love you, Gunnar the Red, even knowing what you are."

He arched back like a bow, bent nearly in half, his muscles so tight she thought he would crack his spine. Spasms ripped through his body, setting him writhing and thrashing like a man having a mad fit, and she recognized that wherever Cwen was, she was trying to counter this. Eleanor fought to keep the amulet in place against his skin. "I do love you. I will not let her win."

Pain exploded through her arms, throwing her back. Ghostly strands of dark smoke poured out of Gunnar, swirled in the moonlight, and wove together, forming a bull that swelled around him and rose into the air. The beast threw back its head, and bull and man bellowed their agony together, a long keening sound that rose and rose. And then the bull vanished, leaving behind only silence and a gleam of dark mist. And Gunnar, limp and unmoving.

Arms too numb to support her, Eleanor crawled over to him on her knees. "Gunnar. Gunnar, please wake up."

Slowly, so slowly, Gunnar pried his eyes open. He lay there staring up at the moon, bright overhead. "It is gone."

"Are you certain?" asked Torvald.

Gunnar reached deep within, trying to find some trace of the bull's spirit, but there was nothing but a strange and wonderful emptiness where the beast had passed. Stunned, he whispered again, "Gone. I am free."

Rain, warm as summer, dropped onto his chest. He turned his head toward a faint sound and discovered it was not rain, but tears.

"Don't cry, sweet lady. You have saved me." He held out his arms and Eleanor came to him, curling down onto his chest, weeping. "Don't cry, love."

"I will cry if I want to," she whispered as Torvald silently drew her gown over their naked bodies. "They are tears of joy."

They were still clinging to each other, Torvald standing over them like a guardian angel, when Brand came back. He took one look at them and started gathering the rest of their clothes.

"I wish I could leave you to each other, but I cannot." He dropped the clothes by their heads. "Dress yourselves. I could not find Cwen. We must leave this place."

BY FIRST LIGHT, they were packed and ready, waiting on the edge of the dene for dawn to shift the others so they could set out. As on the journey to Burwash, only Ari and Torvald would go with them because they could best hide amongst men and their beasts.

But there would be one difference this time. At least, Gunnar hoped there would. As sunrise approached, his trepidation grew, until it felt like an entire hive of bees had taken up residence in his belly. If he changed here, now . . .

"I should move away from her, just to be certain," he muttered in Norse.

"And miss watching the sun rise in your woman's eyes for the first time in nearly six hundreds of years? If you can do it, you are a stronger man than I, Gunnar *inn rauði*. I could not." Brand checked the lashings on the packhorse for the dozenth time and thumped the animal on the rump. He switched to English. "I am the one who must go just now. Fare you well, Gunnar. Lady Eleanor."

"Fare you well, my captain. There will always be a place for you, for all of you, wherever we land," Gunnar vowed.

"Always, *monsire*," echoed Eleanor.

"Your first duty is to each other." Brand started down into the dene, toward where the bear wagon stood. "See to that and the rest will sort itself out."

As Brand disappeared, Eleanor slipped her arm around Gunnar's waist. He pressed a kiss to the top of her head. "Are you ready?"

"Are you?"

"Only for the last six hundred years."

A little later, with the sun just below the horizon, he took Eleanor's hands in his.

"If I start to change, run."

She nodded. "I will. But you won't."

He looked over his shoulder to Torvald, who stood several yards away, still guarding against Cwen, and to the raven who sat on the ground nearby, ready to take Torvald's place. "She is stubborn."

Torvald nodded. "Ari will see her safely away. But he won't need to." He glanced to the east. "Your pardon, my lady." He stripped off his braies, the last item he wore, and stuffed them in the saddlebag with his other clothes. "Here it comes."

Light burst over the distant sea. The sounds of his friends struggling with their changing faded to nothing as Gunnar stared into the sun until he could no longer bear it. Even then he could barely tear his eyes away to turn to Eleanor.

But thank the gods he did. Brand was right. There was nothing as sweet as the sun in Eleanor's eyes. It set them flashing and gilded her cheeks, even the spot where Cwen's magic had left its mark. He touched her hair and felt the early warmth. She was beautiful. She was his.

With a shout of victory, he picked her up and spun her, shouting to the sky, "I take this woman as my wife, Freya, to hold as my own from this *day* forward. Let all men witness it and know that I will give her my sword when we are safe."

She threw her head back and laughed, a joyous sound that went straight to his heart. He spun her again, more slowly, as she spoke her vows back to him, "And I take you, Gunnar, as my wedded husband, to have and hold in sickness and health, for fairer or fouler, for richer or poorer, for all the days and nights of my life. We are wed."

"We are wed. I would bed you this instant," he growled, "but we must ride." Instead, he kissed her, a quick, thorough buss that promised more.

"I am witness that you are man and wife," said Ari as he picked himself up off the ground. "By the gods, it is good to see you, Gunnar. We have much to talk about, but right now I would much like to congratulate your bride."

"Later, and with clothes on," said Gunnar. "We must be away from here. You dress, I'll saddle the horse."

They threw things together quickly, and Gunnar handed Eleanor up onto Rosabelle. As he checked the girth one last time, he looked up at his wife. His *wife*. "You are certain of this?"

She nodded. "Trust me."

"I have little choice, my lady. You own my heart." He swung up on his horse and they set out for Durham.

Only when they were away from the dene and in open country where they could be certain no one was around did they begin to relax a little, although they kept up a fast pace, pushing the horses hard. At some point, Ari started asking questions about what had passed with Cwen. Eleanor offered ready answers, but Gunnar was confused.

"Don't you remember everything that happens when you're the bird? That's what Brand told me."

"I usually do," said Ari. "But last night is a fog. That is what bothers me, that something so important would vanish from my mind, bird or not. Tell me exactly what happened."

Between them, Gunnar and Eleanor put together a complete accounting of the night's events from the moment Eleanor waded into the pool to when she used the true amulet to free Gunnar. Ari listened intently, scratching at his gloved hand, the creases on his forehead growing deeper with every word. "You say the amulet was bloody."

"Aye, Torvald said you—the raven," she corrected herself, "probably snatched it off Cwen's neck." Eleanor flicked her hand at a fly that buzzed around her face. "He told me it would be tainted and that I should wash it off in the pool before I let it touch Gunnar."

"And you did?"

She nodded.

"And that is all of it? You're certain?"

"Yes," said Gunnar.

"No," said Eleanor suddenly. Her eyes widened. "She thanked you for your visions. When she was talking about having the amulet remade, she saw the raven fly overhead and thanked you for your visions. She said you made it simple."

"Visions. Blood." Ari turned the words over and over. He was still worrying at them when the walls of Durham came into view at midday. "My visions. Her blood. Shite."

"What?" asked Gunnar.

"I think I . . . I have to go back. Can you—?"

"We are fine. Durham is in sight. We will soon have Percy's men all around us. She will not dare come near again. Go."

Ari tipped his head to Eleanor. "Your pardon, my lady. But there is something I must learn."

"Then learn it, but be ware, sir. You still owe me my bride's kiss."

"And you will have it, my lady. My vow."

"Go on," urged Gunnar. "Go!"

They watched Ari gallop off, and then turned to each other. A long, silent moment hung between them, and they turned toward Durham.

Now came the troublesome part.

CHAPTER 22

      ·

TEN DAYS LATER, Ralph de Neville, Earl of Westmorland, stood in the meadow outside Raby Castle and stared at the two-dozen tents pitched on his land. It looked like a bloody siege camp, what with flags flying and shields arrayed to show their owners' arms.

He'd come home from court to find them there, and only the fact that the biggest tent belonged to Henry Percy, plus a rumor that Eleanor was present, had kept him from torching the whole mess the first night. He'd ignored them for a full day, and then Percy had sent an invitation so oddly worded, he couldn't resist.

So he was here, as was his wife, who had been part of Percy's strange invitation. "Have you figured out what the puppy wants yet?"

"No. But if you call him puppy to his face, you may find yourself bitten."

"He has no teeth."

"Likely he has simply not shown them to you yet. Shall we see what he wants?"

"Of a certs." Neville put out his arm and led his wife toward the puppy's tent.

"HE COMES, MY lord, and quickly."

Henry Percy looked up from the chessboard. "Just Westmorland?"

"He and his countess, my lord, with only her groom as escort."

"Keep the groom well away from my tent—along with everyone else. I want utter privacy." Henry glanced around to all the people in the tent, his gaze landing at the end on Eleanor's unsmiling face. "Are we ready, my lady?"

She took a deep breath and blew it out between pursed lips. "Yes, my lord."

"Send them in."

The varlet disappeared, and a moment later, the tent flaps opened wide and Henry's steward intoned: "Ralph, Earl of Westmorland, and Joan, Countess of Westmorland."

Westmorland blew into the tent like a whirlwind, half dragging his wife, who quickly shook him free and regained her composure. Henry grabbed Eleanor's hand, and they met her parents mid-tent and did courtesy before Westmorland could take it all in.

"Eleanor." The earl and his lady said it at the same time, each putting a different tenor on it, the lady's pleased at seeing her and the lord's less so. Then Westmorland saw Gunnar. "You."

"Me." Gunnar shoved his bishop forward to take Henry's knight, and then rose and bowed slightly. "My lord. My lady."

"I hope you've married her, Percy, or this knave will surely try to steal her away."

"Oh, I've married and consummated, my lord. Most completely and thoroughly." Henry shot his bride a glance that made her blush like a summer apple.

"And I have married and consummated as well," said Eleanor.

"What?" Westmorland's face flashed through a series of emotions that settled on something dark. "What goes on here? Explain yourselves."

Eleanor's courage wavered in the face of her father's anger. Convincing Henry and Lucy to follow this mad plan of hers had been difficult enough—especially Lucy. Convincing her father . . . But she looked at Gunnar and remembered all she'd gone through to get to this point, and straightened her spine.

"It is simple enough, my lord. I married the man I love."

"And I married the woman I love," said Henry. "They simply were not each other."

Lady Joan looked puzzled. "You have not married each other?"

"No, *madame*," said Eleanor.

The countess looked to Gunnar. "I take it she married you, *monsire*."

"That would be correct, my lady," said Gunnar.

"You!" Westmorland's eyes narrowed, and he whirled on Eleanor. "Was it not enough to spread your legs for him in the forest like some tinker's whore?" He drew back his hand to strike. "I warned you—"

Before he could finish, Gunnar was between them, her father's collar bunched in his fist. He jerked Westmorland close, lifting him onto his toes, and glared down at him. "Earl or not, you will not speak to my wife so. Nor will you ever again strike her."

"Strike her?" Lady Joan rounded on her husband. "When did you strike her?"

"Never."

"Liar! He beat her into marrying Richard le Despenser, my lady, when he knew she wished to marry me." Gunnar released Westmorland with a shove that nearly put the older man off his feet. "That is how her nose was broken."

"Eleanor! You told me you walked into a door."

"Yes, *madame*. I did tell you that. And I told you I was pleased to marry Henry Percy, as well. They were both lies told to avoid my father's ire."

"Ralph!"

"She defied me and dishonored the Neville name."

"You would not listen to me," said Eleanor. "I never wanted Richard or Henry. Your pardon, Henry—"

Percy waved off the insult with a grin.

"But I did want Gunnar. I wanted him all along. So when I left to go to Durham to be wed, I instead set out to find Gunnar. To my good fortune, he found me." She quickly told about Tunstall and the loss of her men and poor John Penson.

Paling, Lady Joan sagged down onto one of the stools at the chess table. Eleanor knelt beside her. "Sir Gunnar saved me, my lady. As always, he was my champion."

"Tunstall would never have taken you prisoner had you done as you were told," grumbled Westmorland. He glared at Gunnar. "You will never see a penny of Eleanor's dowry."

"Oh, Ralph, be quiet," snapped Lady Joan. "Lucy, are you truly married to Percy?"

"Aye, my lady. As he said, married and consummated."

"I have loved Lucy for years, my lady," said Henry.

"I thought it was a flirtation. If you care for her, why on earth did you agree to marry Eleanor?"

Henry's eyes went to Lucy and he shrugged. "It seemed the only way at the time."

The countess shook her head. "Perhaps Eleanor is fortunate to avoid the match after all. But you are foolish, children. So very foolish. I may understand what you have done, but the king will not. When he hears how rashly you have acted, his fury will know no bounds."

"Then I suggest we don't tell him, my lady," said Henry.

"Nonsense," said Westmorland. "Of course we must tell him."

"What Henry meant is that we should tell him what he wishes to hear," said Eleanor. "That Eleanor de Neville married Henry Percy, and that Lucy married Sir Gunnar of Lesbury."

"You propose to trade spouses?" demanded her father.

"No, my lord. I propose we trade selves. That I henceforth will be known as Lucy, while Lucy is known as Eleanor. The king has not seen either of us for a good many years," said Eleanor. "And we were in Northumberland for so little time last year that no one there will know. And with my nose . . ."

"You do look even more alike than ever," said Lady Joan thoughtfully.

"Joan, you cannot be . . . God's toes. Even if I were inclined to go along with this—and I am not—a Percy cannot be married to the bastard daughter of my brother."

"Pardon, my lord, but I already *am* married to her," said Henry. "And I will stay that way."

"I will not tolerate it!"

"If I am willing to feign that Lucy is Eleanor and Eleanor is Lucy," Lady Joan continued, "little difference it should make to you which of them is wed to Percy. They are both your daughters, after all."

Eleanor and Lucy both gasped, and Neville's face turned as scarlet as a robin's breast. "Nonsense, Joan. She is my brother's get."

Lady Joan dismissed that with a wave. "Nonsense yourself. Lucy is as clearly yours as Eleanor is, and I have known it since the day you brought her into my household to serve. As I say, if the world knows her as Eleanor de Neville, if *we* confirm her so . . . then so she is."

"And so I named her to the priest who married us, my lord," said Henry Percy. "The register says Henry Percy married Eleanor de Neville."

"What about you?" Westmorland challenged Gunnar. "There cannot be two Eleanors de Neville running around England."

"I already begin to call my wife Lucy, my lord, although it is difficult to remember," said Gunnar. "Our marriage is not yet recorded, but when it is, it will show her as Lucy fitz Thomas, married to me before two witnesses."

"This is an outrage. You will be found out and declared excommunicate, all of you. And us for supporting the lie." He turned to his wife. "The king will know something is amiss as soon as you stop asking for Percy's title back."

"Then I will not stop. If this is to work, I must throw the weight of my station behind the new Eleanor as firmly as it was behind the old. As must you, husband."

"And if it works, I will owe Westmorland much good-will," said Percy.

"It will not work. People can tell them apart."

"Not so easily now that their noses match. It is ironical, is it not, that in beating Eleanor into marrying one man she did not want, you gave her what she needs to keep you from forcing her into marrying another she does not want." Lady Joan raised her chin, managing to look down her nose at her husband despite the fact she barely reached his shoulder. "You must give the proper dowry to the new Eleanor, just as you would have the old. And of course, there will be lands for the new Lucy and Sir Gunnar."

"He already has lands of his own at Alnwick," grumbled Westmorland. "Let Percy give him more."

"They cannot live so near each other, Ralph, lest people note the deception. You must give Sir Gunnar lands elsewhere. Where is entirely up to you, but they *will* be given. She is our daughter, even if we pretend otherwise for her happiness."

"Happiness should have nothing to do with marriage," said Westmorland.

Lady Joan's expression went flat. "I will keep that in mind, my lord, the next time you come to my bed.

"I didn't mean . . . Joan . . . Shite. When did I stop being earl?"

"You have not," Lady Joan reassured him. "But your

heavy hand has earned you penance. Consider this the beginning of it, and tell Sir Gunnar and his wife what estate they will have."

"Bah. Let me think." Westmorland paced the tent, mumbling to himself, then blurted out, "Penrith. There is an open holding in Penrith."

"Is it a good estate?" asked Lady Joan. "I will not have you trying to starve them out from spite."

"Six knight's fees, with a good profit each year, and if he earns my trust, he will have charge of expanding the castle."

"Excellent." Lady Joan turned to Gunnar. "*Monsire*, what think you of Penrith?"

"I was once in Penrith, long ago. It was a decent enough place." He tugged Eleanor around to face him. "And what of you, *Lucy*? Will you be happy in Penrith?"

"I think, my lord husband," she said, moving into his arms, "that wherever you are is my home and my heart, and there I shall be happy. For I do love you."

"And I, you. Kiss me, wife."

"An excellent idea," said Henry Percy, and grabbed his new-made Eleanor.

"Oh, good God," said Westmorland, and stalked out of the tent.

Epilogue

"THEY ARE FINE, sturdy boys," said Ari, inspecting the new-born and the toddler who had been brought to the solar by their nurses. They both had their father's look to them but for the cap of black hair on each that harkened to their mother. "And you both look well."

"We are," said Gunnar.

"I am better than well," said Lady Lucy. Ari was having problems with that name, this being the first time he'd visited in the dozen years since the two women had traded places. "It took so long for me to catch the first time, I feared we would not have another, but here we are."

"And both born since Westmorland died," said Gunnar. "A part of me suspects the old bastard prayed against us while he yet breathed." Gunnar motioned for the women to take Peter and John back to their nursery. "Now perhaps we can catch up with Percy and Eleanor."

"Why? How many do they have?"

"Seven," said Lucy.

"He told me he aims for an even dozen," said Gunnar. "I think he set out simply to aggravate Westmorland by turning out as many babes as possible. Now he realizes he can breed an army of his own. Have some more ale?"

Ari held out his cup while Gunnar poured. "Does the new earl know of your, um, exchange?"

"I think not," said Lady Lucy. "Richard was a boy and was fostering elsewhere when it happened. I am not even certain his father knew, and I doubt the countess has told him. So far as he knows, it is truly his aunt at Warkworth and a cousin he has seldom met here at Penrith." She said it without rancor, but there was a tightness around her eyes that betrayed a certain sadness.

Ari offered her a sympathetic frown. "It must have been difficult, my lady, leaving behind all your brothers and sisters, never to see them again."

"A little. But we would have gone our separate ways in the end anyway, and I would likely have seen little of them. Most difficult was losing my dearest companion to Alnwick, though we write each other often and she always sends the news from Raby, which she gets in my stead. However, look at all that I have won for such a small price." She gave Gunnar a smile so warm and full of love that it made Ari's chest ache with longing. "And look at this fine castle we are building. I am more than content."

Talk turned to the tower and fortifications Gunnar was finishing for the new earl. When Gunnar offered a tour of the new pitfall he'd designed, Lady Lucy excused herself. "Will we see the others later?"

"Only Torvald, my lady. Brand and Jafri are digging out a cairn near the border."

"Then I will see Torvald for supper. And you again tomorrow. Your pardon."

When she'd gone, Gunnar turned to Ari. "What of Cwen?"

"No sign."

"In a dozen years? Did you learn nothing at the pool?"

"I did. I think. But I do not yet know what it is or how to use it. Come and show me your pitfall. I will try to tell you."

The next morning, while Gunnar sat judgment over a dispute between two smallholders that had disturbed the peace of the village, Ari carried his great book to the castle scriptorium, which had been set aside for him, and opened it to the first empty page. After some thought about how to word it, he recorded Gunnar and Lucy-who-was-Eleanor's life and happiness and the births of their sons, scratching out the words using the same runes he had used from the first days. A few scholars and travelers could still read the old tongue written this way, but it served to keep his saga away from curious eyes.

He started to close the volume, then thought better of it and turned back a page, to where he had last written a dozen years ago:

The water was dark and still when the raven-warrior returned to the pool, the glow faded, the witch Cwen long gone. He studied the currents for a time, and then sliced his hand open.

As his seer's blood spilled into the pool, the water began to stir again. A full vision, the first in many moons, poured into his mind, showing him all that had happened the night before and, more important, revealing what he must do.

Combined with Gunnar and Eleanor's love and enhanced by the mystic light of the full moon, his blood had been nearly powerful enough to break the bull's curse on its own—even without the true amulet. Then, as the night played out, the lady's blood had flowed into the pool, too, carried by that bolt of magical lightning, and the power had grown. And then, finally, Cwen's blood had been added to the mix when Eleanor had rinsed the amulet.

There was power in that pool, both light and dark, and the thought that his blood was the source of some of that power both disturbed and fascinated the raven-warrior. He could draw on that power, he thought, but he was reluctant to sample it. Cwen had once wielded her powers well and for good, until she'd been poisoned by hate. The raven was unsure he could do any better, and did not want to become evil in the quest to destroy it.

So he hesitated, unwilling, standing while the sun faded and more of the magic flowed away with the running water. But in the fullness of the vision he knew that by morning there would be nothing left, so in the last rays of sun, he stripped away his clothes and strode into the pool.

And when he rose out of the water again, his hand, scarred by his own knife in his hunt for visions, was healed but for some faint markings, and his mind was filled with . . .

It stopped there, a void that reflected Ari's comprehension of what he'd discovered at the bottom of the pool.

He had no idea what had happened, what he'd learned, or what to do with it. These two and ten years he'd pondered on it every day, with every breath, and he was no closer than he had been—his attempt to explain to Gunnar yesterday proved that. Only his hand proved that anything at all had happened; his palm remained clear, except for traces of the deepest marks. Unfortunately, those traces formed the runes that spelled Cwen's name—but at least they were fainter than they had been. And best of all, he didn't feel such overwhelming shame each time he saw them. After all, he was not the one who had put them there.

Ari flipped the book closed, fastened the straps and turned the key in the lock that held it all together, then took a moment to trim the quill he'd borrowed and seal the scribe's ink, using the time to think.

As he pulled the door shut behind himself and started

back downstairs to rejoin Gunnar and his lady, he made his decision. He wasn't going to meet Brand and Jafri.

It was time he found someone who could help him sort out what magic he had of his own, what he might have gained from the pool, and how to best use it to overcome Cwen.

It was time he found himself an alchemist who had mastered the dark elements.

HISTORICAL NOTES

This was one of those books where the research very nearly got out of hand.

Eleanor de Neville is a real woman who lived and married much as described, although I adjusted her age to accommodate modern mores. Accurate or not, I can't write a fourteen-year-old heroine. The other members of the Neville clan are also real, as are Henry Percy and Richard le Despenser. Lucy, however, is a fictional character, and her marriage to Henry Percy in Eleanor's stead is my invention.

One of the problems I had was keeping everyone straight while I did my research. *All* Percy earls are named Henry for generation after generation, and nearly all the Nevilles are named Ralph and Richard. Plus the number of Eleanors Neville would stun you. Worse, they all intermarried, so that they were cousins to each other—part of the reason the English had such a hard time sorting out who had the proper bloodlines to be king after Henry VI's heir was killed at Tewkesbury. That difficulty, of course, helped turn the great Percy-Neville feud into the Wars of the Roses.

In the end, the Nevilles won by co-opting both sides of the fight. Eleanor's baby sister, the golden Cecily (later known as Proud Cis), married Richard Plantagenet, 3rd Duke of York, to become the mother of both Edward IV and Richard III. Then Cecily's granddaughter, Elizabeth of York, married eventual Lancastrian victor Henry Tudor (later Henry VII)—a cousin descended through one of the Beaufort uncles Eleanor talks about with Gunnar. Through Elizabeth, Cecily is ancestor to every king or queen of England since, truly the mother of a country.

Confused yet? Me too. If you're curious, you'll find further information and links on my website, lisahendrix.com. But I warn you, you'll be going down a rabbit hole.

ACKNOWLEDGMENTS

As always, it took a lot of folks to make this book happen. Much credit for the development of Gunnar's nature goes to a late night Twitter conversation I had with author Shirin Dubbin, whose insightful questions and comments led me to dig deeper. Thanks, Shirin.

Thanks also go to editor Kate Seaver and agent Helen Breitwieser, who balanced patience and firmness to help me beat this puppy into shape. Assorted author buddies also booted me along the path, including old pal Sheila Roberts, new pal Maisey Yates, and the virtual cheerleaders of Twitter (too many to name).

Finally, because they're most important and I want you to remember them, I need to thank my family. Once again, my husband and kids put up with a dirty house, too much takeout, and general distractedness that must be aggravating as hell—and they did it (mostly) with a smile and offers of coffee and chocolate runs that made it all possible. Thank you and huge, smoochy hugs. And really, I promise to at least try to get on a saner schedule. Or hire a maid. Or something.

ALONE IN JOHN Dee's library for the night, Torvald fetched the *Vox vocis incendium*, the book Ari had asked him to search for clues to how Cwen had worked her magic, and set to work. He was deep in the cryptic scratchings of some long-dead mage when he stumbled over a glyph he didn't know. He lit a stub of candle and carried it to the far corner where Dee kept several grammars of occult symbols, using the light to search the faded titles. He'd just found the volume he wanted when the door creaked open. Before he could think, habits born of eight hundred years of hiding took over; he pinched out the candle and stepped deeper into the shadows, his knife out and ready.

"Master Dee?"

He recognized the low voice as that of his earlier supper companion, even before its owner slipped into the room, candle held high to light her way.

"Is anyone here?" whispered Mistress Delamere, and Torvald heard the murmur of her name in his head the way she'd said it at supper: *Jo-SIGH-un*. Without waiting for an answer, she padded across to the opposite shelves on bare feet.

He eased his knife back into its sheath, ready to step forward and announce his presence. But something held him back, and he found himself lingering in the shadows, watching from the corner as she scanned the shelves and picked out a thin volume bound in green leather and carried it to Dee's desk.

As she pulled the chair out, her sleeping gown pulled taut. With the lamplight behind her, her breasts came into relief against the thin linen. Sudden desire punched Torvald in the gut, and he sucked in his breath, a harsh sound in the silence.

"Oh!" Josian jumped, sending her book spinning across the desk into the folio Dee had left lying there. It slid over the edge, the contents spilling over the floor as she backed away. Her eyes were wide with alarm. "Who's there?"

"Only I, mistress." Torvald hid his extinguished candle on the shelf next to the grammar and stepped out where she could see him.

"Master Rollison." Her shoulders sagged with relief. "I didn't know . . . Why did you not say something?"

How could he answer when he wasn't certain of the reason himself? "I didn't mean to frighten you. Forgive me."

"That makes twice in one evening you have needed my forgiveness. Perhaps you should travel with your own confessor. And perhaps I can borrow him to intercede with Master Dee for jumbling his desk." She bent to retrieve one of the sheets that had fallen from the folio.

"How odd. This is William." She squinted at the other pieces on the floor. "They are *all* of Will."

Torvald helped her gather the unstretched canvases and lay them out on the desk side by side: six of them, all twins of each other, all clearly painted by a single hand.

Josian traced one fingertip over the mark stamped into the corner of the leather folio. "This is Devereux's. Why would he have so many portraits of Will? And why would he bring them to Dee?"

"Dee intends to travel soon. Perhaps young Master Shakeshaft seeks a foreign bride, and these are meant to show prospects what he looks like."

"I hope not. It would not please the English one he already has."

"I suppose not." Torvald started stacking the portraits to stow them away. "Do you know him well?"

"Well enough. He is a cousin of some degree, through his mother, to my father."

They slid everything back into the folio and Torvald arranged it on the desk exactly as it had been. "There. No harm done."

"Good." Her smile faded as an awkward silence stretched between them. She cleared her throat. "I, um, couldn't sleep, so I thought I might read a little. I thought no one would be awake."

Torvald picked up the green book she'd chosen and read the title. "This is a book for deciphering dreams."

"Aye. I have been having odd ones of late. Ever since my husband died. Another one woke me tonight."

"And you want to make sense of them. Perhaps I can help." *Widow, not wife.* Trying to ignore the surge of pleasure that news brought, he settled the book across his palm and opened it. "Of what do you dream, mistress?"

Before she could answer, a faint wooden thunk echoed outside. They both froze, and a moment later, there came a scraping sound.

"Someone's outside," she said.

Torvald put a finger to his lips to shush her, then quickly pinched out both her candle and the lamp. Laying aside the book of dreams, he moved to the window and lifted the edge of the drapery. As his eyes adjusted to the dark, he spied two men hurrying across the moonlit yard. They disappeared into the shadows beside the storehouse.

"Are they robbers?" Josian had hurried to the other side of the broad window, where she also peered out.

"Shh." A faint glow rose over the yard, then vanished; rose again, then vanished. A board squeaked overhead, then another in a different place, and another, moving toward the stairs. Outside, the men came out of the shadows and started toward the library window.

He dropped the drapery. "Someone upstairs was signaling, and now they're headed down to meet those two. Here." He grabbed her arm and started toward the end wall. "Come."

She dragged at him, trying to pull away. "If I am found with you, like this . . ."

Someone started down the stairs at the far end of the hall.

"I am more worried about your safety than your name, mistress. Trust me, and I can protect both."

There was a heartbeat's resistance, and then, "I do trust you."

There was just enough moonlight seeping past the draperies for him to find the right shelf. He reached for the lever, missed it, and had to grope around.

"A priest hole," she breathed, understanding

"Dee showed me, years ago. If I can remember . . . Here."

There was a click, not even as loud as the footfalls now coming down the hall, and the narrow bookshelf silently swung open.

Torvald shoved Josian into the hole and slid in after her. The space was meant to hide one man *in extremis*, not two, and there was barely enough room. He pulled the shelf shut behind them and locked it in place from the inside. He had just enough time to wrap his arms around Josian and wriggle into a comfortable position before the library door opened. Thin beamlets of light spilled through the tiny, hidden screen that provided air.

God's toes. Whoever was out there had apparently marched through the house with a lit candle, and even then they hadn't managed to be quiet about it. With so little cunning,

Torvald was surprised the whole household wasn't after him, even at this hour. Stunned at the unknown man's clumsiness, he listened as the fellow threw the windows open.

"So this is Dee's house." Heavy boots scuffed on the oaken floors as the men climbed in. "I've never been in a witch's den before."

"Dee is more fool than witch," said John Sommerville. Josian leaned her forehead against Torvald's chest and shook her head in disgust or disbelief, or more likely both. Curse Sommerville. The fool was going to get his entire family in trouble with the Crown.

"Does he really talk to angels?" asked the third man.

"So he says. But even the royal whore begins to doubt him. I think he will burn before the year's out, and this devil's library with him. Do you have the list?"

"Half of it. Thom, here, carried the other half from Durham."

"Let's have both." Paper rustled, there was a moment's silence, and then Sommerville made noises of approval. "Well done. With this, Spain will see how much support we have and be far more willing to help us. I will pass it to the next man on the morrow."

"Be careful. If it falls into the wrong hands . . ."

"It won't," Sommerville assured him. "I have an ally at hand, ready to help me if need be, and it will be in Spain within the month. Now go before someone comes. And give our friend my thanks."

There was more scuffling, the click of the window latch, and then silence. But the light still glowed through the screen, and in a little, the scrape of chair across floor told Torvald that Sommerville was studying his list, whatever it was, at Dee's desk.

They settled in to wait, gradually relaxing into each other's arms as Sommerville shuffled papers barely two yards away. The priest hole closed around them, seeming to grow even more cramped as Torvald gradually became aware that the person he was sharing it with was a half-dressed woman. Her scent, her warmth, the press of her unbound breasts against his chest, they all worked on his body in ways he would be happy for in other circumstances, but which were disconcerting just now. He shifted, trying to pull his lower body away from her before his arousal became too apparent.

Josian lifted her head, her uncanny eyes glittering up at him, ghostlike in the thin light, and then she laid her cheek against his chest, accepting. Understanding. She was a widow, after all, not a maid. She knew how men were. He stopped worrying about it and just held her, surrendering to the forced closeness, enjoying the simple pleasure of a woman in his arms.

Perhaps he would go to Warwickshire after they finished here with Dee, he thought as they waited for Sommerville to leave. He could pass some time courting her, perhaps bedding her if she was willing. She might be; widows had more freedom in such things than other women. But it wasn't all about sport. He felt a bond with Josian Delamere he hadn't felt in a long, long while, and whether anything came of it or not, he wanted to enjoy her company for a time.

Eventually, Sommerville started yawning, and not long after that, the door squeaked open and shut again, taking the light and leaving them in pitch black. They waited until the stairs and then the floor overhead, creaked with his footsteps, then a little longer until he must surely be abed. Finally, the darkness grew so oppressive, Torvald worked his hand around and found the bar. The bookshelf swung wide with a snick, and they half spilled out into the library, still clinging to each other as they adjusted to the freedom of a little light and a good deal of sweet air.

"Give him time to go to sleep," Torvald whispered, his lips against her temple.

She shook her head. "No. I must leave now."

"Why?"

"I need to be with my family. I fear for them with John's

foolishness. But also because . . ." She shifted in his arms, lifting to press a kiss to his lips. Not a long kiss, nor a deep one, but a tender one so full of longing and need that it set his blood roaring in his veins. There was the real answer to why, and he was glad for it.

She slipped out of his arms before he could pull her closer. "Thank you for hiding me."

"'Twas my pleasure."

She backed away. "I know."

He couldn't see well, but he thought a smile flickered over her lips. "Josian . . ."

"My sister Catherine is breeding. She asked me to stay with her until she gives birth. At Castle Bromwich. And then I will visit my parents for a time. At Park Hall."

"Castle Bromwich," he repeated. "Park Hall."

She backed into the door and reached behind herself to tug it open. "God's rest, Master Rollison. Torvald."

"Wait. You never told me what dream brought you down to me."

"A white horse," she said from the doorway. "I dream always of a white horse running toward me. I wonder what it means." And then she was gone, her bare feet nearly soundless as she raced back to her bed.

A widow, not a wife. And she dreamed of a white horse.

Thank you, Freyr, keeper of the sun and rain, giver of peace and pleasure. He would have to make a worthy offering for such a gift.

He went to close up the priest hole, making sure the lever tripped and vanished into its hidden slot, so no one else would find it by accident, and then he collected his cloak from the peg and the raven from his perch in the hall and slipped out into the night.

"Warwickshire," he repeated aloud as they rode out the gate. "Castle Bromwich and Park Hall."

And then he turned west, in search of a patch of woods deep enough for him and Ari to face the daily torture that was dawn.